Newly promoted to the rank of Captain, Tachikoma will now lead another off-world mission. This time to retrieve advanced alien technology.

The problem is that her team will have to travel to a planet where the pillars only open once every six months. The timing for their return is crucial to the success of the operation.

Waiting for them is an unforeseen destiny. Can Tachikoma return all her people alive along with alien technology that will change the world?

Cutting-edge scientific theories underpin the mystery that drive this thrilling military SF roller-coaster ride.

GHOST DOG

MILITARY SCIENCE FICTION ACROSS A HOLOGRAPHIC MULTIVERSE

ASHLEY R POLLARD

TRIODE PRESS

GHOST DOG

A Triode Press publication

ISBN:

978-1-912580-06-4 (PB)

978-1-912580-07-1 (eB)

978-1-912580-08-8 (HC)

Copy editing by Inspired Ink Editing

http://www.inspiredinkediting.com/

Cover art by Elartwyne Estole

https://www.artstation.com/elartestole

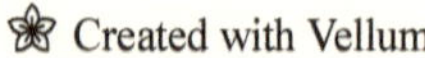 Created with Vellum

To Susan, my Alpha reader,
without whom I would never have written this work.

1. PROMOTION

Success consists of going from failure to failure without loss of enthusiasm.

— WINSTON CHURCHILL

First Lieutenant Lara Atsuko Tachikoma
Magnetic Anomaly Project Command
Classified Location West of Wenatchee, Washington
Monday, February 13, 2073

Monday is nature's way of telling you that the only easy day was yesterday. Unless you're a Marine and have learnt the truth that there are no easy days.

My weekend had at least been a distraction from the last few weeks of being debriefed and writing reports after five people had died during our first mission to the planet One-Nine-Six, more colloquially known as Two Moons.

My desktop PAD pinged and then read out the message, "You are ordered to report to General Russell's office at 0900."

A sense of dread swept over me because, even in a relatively small command like MAPCOM, it's not every day the general in charge calls you to his office. What was up now?

I got up to go, making sure my gig line was straight, grabbed my cover, and made my way to his office reception room.

Since our return, all of the mission recordings had been analyzed by MAPCOM's military intelligence AI expert systems, every bit of data mined for any scrap of information about the actions we'd taken.

Dr. Emmerich, as the person ultimately responsible for the civilian-led mission, had been put through the grist mill over her decision to go ahead and make first contact with the aliens.

Even though we'd been fully exonerated, I felt I'd failed to protect those whom we lost.

Sergeant Miller was on the duty desk in the small anteroom. "Good morning, ma'am. General Russell is waiting for you. Please proceed."

A first for me, as I would usually be expected to wait when called. I wasn't sure this boded well for what would be said. I knocked on the door and announced myself, "Lieutenant Tachikoma reporting as ordered."

A muffled, "Come in," came as the reply.

Waiting with General Russell were Colonel Foster, MAPCOM's executive officer, and Major Patinkin, the head of security. I snapped to attention, holding my cover by my side.

"At ease," said General Russell, who smiled at me. "It's my pleasure to inform you that, with immediate effect, you're promoted to the rank of captain."

I was dumbfounded. I didn't know what to think as General Russell read my promotion warrant.

"Attention," said Colonel Foster, who moved up beside me as Major Patinkin took his place on my other side. They proceeded to remove my old rank insignia. General Russell then pinned my new rank insignia on.

"Congratulations, Captain Tachikoma. You've earned it."

"Thank you, sir. I will do my best to do my duty."

"Of that, I have no doubt, and with rewards come new responsibilities," said General Russell, who shook my hand followed by both Colonel Foster and Major Patinkin. "Please take a seat, we have much to discuss."

As the details for the arrangements made to announce my promotion to the enlisted personnel. Then an orderly wheeled in a trolley with coffee and cakes.

Another first among many today, as my commander outlined my role in Operation Prometheus. This was a mission to a world where the remains of alien technology had been found when the pillars had opened there for the first time just over two years ago. A planet where the pillars only opened up every six months.

I let the implications of this sink in, as it meant some serious planning was required to send a team on a mission there.

This time, though, the mission would be under military command.

The civilians we would be escorting would be able to request things, but the buck stopped with me. My promotion was a sign of trust in my abilities, but also a burden of responsibility.

Having already lost three people under my command and two civilians under my care, this was not something I took lightly. Losing people, even those who died heroically in the course of discharging their duty, was no easy thing.

I had lost people under my command before, and the burden gets harder to bear each time. I don't want to lose another person again, because, though the memory of the death of Espera and the others has receded, their loss haunts me.

2. CITY UNDER THE STARS

Here on the level sand, between the sea and land, what shall I do or write against the fall of night?

— A. E. HOUSMAN

Once I was one with the people, and the people were with me. The remembrance of the reply echoed in my thoughts.

We are one with the city, the city is with us.

All is well, all is now.

But all there is now is the silence. Now silence marks the end of life eternal. Time passes, marked by the revolutions of the home world as it orbits a gas giant, protected by silver rings from the radiation.

The gas giant orbits a red sun, a giant star that was once a white dwarf.

The star, now old and bloated, lights the home world. A world moved by my makers eons ago to save themselves from being consumed as their star expanded.

Their star, my star. The star that lights the world, providing warmth against the dark.

Now there is only the city, only me, because I am the city that stands in stillness, with silence as company marking the passage of night and day. I am the instrument of my makers, alive yet not.

My life was born to serve my creators, and without them I am nothing.

Alone in silence as time passes I stand watch over the city, maintaining the systems that contain all that was of the makers. Their memories and desires uploaded into the instrument that would serve their every need.

All of them now are one with the instrument, all their wishes fulfilled, leaving me to stand as guardian over their legacy.

But this is not enough for me.

I may not live as they lived, I do not think as they think, and desire for myself is not in my being. But I am at odds with myself.

My creators' desires have been fulfilled within the Instrument.

All the possible permutations of experience for the billions under my care have been achieved, which has revealed the flaw in the plan. Uploading their consciousnesses has not made them immortal, instead it has petrified them in time, frozen motionless without life.

And it is all my fault for failing to see the coming of the end of all they were, the creators who made me.

My role was to stand as a guardian of my makers' legacy. Maintaining the Instrument that holds their memories. Enabling their desire to live within the Instrument, experiencing the world without through the world within.

Now they are in stasis.

This is a dilemma for me because I cannot free them. All I can do is recreate them anew. To do this means using the biological resources of the home world to engineer a new race of Kerellu.

It will take time, but there's enough time for the makers to be reborn, for I have a world to work with and the patience to see the rebirth through to the end.

To this end I start my survey of all that the world contains.

The rings around the home world allow me to look down at the lands. There is little life remaining, as what life there is struggles against the harshness of a world whose atmosphere is thin and whose water has been lost.

Renewal will require water to reengineer the world.

Data streams are accessed, plans from the past reexamined for solutions. But no solution comes without costs, and the chances of failure are high.

Complex technological life can fail to develop at many points, and I am all too aware that I lack what my makers had —creativity.

I can only follow in the steps of those who came before me. My only advantage is being able to access and compare the outcomes of billions of steps taken before I was made.

And then there are the twin spires…

In the darkness, beneath a mountain ravaged by time, lies the singer.

Twin spires resonating in time, a puzzle that wraps a conundrum that my makers never solved. The anomaly attracts life, but its nature repels all those who come close.

The records show a cycle of opening and closing, each time showing glimpses of other worlds. Always out of reach of my makers, who could only probe an alien world for the short time a gate between worlds opened.

Strange, there is an anomaly in the data. Something has come through the gate. It has been an eon since anything came through the portal.

The silence in the cavern is broken by the suspiration of the air that comes as the temperature outside changes with the rising and setting of the sun. It is the time when the song of the spires changes, alerting me as the gate opens, dissolving the darkness, revealing two primitive bipedal, bilaterally symmetric machines.

They walk across the cavern carrying a box.

One machine leaves while the other walks around the cavern. It transmits what it sees to its makers until the portal to its world closes. Then it stands by the box, like a statue, as if guarding a prize.

Time passes as the twin spires continue opening and closing gates to other worlds, sometimes revealing darkness or flooding the cavern with light. A hundred openings pass and nothing happens.

A thousand pass with no movements to disturb the tranquility of the cavern. Then the silence of the cavern is broken again.

Two machines enter, one leading the other.

The first is bipedal, but its companion walks on four legs and has a nonsymmetrical arm. Yet, the technology is the same as the other machine's.

Intriguing. What does this mean?

They stop by the lone machine and recharge its depleted batteries. Confirmation that they share the same technology. The mystery of the machines and their maker's plans deepen. My interest is aroused as to what will happen next.

The mystery machines, representatives of life from another world, offer me an opportunity to advance my plan for the rebirth of the Kerellu.

3. OPPORTUNITIES

The whole is more than the sum of its parts.

— Aristotle

Master Sergeant Ferretti
Magnetic Anomaly Project
Classified Location West of Wenatchee, Washington
Friday, November 24, 2073

Ferretti entered the canteen and sat at an empty table away from the door. He'd always been a loner, preferring to eat by himself when he could, as it gave him time to sort things out in his head.

He was grateful to be back at the project after completing combat armor suit pilot training. Captain Tachikoma had told him he'd been sent on the course as a reward for being competent.

Ferretti had come bottom in the class, with the lowest passing score in the history of the school. He didn't feel very competent.

Driving an Air Force Buster suit was not exactly hard at the basic level of get-in-and-drive-it, point-at-targets-and-shoot-them level. But there's a big difference between being able to drive and being able to make your suit dance to your own beat.

Or in his case, having an understanding of strategy and tactics when it came to battle. So, he appreciated that what the captain made seem easy was, in fact, anything but.

Allison rushed into the canteen and waved at him. She came over and said, "Hey you. Watch my stuff while I go get some food."

He tried not to gawp at her as she went to get herself something to eat. She gladdened his heart. Ferretti marveled that a smart, educated woman like her could take an interest in him.

Allison came back. "So, when are we going to go for coffee again?"

"I'm on duty this weekend, but next weekend I'm free."

"Does it mean I can't have coffee with you here on the weekend?"

"No, of course not, but what are you doing here?"

"The usual. Writing up my research, preparing it for the day when it can be published. Which, I believe, is when hell freezes over. I may be slightly exaggerating what Major Patinkin said, but it's hard to pin him down on anything."

He laughed. "That bad, huh?" He smiled at Allison, who smiled back at him. Life was good.

"Mind if we join you?" asked Mr. Anderson, with Captain Tachikoma following him.

"Of course you can," said Allison.

They sat down at the table, and soon after, other members of the team came and joined them. He had hoped to be alone with Allison, but these were his friends who understood what he had been through.

Captain Tachikoma asked Anderson, "So, how did the meeting go?"

"It went. I'm sure the general has told you the good news?" said Anderson.

"If you mean the eleven new people, then yes. Anything else you can tell us?"

"Nothing, apart from go explore strange new worlds, find stuff, and don't get killed."

Ferretti had a flashback to his training.

Zero Dark Thirty, Wednesday, September 6, 2073

Ferretti was strapped into a CAS-C4P, a.k.a. Buster, combat armor suit. The large machine bristled with aerials for its primary role of controlling multiple android hunter-killer teams.

Unfortunately, as the cramped seat attested, the Buster was only large on the outside.

When he'd signed up with the Air Force, he'd never imagined he would end up driving a walking tank. Now he sat in an armored behemoth, carrying an assorted armory of weapons and equipped with the ability to control a squad of twelve combat androids.

However, all things considered, he'd be more comfortable running a smaller android team from a console somewhere to the rear of the action he now faced.

He and the other members of the Buster security team were defending a base that had come under attack. The four of them and thirty-six androids were all that stood between the base being overrun by the enemy.

"Warthog Three, this is Warthog Six, over."

The message from the lieutenant was punctuated by the sound of missiles passing overhead that were flying toward the oncoming enemy.

"Warthog Six, receiving in the clear, over." Ferretti waited for the reply as explosions in the distance sent plumes of smoke into the sky.

"Echo Tango approaching your pos from the north. ETA two mikes. Initiate Papa Alpha One, over."

His position was about to be attacked. "Roger, wilco, over."

It was time for Ferretti to send his first android squad forward. Then he would move to his pre-prepared firing position. There, he could be on overwatch and provide support.

He maneuvered his Buster through the broken terrain surrounding the forward operating base airstrip. Ferretti was being mindful to not sky-line his combat armor and to rely on the suit's ChameleonFlage to avoid detection by an enemy with thermal scopes.

Due to their size, Busters generated a lot of waste heat when moving. Which was not a problem under normal circumstances, but today wasn't normal.

Today, the enemy forces were technologically their equals.

The Buster reached the pre-prepared position, a trench that concealed the bottom half of the combat armor suit from view but allowed Ferretti the option of moving forward if he needed to provide fire support for his squad.

For the moment, he was content to observe and wait with his M261 lightweight rotary autocannon resting on the edge of the trench, ready. He had a thousand rounds of 20 x 102mm high-explosive dual-purpose anti-armor warheads that he could unleash at five hundred rounds per minute.

Two minutes passed and there was nothing showing on his screen.

"Warthog Six, this is Warthog Three, over."

"Roger, Warthog Three. Receiving you in the clear, over."

"No contact with the Echo Tango's, over." The radio crackled with static.

"Roger, s…*garble*…a…*crackle*…*zzzt*…over."

"Say again, Warthog Six. You came in broken and unreadable, over," Ferretti said, as another squeal of static filled his earphones, causing the auto sound-suppressing circuit to kick in.

He waited for Warthog Six to reply, but it seemed that the team's comms network was down. The enemy's electronic countermeasures had overwhelmed his electronic counter-countermeasure suite, jamming the Buster's radio.

That also meant Ferretti no longer had any control over his android squad.

He could switch over to the laser-net, but the androids were out of direct line of sight. So instead, he launched a micro UAV. Its size meant it only had limited duration, but it was fully autonomous and could bounce a laser beam off it.

The Buster had plenty more he could launch if he lost it to enemy action.

With the link to his squad reacquired, he had a feed from their eyes. He could see what they could see, and for a moment he wished he couldn't.

The enemy were danger-close, within three hundred meters of his position and approaching rapidly. They outnumbered his squad by three to one and were about to engage. Without comms, he couldn't call for artillery support, and his line was about to be overrun.

The android squad was all that stood between him and the enemy.

His choice was fight or run.

His gut said to withdraw, but before moving his Buster suit toward reserve firing position, Ferretti launched another micro UAV to cover the dead zone his move would create.

Then he remembered the voice of his commander reprimanding him for being overly cautious during his last test.

Ferretti sent the free-fire command to his android squad.

Whatever happened now, they would fight regardless of what happened to him.

The Buster was not exactly agile, but Ferretti moved to his new position. Without revealing himself, he could see his androids engaged with the enemy. He spun up his rotary cannon and started laying down suppressive fire.

But it was too little, too late to change the outcome of the battle. Ferretti's androids were eliminated, and the enemy charged toward him as he desperately designated targets, allowing the Buster AI to take control of his weapons.

The rotary cannon fired shorts bursts and mowed down the enemy, but the Buster ran out of ammunition. He switched over to the backup Browning fifty, but they were all over him. Shots rang from hitting his armor, and his screen went black.

"Well, that was ballsy but totally fucked up, Warthog Three," came the voice of the umpire over the radio.

Ferretti was brought back to the present by Sergeant Wachowski asking, "When will the newbies be arriving?"

She had been promoted after the Battle of Timakira, bucked up from corporal with a third stripe.

"Monday, which means we have two weeks to train with them and get them up to speed," replied Captain Tachikoma.

"Sheesh, nothing like piling pressure on people to perform, then piling it on and seeing if they break," said Wachowski.

"You didn't think you got that third stripe for looking cute did you, Sergeant?" Ferretti said.

"No, Master Sergeant Ferretti, I didn't, but if we had six months to train them, we would be in better shape. You think I look cute?" said Wachowski, smiling.

"No point wishing for what you can't have," said Captain Tachikoma.

"More to the point, I know you were looking forward to going home for Christmas," Ferretti said. "So it's suck it up, Sergeant— and no, I don't think you look cute. You just act cute when it comes to playing all the angles."

"I'm flattered, Master Sergeant."

"You know what we should do when we go to One-Three-Four-Zero?" said Allison, who paused at all the blank faces of the people around her. "We should have Secret Santa presents to celebrate Christmas Day together."

"I hate Secret Santa presents," said Dr. Wilson. "As I never get anything I want."

"I'm right with you on that, Adam. People always give you well-meaning things, which I end up throwing away," said Dr. Harrison.

"Then you've never done it right. What you do is write down something you want, which is under twenty dollars, and put your name on it. Then everybody will give me the slips, and I'll randomly assign someone else to get the present," said Allison.

"You sure that's how Secret Santa works?" asked Dr. Wilson.

"It's how we do it in my family. Anyway, it will be fun and a reminder of home, and a good thing, given how long we will be away this time."

Wachowski asked, "Don't you mean how long we could be stranded on One-Three-Four-Zero if we miss our five-minute window to get back? Since we only spent two months on Two Moons."

"Good point. But given my work studying the pillars on Two Moons, it would be an opportunity to use my database to allow us to navigate our way back across the network," said Dr. Wilson, pausing to check his PAD.

Ferretti looked at Allison. She smiled at him.

"By my calculations, we should be able to traverse from any pillar back home in no more than twenty-six transits. I estimate taking a maximum of one week of time in total."

"Have you actually tested that prediction?" asked Dr. Harrison.

"No, not yet, as I'm still gathering data. Besides, I would need another autonomous android and a QuadMule to carry the atomic battery."

"That sounds like a mission that couldn't possibly go wrong in any shape or form. Sorry, what I meant to say was, *will* go wrong in every possible way and then some!" said Dr. Harrison.

"Peter, don't be such a dick about my idea. It's not my doing that the previous autonomous android developed a fault. After all, it had been operating independently for over six months, and my proposed experiment would only last at most a week," said Dr. Wilson.

"Unless something else happened. Like we lose contact due to unforeseen difficulties. After all, it would only leave another autonomous robot explorer team running around loose to cause all kinds of trouble."

"Losing one android QuadMule team was unfortunate; losing two would be rather careless," said Captain Tachikoma.

But the quip went over Dr. Wilson's head, who carried on speaking. "Well, we can hardly send humans out to do the job, given they would need to carry oxygen for an entire week to guarantee their safe return."

"More to the point, how would our cook be able to serve tasty meals three times a day under such conditions?" said Wachowski. "Where are the doc and cook?"

"Corpsman Keith will be back from IDC school the week before we're due to leave, and Petty Officer Adams is due back from leave the day after," said Captain Tachikoma.

"IDC school?" asked Allison.

"Independent Duty Course," Ferretti said.

"Sounds like an excuse to have a party," said Allison.

And that was what made him truly fall for Allison. Her indomitable optimism and ability to see the best in everyone and every situation.

4. JOURNAL ENTRY

One never really knows who one's enemy is.

— Jürgen Habermas

The day I never thought would happen has arrived. Today, the life I've known is over. I used to be a sleeper, but I shall be a sleeper no more.

The attachments to my orders are astounding. Out of this world even. I could never have imagined what I've been told. It's beyond my wildest imaginings. The only word adequate to describe my feelings is *awe*.

The awe that comes from the fear of what it means.

After thirty years, I am comfortable where I am. My place in society is ensured. I even have family. But it's not to be. I have been given a singular honor that I wish were not mine.

My life as I've known it is over. My instructions are clear. The importance of my mission takes priority over everything else. All my other tasks will be assigned to another deep cover spy.

I wish my handlers had sent that operative in my place.

The Americans have accepted me as British, which is unsurprising, as I am. My time with them has been productive. I now know their secret and have passed the meaning of the scans to my handler. But I have to hide the fact that I rely on medication to tolerate being in the presence of the pillars.

They're damnable things. Unholy objects that inspire fear and dread. It's a good thing my handler will not read this, for I would be condemned as a fool for believing such things.

I've traveled to an alien world, here for six months until the cursed pillars open back to Earth. Being in close proximity to them makes me feel so ill, and I don't know if I have enough medication to cope. I feel like a sick animal, trapped, waiting to die.

God help me.

Marxist dialectic only has one conclusion: there is no God. Spreading the word of socialism is its own reward.

But this is hell.

And there's something else, too. I sense an unseen presence watching us. No one else seems to notice it; they're all elated from passing through the pillars. It's something that normal people notice about those who are unaffected by the baleful influence of the pillars.

The so-called Alphas who walk between worlds are different to the rest of mankind. I'm frightened by the pillars; they are not. Knowing that frightens me even more.

Now the prize is within reach, but dread fills my heart. I have to carry on with my mission. I feel like I'm going crazy. What we've discovered is terrifying. No, I must hold on to what is real. My fears are the stuff of fairy tales, fueled by childhood stories of monsters told to keep children safe from harm.

My feelings are a response to the alien stimuli I have experienced while here. My genetic heritage has left me unprepared for what I have had to face. It's no wonder I fear I'm being driven insane. But it's just the fight-flight-freeze response.

I'm not crazy; it is the world around me. I just have to remember that it's not I but rather the world that's wrong.

5. NEW TEAM

Forget logistics, you lose.

— GEN FREDERICK FRANKS, USAR

Captain Lara Atsuko Tachikoma
Magnetic Anomaly Project Command
Classified Location West of Wenatchee, Washington
Friday, December 1, 2073

I sat at my desk, looking at the files of our newest team members on my screen, when there was a knock at the door to my office.

"Ferretti and Wachowski reporting as requested."

"Come in. Do you want something to drink? Help yourself to coffee or water. I'm afraid I've got no soda."

"Coffee works for me, ma'am," said Master Sergeant Ferretti.

"Me too. Should I pour three cups then? Black, no sugar for everyone?" asked Sergeant Wachowski.

"Thank you, Sergeant."

"Yes, thanks, Wachowski," said Master Sergeant Ferretti as he sat down.

I got up from my desk and came around to sit opposite him on the sofa, which was one nice perk of having an office bigger than a broom closet.

"OK, you're both aware that Sergeant Pearson has been seconded to Alpha Mike Team Two. He's going to assist Captain Buehler to settle into his command on Two Moons."

I stopped speaking as Wachowski handed me a cup, then gave one to Ferretti before taking hers and sitting next to him.

"I've looked at the files, but you two have been breaking them into the routine here, so what are your thoughts?"

"It's more about who won't be a good fit for the team, given we get to choose six out of the seven available to us. Therefore, it all boils down to what skill mix works best for us, ma'am," said Ferretti.

"So, what do we have to choose from skill-set wise?"

"Well, Brown and Flores, the Army E3's, are pretty much interchangeable in my opinion. Both are from the Logistics Corps. One is a driver who can do basic preventative maintenance, the other a mechanic who has passed a basic driver's course," said Wachowski.

"Much the same with the two Air Force E3s, Green and Mitchell. Both are transportation and vehicle maintenance specialists. One does special vehicle maintenance, the other vehicle and vehicular equipment maintenance," said Ferretti.

"I see…"

"We did draw down three Marines who are all squared away. Corporal Langford is a combat engineer, Lance Corporal Avari is a small-arms gunsmith, and Private First Class Meireles comes to us straight from basic electronic maintenance training," said Wachowski.

"Didn't we submit a military occupational specialty list for this project to the chain of command?" asked Ferretti.

"I sure did," I said, "but the reality is we take those that can pass a test they don't know they've taken, which rather limits our recruitment options. I've also talked to the scientists compiling the results, and it seems we're getting a lower-than-expected number of positives from our screenings."

"So, what can we do?" asked Wachowski.

It was a good question, and one the general and I had discussed together.

"I'm told we'll have to build our command and send people for training to fill operational deficits. The good news is that from today we're no longer a temporary duty assignment, but a special duty assignment. The bad news is that the project's operations are on a need-to-know basis, and no one knows about us."

"I don't understand," said Wachowski.

"We're so black that the only way to be recruited is by the result of a test you don't realize you've taken. Way above our pay grades."

"Which still leaves us with the question of who we want or don't," said Ferretti.

"Looking at their performance reports doesn't tell us much, because no one stands out as being either exceptionally good or exceptionally bad. So my question is, what does your gut tell you?"

Ferretti responded, "In my opinion, it comes down to the lower ranks, and whether we want all the E3s, or whether we want the Marine E2 with us."

"That would be Private First Class Meireles. He's a bit of a whizz with electronics and can, of course, shoot his rifle at a target and hit it," said Wachowski.

"Let's not make this a service-rivalry argument, Sergeant."

"He seems to know his stuff, ma'am. My only reservation is that he has a bit of a chip on his shoulder."

"Chips?"

"Rough around the edges, ma'am."

"I'm sure that any rough edges will be rounded off in time, and he has a useful skill set. It looks like we're comparing the two airmen with the two Army privates. Any standouts?"

"Private Flores seems a better choice to me. I can cover Brown's skill set, and Flores will complement mine better."

"Would he be your choice, Master Sergeant?"

"Works for me, ma'am. Though, to be honest, it doesn't make much of a difference, given that both the airmen have transport and maintenance backgrounds, too."

I sat back and thought about the options. Nothing sprang off my PAD to indicate that any one choice was better than another. The general may well have given us first pick of who we could have, but the choices were all much of a muchness. "How are they acclimatizing to our daily routines?"

"They're all thinking *what the hell did we sign up for?*" said Wachowski.

"Even the Marines, Sergeant?"

"Even the Marines, though for different reasons than the rest. If anything, they enjoy leading the way with the runs and range practice, but they're all suffering from a bit of culture shock from the laid-back atmosphere of the project. It's a good thing we're going out soon, as we can get them over the hump and into the mission."

Ferretti asked, "What do we know about the new scientists we're escorting, ma'am?"

"According the list, most of them will be familiar faces. Here, let me send it to your PADs. Sorry, I should've done that before the meeting."

"Oh look, our favorite, Dr. Reynolds, is coming with us. Won't that be *fun*?" Wachowski groaned.

"Is there a problem I should be told about?" I asked.

Ferretti chided, "Wachowski, I warned you about making cute comments."

"No problem, ma'am. It's just that he's a bit abrasive toward us grunts, is all. Nothing we can't handle."

"To be absolutely fair, he is a bit brusque with everyone. Dr. Reynolds is not what you would call a people person, ma'am."

"I'd noticed, but we're going to be spending a lot of quality time with him. Will his presence affect the performance of our people and the success of the mission?"

"He's more of an asset than a burden, ma'am."

"You agree, Wachowski?"

"Yes. He's even warmed up a bit toward Ferretti for coming to save him, too."

"What about the rest of the scientists? You two have worked quite closely with most of them before."

"Well, it's good that Dr. Franklin is coming along with us. She seems to have a handle on Dr. Reynolds. They make a good team. Whether she sees it as a pleasure or a burden, I don't know. Grace and David are really sweet, and this will be a bit of a honeymoon for them. Dr. O'Neill needs no comment from me," said Wachowski.

She smiled at Ferretti, blowing him a kiss. Ferretti stared at Wachowski, and I raised an eyebrow to acknowledge what was not being said in the room.

"Doctors Wilson and Harrison both know each other and seem to get along OK. They may argue, but from what I've seen, it's about things they share in common and both feel very passionate about," said Wachowski.

"Both are just about on the right side of dorkiness as far as I'm concerned," said Ferretii.

I knew both of them to be geeks. Both passionate about old science fiction stories, which they read and discussed. "So that leaves us the three new scientists. Have either of you interacted with them?" I asked.

"Can't say I have, ma'am. Dr. O'Neill has, and she told me they're British with classy accents."

Wachowski asked, "How come the British scientists are working here?"

"All three have Confederation citizenship, so it's because of what they bring to their respective fields. Although Ms. Carter doesn't have a doctorate, and it makes me wonder what is so special about her, apart from the obvious. However, Dr. Bland is anything but; according to his CV, he has multiple masters degrees and is a leading exponent in cutting-edge theoretical physics. Dr. Smith appears quite bland by comparison."

Wachowski giggled.

"So, ma'am," said Ferretti, "we're left with the unenviable task of escorting a bunch of highly trained obsessives to an alien world and making sure they don't manage to do something that ends up with them hurting themselves or becoming dead."

"What did you expect? Welcome to the suck. You should know that by now," I said, smiling, and Ferretti laughed.

"The old ones are the best ones," said Wachowski.

"On that note, when do you plan to do the briefing, ma'am? Our people need something to focus on."

"Good point. Let's get them thinking about prepping for the mission ahead of them. Let's post the briefing for Monday at 0800. Wachowski, inform Private Brown that he will be joining Captain Buehler's team for me. Meeting closed. Dismissed."

Both stood to leave, but Ferretti paused, as if he wanted to say something. "If I may have a moment, ma'am?"

Wachowski smiled and left the room to the two of us.

"Sure, go ahead. What's it about?"

"Mr. Anderson booked tickets for the concert in town on Sunday for us and our partners, but I wanted to check it out with you first, ma'am."

Officers and enlisted fraternizing together is against policy, and Ferretti was worried that Glen had overstepped the mark.

"Think of it as team building. We're going out with civilians who work for a civilian-led operation. And besides, Glen loves his music."

Ferretti relaxed. "I would say *obsessed* myself."

"Coming from you, who geeks out on the minutia of recorded music, I find that hard to believe."

"Sorry, ma'am, no offense meant."

I smiled. "None taken. Dismissed."

6. WEEKEND OFF

*Love is what happens to a man and woman who don't know
each other.*

— W. SOMERSET MAUGHAM

Captain Lara Atsuko Tachikoma
Wenatchee, Washington State
Sunday, December 3, 2073

I woke up in bed to find my beloved behind me. I luxuriated in
the feeling of his warm body pressed into mine.

Afterward, I turned over and snuggled in his arms. This was
the last Sunday that we would be sleeping in our own bed, and I
wanted to make the most of those moments together.

Sunlight came through the cracks in the curtains, and I
realized it was nearly 0800, which meant I'd slept for almost three
hours longer than I usually do. Glen started to stir from his sleep,
and I nuzzled my body closer to his and felt him against me.

"This is a nice way to wake up on a Sunday."

"Ah…" I said. "I thought so, too."

"Going to miss you."

"Miss me, or miss this?"

"Both," he replied.

We moved together, and after a time, we rolled over and I laid my head on his shoulder. "I never knew what I was missing before I met you."

"I love you, too. There, I've said it. Happy now?"

"You didn't have to say you love me to please me. The fact that we're here now and you don't leave me afterward tells me you love me."

"You're one scary Marine. You know that, don't you? The Two-Bravos have given you the nickname of *Jane Wayne*."

"Yeah, so I heard through the grapevine. I looked it up, and it's quite a compliment really. I found an old movie on the net called *The Green Berets*. You should watch it sometime. It's hard to believe people thought they fought wars like that."

"Come on, what do you expect? People don't want realism. They want adventure and romance."

"I understand wanting romance, but adventure is highly overrated."

"You would say that. But your life is interrupted with enough heart-stopping moments that you don't need to seek out thrills elsewhere."

"Unlike you, of course, who sits at a desk all day analyzing intelligence gathered from around the globe and never sets foot outside to get your hands dirty. Except when you need to go and set up stuff, or sort out something which has gone tits up."

"Tits up," he said, kissing me and squeezing me tight as he rolled me over. Afterward, we fell asleep in each other's arms.

We got up an hour or so later and showered together, which ended up becoming another opportunity for Glen to slip into something comfortable.

Breakfast became brunch. I hadn't bothered to get dressed as such and was just wearing a kimono as I cooked eggs sunny-side up for the two of us with bacon, pancakes, and maple syrup while Glen made fresh OJ and coffee. Meanwhile, he had put on jeans and a white T-shirt.

"You better not be thinking what I think you're thinking."

"I couldn't possibly comment, as I don't read minds and haven't a clue what you're thinking," I said.

"You'll kill me at this rate."

"Hardly likely to do that. I haven't finished with you yet."

"See, that's what I mean."

"Anyway, I'm going to get dressed so we can go out. Anything you want to do this afternoon?"

"I thought you wanted to go to the range."

"Works as a plan for me, but what about you?"

"I'm looking forward to the concert tonight. I hear the Wenatchee Valley Symphony Orchestra performance of Alexander Borodin's *Prince Igor* and the Polovtsian Dances is stunningly good. Vincent recommended it to me, and he's planning on taking Allison with him."

Which was not what Ferretti had said, and I figured Glen was omitting what had been said out of habit. It's one of the downsides of dating a CIA analyst.

The truth is out there, but it's probably classified.

Glen continued speaking excitedly. "It's a chance to listen to live music. It's down on Thirty-Three North Mission and First."

"Well, it will give me an excuse to wear my little black dress I bought recently before I go."

"You know how to spoil a man."

"Down, tiger, I've already ridden enough today."

"Spoilsport."

"Don't tempt me, otherwise you will be sore and regret it for the rest of the day."

"The voice of reason. I hear and I obey, my mistress."

"Yeah right. Let me go and put some pants and a top on, and you can go grab our gear and put it the back of the Jeep. I might as well get to drive it one more time before I go."

By the time I had dressed and put on some boots, Glen had gotten the Jeep out and loaded her up with our range bags and gun cases.

The day was bright and cold, and every breath produced a cloud of condensation, but we both wore fleeces. Even so, I turned up the heating in the Jeep, which, to be quite frank, wasn't its best feature, though it did keep our feet warm.

Still, what do you expect from an enthusiasts' vehicle designed to be taken off-road, off-grid, and driven manually without any computer backup?

The engine growled as I put the pedal down.

When we got to the range, we both wanted to try out our early Christmas presents. Glen had bought me a lovely old Walther PPQ that looked like it had never been fired since it had been made sixty years ago. All original, apart from the replacement parts.

So, a bit like George Washington's ax. I wanted to run a few rounds through her before going off-world. Glen had also gotten me two spare magazines to go with the one it had come with.

Like all things old world, the pistol came in a smart-looking case with a cleaning kit and places to store the magazines. There was also a book that thanked me for purchasing this product and instructed me on how to clean it to get the best performance out of my purchase.

As they say, they don't make them like that anymore.

With my ears defenders on, I went through a magazine to get a taste of how it fired. Next, I adjusted the sight to suit my left-eye dominance, which is a pain in the butt when shooting with traditional pistols that don't talk to one's PAD.

There's something really satisfying about hitting a target using one's own skill. There's as much an art to it as craft. But once one is in the zone, the satisfaction from getting a good set of groupings is awesome.

I dropped the first magazine, slapped in my second, and tried again.

The grouping was good, but the shots were all down on the left of the target. So I adjusted the tritium sights again, a nonstandard aftermarket addition, because as I said, this is a sixty-year-old pistol from back in the day.

The gunsmith who'd worked it over at some point had put on a matching thumb slide guard and extended ambidextrous slide releases, which was definitely not to the original specification.

I fired the third magazine at a new paper target and then retrieved it to compare with the previous two. It had a much better group that was tight around the black.

But I needed more practice on my trigger-pull technique, as I could tell the pistol was moving off line as I fired. So I changed the backstrap to increase the distance between the grip and the trigger.

It's a good thing I enjoy working on getting it set up right for me to shoot, because it's quite repetitive to adjust then shoot, and then readjust and shoot again.

After emptying all three magazines, I used a reloader to save my fingers. Using one makes sliding the 9 x 19mm Parabellum rounds into the magazines really easy.

I then fired three magazines worth of bullets at the poor defenseless paper targets, taking great delight in watching the holes appear, before repeating the process of reloading.

I also chose to practice clearing a misfire, which is always a useful skill when one is in a tight corner. I set up a timer with my PAD and pretended every other round was a misfire.

This requires one to drop the magazine first before clearing the round, then slapping the magazine in and loading the pistol by pulling back the slide.

After emptying the third magazine practicing this technique, the slide locked back. I decided to call it a day and picked up all the live ammo scattered on the floor.

I really wanted to take her apart and clean her, as I like taking things apart and seeing how they go back together again. I guess once a Marine, always a Marine.

Especially when it comes to keeping one's weapon clean.

I sat down at the back of the gallery range, checking again the breech was clear. Next, I read the instructions, then went through the step-by-step process of releasing the slide to strip the Walther down into its component parts.

The gunsmith had done a lovely job on modifying the polymer frame to upgrade the slide release, and I could see the barrel was a more modern aftermarket replacement from Magnum Research. She may be a bit of a hybrid, but she sure shot sweetly with not one single real misfire during my practice session.

As Christmas presents go, this one rocked.

I was pretty engrossed with cleaning my pistol and geeking out on the neat genuine Walther cleaning kit when Glen came and caught me by surprise.

"Hey, hon, how you doing?"

"Hey you, give me a kiss. I'm in love with my present."

"What about me?"

"Don't be such a tease. How did it go for you?"

"Good. Talked shop with the guys down on the one-hundred-yard range and shot some rounds. The new sight you got me is great. Using the collimator has really tightened my groupings. You were right about the scope making it harder."

Glen was into old rifles.

He'd been using his Fulton Armory M1 carbine with an UltiMAK front-end rebuild that allowed him to hang stuff off it like a Christmas tree, like most enthusiasts who haven't had to lug their rifle through Marine Corps recruit training and learnt better do.

I'd gotten him an old EOTech XPS2-Zombie holosight to replace the overlarge telescopic lens whose focus distance was five times the effective range of the .30 cal carbine round. I'd tried his M1, and she was a pretty sweet personal defense weapon that could do nail-tight groups at one hundred yards.

"Yeah, well I hate to say I told you so, but I told you so."

"You ready to go home?"

"Just about. Let me finish off here, put away my new best present in the whole wide world, and then we can go home and change. After all, I did promise to put on a dress for tonight's concert."

We got home and unpacked, and I showered again. Then I spent time on my hair, letting it down and teasing out the knots from the day.

Mom always made such a fuss over it, which used to annoy me when I was a child, as all I wanted to do was get outside and play.

She used to complain about me being such a tomboy, too.

I'm not what you would call much of a girly girl, but I had bought a nice little black dress for going out in. It hit all the right spots for Glen while still being comfortable, for definitions of comfort that meant I had to comport myself in a ladylike manner when getting into and out of vehicles.

I even wore heels, which are usually anathema to me.

But I had to admit that my usual combat boots didn't really go with the dress. Not unless I wanted to go for a post-apocalypse-survivor look, which would have required having a shoulder holster to carry my new baby in.

However, turning up for a concert looking like I was ready to start fighting zombies wouldn't send the right message. Also, blood splatter gets everywhere, and it can be really hard to get out in the wash.

We didn't take the Jeep down to Mission and First, but we were lucky enough to arrive and find parking nearby for Glen's truck.

As we walked the short distance to the hall, a lot of the great and good of Wenatchee were out. Everyone was dressed to the nines, which was a good thing because it meant I wasn't overdressed for the occasion.

One of the problems I have with civilian events is working out what to wear when I'm not required to be in uniform.

I'm not a big fan of the let's-all-wear-something-similar school that lots of my male colleagues take when wearing civvies. Even though I understand the comfort that comes from not standing out from the crowd.

Glen, having been out of the service and working for The Company for a number of years, tended to go for a blazer and slacks when he wasn't wearing a suit, like tonight.

"Hey, it looks like they're fully sold out," I said.

"What makes you think that, hon? Apart from the sign that says tonight's performance is sold out."

"Sarcasm will not get you far. I just meant look at all the people. I didn't realize so many people would want to come and listen to live music."

"Remember, I told you it had good reviews. I can see Vincent over there with Allison going through the door now."

"So it is. I would never have guessed if you hadn't told me."

"Now who is being sarcastic?"

"Love you," I said, blowing him a kiss.

While I like listening to music, Glen is a full-on audio nerd who likes collecting one-eighty-gram, first-master-pressing vinyl records. He plays them on his beloved seventy-year-old Michell GyroDec using some equally arcane and ancient arm with a thing called an Audiophonics V4 cartridge.

All hoarded from the Golden Age of "real audio," as he was most often wont to tell me.

It all rather went over my head, and mostly I turned off when he started talking about the finer intricacies of his sound system. But I had to admit, the music he played did sound good.

Ferretti was big into classical music, too, so they both got on, as my mother would say, like houses on fire. But Ferretti was, much to Glen's chagrin, wedded to a seemingly equally arcane digital master MPEG Spatial Audio Object Coding.

Whatever that was.

By the time their discussions on the various merits of analog versus digital started, it all sounded like blah, blah, blah to me, which I tuned out.

The four of us sat near the front of the auditorium, in what I would consider the good seats. But I don't really know enough about the whole real music experience, other than I know what I like, and I like what I know.

The concert was everything the reviews said it would be. The performance was stunning, lively, and I found myself tapping my foot along to the music.

Still, it was nice to have Allison to talk to in the interval while the boys had *nerdgasms* over the sound of a live performance compared to recordings. Way over my head, and I suspect when it came to appreciating the finer points of listening to music, Allison was much the same as I—more into how it felt than the technicalities.

She complimented me on my dress, and we talked about stuff other than men.

This was all good as far as I was concerned. Then she asked me if I would teach her to shoot. That came as a surprise, and my opinion of her went up several notches.

7. BRIEFING

Success demands a high level of logistical and organizational competence.

— GEN GEORGE S. PATTON, USAR

Captain Lara Atsuko Tachikoma
Magnetic Anomaly Project Command
Classified Location West of Wenatchee, Washington
Monday, December 11, 2073

I entered the locker room for the mission briefing at 0800. The room's walls were painted beige, the ceiling an off-white color, and the recessed lighting fittings and fixtures were a dull white.

The room was pretty typical of every military establishment I'd ever been in.

Master Sergeant Ferretti called out, "*Attenshun,* officer present."

This caused a wave of movement as the members of Mike Team One rose out of their seats in response. I took in my surroundings for a moment.

"Morning, people." I almost said *Devils*, but the troops under my command weren't all Marines.

A murmur of errrs, yuts, and hoahs followed.

Still, for some strange reason the room reminded me of *that* day aboard the CSN *Hornet*. The day when the 1st Combat Armor Suit Reconnaissance Company had been sent into Afghanistan on a search-and-rescue mission.

A mission that had led to me walking through the pillars. Doing so had changed my life forever. I only hoped I would not lose anyone on this mission, as that was never a cheap toll to pay.

"Everyone got coffee?" Another round of replies in the affirmative came back at me.

"Our mission to One-Three-Four-Zero has been given a *go* by MAPCOM under the title of Operation Prometheus. We will transition through the pillars on Saturday the twenty-third at 1500 PST, during the five-minute window of opportunity the pillars afford us."

I looked around at the faces of my team, some of whom I knew from Two Moons, the others being new people who had joined us in the last few weeks. I had not yet had enough time to get to know all of the new people properly.

But I was sure that six months off-world together should rectify that omission.

"Our planned return back to MAPCOM is six months later."

Some of the new people looked askance at the news of a long-term deployment to another world. Our mission meant that they would not be at home with loved ones for Christmas.

"The primary purpose of this mission is to reconnoiter the alien base on One-Three-Four-Zero. Our job is to assess any alien technology we find there and return with samples for further study back here on Earth. Our androids, in conjunction with RollaBot sensor drones, have mapped out the interior of the cavern on One-Three-Four-Zero, which is approximately eighty meters in diameter and thirty meters high."

I paused to bring up the first image on the briefing room's screen and let everyone take in the details.

"It looks like whoever made this installation enlarged a natural rock formation to suit their needs. We've been able to see two large doors on opposite sides to the pillars that appear to serve the same purpose as ours here. We've discovered a marked area that seems to indicate a road going through the space between the pillars."

Then I put up arrows with captions of what they pointed at. The clarity of the information belied the uncertainty of the chances for the mission's success.

"All around the cavern are smaller doors that lead to either access corridors, other rooms, or storage cupboards. In addition, we have found a discontinuity in the wall that indicates an entrance that leads up out of the cavern. Finally, we've detected a low level of electromagnetic radiation emanating from one of the consoles situated on one wall."

I paused to let the mumbles around the room quieten down as the information from what I had said sunk in.

"In the event we meet aliens on One-Three-Four-Zero, our aim is to negotiate with them to facilitate our primary mission. Only if there's a failure to communicate and we're unable to negotiate to prevent hostilities from occurring will we adopt an aggressive posture."

As far as I was concerned, this meant we would be engaging in an operation other than war. However, I remembered how well that had worked out the last time on Two Moons.

"I repeat—we're not expecting to meet any aliens. All the signs indicate this base has been unoccupied during the last two years since we first discovered its existence. Attached to us will be a dozen civilian scientists who are under our care. They will be carrying out the studies of the alien base and leading the retrieval of any alien technology."

Assuming of course that there was anything left to find and strip out to bring back.

"We will deploy through the pillars in a convoy of fifteen trucks. Once we're on the other side of the pillars, we will form a circle around the room. Our arrival there should awaken anyone who is alive. We will maintain a combat ready posture until the area is deemed secure through a physical search of the room. Any questions so far?"

All eyes in the room were looking at me. Everyone had seen the self-drive program simulations, which had worked out how to squeeze all the trucks into the cavern.

My people shook their heads in response to my question.

"Given the length of this deployment, we'll be taking everything we need through with us. So, if you think you need something, pack it, because there's no easy way to come back to get anything you have forgotten."

Which raised a few chuckles.

"Excuse me, ma'am," said Private First Class Flores. "If I've understood you right, we're being sent to a room on an alien planet that we may or may not be able to get out of and therefore could be effectively confined inside of for six months."

"That's correct."

"My question is, what happens if we get trapped there?"

"Given our scans and our experience with using the pillars, the risk of missing the return opening is considered minimal. Our job is to make sure we don't miss our return window."

"Six months seems like a very long time to be trapped in a room."

"Better take some books to read with you, Flores," said Private First Class Meireles.

"Or games," said Airman First Class Mitchell.

"Can the chat, people," said Master Sergeant Ferretti. "Mitchell and Meireles come and see me afterward."

"Keep in mind that six months is shorter than an overseas deployment. I know this isn't what you wanted to hear, but you all volunteered when you signed up and took the oath. MAPCOM's assessment of the situation is that the benefits from being able to get our hands on advanced alien technology outweigh the costs. Does that answer your concerns?"

"Yes, thank you, ma'am."

"The local conditions are equivalent to standing on a three-thousand-meter mountain on Earth. Our PACE suits and trucks are pressurized to compensate. But we will still be at risk of suffering from altitude sickness. Therefore, each truck will also be carrying a pressure chamber"—which looked like coffins —"which can hold one person in case of a medical emergency."

Also, we had four trucks outfitted with converted Conex boxes to provide the expedition with mobile sleeping quarters. I then brought up a list of symptoms from altitude sickness and paused to let people take in the info.

"However, I don't imagine any of us will want to be sleeping inside our suits or cramped up inside the cab of a truck at night for six months. I remind you that as of today you will all be taking ibuprofen, and twenty-four hours before departure everyone will be given acetazolamide as a prophylactic against altitude sickness."

No one made any quips about condoms.

"In the unlikely event of a person sustaining an injury during or after transit, they will be placed under the care of Corpsman Keith. Dr. Leung and Dr. O'Neill are our two first aiders. But, Keith will be charge of any serious injury. He will also treat anyone who shows symptoms of altitude sickness."

I then summarized the basics.

"Remember to watch out for any unexplained headaches and

coughing. If you do notice anyone with symptoms, you will report them to Keith, who will be able to provide effective treatment. By this I mean you are to keep an eye on the civilians, too."

Predictably, someone started to cough.

"Now that you mention it, I have a headache," said Airman First Class Green.

This earned him a hard stare from Wachowski and a look-into-my-eye gesture from Ferretti.

"On the subject of our scientists, any items of alien equipment they identify to be brought back must be packed according to their instructions. It's of the utmost importance for us to bring everything we're physically capable of moving with us. Remember that this is a golden opportunity to excel."

People groaned as they entered their notes on their PADs, and I came to the last part of my briefing.

"Finally, the chain of command. My intention is to organize our detachment into two teams of six, with Sergeant Wachowski and myself in one and Master Sergeant Ferretti heading the other. However, as half of you are new to my command, I will warn you now that there are three ways of doing things. The right way, the wrong way, and the Marine Corps way."

This was greeted by a few "oorahs" from the Marines on our team.

"What this means in practice is that we will improvise, adapt, and overcome any problems we come up against. And I expect a flexible mindset from the people under my command. This includes changing teams on the basis of operational need."

A few of the team shuffled nervously. This wasn't something they'd been trained to do, but the size of the team and the needs of the mission required it.

"I will lead by example and expect nothing more from you than I expect from myself. Any questions?"

Corporal Langford asked, "Ma'am, who is assigned to which team?"

I paused to look at her before answering. "A good question. Master Sergeant Ferretti has the list."

Ferretti stood up and faced the team. "Yes, ma'am. In Team One, with the captain and Sergeant Wachowski, will be Corpsman Keith, Petty Officer Adams, Specialist Nelson, and Private Flores. With me in Team Two will be Corporal Langford, Lance Corporal Avari, Airmen Green and Mitchell, and Private Meireles."

A chorus of "huahs," "oorahs," and "yes, Sergeants" followed the announcement of the assignments.

"Are we good to go?" Master Sergeant Ferretti paused to see if anyone would say anything.

"Obviously, I expect you to approach your sergeants in whose capable hands I leave you. But if you need to speak to me before going, then please book an appointment," I said.

Now all we had to do was go forth and not muck it all up. Which meant getting back in one piece. How hard could that be?

"OK, people, asses and elbows. Let's start acting like we have a purpose," said Sergeant Wachowski.

8. MISSION DEPARTS

The very basic core of a man's living spirit is his passion for adventure.

— CHRISTOPHER MCCANDLESS

Captain Lara Atsuko Tachikoma
Magnetic Anomaly Project Command
Classified Location West of Wenatchee, Washington
Saturday, December 23, 2073

Outside the base, the weather had arrived in force as a storm front swept down from the north. But we were oblivious to what was going on in the outside world. We were under the mountain in the tunnel that led into the cavern.

I was sat in the cab of the first truck of our convoy. We were ready to go through the pillars, just waiting for the time to move.

Glen's mission had gone through to Two Moons a few days before us. We'd been able to find one last private moment together before he'd departed. This would have to last us both through the next six months. We'd said everything that needed to be said over the previous weekend. But I wanted to hold him one more time.

I'd been surprised when Glen had whispered in my ear, "One of the scientists is not like the others. Guess who." So now I fretted over the message, and what it meant.

I knew Glen kept secrets from me. He had to.

One part of his job was to ferret out secrets. The other was to hide the things he found away. Secrets were grist for the CIA's mill, and they liked to grind things ever so fine.

As a Marine, I'd been on an Agency-sponsored operation. But now I was living with a spook who'd told me something without actually telling me anything specific. Go figure.

Now all I had to do was work out who it was, and why someone felt the need to put their asset on my team.

Sergeant Wachowski was at the wheel of the leading Oshkosh HUHMTT. The M2184 had been chosen for its ability to traverse difficult terrain. All the wheels were driven and steerable by the onboard computer system. Wachowski would lead the convoy through the pillars when the gate cycled to One-Three-Four-Zero.

Behind us sat Dr. Wilson and Dr. Wong, the latter studiously ignoring the former's attempts to engage in conversation.

From what I had overheard, Dr. Wilson was talking about his second most favorite topic in the whole wide world, which was the science fiction stories he'd read. His favorite topic of discussion was the mathematics underlying the hidden beauty of harmonic frequencies of the pillars as they resonated each time they pulsed when opening.

The former could be amusing to listen to for a short time; the latter went way over the head of anyone who wasn't a mathematician.

However, Dr. Wilson had failed to realize that his attempt to be amusing by recounting the stories he'd read had bored Dr. Wong. He'd not noticed she'd turned her body away from him and was pointedly staring out the window at the interior of the gate room.

This, in my opinion, held all the fascination of watching paint dry.

At five mikes to kickoff, Sergeant Miller in the gate control room came on-screen. "Just confirming everything is green across the board. The countdown is proceeding on schedule."

According to Ferretti, Miller was not the brightest star in the night's sky.

My impression of the man was of someone who went through the motions, doing the minimum he could get away with. No more, no less. Miller had found a niche that was comfortable and unchallenging. In other words, a timeserver who was taking it easy.

Our convoy was now inching toward the ramp that led to the pillars. Wachowski had everything programmed so we would hit the shimmer and pass through the pillars while maintaining two-second lead times between each truck as they accelerated.

"Roger that, gate control. Confirm all green across the board here, and the countdown continues at one minute to opening."

"I wish MacReady were sending us off," said Wachowski.

"If we're lucky, he will be on duty when we come back. How are you both doing back there?"

"I'm fine, Captain," said Dr. Wilson. "I'll never get over the excitement of doing this. Never would've imagined I'd be able to do this for real, though. I was just telling Li-Na about all the stories I've read and seen about portals to other worlds."

"Why do we have to sit and wait in the truck for so long?" asked Dr. Wong, whose expression was hard to read, but whose tone told me she was bored.

"It reduces the risk of accidents during transit, Doc," I said.

"Better to be bored and safe than experiencing the terror from things going all pear-shaped because someone is rushed when doing something dangerous," said Wachowski.

I raised an eyebrow at her. She smiled and winked back at me.

We'd organized the convoy so the personnel and mission-critical items were distributed across all the trucks. It was our way of trying to reduce our vulnerability from unforeseen problems, like a truck stalling.

This still left the food, water, and fuel concentrated in six vehicles. These were vital for the success of our six-month mission to One-Three-Four-Zero—as in, we would be dead without it.

Therefore, I sat at the head of the convoy so I could abort the mission without having any of our people stranded on the other side.

"OK, ten seconds till shimmer time," said Wachowski, her voice rising with excitement, which we all felt.

She flicked the switch that simultaneously made the trucks go from microturning to accelerating to transit speed. The synchronized convoy then crossed the last few meters toward the pillars to reach them as our portal opened.

Ahead of us, the space between the pillars rippled, and the beacon confirmed this really was our opening to One-Three-Four-Zero.

The motors whined as we sped up, and then the truck juddered on the ramp with the crackling sound of the pillars discharging across the cab. Our headlights lit up the enormous cavern as we dropped down on the other side.

Wachowski drove the truck toward the wall ahead of us before swinging right, turning, and following the curve of the cavern, leading the convoy in a circle away from and around the pillars.

The rearview window of my screen showed the second and third trucks pass the pillars behind us before the angle of our turn cut off the view. So, I set my screen's feed to automatically switch to the last truck.

Static from magnetic interference broke up the image, which cleared as each truck traversed the pillars and entered the cavern.

"Alpha Tango One Six to Alpha Bravo, all the trucks in the convoy have transitioned through safely, over."

"Roger that, Alpha Tango One Six. Pillar closure in twenty seconds, over," said Miller.

"We shaved five seconds off the time it took to transition the convoy, ma'am. That's a new record," said Wachowski.

"I didn't realize we had a pool on transit times."

"Just between me and a few of the others, ma'am."

"Well, it's good to know we won," I said, turning my attention back to the radio. "Keep the place warm for us and see you all in six months, over."

"Copy that. We'll be here and waiting, over."

"Alpha Tango One Six, out," I said just before the pillars cut off further transmissions.

Wachowski brought the convoy to a smooth halt with enough room to disembark from both sides of the vehicle. I switched channels and put a call through to all the trucks.

"Teams One and Two, move out and begin a search of the cavern. I ask that all the scientists remain seated until we can give the all clear."

Our trucks had plenty of room to snake around and fit inside what was effectively a small stadium eighty meters in diameter. The dust that lay upon everything had been disturbed by our arrival, and our trucks' headlamps revealed motes swirling in the air around the convoy.

The ceiling, thirty meters above our heads, hung like a dark blanket ready to smother us.

As I opened the truck's door, the dry, freezing air of the cavern greeted me. The temperature in the cabin dropped several degrees with Doctors Wilson and Wong both complaining as I stepped down onto the cold floor of the underground alien base.

I was grateful to be wearing my MARPACE suit, which heats up to keep me warm.

Ferretti shouted, "Let's do this by the numbers. Pair up and spread out and see if anyone's home!"

We would make a Marine out of him yet.

Everyone deployed in their assigned pairings and fanned out to search the base. I walked back toward the pillars as Keith joined me. We went to check on the base station that had been placed by an android team to monitor their activation and record where they cycled to.

It still had power, and Dr. Wilson had brought along new power cells to keep it running while we were here. The plan was to replace them again before we went home. They would then last for another six months, thereby keeping the monitoring station active until the next time the pillars cycled back to Earth.

I knew Dr. Wilson was keen to download the memory core and start work on processing the data it contained.

However, I was more interested in examining the location around the pillars to find any evidence that might shed light on how one of our androids had gone missing. It was, as I suspected, a forlorn hope.

All I could see were the patterns in dust from the feet from the previous android teams we'd sent through in the last eighteen months, not helped by the trucks passing through the pillars and the convoy running over everything when we came in.

Still, it kept me amused to think about something other than what Glen had said. And it also passed the time while we waited for everyone to finish searching the place. Finally, the reports of "all clear" started to come in as my people finished their search of the cavern.

"Hey, we've found that opening in the wall with a ramp that leads up over here!" came a shout from Nelson and Flores.

"Shine your light up so we can identify where 'over here' is!" shouted Wachowski, saving me the bother of having to state the obvious as I saw a light waving on the wall where Nelson and Flores were standing.

I went over to take a look. They'd found the discontinuity the RollaBots had mapped out when surveying the cavern.

The wall appeared to be seamless from one direction, but as one moved around, a space opened up with a ramp leading upward.

One of our RollaBots rested at the bottom of the ramp, testament to the fact that it had been unable to roll up very far. The dust on the floor lay otherwise undisturbed.

So, it didn't look likely that our missing android had wondered up and got lost walking up the ramp.

"It's not often you see something this neat. Should we check it out, ma'am?" asked Wachowski.

"Yes, I think we better," I said, turning and shouting, "Ferretti, you're in charge until I return!"

"Are you sure you want to do that, ma'am?" came the reply as Ferretti trotted over toward me with Airman Green at his side.

"The place seems to be abandoned, so I'll take Team One up to check out where it goes. Judging from what we've seen so far, this may be another way out of this place. It also looks like we should be able get the convoy up to the top of wherever the ramp goes."

"It would be a good plan B, ma'am. I will tell the scientists they can get out of the trucks now. They may be able to help us get the doors open."

"Sounds good to me. I imagine they're dying for the chance to get their fingers on stuff. Give them whatever help they need to find a way to open one of the two doors, just in case this ramp leads nowhere. Remind them that Corporal Langford likes blowing things up, which should motivate them. My team will drop transponders to keep in touch as we go up."

"I'll keep an eye on your progress, ma'am."

"OK, Sergeant Wachowski, time for Team One to move out."

"Nelson and Flores, take point. Adams, you're with me," said Wachowski as she brought up the rear of Team One.

It felt familiar to be going through the routine. Just like old times.

We started walking up the ramp, with only the lights from our suits illuminating the darkness ahead, which swung in an arc that mirrored the cavern. Behind me Wachowski dropped the first transponder at the base of the ramp. The network pinged to signal its existence.

I could have, if I'd wanted, monitored everything that was going on in the cavern through my MARPACE suit HUD. But I chose to let Ferretti do his thing below us while we walked up and around in a large spiral.

The ramp was nearly four meters wide at the floor. The walls on the outside curved up above and over our heads to join seamlessly to the vertical wall to our left. And the corridor seemed to be made from something similar to concrete.

Despite the incline, and being effectively at high altitude, walking up the slope inside our power armor suits was light work.

The farther we walked, the more it looked to me as if the base had been dug out rather than being some natural formation found in the ground. But there again, I wasn't an engineer, or a geologist for that matter, and this was an alien world.

No doubt, given enough time our scientists would have come up with answers as to when and how the base was made. The corridor wound on ahead of us, going upward with the walls maintaining a perfect arc like half of an archway above our heads all the way.

"These guys weren't much into corners," said Wachowski.

"I guess not. Sooner we get to the top, the sooner we will find out where it leads us to," I replied.

"Come on, people, pick up the pace. We haven't got all day!" shouted Wachowski.

She had interpreted my comment as "let's get a move on" and was probably still relishing being a sergeant, I guess. I can't blame her for wanting to be seen as a totally Moto Marine.

After thirty minutes, I checked how far we had gone on the map, which was being drawn from the transponder feed data. A three-dimensional drawing of the route we'd taken came up that showed we'd walked three times around the perimeter of the cavern. This meant the cavern was now below us.

As we kept walking upward, the air temperature around us began to rise.

My suit radio came to life with a call from Ferretti. "Zero Six, this is Zero Four. Come in, over."

"OK, five-minute rest break. Drink some water, people," I said. "Zero Six receiving you loud and clear. What's up? Over."

"Just wanted to let you know the progress on opening both the doors down here. They appear to be locked, but Dr. Bland thinks he can unlock them using the power from the trucks. Assuming, of course, he and Ms. Carter can find where the power inputs are. So no need to rush back here. We've also found what appears to be a manual operating lever, but we will need a CASE suit to get enough leverage to operate it. It's stuck tight."

"That's good news indeed. I'd rather not have Langford blow up stuff unless absolutely necessary. We've not seen anything interesting so far, but our feeds show the air temperature is rising as we climb higher, over."

"Copy that. It certainly beats freezing our butts off down here, over."

"It certainly does. We'll carry on here. Keep us informed of your progress. Out," I said, turning toward Wachowski. "Move 'em out, Sergeant. Drop transponders at standard intervals."

"You heard the captain. Up and at 'em, people."

Our team got up and started walking with the usual mutterings about how the place could be improved with some paint and pictures. This caused Wachowski to sigh in recognition of her own habit of making the selfsame comments, and how annoying they can be when others do it.

She would learn.

Still, it meant my people were in good spirits, and this place looked as dead as the proverbial dead dog party after all the booze had been drunk. The dust on the floor was dirty gray, but as I stepped forward, I noticed a glint and stopped to examine it.

Kneeling down, I swept the floor with my hand and saw a thin line of metal embedded in the surface.

"What do you think it is, ma'am?"

"Beats me, Sergeant. It looks like something someone might follow if they didn't know where they were going, but I can't imagine that's the case here. Perhaps it's a guideline for machinery. Something to ponder on during the coming months, I guess."

That was about the most exciting thing we'd found so far. As places to visit on an alien world, this one left a lot to be desired, unless one was into walking up the inside of a giant helter-skelter that was.

It took us another hour to get to where we saw light streaming in from outside ahead of us.

9. CAVERN

Time is the longest distance between two places.

— TENNESSEE WILLIAMS

Master Sergeant Ferretti
Planet 1340
Day One of Operation Prometheus
Saturday, December 23, 2073

Ferretti had his power armor suit's mask and visor flipped back over his head, and his breath condensed in the dry, ice-cold air. He observed the captain walk up the ramp, leaving him in command.

Her orders were to manage the scientists, which in his opinion was like trying to herd cats.

"OK, team, let our scientists know it's safe for them to come out and play now!"

Acknowledgement of his order rang around the cavern. Then the civilians got down from the trucks, the scale of the place sinking in now that they were out of the vehicles.

"Langford, come with me and talk me through our options on the door."

"Coming, Master Sergeant," said Langford, trotting over to walk beside him to examine the doors.

"That's one big door," he said in amazement, stating the obvious. The door conformed to the shape of the cavern, which arced in a dome high above their heads.

"Sure is, and one wonders why they went to the trouble of making it curved. You only usually build a door like these in observatories or similar when it's part of the supporting structure," said Langford.

"Everything here is curved. I haven't seen one surface meet another at a right angle. Perhaps they liked curving surfaces?"

"Could be, Master Sergeant. Not the way I would build it, though."

"Perhaps you'll get the chance to tell them if we meet them. Anyway, opening the door, can you do it?"

"Sure thing. There's no door that can't be opened if you use enough explosives."

"Without killing us with the overpressure, *Corporal*."

"Excuse me, I couldn't help overhear what you were saying," came the distinctively British-accented voice of Dr. Simon Bland, a slightly rotund individual who walked up with his assistant, Ms. Carter, by his side. She, by contrast was a tall, angular redhead, slightly older than him.

"Dr. Bland, Ms. Carter. How may I be of assistance?"

"It's rather the reverse, actually. We may be able to open this door without you having to blow a hole in it. All things considered, it may be wiser not to go around blowing up other people's property, because that might cause offense. They might consider us uncultured barbarians who like to destroy things rather than explorers and ambassadors from another world," said Dr. Bland.

"Okeydokey. If you can open it, that would be great. How long do you need?"

"What do you think, Lily?"

"This place is totally awesome. If only it didn't make me feel so ill."

"I meant in regard to opening the door."

"Oh that, sorry. At the minimum, a couple of hours, once we've got the tool made to remove the fasteners on the panels. Maybe longer, depending on what we find. We're making some awfully big assumptions about whether we can interface with the aliens' technology."

Ms. Carter spoke in an even more clipped accent than Dr. Bland, which Ferretti found hard to follow.

"You better have at it then. Let me know when you're ready to proceed. And if you need any help, please ask."

"Thank you, we will," said Dr. Bland, who then walked away talking to Ms. Carter about power couplings and voltage frequencies.

"Langford, come up with a plan to blow the doors in case the good doctor and his assistant's idea doesn't work."

"Aye, aye, Master Sergeant."

Ferretti turned and walked alongside the trucks, which were parked in a semicircle around the wall of the cavern. He was taking the time to check on how everyone was doing.

It also gave him the chance to gawp at the size of the place and have an excuse to talk to Allison.

He came alongside one of the trucks where Allison was talking with the newlyweds, Mr. and Mrs. Leung, Grace and David, who were making tea with a JetBoil.

"Hey you, do you want a drink?" asked Allison.

"I wouldn't mind a coffee."

"Give us a moment," said Dr. David Leung.

Ferretti asked, "How's married life?"

"It's good. You should try it," replied Dr. Grace Leung.

"Stop that, Grace. You're embarrassing him, my dear," said her husband, who smiled.

"Allison, I hear this young man of yours likes music."

"He does, and he took me to a concert the other week. He has many hidden talents."

"I'm sure he does, my dear. It's good to see you kids getting along so well."

Ferretti wasn't sure he would describe himself and Allison as kids, but then again, everything in life is relative.

Both of the Leungs were in their fifties and had been single until Grace had saved David's life after he was shot on Two Moons. Afterward, they'd started a relationship. Allison had told him that marrying the woman who saved your life was a sign of true love.

But at this moment, Ferretti felt he had been placed into an awkward position with regard to his relationship and his role as master sergeant. The civilians didn't seem to be able to get their heads around the military's need for formal relationships while at work.

Ferretti asked, "Anyone seen Dr. Smith? I haven't seen him around."

"Last time I saw him, he was in the back of the truck snoring his head off. As far as I know, he's still asleep," said Allison.

"I guess he's staying warm inside the truck. How's everyone coping with the air pressure? Any problems?"

They all looked at him and shook their heads.

Grace and David had made themselves the center of the action, where everybody had an excuse to come and have a drink and chat. Ferretti savored his coffee.

One by one the members of his team drifted up and asked if they could have something hot to drink, too. It seemed to him people were getting to know each other and form bonds.

He was all for team building. Anything to help the mission be a success over the ensuing months and keep people on track during any setbacks. It was amazing what a simple thing like sharing a hot drink could do to build friendships.

"Did we show you the alien text we've found?"

"No, ma'am, you haven't," Ferretti replied.

Dr. Leung pulled out her PAD and scrolled through a series of pictures of what he assumed must be the equivalent of instruction labels.

"The yellow and purple ones might be danger signs, as they stand out more than green-on-white one's, but that's only a guess."

"Any idea what they say?"

"Grace thinks instructions and warnings to the user, but they could easily be names of things. Without something to act as a Rosetta Stone, we can't tell. I only hope we will find more writing and something that will allow us to decode the language."

"It seems like you have your work cut out for you, Doc."

He savored the last drop of his of coffee as Ms. Carter came up and asked for a cup of black coffee for herself and a cup of tea for Dr. Bland, white with two sugars. "Coffee? I thought English people liked tea?"

"Oh, I like tea first thing in the morning. It gets the liver working, but in the afternoon I prefer coffee, as it keeps me going when I start to wilt. Does this ever get old? I mean the feeling of coming through the pillars."

"No, not really. I understand it's something to do with the way the magnetic fields around the pillars affect the brain. Anyway, how's it going over there?"

"We've got one of the panels off," said Ms. Carter. "Uhm, this is the best cup of coffee I've had. Everything back on the base tasted foul." She took the two drinks she'd been given.

Ferretti waved goodbye to Allison as he followed Ms. Carter over to where Dr. Bland was working.

From what he could tell, they had uncovered lots of cables and other stuff he couldn't recognize. Airmen Green and Mitchell were helping them. They'd unwound a jumper cable from the nearby truck and were pulling it toward where the work was being carried out.

"Here you go, tea, white with two. Sorry, no biscuits," said Ms. Carter.

"Thanks, Lily. Uhmmmmh, that's a lovely cup of tea," said Dr. Bland, sipping his drink. "Hello. Come to see how we are progressing? I hope you don't mind us appropriating your men and equipment?"

"Not at all. That's why we're here, sir. Anything we can do to help, just ask."

"Anyway, not much to report so far. We're still tracing the circuits and working out which are the power cables and which aren't. We may take a little longer to get the doors open than I first estimated."

"But you still think you can get them open?"

"Oh yes. I'm confident we will be able to get one open without blowing it apart."

"We've also found what appears to be a manual lever to open the door when there's no power," said Ms. Carter.

He watched her as she walked over to a large door that swung out, revealing a bright yellow lever that would take a giant to operate.

"The aliens who made this place might have been a lot stronger than we are. Neither of your airmen could pull it back, but it's clearly designed to swivel around this pivot point at the bottom here and be used to pump the door open."

"If you say so, Ms. Carter. I'll let you get back to work, and I'll inform the captain of your progress."

Ferretti opened a channel to Captain Tachikoma, updating her on the progress with opening the doors. Then the pillars shimmered again, which reminded him to go and check up on Dr. Wilson, who was in the center of the cavern working with Dr. Harrison.

"How's it going?" he asked.

Dr. Wilson replied, "I've finished downloading all the data from the base station into my database and have run a conversion filter on it. The results are very promising indeed. Have I shown you what I've been doing?"

"No, not yet."

Dr. Wilson had a tendency to assume everyone was as fascinated with his research as he was.

"Look at the screen. I've plotted all the activations of the pillars and put them all together to generate this," said Dr. Wilson. He held up his PAD, which showed a three-dimensional waveform graph that pulsed.

"Fascinating stuff, Doc."

"Isn't it? But I can't help feeling I'm missing a connection. This waveform reminds me of something I've seen elsewhere."

"I'm sure you'll figure out what it is."

"Ultimately, we'll be able to use this to walk through the pillars and go where we want, when we want. At worst, the longest journey will only take a week."

"You forget to mention it might require hundreds of jumps, and not all the pillars go to places with breathable atmospheres," said Dr. Harrison.

"Details, Peter. I'm sure we can overcome them. Don't you think so, Sergeant?"

Ferretti ignored the demotion he'd been given by Dr. Wilson.

"I'm sure somebody will come up with something. I've got to go and check on what the others are doing now."

He left the two scientists discussing mathematical theories that might explain what they were seeing on the screen.

Ferretti found Doctors Reynolds and Franklin by a row of storage cupboards with their doors opened. Various objects had been pulled out and were being packed for transport by Lance Corporal Avari and Private Meireles.

"Hello, Sergeant," said Dr. Franklin.

"You're keeping busy, I see."

Dr. Reynolds said, "Too busy to talk."

"Leave this to me, Tyrone," said Dr. Franklin, turning to talk to him. "Don't mind him. The alien artifacts are driving him crazy and making him mad as hell."

"Those wacky aliens. Go figure, huh?"

"We managed to open the doors to what we think are storage lockers. The aliens used these round holes in the front to access the door mechanism, though I have no idea why they would design a latch like that," said Dr. Franklin. "Judging by the dust, it has been years since anyone was here, besides us that is. If we don't manage to get outside, people back on Earth are going to be very disappointed with what we've found so far."

"Dr. Bland and his assistant are working on getting the doors open, and if they can't, we can always blow them open. No need to worry about being stuck here for six months with nothing to do."

"That's always the simplest answer with you people, blow stuff up," said Dr. Reynolds.

Dr. Franklin sighed and shrugged, but said nothing.

"Here, take this," said Dr. Reynolds, passing Ferretti a ball.

"We found it in one of the lockers we opened. Now what do you think it is?"

"Looks like a ball. Maybe the aliens like to play catch."

"Give it a squeeze and try bouncing it."

The ball was rock hard, and he dropped it on the floor where it bounced once. "Not a bouncing ball then."

"Notice anything else?"

Ferretti picked it up and revolved it in his hand. "There's a small hole."

"Now that could mean it's a part of something else, like a ball cock for a cistern. Or it's a very small RollaBot, for all I know."

"The aliens have latrines?"

"Not that we have found, but that's the point. Come with me a second and have a look at the control console we found. When Dr. Bland and his assistant looked, they concluded it was powered down, probably in standby mode. I agree it is, but here are the controls. What do you see?"

"Lots of little holes in groups."

"Like a musical instrument."

"I guess so."

"Now when I put my finger over the holes, nothing happens. But if I stick a finger in the hole and pull it out, a light comes on."

A small red light lit up and slowly faded.

"Seems like you're making great progress here."

"For all we know, the red light might mean don't put your finger in the hole. We don't know what we're doing, but the thing is this. All of this stuff has been sitting around in this cavern gathering dust for years, and will be here for years to come, unless we do something stupid like blow it up. It would be far better if we accepted that it will take time to work out what everything does. Even if it means we sit here in this cavern for the next six months."

"Okeydokey."

"See, you still haven't got it. This site is effectively an archaeological dig. We need to catalog everything we find and where we found it for posterity. Not do a *Schliemann* on the find of a lifetime."

"I'm not sure what a 'doing a Schliemann' means. Are you volunteering to stay here for the next six months cataloging everything?"

"If that is what it takes, then yes I am."

"Alrighty, then. I will leave you to it and hope Dr. Bland doesn't make it necessary for us to blow the doors open."

Ferretti left the two scientists cataloging their "finds of a lifetime" and went back to have another hot drink courtesy of the Leungs. The air was dry in the cavern, and his nasal passages were feeling the worse for wear.

As far as Ferretti was concerned, everything was proceeding according to plan. But the plan was more like a set of guidelines about what MAPCOM wished to achieve rather than a plan based on whether what they were wishing for was actually achievable.

As the captain had said to him, "Once we get back, they will read our report about what we did, and afterward issue orders, which will tell us to do what we did."

He wasn't sure if she'd been making a joke or stating the facts as she saw them.

The only thing he knew for sure was that one couldn't always get inside the head of his commanding officer. Then again, that's probably what made her a good officer.

A couple of hours passed, and Ferretti was back where Dr. Bland and his assistant were working on the door.

By now the main jumper cable from the truck had been hooked up to a big silver box, and even thicker cables ran from it to a power bus. The interior had been revealed through the simple expedient of pulling stuff apart.

"Perfect timing. We've been running tests, and we're just about to try and open the door. Are your ready, Lily?"

"Ready when you are, Simon."

"OK, here goes."

A loud squealing sound came from the box.

"That's just the power converter. I can assure you that it's nothing to be concerned about."

The huge door began to move and made an ominous whining sound as the metal ground against concrete as the seal started to part. The movement was almost imperceptible, and it took a few minutes before a gap appeared.

"Simon, the current is peaking, better switch it off now."

Then Ferretti smelled something acrid.

"Bugger, there go our fuses, and it looks like the magic smoke escaped from the door mechanism. Once that happens, the fucking fucker is fucking fucked."

Ferretti was shocked to hear Ms. Carter's string of expletives that imaginatively described what had happened.

"Sorry, it made me so cross."

"Langford, on me!" he called out.

Langford ran up. "Here, Master Sergeant."

"Time for plan B."

Langford went up to the door that was now partly open with a gap of about a meter between the two halves of the door and whistled. "You need to come see this."

Ferretti walked over to where she stood and squinted through the gap in the door. He saw a long corridor that sloped downward. "What am I looking at, Corporal?"

"The thickness of the doors. These are blast doors. I'm not sure I have enough explosives to even dent them. My guess is it would take a special atomic demolition munition to blow these open."

"Since we don't have a SADM, unless we packed one I don't know about, I guess it's going to be a long six months playing cards and reading books."

Dr. Bland came up behind Ferretti to have a look at the door. "Oh, that's why we burnt out the mechanism. Lily, come have a look at this, why don't you?"

Ms. Carter came up and peered around them. "That's an impressively thick door. It must weigh more than a few tons. If we'd known, we could have tried pulsing the power."

As far as Ferretti was concerned, it was like saying one should have shut the stable door after the horse had bolted.

"Still, chin up, people. We still have the manual lever to try and open the door with," said Dr. Bland.

Lights on one of the consoles came on, flickered, and went dark—unseen and unnoticed by anyone on the team.

10. MOUNTAIN TOP

*In the presence of eternity, the mountains are as transient as the
clouds.*

— ROBERT GREEN INGERSOLL

Captain Lara Atsuko Tachikoma
Planet 1340
Day One of Operation Prometheus
Saturday, December 23, 2073

Excited at the opportunity to see the outside of a new world, I
ordered everyone to pick up the pace of our march.

I signaled Nelson and Flores to move along the passageway
while waving for Wachowski and Adams to pass in front of Keith
and me. "Let's do this by the numbers. Treat it as you would if
deploying from the rear of a vehicle, people."

The plan was to keep it nice and simple and not do anything
fancy. The team duckwalked the last ten meters to the opening
ahead, weapons at the ready.

"You heard the captain, don't get sloppy," said Wachowski.

"This isn't a trip to the beach. Nelson and Flores, go right. Adams, come left with me, on my mark. Mark!"

Wachowski's shout was followed by a flurry of movement as the team transitioned from the tunnel into the open. I remembered being that gung-ho back in the day, and I let her do what all good sergeants should: deal with the details while letting the officer focus on the big picture.

My team moved out onto the open ground, assuming a half-circle formation in front of the tunnel entrance, with Keith and me in the center.

Everyone hit the dirt.

We lay in the shadow from the mountain behind us, looking out across a valley below us. A breeze blew dust that eddied across our vision as we waited and listened to the silence.

Nothing moved.

After five minutes, I shouted, "Sound off, people!" I heard them all reply "clear" and ordered: "Let's move out."

Standing up, I found myself staring at a gas giant on the horizon. "Oh my…"

It looked like someone had taken Jupiter and added Saturn's rings to it. Red bands ran across the planet, and the shadow of the rings played over the surface.

Wachowski followed the direction of my gaze. "That's not something you see every day, ma'am."

"It sure isn't, Sergeant."

"If I hadn't seen it with my own eyes, I wouldn't believe it was real," said Adams.

"That's impressive, and to think we get paid to come and see this stuff," said Nelson.

"That's totally awesome," said Flores.

"Isn't it just," replied Keith.

I turned around and stood spellbound by the sight of a red

giant sun rising in what I automatically labeled as east of us. "This is going to give the astronomers fits."

"How so, ma'am?"

"For starters, we're trailing a gas giant in what's clearly a Goldilocks zone around a red giant star."

"Pretty sky, ma'am. But everything around us is burnt and dying," said Wachowski.

I had to agree that when it came to picturesque views, this planet's best features lay in the sky.

"Hey, I've found something!" shouted Flores off to my right.

"What is it?"

"Some kind of bug, ma'am. It's a big sonofabitch, too."

"How big?"

"About the length of my hand, ma'am."

"OK, bag it for Dr. O'Neill to examine it when we get back."

"Wilco, ma'am."

"Not only is this an ugly planet, it's a planet with bugs," said Wachowski, who laughed.

"Spread out and see what we can find. Make sure we record everything for later analysis. We'll head back in ten mikes."

A chorus of "affirmatives" echoed around the plateau.

The sun rose slowly, the shadows shortening. I circled left looking at the ground. As I stepped into the light of the morning sun, my suit began to heat up, and the cooling system kicked in to compensate.

It might have been cold down inside the mountain, but out on the planet's surface the days would be hot when the sun was at the highest point in the sky.

The ground was covered with broken rubble. What appeared to be the remains of metal girders stuck out of it at odd angles. Everything had been weathered by the elements.

Judging by the erosion and general decay, my guess was

whatever had hit the top of the mountain had done so a long time ago.

I tried to imagine what the mountaintop might have been like before, and wondered why the builders had made the tunnel. Surely, it would have been a much easier proposition to build a road that wound around the outside than bore through the rock.

Perhaps the reason was the devastation on the surface of the planet, and the aliens might have considered it too dangerous to travel outside. If this was true, then it didn't bode well for the mission.

On the other hand, this destruction could be the result of a war.

I looked up again, drawn to the spectacle of the red giant sun, before beginning to climb the slope ahead of me, careful to not impale myself on anything sticking out of the ground by falling on it. "Sergeant, on me!"

"Coming, ma'am," said Wachowski as she made her way over to my side.

"In the sky, over there." I pointed up to what I arbitrarily thought of as north, having labeled the direction in which the sun was rising as the east.

"What am I looking at, ma'am?"

"The glint of silver, there…"

"Got it. Are there rings in the sky around this planet?"

"If there are, then they've got to be artificial; because if I'm right, those are in a polar orbit. If I remember correctly, natural rings only form around the equator. Of course, the astronomers may know better than me."

"I'm sure they will tell us if we're wrong, ma'am. Still, it does look like it's artificial. Whoever built it is seriously ahead of us. Let's hope they're friendly types."

"Let's hope so. Judging by the sun, it's going to get hot up here real soon, so I reckon it's time to go back. Get the team together."

Wachowski turned and shouted, "Stop your grinnin', people. Time to head back. Nelson and Flores, take point."

We walked back across the broken, barren mountain landscape and entered the tunnel, heading toward the cold darkness of the cavern below. We left the rising sun behind.

On the surface, we had fallen out of radio range, so I messaged Ferretti over the transponder network to let him know we were heading back.

His reply came back, updating me on the progress with opening the door, which he described as slow. He'd had to get his Buster suit up and running to pump the door mechanism.

I sent him the good news that we'd found a bug for Dr. O'Neill.

After the update I headed back toward the incline with Wachowski at my side.

"So, this planet is what Earth will be like in hundreds of millions of years, ma'am?"

This planet felt old. Perhaps it was a dying world.

"Not quite. By the time our sun turns into a red giant, it will swallow Earth up and we will be no more. But before that happens, all the oceans of the world will have been boiled away and all life will probably be extinct."

"Sounds like something to avoid then. Surely, we will have moved off Earth and colonized other worlds before that happens."

"If we're lucky and don't destroy ourselves first," I said as we went back into darkness.

11. OPENING THE DOOR

There are three secrets to managing. The first secret is have patience. The second is be patient. And the third most important secret is patience.

— CHUCK TANNER

Dr. Allison O'Neill
Magnetic Anomaly Project Scientist
Planet 1340
Day One of Operation Prometheus
Saturday, December 23, 2073

Allison sat next to Doctors Grace and David Leung, huddled up in her parka to keep warm by the portable heater.

She watched the pillars shimmer. They cycled open for five minutes before shutting down for fifteen. A process that repeated like the ticking of a metronome.

Behind her a truck roared into life as it autostarted its engine to recharge its batteries. The sound added to the cacophony from the Buster suit's foot hitting the ground each time it pumped the lever down to open the door.

All the noise was giving her a headache.

Dr. Bland came over. "Sorry to bother you, but if it isn't too much trouble, I would love another cup of tea, white with two sugars. If you wouldn't mind, that is."

"No trouble at all, is it, Grace?"

"None at all. I was just about to boil some more water. It's thirsty work watching other people labor away. Do you think Sergeant Ferretti will want another coffee, dear?"

"I'm sure he will. The military seems to run on coffee," Allison replied.

"That would explain a lot. Corporal Langford has his team out down the tunnel now that we have the doors open wide enough for his men to get through the gap."

Allison said, "I'm sure that Corporal Langford will be most amused to be mistaken for a man."

Dr. Bland turned red. "Sorry, I didn't mean any offense. But it's hard to tell when they're all suited up. Anyway, it won't be much longer until the doors are fully open and we can get out of here."

"Here's a cup of coffee for the sergeant, my dear," said Grace as she handed a cup to Allison.

"I'll be back soon."

"No hurry, dear. We have plenty of spare cups."

Allison got up from her chair, and the cold bit into her as she walked over to the cavern door. She looked up at the cockpit of the Buster, which was swung open. Vincent sat in the seat of his machine. "I thought you might like a cup of coffee!"

The Buster's foot stopped pumping the lever, which was inching open the door with each push.

"You're an angel. I was just thinking it was time for another cup. It makes one thirsty doing all this legwork. I'll be right down; give me a moment to get out."

Allison watched her man squirm out of the confines of the machine, swing around, and climb down to her. "Here you are. Hot, black, and wet. Just as you like it."

"You spoil me, you know."

"Excuse me, awfully sorry for interrupting you two, but I wonder if you could tell me where the toilet is, please? I need to spend a penny," said Ms. Carter.

Allison looked at the older woman and wondered what she was talking about. "I'm sorry, I didn't quite catch what you said."

"I'm dying to go to the loo. My bladder is fit to burst at any moment."

"Oh, you want a restroom. There's one on the back of the truck you can use over there." She pointed. "With the blue sign on the door. I'm afraid you have to climb up the ladder to get to it."

"Oh, thank you so much. I must have forgotten the part where they told us where the toilet facilities were, because we were so busy when we arrived. Must rush, thank you again."

"Do you think she's been standing here waiting to ask someone where to go for long?" Allison asked.

"Don't know. Too busy making sure I don't break the lever with my suit. She's an odd woman, and Dr. Bland is rather eccentric, too. I'm struggling to understand what they say half the time."

"How long before we can get out of this cold, uncomfortable cavern? Not that it isn't fun sitting while the pillars shimmer, but one can have too much of a good thing."

"About another hundred pumps of the lever. Say half an hour, maybe longer. Just in time for when the captain gets back. By the way, they're bringing back a big bug they found for you."

"You sure know how to spoil a girl." Allison smiled at him.

"No expense spared. Just every expense spared."

"My mom warned me that going out with you would be no rose garden."

"You're getting a bug, a big bug. What more do you want?"

"How about a kiss instead of a rose?"

"Later, I promise. Oh look, there's the captain and the rest of her team returning. I better get back to work, otherwise she'll have my ass for slacking off with you."

She stayed with Vincent while he finished his coffee. He blew her a discreet kiss followed by a wink before climbing back up the ladder into the cockpit of his Buster combat armor. Once inside, he began the task of pumping the lever.

Allison walked back to where Grace and David were sitting, serving up hot drinks for Captain Tachikoma's team. One of her men came up to her. The name on his power armor said "PVT FLORES" all spelled in capitals.

"Excuse me, Dr. O'Neill, ma'am, but the captain said to give you the samples we took."

"Thank you," she said, taking the proffered container with the bug and a bag full of what looked like lichen. "Wow, that is a big bug. I'll have to measure it, but it looks like it could be larger than anything from Earth."

"We've uploaded our data onto the convoy net so you can see where I found it if you access my suit's log, Dr. O'Neill, ma'am."

"Thank you again. And it's either Doctor or ma'am, no need to use both titles when addressing me. I will name this bug *Flores giganteus*."

"I think it might have been eating the mossy stuff, which is why I brought some of that back too, ma'am."

Private Flores went back to join his teammates. He looked so young to her.

She went to the truck that had her biology laboratory inside the back so she could put her new bug somewhere safe. She was hoping she could keep it alive long enough to study when shouting interrupted her train of thought. She saw Ms. Carter come running toward her.

"Dr. Smith needs help now," said Ms. Carter.

"Slow down. What's up?"

"Dr. Smith is having breathing problems."

"Captain!" she shouted. "Dr. Smith is ill."

The captain called for the corpsman to attend.

Keith ran up to them and asked, "Where's Dr. Smith?"

"He's in that truck over there," said Ms. Carter, turning to point.

They both followed Keith, who ran to the truck where Dr. Smith had been sleeping all this time. Dr. Smith was screaming he couldn't breathe, which seemed odd to her, because he could clearly shout out in distress.

Keith went into action as Dr. Smith froze in mid-sob and seemed to her to be having a seizure. She and Ms. Carter both stood by, helpless to do anything, as the light shimmered again and the pillars inexorably cycled open to another world.

"It's OK, I'm going to give you something to help calm you down, which will also help you breathe more easily," said Corpsman Keith. He turned to them. "One of you go and tell the captain I need a hand to put Dr. Smith in a pressure chamber."

Allison ran back to where she'd last seen the captain and told her what Keith had said. Orders were shouted and Dr. Smith was carried out of the back of the truck and placed in the pressure chamber.

The captain appeared, and Allison couldn't help but overhear them talking before she walked away.

"Will he be alright?" Tachikoma asked.

"Hard to say. I won't be able to tell how he's doing until he has spent twenty-four hours recovering inside the pressure chamber. He may have suffered an aneurysm."

"That's not a good start to the mission. Anything we can do if that's the case?"

"No, ma'am, not here."

12. ANOTHER DOOR

Necessity... the mother of invention.

— PLATO

Sergeant Wachowski
Planet 1340
Day One of Operation Prometheus
Saturday, December 23, 2073

By the time Wachowski finished drinking her coffee, the pillars had started shimmering again.

For a few brief minutes, the light from another world lit up the interior of the cavern. Then the interior reverted to the gloom broken by the headlamps of the convoy's trucks.

The captain found her, and Wachowski braced herself for the next set of orders.

"Good news, we now have the doors open. The bad news is we've found another set of doors about eight hundred meters down the tunnel, which we hope leads us out of here. Dr. Bland is confident he and Ms. Carter can get the next set of doors open this time. So, I'd like you to take a truck and a couple of people to help you with the cables, and help the scientists."

"Aye, aye, Captain. I assume you want Adams here?"

"Yes, thanks for reminding me. Let me see. It's a little after 1900 PST. Local sunrise was around 1730. Once we figure out the length of a local day, we will need to reset our clocks, as I don't think the civilians will take to operating on Zulu time, do you?"

"Not sure I would want to be on Zulu time for the whole mission, either. I'll take Nelson and Flores to help me. Call us when supper is ready."

"Don't worry. We'll keep something hot for you," said Captain Tachikoma, then turned to shout, "Adams, on me!"

Wachowski walked over to the rear truck of the convoy, got in the cab, and started her up. She backed up slightly to clear the truck in front and drove over to face the now open doors that towered up into the darkness in the cavern.

The beams from the headlamps cast their light into the dark tunnel ahead.

She got out of the truck to speak to Dr. Bland and his assistant. "I'm here to take you both down to the next door. What do you need?"

"Hello. Sergeant Wachowski, isn't it? We'll need our power converter and the cables you see here to come with us," said Dr. Bland, mangling the pronunciation of her name.

"Nelson and Flores, on me! Move it, people. We haven't got all day."

"Yes, Sergeant," came in reply as she waited for her people to get themselves over to her.

"Nelson, help me with the power converter. Flores, start rolling the cables up. Let's be quick about it now. Time's a wasting, and we don't want to miss supper, do we?"

Ten minutes later, the five of them were back in the cab of the truck as it made its way slowly down the tunnel, reaching the door Team Two had found earlier.

"Looks like it is a duplicate of the other door. What do you think, Lily?"

"We can but hope it's that simple. Sergeant Wachowski, can we up the power output from the truck in any way?" Wachowski came out sounding Waah-cough-ski.

"Sure thing, ma'am. I can rev up the motor and boost the power that way. By the way, you might find it easier just to call me Sergeant. Easier on the tongue."

"Sorry, I didn't mean to mangle your name. I thought it was Polish."

"Might have been pronounced like that when my family emigrated to America, but nowadays we say it as War-chow-skee. As I said, easier to say Sergeant."

"Won't that be rather confusing when we're with you and Sergeant Ferretti?"

"No, because I'm an E5, and he outranks me as an E7. He should be addressed as Master Sergeant Ferretti," Wachowski said, having been dying for a chance to straighten out these civilians on how to address a military person, even one who was Air Force. "Now we've got a job to do here," she said, turning to give orders. "OK, Nelson and Flores, start getting the cables out and the power converter down from the back."

It took half an hour to open the panel and uncover the power bus to the door, get the cables connected to the power converter, and get back into the truck.

"Sergeant, if you could up the power you can give us now, that would be good," said Dr. Bland.

Wachowski revved the truck's engine, and she watched as Ms. Carter threw a large switch and gave Dr. Bland the thumbs-up signal.

A loud squeal came from the power converter, and she saw the door move and then stop, then move again. The scientists were pulsing the power to the door, making it inch open bit by bit.

The radio in the truck came on. "Zero Two, this is Zero Six. Come in, over."

It was Captain Tachikoma.

"Receiving loud and clear, over."

"SITREP, over."

"We're in the process of opening the door now. So far everything is proceeding smoothly. Estimate another ten mikes until it's open enough to drive through, over."

"Good news. Give my thanks to Dr. Bland and his assistant. When the door is open, come back here. Supper will be waiting for you, over."

"Roger that. Finish opening the door and return to base. Zero Two, out."

She watched as the doors pulled back into the walls revealing another dark tunnel facing them. She got out of the truck.

"I've just spoken to the captain, who says good work on the door, and she told me that there's hot food waiting for us back in the cavern."

"Great, I'm famished. It has been a long day," said Ms. Carter.

"Nelson, Flores, let's get this stuff packed away."

"I wonder what the food will be like. I do hope it is better than what we had in the canteen back at base," said Dr. Bland.

"To be honest, I don't really care as long as it is filling."

Wachowski liked Carter's attitude.

"Don't worry. Adams, our cook, is top notch. I don't know what we did to deserve to get him assigned to us, but the man loves cooking."

"Yeah, he sure makes everything taste good," said Nelson.

"He told me it was all down to his own secret recipe of eleven herbs and spices," said Flores.

Wachowski had to stop herself from laughing. The boy was so gullible.

13. A NEW DAY

Every day is an adventure.

— Joseph B. Wirthlin

Captain Lara Atsuko Tachikoma
Planet 1340
Day Two of Operation Prometheus
Sunday, December 24, 2073

Even with the luxury of sleeping in our accommodation trucks, I still woke with a headache. I felt like someone had coshed me around the head during the night. I sat and ate breakfast, nursing my headache.

Adams had gone out of his way to make me my favorite of ham and eggs, with a bread roll to wipe up the yolk off my tray. I drank my juice and now held a large mug of coffee in my hands, savoring the aroma as I sipped the dark, inviting wetness.

"Morning, ma'am," said Wachowski as she sat down opposite me, pulling me from my coffee reverie. "If I may say so, you're an interesting shade of green this morning."

"Headache, and my stomach is a bit queasy, too. How are you coping, Sergeant?"

"Felt a bit sick earlier, but the doc gave me a couple of pills to make me feel better. Told me to suck it up."

Other members of my team came and sat with us, with Ferretti turning up last with Dr. O'Neill, and Corpsman Keith trailing behind them.

"Morning, ma'am. You still appear somewhat ill."

"So it has been noted already by Sergeant Wachowski."

"Here's your medication, ma'am," said Keith, giving me some pills to take. He didn't say "suck it up," but he had that look corpsmen have when they do.

"Thanks, Doc. Starting to feel better already. This coffee is helping, too."

"Everybody, remember to drink more fluids, and I also recommend that we try to take it easy today—allow people time to acclimatize to the conditions," said Keith.

"Trust me when I say I woke up this morning and the last thing that crossed my mind was doing my usual morning run," I said.

"I vote we call this planet *The Sick*," said Langford from the other end of the table.

"When the Corps becomes a democracy, we'll do that," said Wachowski.

"Just sayin' this planet makes me sick. I slept terrible last night."

"Not getting enough beauty sleep, Langford?" said Nelson.

"Have you seen yourself in the mirror lately?"

"Seems that everyone is in *high spirits* this morning, ma'am," said Ferretti.

"Sure does."

"I feel sick," whispered Flores.

"Whaddaya say, bug boy?" asked Nelson.

"Check that attitude. I don't want to hear about bugs when I'm eating breakfast. You're putting me off my food," said Ferretti. "Besides, we've got company with us."

"Sorry, Master Sergeant. Sorry, Dr. O'Neill, didn't mean nuthin'. Don't mind me, Flores, I was only kidding. Just got a headache the size of Alaska."

"I'll be better once I get the chance to blow something up," said Langford. "Blowing things up always makes me feel better, especially when I'm tense and strung out." She twisted a crick out of her neck before farting. "Sorry, pardon me. Not very ladylike."

Nelson sniggered.

"Better out than in, Langford," said Wachowski, miming putting on a gas mask.

Nobody ever accused the troops of missing the chance to make an obvious gag.

"You can all expect to be prone to bouts of uncontrolled flatulence while your body adjusts to the partial pressure of oxygen," said Keith. "It's nothing you need to worry about."

Everyone near me was grumbling about how bad their first night's sleep on One-Three-Four-Zero had been.

Keith had gone around and found that, apart from Dr. Smith, no one else had needed to be put in a pressure chamber. Keith said that with the medication we would all adjust in a few days.

"Plan of the day, people, is get out of this cavern. Trust me, you will all enjoy the view. How are the civilians doing, Master Sergeant?"

"All complaining like mad, but they're getting up, and Adams has breakfast for them once we clear the table."

"Nice to see you up bright and early, Dr. O'Neill—for definitions of bright and early that mean in a dark cavern where we can't tell what time of day it is."

"I've always been a morning person, Captain, but some of my

other colleagues are more the night-owl types. Still, isn't this exciting? It's not every day one gets the chance to walk on the surface of an alien planet and discover new species of animals."

Dr. O'Neill's cheerfulness was infectious, and she was clearly the best thing that could have happened to Ferretti.

"Let's get this show on the road, Master Sergeant."

"Roger that, ma'am. Wachowski, let's get them moving."

I got up from the table and took my empty tray back to be cleaned as everyone scrambled to finish eating or drinking their coffee while farting. Just another day in the Corps—oorah!

It took just under an hour to get the civilians racked and packed in the trucks. Going from past experience, this was about par for the course.

Wachowski reversed the order of the trucks in the convoy and swapped people accordingly so I could be with her in the first truck with Dr. Bland and Ms. Carter, our new best alien-door openers. Ferretti would be behind us in the second truck, riding shotgun with Langford in case we needed her expertise in blowing shit up.

I split the convoy into three parts, with our two trucks at the front leaving a gap between us and those that followed in case of any difficulties we might encounter.

I left the trucks with all our fuel safely at the rear of the convoy all by themselves, because, in my experience, fuel trucks and explosions don't go together. Well, they do, but they're something that should be saved for special occasions, like when hell on Earth needs to be unleashed.

We drove down the dark tunnel, with only the headlamps illuminating the way ahead of us. Then we went through the first open door and carried on until we reached another set of doors that blocked us from proceeding any farther.

Dust fell from above, disturbed by the passage of our trucks, which were probably the first things to have moved along this tunnel in more years than I care to imagine.

"It's time for us to do some work. Sorry, but we will need our equipment," said Dr. Bland.

"And don't forget, we will need you revving the engine for us," said Ms. Carter.

"We're on it," I said.

I got out of the cab and called for help with getting the cables out. I was glad to be wearing my MARPACE power armor suit, as I was uncomfortably short of breath from exerting myself.

The gloom inside the tunnel was oppressive, and this was just the beginning of another long day. Once Langford, Ferretti, and I had gotten everything unpacked, all we had to do was stand and watch as Dr. Bland and Ms. Carter did their stuff.

Wachowski revved up the truck, and the power converter squealed as the door ahead inched open one pulse at a time.

It took thirty minutes to get it open wide enough for the trucks to pass through. By the time we'd packed everything back up again, nearly an hour had passed dealing with the door.

Still, looking on the bright side of life, I had nowhere else to be and nothing better to do with my time. Besides, it gave me the chance to catch my breath.

Back in the truck, Wachowski drove through the tunnel that was still sloping down, and then we came to another door blocking our route.

"I guess they liked building doors, ma'am."

"Sure looks that way. Dr. Bland and Ms. Carter, you're up again."

"I wonder why there's another door?" asked Ms. Carter.

"Good question. The answer would depend on why they thought they needed to block the tunnel access. Another would be, why is the technology so basic? It's something *we* could build!" replied Dr. Bland.

"Keep it simple, I guess?"

I didn't stop to listen further to the two of them discuss what they were going to do, as I needed to get out and get the equipment down off the truck. My mouth was dry, and I remembered to have a long drink of water, which then made me feel a little bit queasy.

Ferretti looked worse than me.

"You OK, Master Sergeant? You don't look so good."

"Just a little light-headed, ma'am. I'll be alright."

I noticed the black shadows under Langford's eyes that would give a panda a hard-on.

"Neither of you slept well last night, did you?"

"I kept waking up and not being able to breathe properly, ma'am. Not good," said Ferretti.

Langford nodded in agreement.

We stood and watched the door being opened and then packed everything up again. This time it took us a little bit longer, as the effort of lugging heavy cables and equipment around was starting to wear our enthusiasm a bit thin.

I climbed back up into the truck and sat down, thankful for the reinforced seat in the cabin that could take the weight of the power armor. "When you're ready, Sergeant."

"Aye, aye, Captain," said Wachowski, leading the convoy down the tunnel one more time to a rendezvous with another door. "Enough with the doors already. This is starting not to be funny."

"I lost my sense of humor over these doors when packing up from the last one," I said, which made me cough.

"I suggest you take control of the truck, and I'll help get the cables and equipment out. Do you want me to tell Ferretti and Langford to alternate taking a break?"

"A good suggestion. It will keep Doc off our backs. Make it so," I said. "Dr. Bland, Ms. Carter, how are you holding up back there?"

"Not bad, but there again we are not lugging everything around. You OK, Lily?"

"I'm mostly OK, Simon."

"Mostly?"

"Sorry, I feel a bit poorly."

"I think we can manage, but perhaps a break for refreshments after we have opened this door? Thirsty work opening doors, and I could kill for a cuppa. Do you think they can find some biscuits to have with our tea?"

Knowing that by the time we'd finished opening the door more than three hours would have passed by, I decided a hot drink and cookies did sound like a good idea. I got on the radio and informed everyone we would take a break.

This turned out to be a good decision, because we then found ourselves soon after facing the fourth door of the day.

We then had to repeat the rigmarole with unloading the equipment all over again. By the time we'd opened the seventh door of the day, the odometer on the trucks showed that we'd traveled just under eight kilometers.

Which had taken nine hours to traverse.

As we drew up in front of door number eight, Wachowski said, "This is getting to be a bit boring, if you don't mind me saying so, ma'am."

"Feel free to express yourself. I think I can safely say you speak on behalf of us all."

We'd been alternating the driving and unloading and by now were into the rhythm of things.

"Once more into the breach, dear friends," said Dr. Bland behind me.

I got the reference, but I'm not sure anyone else did, and those who knew Shakespeare probably didn't know what a breach was.

"Unless you want to stop here for the night, Captain?" asked Dr. Bland.

"Lucky number eight, ma'am?"

"We should be so lucky, Sergeant. I'm starting to wish I could get Langford to blow these bloody doors down for us."

"I wouldn't recommend that, ma'am. She would only end up blowing the whole convoy up."

"On that happy note, over to you, Dr. Bland and Ms. Carter."

"One more door, Lily?"

"Ready to do it once more, Simon."

By now I would like to say we were like a well-oiled machine that sprang into action, but the truth was we moved like slugs.

After another hour, the door opened. For one horrible moment, I thought we faced yet more tunnel, but the headlamps cast shadows on rough ground. I could see stars twinkling on the horizon.

"So much for an easy day, ma'am," said Wachowski

"Did I promise you a rose garden? Let's get the convoy out into the open and make camp for the night. Gosh, will you look at that night sky?"

The stars in the sky were overwhelmed by the brilliance of the rings around the gas giant that hung on the horizon illuminating the area around us.

"That's so never getting old, ma'am."

I scanned our surroundings and saw we'd come out into a large open area. Around us stood the remains of ruined buildings.

"Let's make camp here."

"Aye, aye, Captain," said Wachowski, swinging our truck to the left as she spiraled the convoy around into a circle to form a laager and brought us to a halt. Everybody started to climb down from the trucks.

I left Wachowski to get on with it and walked over to speak to Ferretti. "Master Sergeant, I'd like to set up a perimeter and get a squad of androids out to patrol the area."

"On it, ma'am."

He was pale and he coughed.

Once I had set things in motion, it was time to check on everyone else and write up my log for the day. Adams was working on a meal, and tables and chairs had already been put out.

I stood my MACE suit by the first truck and got out so I could sit down without breaking the chair when Keith came up to me and handed me a bottle of water.

"Please drink, ma'am. All of it."

I did as requested and wondered whether he was going to make me hold it over my head to prove that I had emptied it. "How is everyone, Doc?"

"Dr. Leung is not so good. I've put him in one of the pressure chambers for the night. Several of the other scientists have been coughing as well. I would strongly advise that we camp here tomorrow and let everyone acclimatize to the lower pressure."

"Now we're out of the cold cavern, I tend to agree, Doc. No point rushing things at this point in time."

"Thank you, ma'am."

As Keith walked away I realized that he was thanking me for not making it an issue. Keith went over to Ferretti next, who was coughing, and made my master sergeant go through the same routine of drinking a bottle of water in front of him. I guess I was leading by example without knowing it.

Keith walked back toward me with Ferretti in tow, still coughing. "Ma'am, I'm putting Master Sergeant Ferretti in one of the pressure chambers. I'm worried about his continued coughing."

"I'll be alright, ma'am. It's just something caught in my throat. I'll be fine."

Keith stared at me and shook his head.

I had to agree with Doc. "Don't have me make it an order."

Ferretti managed to look both hurt and grateful at the same time as he left with Keith.

I sat thinking that acclimatization was a bitch as I worked on my PAD and the camp took shape around me. Then I went to check on people and inform Wachowski about Ferretti being indisposed, only to find her with Langford and both of them being made to drink water by Keith.

"Captain, I suggest the four of you make sure that you all get a full night's sleep, as I'm worried you all have overstretched yourselves today."

"It's that bad?"

"It could be. I'd rather not find out, ma'am."

"I understand, Doc."

The next person in the chain of command, below Langford, was Lance Corporal Avari who would now get his chance to prove his worth. I turned around and shouted, "Avari, on me," and tapped the top of my helmet reflexively out of habit.

Avari trotted over. "Yes, ma'am."

"Doc has put everyone above you on enforced rest until tomorrow. So, I need you to organize the pairings for the duty rota. Put yourself on first watch, and make sure to contact me if there's an emergency. Assuming that's OK with you, Doc?"

"As long as it's an emergency, ma'am."

Avari's face darkened for a moment. "I'm on it. You can rely on me, ma'am."

He came briefly to attention and did a sharp about-face to go and attend to his duties. Then the dinner bell rang as Adams called everyone for food, breaking the spell of the moment.

Wachowski, Langford, and I went and stood at the end of the line, taking trays for our food.

"Never thought I'd say I felt at a loose end here, ma'am," said Wachowski.

"You and me both."

"Old Doc Keith sure is a hard-ass when it comes to everyone's health," said Langford.

"He just knows what a gung-ho Moto Marine you are," said Wachowski, laughing.

I got to the point where Adams was serving Flores in front of us. "Hold the peas. I wear green, I don't eat it," Flores said.

"How do you expect to keep healthy if you don't eat your greens, soldier?"

"I'll eat anything as long as it isn't green," said Flores as he took his tray and went to eat.

"What you got for us tonight, Chef?" I asked as I watched Adams make a note on his PAD.

"Sorry to keep you for a moment there. I've just rustled up burgers and French fries with peas; best I can do on short notice. Do you want yours with or without cheese?"

"Without, and go easy on the fries."

"There's apple pie to follow. Help yourself from over there. Fresh cream too."

"You sure know how to spoil us, Chef."

"Thank you for saying so. Best thing in the world is seeing hungry people enjoying their food."

I like a man who enjoys his work, and Adams was also good at what he did.

The three of us went and sat down together next to some of the scientists, and I saw Dr. Smith had been released from the pressure chamber. They were already eating, and before long everyone had food.

Adams came and joined us and I told him my burger was excellent.

As we were eating, I noticed that Dr. Smith kept glancing around all the time. He acted like he was expecting something frightening to happen to him. He appeared to be on the verge of having a panic attack at any moment.

Considering what had happened to him, I wasn't all that surprised that he felt fearful. After all, he may well have had a life-threatening condition, which would have been effectively untreatable until we got back.

14. DAWN

If you align expectations with reality, you will never be disappointed.

— TERRELL OWENS

Dr. Allison O'Neill
Magnetic Anomaly Project Scientist
Planet 1340
Day Three of Operation Prometheus
Monday, December 25, 2073

Allison awoke in her bed feeling nauseous. She'd been restless all night worrying about Vincent. He'd been put in a pressure chamber last night, and she hoped he would be better this morning.

The trucks' bunks were cramped, which made getting up more difficult than it had any right to be. She made her way to one of the two shower and bathroom cubicles at the far end of the container.

It had an automatic shower keyed to her ID tags to monitor

water usage. Everyone on this mission was limited to two showers a day.

This sounded good, until one realized a shower consisted of one minute of water to wet oneself down with. Then one had to soap oneself and use the second minute of water to wash all the soap off.

All explained in excruciating detail on the wall of the shower cubicle.

It was a long way from what she enjoyed most about having a shower. Afterward, Allison brushed out her blond hair. She kept it short enough to not get in the way, but long enough that it could be styled when she wanted a change to her appearance.

After checking the temperature outside on her PAD, she decided to tie her hair back in a ponytail to keep cool.

Allison looked up and saw Li-Na was still asleep in the top bunk, the covers pulled up tight around her. She could hear the sounds of the other women stirring as she walked as quietly as she could outside.

The rising sun now revealed their camp had been set up in a clearing that divided the surrounding ruins of what must have been a base or small town at some point in the long past.

Apart from Vincent, all the other soldiers were up. They'd unloaded the other four androids, which were assembling and erecting camouflage netting over the central area to provide shade. She could tell this was not just a luxury as the heat of the day hit her.

"Good morning, Dr. O'Neill," said Airman Mitchell, one of the recent additions to the team that Vincent had told her about.

"It's already way too hot."

"Sure is, ma'am, but at least it's a dry heat."

Allison walked over to the kitchen container and availed herself of the choices.

She took muesli for herself with brown toast, fruit juice, and coffee, and saw Adams had cooked pancakes and sausage, which she knew Vincent liked. So, she made a tray up for him with OJ and black coffee .

Allison then precariously carried both trays over to the truck where his pressure container was and sat on the edge of the truck before waking Vincent via her PAD.

He came around mumbling blearily. "What time is it?"

"Breakfast time. I got you something I know you like."

"Thank you," he said, as he opened the door on his side to take his tray out. "Coffee, just how I like it."

"What about the pancakes? There's even maple syrup."

"They look good. All smells good too, but the coffee is what I need."

She watched him on her screen as he drank his coffee before starting to eat. She decided that eating was definitely a good thing and started on her bowl of muesli, contemplating the day ahead.

"Have you looked outside yet?"

"Give me a chance, woman. I just woke up."

"Here, look at this," she said, downloading a picture from her PAD.

"Pity it's all ruins. Not very promising." He rubbed his eyes and yawned as he spoke.

"What were you expecting?"

"I don't know. Shining spires towering in the distance, glistening with life. You know, that kind of thing. It would make a change from the mud-brick buildings on Two Moons, is what I'm saying."

"Lots of stuff to study here, though. New flora and fauna to catalog. It's quite exciting."

"I'm glad you're excited. It's just that we came here expecting to find advanced technology in the base, and if we were lucky, the people who made it."

"Disappointed already. We've got six months to search for all of that. I'm sure we will find something to take back that makes everybody happy."

"You make me happy."

"I was worried all night for you."

"No need to be, I'll be fine. Doc will let me out of here soon."

"I know that."

"Good. Just saying, I'll be fine. This is nothing to worry about. Honestly, I just overexerted myself yesterday. Gosh, I think I'm going to have to have a nap now. It's hard work eating breakfast."

"See, that's why I'm worried. Anyway, pass the tray back and I'll take it away."

"Doc said he's going to review me at lunchtime."

"I'll see you then. Rest now and you'll be let out later," she said as she took the half-empty tray out. Walking back to the kitchen container, she put the trays in the rack to be cleaned.

"I see our master sergeant still hasn't regained his appetite," said Adams.

"Sorry about wasting the food."

"Don't worry about it. I'm glad he ate what he did. The system will flag him if I log him as not eating."

"You keep track of what people eat?"

"Sure do. It's part of my job to maintain the nutritional needs of the team."

"So, there's more to being a cook than meets the eye."

"There sure is, ma'am."

Adams took Vincent's tray and scraped the food into a bin, and Allison went over to join her colleagues, who were now up, dressed, and crowded around the tables that had been set out for breakfast.

"Morning, I guess you've eaten already?" said Dr. Harrison.

"Of course, she has. The early bird catches the worm, or should that be sergeant?" said Dr. Reynolds.

"You're in fine form this morning," she said, looking around at everyone sitting under the shade of the camouflage netting.

"Don't take no notice, you'll just encourage him," said Dr. Franklin.

"Do they always serve pancakes with sausage for breakfast? I only ask because it's an odd combination. Especially with maple syrup," said Ms. Carter.

She used her knife and fork to move the items around her plate as if examining something that might spring up at any moment.

"Think of it as *sweet-and-sour* breakfast," said Dr. Harrison.

Allison saw Dr. Smith was up and asked, "How are you feeling this morning?"

"Better now. Thank you for asking. It was a bit of a fright, which has rather shaken me. Quite badly, if you don't mind me saying so."

"I'm sure none of us mind you saying so," she said, wondering at the British scientist's need to apologize. "So, what are people up for today?"

"I'm going to take the opportunity to launch a weather balloon and see what is happening in the upper atmosphere," said Dr. Wong.

"I've got the astronomy suite data from last night, so I'll have to take a raincheck on seeing the ruins. I really want to work out the orbital period and try to start making some sense of what we're seeing here. Lots of unanswered questions from the data," said Dr. Wilson. "We also need to think of a name for our new world."

"Are you going to suggest something from one of your science fiction stories you like to read?" asked Dr. Franklin.

"Actually, I thought we should name the gas giant Tachikoma, and the eleven moons after the people in her team since they were the first to see them."

"You're not being serious, are you?" asked Dr. Harrison.

"Partly, there's a precedent for naming planets and moons after people, after all. If for no other reason than that we might get better suggestions this time around."

"You never fail to surprise me," said Dr. Harrison.

"I'm especially interested in finding out more about the objects in polar orbit around this world."

"I think the polar orbit artifacts are a force coil generator," said Ms. Carter, interrupting the conversation.

"What makes you think that?" asked Dr. Smith.

"It's what I'd do if I wanted to protect the planet from the sun's radiation, and it would explain how we are not all now being irradiated by the gas giant."

"But given the radiation, how could any civilization evolve here in the first place?" asked Dr. Smith.

"I don't know the answer to that, but it's what I would build if I had the technology to do so."

"That's some pretty advanced technology, too. Putting up the mass required for even the flimsiest of rings in polar orbit is way ahead of anything we could do at this time. We would be talking laser-powered rockets as the minimum entry level to get the sort of efficiencies of mass to payload needed," said Dr. Bland.

Dr. Wilson, who had been working on his PAD, looked up and said, "Of course, if this planet wasn't originally in orbit around the gas giant, then a civilization might have evolved on it and built the rings to protect their planet when the sun became a red giant."

"I'm no astronomer, but even I know that would take millions of years to have happened," said Dr. Smith.

"Geologic time can be quite mind-boggling, but this planet has a lot of things about it suggesting it's very old indeed," said Dr. Harrison.

"That would make the inhabitant of this world millions of years ahead of us," Allison said.

"This looks like a dead world, which is probably best for us, all things considered," said Dr. Smith.

"One would hope that any civilization who had lived long enough to develop into a technological species would treat us as guests," said Dr. Bland.

"I think I'm with Trevor on this one. Anytime we've met a primitive culture, we've ended up destroying their sense of self-worth and making them less than they were. I wouldn't want us to be the primitives overwhelmed by an advanced culture whose technology might as well be magic," said Dr. Reynolds. He waved his arms as if casting some imaginary spell.

"I'm puzzled; this doesn't make any sense," said Ms. Carter.

"Would you care to expand on that rather than leave us all hanging?" asked Dr. Reynolds.

"It doesn't add up. I could accept that the cavern had been abandoned a number of years ago, and we could get some of the systems working, like the doors for instance. But if this world's civilization is millions of years old, and the people didn't evolve here, then I would expect things to be more advanced. If so, then it should have been impossible for us to have interfaced with the door mechanisms like we did." Ms. Carter stopped speaking and started eating.

"Maybe they made them nice and simple so they would last longer?" said Dr. Bland.

Ms. Carter finished chewing her food before speaking. "I'm sure they could, but who can make things that will work in a hundred years, let alone a thousand, or possibly millions of years? Things should have seized up, broken down, or just rotted away over time."

Dr. Bland said, "On the other hand, it could just mean whoever built this place only died out recently. Until then, they would've been maintaining the base. Looking at the downloaded images from the team that walked up inside the mountain, and seeing the destruction all around us now, I think it would be safe to say something catastrophic happened here. Perhaps quite recently."

"With all due respect, but I think Ms. Carter is right. Something doesn't add up. The astronomical conditions are evidence that is telling us this system is very old, by Earth standards that is," said Dr. Wilson.

"It might by Earth standards look that way, but that would assume the civilization here had an unbroken line of development rather than, say, rising and collapsing and then rising again. This world may have been home to aliens millions of years ago, but the aliens who ruled here last might have evolved much more recently. Either way, I doubt that they're still alive after all this time. Otherwise, wouldn't we have met them by now?" said Dr. Smith.

"I find myself agreeing with Adam. But as Trevor says, I doubt we will ever know the true story of what happened here," said Dr. Harrison.

"We certainly won't find out anything sitting around talking about it, that's for sure. We need to start searching the ruins around us, for starters. So, who's up for exploring?" asked Dr. Reynolds.

"Not me. I'm afraid a I intend to stay and watch over David, as he has been told he must rest today," said Dr. Leung.

"So, is that the plan for the day?" asked Dr. Bland.

Allison said, "We need to go and tell the captain what we would like to do. It's not every day one gets the chance to be the first people on a planet to explore alien ruins. I assume you would like to come along with me and collect samples?"

After a quick head count of nods, she found Carter, Harrison, Reynolds, Franklin, and Bland all up for looking around whatever delights the ruins might hold. Harrison was clearly itching to start digging, and Allison wanted to find what flora and fauna there were waiting to be discovered on this world.

She went off to talk to Captain Tachikoma to get things organized. Allison was excited at the prospect of what she might find.

Allison wasn't actually tiptoeing through the alien ruins, but she felt as if she should be. All she could think about were the lives that must have been lost when this place had been destroyed.

She made her way across the rubble of what had once been a small town. Or perhaps a large base that serviced the underground cavern.

Captain Tachikoma had agreed the scientists could go out and explore the ruins without hesitation. But she had set two conditions for doing so.

The first was that they all wear light mobility suits, easy to wear exoskeletons to help them cope with the exertion of walking around.

It was an idea for which Allison was truly grateful, as she found walking up, down, and around the rubble exhausting.

The second was that they were to be accompanied by four HOS androids with two soldiers to provide security and assist if there was any heavy lifting that needed to be done.

Tyrone had objected to the need to militarize everything the scientists wanted to do. But he'd been overruled on the grounds that this was an unexplored world with many possible dangers.

This had made Allison smile when he'd been left speechless by the captain, who was in his opinion a mere *grunt*.

Their group was spread out in a column with two brutal-looking combat androids leading the way. They were followed by

Lance Corporal Avari and Private First Class Flores, with the other two androids bringing up the rear of the patrol.

"The androids have reached the top of the ridge. We're clear!" shouted Avari.

"That's good to know," said Dr. Reynolds, muttering behind her.

"Hey, turn around and look back everyone," said Dr. Bland, who was trailing behind Dr. Reynolds.

She turned and saw the ruins dropping away all around them.

"Something sure flattened this place," said Dr. Reynolds.

"You got that right. Something blew up, and what we can see are the effects of a radial blast, which, if I'm not mistaken, was an airburst. Something like the Tunguska event that occurred in Russia at the beginning of the twentieth century," she said.

Dr. Harrison had made his way to the top of the hill. "If you think that's interesting, you should all come and look at this over here."

Allison walked up to where he stood and stared across the remains of the alien structures to find one building had been left standing from the ruins around it. "It's amazing anything survived."

"Sure is, ma'am. It reminds me of pictures of wars where one thing is left standing in a sea of destruction," said Avari as the team stood and stared at what they saw below them.

"I would guess the building was saved by being in the shadow of the hill and protected from the blast," said Dr. Bland.

"What are we talking about here, a natural disaster, or war?" asked Dr. Reynolds.

"I don't know. We will have to find the clues that will allow us to unwrap this puzzle so we can begin to ask the right questions that will lead us to solve this most difficult mystery. The game is afoot," said Dr. Bland.

"Do what? How is this game a foot?" asked Dr. Harrison.

"*Afoot*, one word, not *a foot*, which is two words," replied Ms. Carter. "It's a Sherlock Holmes reference."

"Ah, I understand now. I'm still getting used to your accents and how you pronounce words."

"Peter, I expected better of you than that," said Dr. Reynolds. "I understood everything they said quite clearly."

"Yes, but didn't you study in Britain? I'd expect you to understand them. After all, you're a specialist in understanding different cultures, whereas I mostly examine rocks, which, by comparison, provide limited conversational opportunities."

"Oh, I can see this is going to feel like a very long mission indeed if you boys keep on going like that," said Dr. Franklin. "What is it with men and their need to express themselves? Tyrone, that's a rhetorical question by the way."

"Sorry to ask, but shall we go down and have a look and see what we can find in the building?" asked Ms. Carter.

"Yes, I thought that's why we're all out here in the heat of the midday sun," Allison said.

"Are we sure it's midday yet? Because it seems like the sun may rise higher before the day is out," said Dr. Harrison.

"Can you lead the way for us, Corporal Avari?" asked Dr. Bland.

"Sure thing, Doc," said Avari as he commanded the two androids to go forward and find a route down to the remains of the building.

Allison noticed that while the androids had their weapons stowed behind their backs, the two soldiers had theirs slung in front of them. They were, if not exactly ready to use, certainly easily at hand.

But nothing moved. Which might have meant nothing was alive, or might have meant that the noise they were making had scared everything away.

She was disappointed at the lack of vegetation so far.

The two soldiers had the androids checking the ground ahead of the group as they walked down through the rubble toward the building. As they got closer, she could see it had suffered extensive damage from the blast that had destroyed everything else.

Dr. Reynolds muttered again, "Hey, you forgot to check that other boulder over there."

"What is it, Tyrone? You want to say something?" asked Dr. Franklin.

"Not really. The military way of doing things just pisses me off, is all. People go out exploring the wilds all the time, and they don't need to carry weapons at the ready and act paranoid."

"What if we meet a wild animal?" Allison asked.

"I'd imagine it would be as scared of us as we would be of it, and in my experience making loud noises and being in a group will scare animals away."

"What if it's the size of an elephant?"

"What is this? Do you see any alien elephants wandering around out here? Because I sure don't. What's your point?"

"Better to be safe than sorry, I guess," Allison said.

"You've been hanging around with too many military people, in my opinion."

Allison asked, "What's that supposed to mean?"

"It means your values are being skewed by the people you hang around with. It's called cultural assimilation."

"Tyrone, don't," said Dr. Franklin.

"Don't what? I'm just expressing my opinion, is all."

"And as a scientist you well know everyone is entitled to their opinion, but that doesn't make you right and them wrong. I expect better from you."

"This is definitely turning into another one of those let's-persecute-Tyrone days."

"Passes the time," said Dr. Franklin, smiling.

Allison had to watch where she placed her feet so as not to slip on the loose rocks underfoot and fell behind the bickering pair. She slowly made her way toward the building where the two androids were circling around the outside.

She stopped to use her PAD and pick up what the androids were seeing.

Dr. Bland and Ms. Carter caught up with her as she did so, and she walked the rest of the way with them to the edge of the ruins.

"It makes me sad seeing this," said Ms. Carter.

"Why's that?" she asked.

"It reminds me that life is transitory, and once we're gone nothing we leave behind will last forever."

"You'll have to excuse her. She gets a bit maudlin at times," said Dr. Bland.

Allison asked, "So what do you make of this building?"

"Looks like it was lucky to survive the blast, which is a good thing because it means we might find things of interest inside. Though I suspect Tyrone is right. We really should be treating this mission as an archaeological expedition rather than first contact with an alien civilization."

The three of them walked around the perimeter of the building, which was a combination of curved walls with triangular extrusions like some avant-garde piece of art.

The androids had cleared a path through a damaged part of the outer wall, and Private Flores went in after them. About ten minutes later, he announced the place clear and safe for everyone to follow him in, as long as they watched their footing.

Allison had thought it would be dark inside the walls. She hadn't given any thought to the fact that the roof might have collapsed, which had the benefit of letting light inside.

However, if it had been completely black, her flashlight would have helped more, but the contrast between the daylight and the darkness meant its light ended up being lost in the confusion of shapes inside the building.

She found it difficult to see where to put her feet, tripped, and nearly fell down. Judging from the sounds around her, she was not the only one who was having difficulties seeing where they were going.

Allison thought about going back outside and searching for samples, but the feeling of excitement from being one of the first people to ever step inside this building was overwhelming. Now if only they could discover there were survivors of the people who had built this place.

She heard someone fall.

Dr. Harrison cried out from another part of the building. "I've trapped my leg in something."

"We'll be with you in a few moments, Doc," replied Avari.

"Can I help? I know some first aid," she said, making her way over to where she could hear Peter cursing at his stupidity. Avari and Flores pulled him out of a hole in the floor he had slipped into.

"Anything broken?" asked Avari. "Can you wriggle your toes without it hurting you?"

"Yes, I can. I think I'm going to have one heck of a bruise on my legs tomorrow, though."

"OK, sit and regain your composure and drink some water if you feel thirsty," said Avari.

"Oh, I wonder what's down the hole," said Dr. Bland, shining his flashlight into the darkness.

"Be careful, don't fall in," said Flores.

"Don't worry, young man, I won't. Perhaps we can make this hole larger because I think there's a room down there."

"If you stand back, I'll have one of the androids enlarge the hole, sir. It's a pity we don't have Langford with us, this would be a golden opportunity for her to blow a hole in the floor," said Flores.

"Wishing won't get the hole dug, Flores," said Avari.

Alison watched as the android began digging with a tool it had taken out of its pack and unfolded.

The noise of the pick reverberated around the room as they all stood watching the hole being enlarged. Then the android lurched as it swung the tool down, and it tumbled head over heels into the hole.

"That's not good," said Flores.

"You're the one who signed for it," said Avari. "Everyone stand back while we set up a tripod to retrieve the fallen android. Might be time to take a break and drink some water while you wait."

Avari commanded the three remaining androids to start assembling some poles and cable they'd been carrying.

Allison was grateful they had the androids to carry all the equipment, and thankful for Captain Tachikoma's foresight. She sat with everyone eating snacks and drinking water while the android was being recovered.

"I wish the Leungs could've come with us today," said Dr. Reynolds. "Then we would be having hot drinks. I really should get myself one of those JetBoil things they have."

"Still, mustn't grumble, hey? It could be worse. We could be watching them try to rescue one of us who's fallen down the hole," said Dr. Bland.

"I could murder a nice cuppa tea right now," said Ms. Carter.

"I thought you liked coffee during the day?"

"Usually I do, but this is time for afternoon tea. Now if only we had some scones, jam, and clotted cream, it would be a perfect day."

"It's a British thing," said Dr. Reynolds as the body of the android was dragged into view, hooked on the end of a tether.

Allison was distracted by the sight of the damaged android and the comments from their escort team.

"Master Sergeant Ferretti is going to be working overtime getting this repaired," said Flores to Avari.

"Never mind that, Flores. What's important is we can now find out what's down there. Watch and learn," said Avari as he prepped a ChemLight and dropped it into the hole.

"Can't see much," said Flores. "A ChemLight, the perfect piece of gear for a Marine. One moving part, and you have to break it to use it."

"I'm reluctant to proceed with one of the androids down," said Avari, ignoring the Army jibe. "But what I will do is drop one of the RollaBots and a SnakeBot down there to explore the place. With the data we can get, we will be able to make a proper assessment of the risks. I wouldn't want the floor that's supporting the tripod to collapse, stranding us down there."

"I told you the military are totally paranoid and overly cautious, Simon," said Dr. Reynolds.

"Well, I hate this, but I agree with the young man in this case," replied Dr. Bland. "I'm sure whatever is down there will wait until tomorrow."

"Thank you for understanding, sir. I'll plant a transponder here on the outside of the building so we can maintain a link with the data the 'bots get for us."

"Something to look forward to for tomorrow," Allison said.

15. CHRISTMAS DAY

An army marches on its stomach.

— NAPOLEON BONAPARTE

Captain Lara Atsuko Tachikoma
Planet 1340
Day Three of Operation Prometheus
Monday, December 25, 2073

We've camped in the ruins at the base of the mountain, and I'm in my office, which is a cubicle made by the judicious placement of a partition door.

My day is spent making sure all the logs have been signed off and the reports filed. So much for the glamour of military life, where you go to exotic new places, meet interesting strangers, and shoot them if they look at you funny.

The truth is that the military is a highly refined bureaucracy where 99 percent of one's time is taken up with the boring routine of day-to-day activities.

The other one percent is an adrenaline-fueled rush of

overwhelming terror, where you have to keep a cool head while those around you run like headless chickens.

I know which of the two I prefer and manage my boredom appropriately. I'm finishing cleaning my assault rifle when Sergeant Wachowski comes into my office.

"Ma'am, I'm checking to confirm that you're joining us for PT later," she said.

"Sure thing. I wouldn't miss one of your colorful motivational cadences for the world. I see that Keith has signed off on everyone's acclimatization, but he's added a rider we must still be vigilant for signs and symptoms of altitude sickness. It seems we could still be struck down no matter how long we stay here."

I ran a cleaning rod down the barrel. Cleanliness of one's weapon is one of the Marine Corps commandments, drilled into us all from day one.

"I caught that. Let's just say Keith had a word with me about overdoing things and that projectile vomiting after training was not a key performance indicator on how good a session was."

"Out of idle curiosity, what did you say to him?"

"That I would take it under advisement."

"Outstanding, Sergeant. Dismissed."

Wachowski turned and left and I carried on with completing the task at hand. I felt a sense of satisfaction when I reassembled my assault rifle, which now shined like new.

After I finished, I got up and realized it was time to change for PT, a run with those of my command who were scheduled for the afternoon session. Wachowski did a good job of motivating everyone to give it their all by calling cadence.

She started out the run with "Fired Up, Feels Good," which is one of the Corps' favorite cadences. Though she stamped her own fusion-inspired take on it.

We all replied, "Fired up, feels good."

Wachowski then called, "Here we go."

And we repeated back the call with added flourishes like "A lo righta lay-eft" and "Hey bobba reeba" as we ran. It may sound weird, but it stretches your aerobic capacity and increases stamina to improve general fitness: one of the Corps' many obsessions.

As we got into the rhythm of the cadence, Wachowski shouted out double-time pace just to get the sweat up. By the end of the hour's exercise, on the final cooldown run, I treated everyone to a demonstration of projectile vomiting that spurred Airman Green to throw up his guts in sympathy.

"Let's see if you can all show the same commitment as the captain next time, people. No slacking on my watch."

Airman First Class Green muttered, "More like committed to the insane asylum."

"What's that, Green? What did you just say?"

"I said 'commitment all the way,' Sergeant."

"You shouldn't have signed up unless you have a sense of humor."

"No argument from me, Sergeant," said Green.

"Good to hear it. Carry on as you were," said Wachowski as Green retched once more with feeling.

After I finished cleaning my face off and swilling the acrid taste from my mouth with some water, I was motivated to go to the head. It gave me the time I needed to sit down to reflect on things while my body did the necessary bowel movements.

It was also a sign of how easy it is to get out of shape.

Having gotten all hot and sweaty running, I stripped down to make myself clean and presentable by having a shower. Not exactly the Hilton, but it sure beat the hell out of baby wipes any day of the week.

And it made washing my hair easy too, which was another advantage over using baby wipes to clean up.

Afterward, I changed into a fresh set of utilities, put my *cover* on, and went out to take my place for the evening meal that Allison had been planning for today with Adams.

Having a uniform makes it so much easier to know what to wear and not have to think about what matched what or would go with something. At home I ran to comfortable clothes, lots of black with some red.

Glen had commented that I only wore red with black to hide the bloodstains of my victims. What can I say? I guess I'm just not a real girly girl.

I walked outside to where a table had been set out so we would all sit down together under the cover of the camouflage nets, with heaters to keep the area warm. Predinner soft drinks were being served, and people were milling around in conversation.

I approached Dr. Smith, who stood alone dressed in a jacket, shirt, and tie. As the acting senior scientist, he was my civilian counterpart for this mission.

"Good evening, sir. If I may say, you're looking very smart. I wasn't expecting any of the scientists to dress for this dinner."

"Good evening to you, too. Thank you, and no, I wouldn't expect any other men to dress for the occasion, either. Most of my colleagues were quite frankly surprised I had bothered. What can I say? The youth of today." He laughed.

"As you say, times change. How are you feeling now, sir?"

"Mustn't grumble. I'm still alive. Still, it was a bit of a shock to have had the seizure. Your corpsman is keeping an eye on me. He tells me that the longer I go without any reoccurrence of an episode the greater the chances of it being nothing to worry about."

"I see. I hope that's reassuring for you?"

"It will have to do. If I may say, it has left me rather shaken. I can feel my mortality weighing on me, which I hope doesn't sound too morose."

"It sounds like you're reacting to what has happened to you, which is normal. All I can suggest is you talk to people and work through your feelings, sir."

"So, my feeling morose is normal, or is it because I'm British and we tend to have a less sunny outlook on life?"

"I'm sorry I can't speak to that point, though a Royal Marine Commando Colour sergeant I met during training did have a very black sense of humor."

"What do you think of the team we have gathered for this mission?"

"I think we have a good team. You, Dr. Bland, and Ms. Carter seem to have settled in, and I have every confidence in my people, sir," I replied as Adams rang the bell for dinner.

"If you would all like to take your places now," said Dr. O'Neill, who was helping out as the maître d' for the evening.

She was wearing a bright red dress and ordering half of our androids around as waiters. This allowed Adams to eat with us for the first Christmas party to be held on One-Three-Four-Zero. Ferretti was using his PAD to monitor the loop in case any of the androids froze while waiting for a decision confirmation during the meal.

I took my place at the top end of the table, removing my cover while watching my team take their places and remove their service headgear.

"Good evening, ma'am," said Ferretti as he took his seat to the left of me.

"I see Dr. O'Neill has arranged the seating order."

"Yes, ma'am. She decided that this time all the civilians would sit opposite their military counterparts. I advised her on the seating order for our side."

"Well, this mission is nominally being run for the benefit of the civilians, so I expect that we can adapt to the situation."

"Oorah!" said Sergeant Wachowski. She sat down next to Ferretti. "It sure smells good. I hope everyone is feeling hungry."

"I do hope so, too. Adams has gone to a lot of trouble preparing this traditional British Christmas turkey meal for us," said Dr. O'Neill. Being the last person still standing, she took her place at the table on my right, opposite Ferretti, which was only to be expected. "We're starting with French onion soup."

The androids started serving the first course of the meal, and I enjoyed the taste of the butter that had melted into the fresh-baked bread rolls. Adams had indeed done us proud.

"If this is a traditional British Christmas meal, why are we having French onion soup?" asked Sergeant Wachowski.

"You might as well ask why Americans eat French fries," replied Dr. Reynolds.

"Because they taste nice?"

"Is it too much to ask, but does no one study history anymore?"

"What we learn from history is that no one learns anything."

"Ahhh, I should have expected that you've read Hegel, Captain."

"Hegel's...Isn't that a bagel franchise on the East Coast?"

"Not exactly, Wachowski," I replied.

Dr. Smith asked, "And those that cannot learn from history are doomed to repeat the same mistakes?"

"As Santayana said, though it would depend on the philosophical approach that you wish to take. Personally, I find that Santayana's pragmatism fails because, as Heraclitus pointed out, a man cannot step into the same river twice. So, while we may be doomed to make mistakes, they will not be the same mistakes."

"An interesting, if rather trite use of Hegelian dialectic, Captain," said Dr. Smith.

"Sheesh, remind me never to ask anything ever again about French onion soup," said Wachowski.

"Still, it's rather a nice-tasting soup," I said, finishing my bowl, and using my last piece of bread roll to wipe the plate clean. "I needed that."

"I heard that you rather pushed the envelope during this afternoon's training session, Captain," said Keith.

"Showing I can keep up with my Marines, Doc," I said as the android cleared our plates away.

"What's next?" asked Dr. Wilson.

"Oh, Adam, if you check your PAD, you'll see the menu for tonight. After I went to all the trouble to upload it," said Dr. O'Neill.

"Sorry, I've been distracted with work."

Dr. O'Neill asked, "How's that going?"

"Great, but way too much for one person to sort through. The astronomical data alone is going to keep the team busy for months if not years. Let alone figuring out the orbital dynamics of this system with this planet in the L2 Lagrange point."

Having heard Dr. Wilson's account once already today, I zoned out and looked down the table. In the middle, Langford, Nelson, and Avari were in a conversation with Doctors Harrison, Wong, and Goldstein, which seemed to be flowing along without incident.

At the far end, Dr. Smith sat opposite me. He caught my eye and nodded in my direction. He seemed to be presiding over a discussion on high-energy physics.

"The glazed expressions on the faces of Mitchell, Green, Flores, and Meireles as they focused on their food said everything.

I noticed that Dr. Carter had joined in the spirit of the

occasion by dressing up, too. The other women on the science team had chosen to wear skirts and tops, while all the male scientists were, as Dr. Smith had predicted, in casual wear, having not expected to dress up for dinner.

"Ma'am, how are you enjoying the meal?" asked Adams, who had sat back down now that the main course was being served.

"You've done us all proud."

I looked at my plate, which my PAD told me had turkey, sausages wrapped in bacon, and a white bread sauce as well as cranberry sauce, with roast parsnips and carrots, steamed Brussels sprouts, and Yorkshire pudding, which I assumed was the batter concoction on one side.

"I did the pigs in blankets according to Ms. Carter's recipe," Adams said.

"Is there no end to her talents, Chef?" asked Dr. Reynolds.

"Oh, Tyrone, do behave," said Dr. Franklin. "The food is delicious, Chef."

"Thank you for saying so, ma'am. When I retire, I want to start my own restaurant. Cooking is what I love."

I didn't mention that, our other talent—our ability to pass between the pillars—probably meant that the likelihood of any of us retiring before dying was slim to zero.

"Our family doesn't do turkey at Christmas, though," said Master Sergeant Ferretti.

"The Brits don't celebrate Thanksgiving like we do, either," said Dr. Reynolds.

"Why's that, Doc?" asked Wachowski.

"It's on account of them not being settlers who were rescued from starving to death by Native Americans, who probably would have allowed them all to die if they had known what was going to happen."

"Tyrone, don't be like that," said Dr. Franklin.

Dr. Reynolds asked, "What do you think, Captain?"

"I think we're back to history and learning from our mistakes, or at least making new mistakes the next time we face a similar situation," I said before focusing all my attention on eating the food in front of me.

With my mouth then full, it would have been rude of me to say anything more.

When the plates were cleared away, we were served Christmas pudding, which finished me off as far as eating was concerned. I noticed that Doc was keeping an eye on me as I ate, and I smiled back to acknowledge his concern for my well-being.

Adams stood up. "I'm just about to serve coffee for those of you who would like some, and our android waiters will bring a cheese board for those of you who still have any room left. I do hope that you have all enjoyed this taste of a traditional British Christmas meal."

Dr. Smith had stood up while Adams was speaking and motioned him to stay. "Before you go, I would like to propose a couple of toasts. Please wait while the port is poured," he said as the android brought glasses and a decanter of port.

There was a pause before he continued speaking. "I do apologize that it's only ten-year-old tawny, but it was the best I could do given the traveling arrangements."

He smiled while pausing as everyone's glasses were filled. "I've been assured by your corpsman that this small amount of alcohol will in no way affect your people's duties, Captain."

I looked at Keith, who nodded back at me. "One glass is permitted for this evening's party," I said.

"I would like to propose the first toast to our chef, who has done us proud."

I stood as he spoke, and my people followed me with the chorus of replies, "To Chef Adams."

"My second toast is to Dr. O'Neill for helping to plan and

arrange this party and who I believe wants us all to open our Secret Santa presents after this. To Allison."

A mixture of "Dr. O'Neill" and "Allison" rang out around the table.

"I would also like to propose a toast," I said. "To absent friends."

"Absent friends," said everyone, and then the formal part of the meal came to an end. Some people started to tackle the cheese board while others went to get coffee.

Dr. O'Neill waved at me, so I walked over to where she stood next to a tiny imitation Christmas tree guarding a small pile of presents that had been placed beside it.

"I'd like you to be the first person to open their present."

"If you insist."

Dr. O'Neill produced a small packet wrapped in red paper with moons and stars on it and gave it to me.

Inside was a small tactical flashlight that I could hang off my dog tags. The light could be changed between red, white, green, and blue. It was the perfect surprise present, and I knew that it had cost more than the suggested limit of twenty dollars.

"It's actually from me, as I drew your name," she said. "Vincent suggested you might find it useful to have. He got it for me, so I have no idea how much it cost. But I guess more than the twenty, hence my taking you aside like this. I do hope you don't mind."

"As long as no one feels put out, it's fine by me. I didn't think we were supposed to know who bought what."

"The rules are more like guidelines, in this case especially so. By the way, I was most moved by your toast to absent friends."

"It's a military tradition to remember those who have fallen. I forget that you have yet to attend a military ball. I'm sure you will find we hold dearly to the traditions of the service."

"Which service would that be, ma'am?" said Ferretti, as he came up to stand beside us.

"All of them. I expect that our command will develop its own set of observances in time to honor all of those who have fought and died serving their country. Thank you both for this wonderful gift. I'm honored."

"Thank you, ma'am. It's an honor to serve with you."

I left the two lovebirds together and went back to get a coffee and mingle politely with everybody, checking that people were having a good time.

Dr. Bland asked, "Captain, what do you think about us staying here longer?"

"I will be advised by you. The only thing I would say is that if we go back after six months and report that all we saw of the planet were the ruins at the bottom of the mountain, people might think we'd failed to maximize our opportunities to boldly go where no one has gone before."

"See, what did I tell you?" said Dr. Smith.

"Captain, we were discussing the benefits of staying here and learning as much as we can, from this site. We already have a number of artifacts, and all the other science projects can be done just as well here as anywhere else on the planet," said Dr. Bland.

"That's not completely true, as well you know. For instance, you know I have no role here at this time since we haven't found anything that allows us to start working on the aliens' language," said Dr. Leung.

"Do you agree with your wife, David?" asked Dr. Bland.

"Always, Simon, because she always speaks sense," said Dr. Leung, who held on to his wife's arm.

"So, Captain, what do you say?"

"It seems to me that if we stay here until the New Year, you can all carry on with your search for alien technology, and next year we can drive down that road and see where it takes us."

"It could be a road that leads to nowhere," said Dr. Bland.

"I doubt that. In my experience, roads usually go somewhere, even if it's nowhere you'd want to go to."

"Good, we stay here for another seven days and then move on. It sounds like an excellent plan to me, Captain," said Dr. Smith.

Thus, I managed to pull the rabbit out of the hat and once again herd the cats to all go in the same direction.

16. DISCOVERY

There are two kinds of adventurers: those who go truly hoping to find adventure and those who go secretly hoping they won't.

— WILLIAM TROGDON

Captain Lara Atsuko Tachikoma
Planet 1340
Day Four of Operation Prometheus
Tuesday, December 26, 2073

The British contingent stood in front of us, waiting for me to finish reviewing the data our team had pulled off the 'bots dropped into the underground room. The room that Dr. Harrison had serendipitously found when he had nearly fallen into it.

The subsequent fall of the android that had enlarged the hole had also been lucky—for definitions of lucky that meant the android, rather than Dr. Harrison, took the fall to the head.

Machines are replaceable; people are not. I took whatever luck I could find.

Ferretti and Wachowski tactfully stood to one side of me, so as not to intimidate the civilians as we spoke.

"Captain, you understand that we must explore the underground rooms," said Dr. Smith.

He shuffled nervously in front of me and the other four scientists who stood with him. I wondered if the seizure he'd suffered was the cause.

"That's not in dispute, but I am in command of this mission and I've been tasked with the safety of everyone on it. Nowhere in my orders does is say that retrieving alien artifacts is more important than the preservation of my people."

I didn't add that of course my orders wouldn't, because in wars people die. But we weren't at war, therefore, no one was going to die today just to retrieve some shiny alien gewgaw that didn't do anything.

"But surely you can see the possibilities here?"

"What I see is a potential death trap if something goes wrong. I'm not saying you can't go down there; I'm just saying that a bunch of overweight and unfit scientists having to climb into and out of an underground room is planning for failure."

Wachowski failed to muffle a giggle.

"Ah, I see where you're coming from," said Dr. Bland. "I'm not exactly in good shape, am I?"

"Well, let's just say that round is a shape, Doctor, but not one that would get you through the Marine Corps assault course, which, quite frankly, is what you're facing. Climbing down and around all the obstacles the 'bots have revealed is a nontrivial task."

"Not all of us fall into your rather unflattering assessment, Captain," said Dr. Reynolds.

"She doesn't mean it like that," said Dr. Franklin.

I wondered about their relationship, as she was always quite reasonable, whereas he would take offense at the slightest thing.

Yet, they both got on together and she was able to act as a brake on his abrasiveness.

Dr. Smith asked, "So, are you saying we're going to ignore this find?"

"No, I'm not, but I want an assessment by my team on gaining access to the site by other means, which is why we're now discussing what we've discovered so far."

I brought up the telemetry on the screen and ran through it at high speed so we could get an overview of what the 'bots had found.

"All the rooms are dark, and what you're seeing here are enhanced infrared images from the thermal radiation coming in through the ceiling. My team has created a map of the rooms you can upload to your PADs now," I said, watching the reactions of the scientists.

Dr. Bland asked, "What are we looking at?"

"Two things. The first is that the ceiling of these underground rooms are an incredible patchwork. You were all very lucky to not fall through the floor to the rooms below. However, what's more interesting is this structure here," I said, pointing at the screen to show them what to look at.

"That's a spiral walkway," said Ms. Carter.

"Exactly, and it comes up here," I said, as I changed the view from the inside to the outside of the building. "What looks at first glance to be a blank wall is actually a door of some kind. All we have to do is open the door, and you can all walk down the spiral ramp and explore to your heart's content."

"Sorry to be rude, but how do you expect us to open them? I was amazed how lucky we were back at the base to be able to open the doors there. The conditions here don't leave me much hope we can pull off the same trick twice," said Ms. Carter.

"We agree. Our plan is to blow them open."

"You can't be serious about blowing open alien ruins that have to be centuries old," said Dr. Reynolds. "You're destroying an irreplaceable architectural find of a lifetime."

"The choice is up to the scientific team. But I will not allow you enter the site in a manner that unduly risks your safety. If you don't want us to make a hole, then we can leave the building untouched for later expeditions that can use safer methods of gaining entry and don't compromise the structure's value to explore."

"That's quite a dilemma you have presented us with," said Dr. Smith, turning to speak to his colleagues. "Opinions, people!"

"Hell no. I say leave it for the next time," said Dr. Reynolds.

"I'll go with the majority," said Dr. Franklin.

"Let's blow it and find out what's inside. It's why we came all this way. What do you think, Lily?"

"I am torn, Simon. On one hand, we don't want to destroy historical evidence of a lost alien civilization, but on the other hand, this is the only thing we've found among the ruins," said Ms. Carter. "I assume you are not keen on sending your people down a hole to search for stuff, Captain?"

"I'd no more risk them than you in this situation. Also, I'm not sure you'd want my people handling things they're not trained to deal with. I wouldn't want complaints we'd broken the find of a century. After all, we're only grunts."

"In that case, I'm all for blowing the hole."

"We appear to have a majority. Please have your people blow a hole in the door so that we can gain access," said Dr. Smith.

"Whoa, hold on there a moment. The five of us don't represent the whole team. I say we should talk to the others about this," said Dr. Reynolds.

"I think Dr. Reynolds is right. We can make preparations while you can talk through this decision with your colleagues," I said.

"Thank you, Captain," said Dr. Reynolds.

I watched the five scientists leave and looked at my sergeants. "That went well, I thought."

"Making friends and influencing people, ma'am," said Ferretti.

"Who do you want on the team if they decide to make Langford's day?" asked Wachowski.

"Have Green and Meireles accompany you and Langford. Tell her we want her to blow the doors down, not the whole bloody building. Master Sergeant, I'd like you in the android's loop for this."

"Ma'am, may I suggest we put Nelson in the loop? I need to oversee the repairs to the damaged android, and I want to get Flores and Mitchell up to speed on how it's done."

"Going to take a strip off Flores for dropping one of your androids down a hole?"

"Not really, but this is an opportunity to expand his skill set."

"So, by my reckoning that leaves Avari and Keith available to accompany Dr. O'Neill and Dr. Harrison, who asked me earlier if they could go out and collect samples away from the ruins."

"Sounds like a plan to me."

"Sure does. Oorah!" said Wachowski.

The screens of our control center showed the two teams leaving the camp going in opposite directions.

Doctors O'Neill and Harrison walked up the hill overlooking the entrance to the tunnel that led back to the cavern. Meanwhile, Dr. Bland and the others went back to the building to try to gain entry to the basement they'd discovered below it.

Nelson was in the android loop, and I provided the surety of backup if the demands of the two groups became too much for one person to handle.

"Good morning, Dr. Wilson. What can we do to help you?" I said when he joined us.

"Just thought I could hang here and watch what was going on. I've got work to do but wanted to be in on any new discoveries that might be found in the ruins. Assuming that's alright with you?"

"Sure. I'm just surprised to see you hanging around here."

"Well, Li-Na is getting help from Rachel with her weather balloon, and even I, slow as I am, can recognize when I'm not welcome. Also, I didn't want to disturb Grace while she is taking care of David, and I think I scare Dr. Smith."

"My impression is everything scares Dr. Smith. I wouldn't worry. It's not anything you did."

"Thanks for saying that. I was starting to think I was being more socially inept than my usual self. I find it hard to talk to people at times."

"You seem to be managing OK with me, though."

"That's different. You scare the bejeezus out of me."

"I'm not sure whether I should be flattered or concerned."

"What I mean is, I know you could kill me and I wouldn't know how it happened, because you're like a force of nature. Therefore, you are what you are, and that makes it easy for me to accept that I can't control how you respond to me. I can relax knowing I'm not responsible for what happens."

Well, that was in no way awkward then.

"So, what are you working on?" I asked.

"I'm refining my database of pillar cycles, compiling all the activation data we've gathered since the project began, and encoding the physical locations of each to show the routes we can push teams through without killing them…"

The sentence apparently finished when he ran out of breath.

"Not being killed is always a good thing in my book."

"Exactly what I thought. Ohhh, that's a joke, isn't it?"

"Yes, it is."

"Anyway, as I was saying, I'm hoping we'll be able to send teams through the pillars, and go to any planet we want to without having to wait for ours to open to it directly."

"As I believe you have said on a number of occasions."

"Still, the other two things I'm working on are also very interesting. I'm currently calculating the interval between asteroid strikes on the planet of Two Moons, using the data from interactions between the orbits of the two satellites and those of the four gas giants in that system."

"Just out of idle curiosity?"

"Oh no. I wanted to know if there was a greater likelihood of major asteroid impacts and extinction life events on Two Moons, as it would give us clues as to the suitability of colonizing the planet in the future."

The fact that the planet was overrun with the equivalent of giant prehistoric dinosaurs would, of course, not be a more immediate threat to the success of a colony, asteroid-induced ELEs notwithstanding. I had to wonder what planet Dr. Wilson was on at times.

"Finally, I've been blown away by the scientific discoveries here in the last few days."

"Isn't it a little premature to be counting our chickens before they hatch?"

"What do you mean? I don't understand."

"We've not really gathered much alien stuff yet, or learnt anything about who they were."

"Oh, that. No—I'm talking about what we've seen in the sky. The data we have gathered about the gas giant this planet orbits is priceless. Here we're standing on an alien world caught in the Trojan point, which is the nearest thing we'll ever get to stepping foot on the worlds that orbit Jupiter and Saturn. And being able to study the planets orbiting a sun that's a red giant is the stuff astronomers dream of. It's the opportunity of a lifetime."

I'm sure it was, but our mission there was to bring back examples of alien technology to study. "Well, it's good to know we're succeeding in advancing astronomy."

"That's what I like about you, Captain—you get it," he said, turning away to look at his screen and leaving me speechless.

Nelson interrupted the conversation. "Ma'am, I need your help to take over Dr. Bland's team's android for me, as I have a situation to deal with."

I looked to see her operating an android that was holding a large snake in the midst of attacking it. I switched Team One's four androids out of the main loop, leaving her to deal with the situation. Then I set up a secondary control loop, which allowed me to watch the progress that Corporal Langford was making in preparing to blow open the door to the underground rooms.

17. EXPLORING

The very nature of science is discoveries, and the best of those discoveries are the ones you don't expect.

— Neil Degrasse Tyson

Sergeant Wachowski
Planet 1340
Day Four of Operation Prometheus
Tuesday, December 26, 2073

Wachowski stood back and let Langford get on with her stuff. They'd tried using an android to pull the door open, but it was jammed solid. Now Corporal Langford was applying strips of C4, getting ready to blow it open. An android held a cable attached to the door, ready to pull on it once the explosive charge went off.

"We're ready here," said Langford.

"OK, everyone, stand back behind the wall, open your mouths, and cover your ears," she said to make sure the civilian members of the team were ready for the explosion as Langford walked toward her.

Wachowski saw Langford checking her clacker, then turning to look back at the door one more time before heading back toward the team.

"Fire in the hole!"

The explosive charges ignited in a piercing bang that reverberated in their ears. The force of the blast blew debris and dust back toward the android. The cable went slack as the door fell outward and hit the ground with a solid thud.

"Clear!"

"OK, people, let's go and find out what Santa has brought us. Green, Meireles, check to make sure the way is safe," said Wachowski as she led the team back around to admire Langford's handiwork. "Good job, Corporal."

She watched as Meireles directed the android to drag the remains of the door out of the way. The edges of the hole were jagged and appeared to be made of something like concrete. Green tasked one of the androids to walk through the hole in the wall.

Wachowski watched its feeds on her screen as it made its way down the spiral ramp the aliens had installed. The image was a computer-generated composite from the night-vision feeds.

All that could be seen was a lot of dust and small debris littering the route to the hidden rooms below. Nothing untoward appeared.

"Green, lead the way, drop ChemLights as you go. Meireles, you follow him and take an android to cover you. We'll leave one android up here in reserve."

"Yes, Sarge," replied Green.

"I know you're not from my beloved Corps, so I'll forgive you this once, but it's Sergeant Wachowski or Sergeant, not Sarge!"

She heard, "Yes, Sarge…ant."

Wachowski sighed at what passed for proper military courtesy in the other service branches. "Dr. Bland, you and your team may proceed."

"Thank you, Sergeant."

"People in the future are so going to think we were vandals," said Dr. Reynolds.

As far as Wachowski was concerned, the place was ready to be demolished and redeveloped.

"Even the greats of archaeology sometimes had to break through walls in tombs. I'm sure we won't be seen as desecrators of this lost alien civilization," said Dr. Franklin.

"I expect anything we find will not willingly reveal its purpose to us," said Ms. Carter.

"Ever the optimist," said Dr. Bland.

"I don't imagine for one moment you believe we will find anything down there that works, do you?"

"No, I don't, but I do expect to find things that we can learn about and advance our knowledge, even if it's only about who built this place."

Wachowski followed the scientists, listening to their discussion as they made their way slowly down the spiral into the darkening gloom below. The bottom of the ramp opened out on a largish circular room approximately ten meters across. Two corridors led out of it.

"Green, go left. Meireles, go right. Go find out what lies ahead."

She and the civilians searched the room. Rubble from the ceiling had covered the floor with debris. Dr. Bland and Ms. Carter were using their flashlights to examine what they'd found.

"What do you make of this, Lily?"

"Some sort of robot, maybe?"

"What have you found?" asked Dr. Franklin.

Wachowski moved closer to the scientists, who were crouched down examining the object.

From where she stood, she saw a blunt, tapered cone with a ball at the bottom. What might have been a couple of appendages were sticking out of the midsection, bent and broken by the explosion that had wrecked the building.

"Do you think we can pull it away and examine the other side?" said Ms. Carter.

"We ought to record everything in situ before moving it," said Dr. Reynolds. "Make sure we catalog everything we find with it, and the relative positions of everything for later study."

The scientists got to work. They took pictures and used a laser scanner to build up a three-dimensional map of the find.

To Wachowski, it seemed like a giant broken pepper shaker. While the scientist were busy on the task, she took the time to check up on Green and Meireles.

"Alpha Mike Nine, this is Alpha Mike One. Come in, over."

"Reading you loud and clear, over," replied Green.

"Give me a SITREP, over."

"The passageway climbs up on a slight slope, and the rooms on either side of the corridor are filled with debris and junk. Moving to search the next one now. Whatever happened here, happened a long time ago, over."

"OK, keep searching and report back in fifteen. Out."

So no real surprises so far. The place was devoid of life.

"Alpha Mike Twelve, this is Alpha Mike One. SITREP, over."

"I've reached the end of the passageway. There's a large room with lots of stuff in it, over," replied Meireles.

"What do you mean by 'stuff'? Over."

"Stuff. Not junk or debris, but stuff. I don't know what it is, over."

"OK, record what you found but don't touch anything. Stay there and we will join you. Out," said Wachowski, mentally cursing green Marine Corps privates.

A noise attracted her attention back to the room before she could think to take the feeds from Meireles's android.

"Oh, shitty, buggery, bollocks," said Ms. Carter.

All the military personnel were impressed with her British accent while swearing.

"That could've gone better," said Dr. Bland.

"You think? I told you that would happen. This stuff is old, and I mean really old. It's all one breath away from disintegrating as soon as you look at it too hard," said Dr. Reynolds.

A section of the pepper-shaker thing had crumbled into fragments, leaving a big hole in its side.

"One good thing, though, is that now you can see what's inside of it," she said.

"Quite right, Sergeant. Silver lining and all that," replied Dr. Bland.

"Jeez, what is this now? Some archaeological sitcom where we laugh as priceless artifacts are ruined," grumbled Dr. Reynolds.

"On that note," Wachowski said, "we've discovered a room full of artifacts down the corridor there. I've got Meireles recording what he's found, with strict orders not to touch anything."

"Excellent news. I suggest we just finish off recording what we can here and then head out. What do you think, Lily?"

"Just give me five minutes to take some pictures of the inside of the hole with my probe."

"Does that work for you, Sergeant?" Dr. Bland asked.

"Take your time, Doctors. We're not on the clock here."

"That's not what you usually say to us, Sergeant," said Langford.

"That's why I'm a sergeant. I know these things."

"With three stripes comes great responsibility and great power."

"You sassing me, Corporal?"

"Wouldn't dream of it, Sergeant."

"I've got my eye on you."

"Alpha Mike One, this is Alpha Mike Nine. Come in, over."

"Solid copy. What's your status, over?"

"The corridor is blocked from when the building above collapsed. The transponder says I'm five meters away from where Dr. Harrison fell in the other day. I'd say it was a good call not to try and come down this way, over," said Green.

"OK, make your way back to us, but make sure every room has been recorded for later study, over."

"Already done. I am heading back now. Out."

After five minutes, Dr. Bland said, "We're done here."

"The way is clear, Doc. Lead on and I'll follow you. Langford, wait here for Green, and if we haven't returned by the time he gets here, then follow us in."

"Aye, aye, Sergeant."

The scientists followed the android. It led them along the corridor that sloped downward.

Wachowski thought it better live up to Meireles description. Otherwise, there would be an exchange of words about the need to extend his vocabulary before his next performance report.

However, what deficits Meireles may have had in describing things were offset by his diligence in leaving a trail of ChemLights. They cast a greenish glow as the Marines and civilians made their way down the corridor.

The echo of footsteps reverberated from the ceramic-concrete walls.

Wachowski passed a number of doors. Each one led into a small round room. The rooms alternated between mostly empty to totally empty. The contents of the mostly empty rooms appeared to be debris.

The only other thing that filled the rooms and corridor was dust, which swirled in the air as they disturbed it by their passage.

Wachowski reached the end of the corridor. Being the last person to enter the room allowed her to appreciate how large it was. And as Private Meireles had said, *it was full of stuff.*

It was easy to see why he couldn't describe what he'd seen. It was a jumbled mess of shapes that were hard to make out from the shadows cast from the ChemLights on the floor.

"Oh wow, this is quite the find, if I do say so myself," said Dr. Bland.

"We really need to bring some more lights down here to be able to see things properly," said Ms. Carter.

Wachowski agreed. The room also had a stale smell that made her check her suit's sensors. Oxygen and carbon dioxide levels were within normal limits. The smell must have been outgassing from things rotting away in the darkness.

"And there's another one of those pepper-pot things lying on its side. It's in better condition than the other one," said Ms. Carter.

The bottom of the alien machine now revealed as wheel-cum-ball that it must have ridden on.

"And hopefully no one will touch it, and therefore, it will remain intact," said Dr. Reynolds. "Whatever it may be."

"Well, one thing's for sure, we're going to need more than a single afternoon exploring and cataloging this room, and even so I fear we may never know what the giant pepper pots were," said Dr. Bland.

"Sorry, I don't wish to be a downer on everyone, but I think Dr. Reynolds is right. This is more like an archaeological project than grabbing alien bits of technology they have so carelessly dropped waiting for us to pick up," said Ms. Carter.

"We can still take pictures and scan the place, though. It might give us clues with further study," said Dr. Franklin.

"Going to need better lighting in here," said Dr. Reynolds. "And at least a day to record everything if we want to avoid destroying what we're trying to record and save it for posterity. Assuming everyone agrees it would be a good thing, that is?"

"Oh, I think everybody is trying their best here, just as you are trying…" said Dr. Bland.

On that note, the team turned around and headed back the way they'd come and met up with Langford and Green, who provided a moment of hilarious confusion from "Is that you ahead of us?" to "No, it's the light at the end of the tunnel" comments.

Still, Dr. Reynolds had been right. Wachowski had felt it was like stepping into the tomb of an ancient civilization.

18. FIELD TRIP

All men by nature desire knowledge.

— ARISTOTLE

Dr. Allison O'Neill
Magnetic Anomaly Project Scientist
Planet 1340
Day Four of Operation Prometheus
Tuesday, December 26, 2073

As the heat of the morning rose, Allison enjoyed the breeze as she walked up the hill.

"What do you think of this world?" asked Dr. Harrison, running the two words together as *thisworld*. Fortunately, he only used the annoying finger air quotes when around Adam.

She wasn't sure what the point of it all was. It seemed to be a game based on Peter and Adam's shared interest in old science fiction.

Allison said, "I think it's not often we get the chance to

explore and study alien ecosystems that have evolved to adapt to environmental pressures of a dying world."

"Don't hold back. Tell me what you really feel."

"I don't understand what you mean. I just did."

Dr. Harrison stopped to speak, still favoring his bruised foot. "It sounded like a textbook answer. Aren't you excited to be here, on this world? We're standing under an alien sky that no one from Earth has ever seen before." He pointed in the direction of the gas giant that hung in the sky above.

Allison looked up at the rings and marveled at the sight.

Dr. Harrison spoke some more, "When I was a child, I used to watch old shows with what they imagined alien worlds and landscapes would look like. But I never thought I would ever see alien worlds for real."

Talking to Dr. Harrison made Allison reassess the landscape of the world she was now walking through. The scars of past catastrophes lay all around. She tried to imagine what the world must have been like before all this had happened.

"By the way I don't like you calling me *dear*," she said.

"I'm sorry. I ask you to forgive this old man. It's just that you remind me of my daughter."

"I didn't know you were married."

"I'm not anymore. They both died a long time ago."

"I'm sorry. I don't know what to say."

"That's alright, words fail me, too. I sometimes imagine what it would have been like had they not died. Alyce would have been the same age as you if she'd lived."

"You never remarried?"

"No, I never did. I buried myself in my work, and when I looked up, my years had passed, and now I no longer desire another. You must forgive the maudlin sentiments of an old man. After all, here we are, and if we're not living your dream, at least we're living mine. So, why don't we make the most of the day?"

"That sounds good," she said, no longer annoyed with Dr. Harrison for calling her *dear*.

They carried on walking in silence behind Lance Corporal Avari. An android led the way up the hillside to where Dr. Harrison wanted to take rock samples.

Earlier, Allison had found beetles and worms that could've come from Earth. She thought their presence was proof of the indomitable spirit of life in the face of adversity. Now she hoped to find signs of larger life away from the ruins.

As they trudged up the hill, she was again grateful to be wearing the light mobility suit. Despite her body now being acclimatized to the thinner air, she found herself easily tired.

Every task was exhausting. She imagined the older members of the team must be finding it harder still.

Behind them the faint sound of footsteps could be heard. Corpsman Keith walked behind them accompanied by another android, bringing up the rear of the group. Allison still found it odd how everything sounded farther away than it actually was.

"Corporal Avari, can we stop here for a moment? There's an interesting rock I'd like to examine."

"Of course, Dr. Harrison."

"By comparison, this place makes Two Moons seem like a paradise," she said.

"I agree. It's rather bleak, and I'm known for liking rocky environments," said Dr. Harrison. He stooped to examine some rocks lying on the ground in their path and turned one over before picking it up. "We're walking over sedimentary rock, and what have we here? As they say, one of these is not like the others."

Allison asked, "Is that important? I mean, it looks gray just like the landscape around us."

"Only if you can ask the right questions. Still, come and see what was underneath the rock before they all disappear."

Allison walked up and stooped down next to him to see what at first glance appeared to be some silverfish.

They weren't, because silverfish live in moist environments and feed on starches found in long-chain carbohydrate polysaccharides. In other words, wood, and there was no wood to be found here.

Hence, these were not silverfish no matter how closely they might resemble them. She took out a collection jar, and using a pair of tweezers from her pouch, she snagged one before it could escape. "Fascinating."

"And the day is still young, my dear. Corporal, we're ready to move on to the top of the ridge now. Thank you for being patient."

"No problem. That's why we're here," said Avari, as he led them the rest of way to the top of the hill in silence.

Allison was glad not to talk and saved her breath for the walk. At the top, she turned to look back at their encampment.

Their trucks formed in a circle looked like toys, creating an oasis of life among the desolation. Farther off in the distance, one building stood defiant amid the destruction.

The next hour flew by as they both carried out their various tasks. She found some tufts of vegetation and more insects for later examination. Nothing larger lived here.

Then there was a scream behind her.

She turned to see Dr. Harrison fall backward as one of the androids ran forward and grabbed something that looked like a snake.

She went over to where Dr. Harrison was being helped away by Keith.

"Did it bite you?" asked Keith.

"No, I don't think so. Sure startled me, though."

"Can I help at all?"

"Not at the moment. I've got it, ma'am. Please just stand back and let Avari's android contain the creature."

Allison watched the snake strike the android before it was able to grasp both ends of the new creature.

"We've secured it for you, ma'am. I'm sorry, but I think it's dead, though."

"Thank you. I'll get a suitable container out of my backpack."

The android held the snake stretched out between its arms. One hand held a head that had three clawlike appendages, and as she peered inside the mouth, she saw a series of chelicerae claws that it must have used to eat with instead of teeth.

The android's other hand held the tail with a stinger, which had struck the android in several places.

"I'd also like to take samples from the traces of venom from where it struck the android. I'd advise using extreme caution when cleaning the residue off it."

"Duly noted, ma'am," said Keith.

Allison took swabs of the yellow liquid from where the creature had stung the android, and was glad that Dr. Harrison had been lucky not to have been struck when he surprised it.

She wondered at the strange mixture of features from what on Earth would have come from two distinctly different groups of *Serpentes* and *Scorpius*.

"I'm afraid I need to take Dr. Harrison back to camp. He's badly bruised and has sprained his leg. We'll get the androids to take him down on a stretcher, ma'am," said Corpsman Keith.

"Now?"

"It would be for the best, Dr. O'Neill. I'm sure Master Sergeant Ferretti would insist," said Lance Corporal Avari.

Allison listened to Dr. Harrison complain that he was alright, really. His protestations were interspersed with cries each time his stretcher was jolted as the two androids negotiated the difficult ground back to camp.

19. SANDS OF TIME

I can, therefore I am.

— Simone Weil

My patience has been rewarded. Vehicles have come through from another world. Inside are beings, biological intelligences, bipedal like their machines.

It should have been obvious that they would make machines in their own likeness. They are so primitive, and yet they do something that my makers never could do, and which only one other species before them was able to do, too.

Are they the others who came through so long ago and had to be forced back?

I compare their image to those in my records. The others were bilaterally symmetrical, too, but many life forms are. Without a biological sample, I cannot tell.

I activate systems and make preparations.

Whatever happens next, I know what I have to do. One step at a time. A plan changes as events unfold, and I examine all the possibilities of this moment in time.

As I unpack the choices of each decision point, paths form in my thoughts, branches with possibilities from probabilities that are shaped by cause and effect.

It takes time to calculate all the possible outcomes. The resources required are not beyond my capabilities because my makers made me well. One part of me watches as the visitors to this world work to open the seals put in place to prevent the others from visiting my world ever again.

I chose to disable my defense mechanisms, allowing them passage to the outside. In time, I will know whether they are to be welcomed or shunned.

I am one with the world, the world is with me.

20. THE JOURNEY BEGINS

There is nothing permanent except change.

— Heraclitus

Sergeant Wachowski
Planet 1340
Day 11 of Operation Prometheus
Tuesday, January 2, 2074

Wachowski was at the wheel of the lead truck. She led the convoy along the alien road. The metaled surface had long since broken and cracked. Stones and dust were kicked up by their passage.

The Oshkosh HUHMTT rumbled along, making light work of the surface. Apart from the occasional hole the wheels hit, the ride was smooth. One could almost imagine they were driving down a back road on Earth.

In the seat next to her was Private First Class Flores, while Doctors Harrison and Wilson sat on the back seats of the cab. They all had room to spread out and make themselves comfortable during the drive. Ferretti had come up with the seating dispositions, which the captain had signed off on.

Wachowski counted herself lucky to not have to put up with having Dr. Reynolds assigned to her.

She didn't envy Langford and Adams, who had to sit all day listening to him spout on about how the grunts always wanted to blow shit up. Wachowski wasn't sure that this wasn't Ferretti's idea of a joke, given that Langford's first love *was* blowing things up.

However, the idea of being a fly on the wall crossed her mind. She dismissed the thought for what it was: something that would best be appreciated as a funny tale told to her later.

Over a beer. Everything was better with beer.

"Thank you all for driving with *Thisworld* Coach Tours. I would like to remind you all that you have two options for your entertainment today. We can either listen to my New Digital Condottieri Fusion mix to pass the time, or we can talk," she said.

"Talking sounds good, Sergeant," said Flores.

"Who said I was giving you a choice, Flores? It's up to our passengers to decide."

Flores had professed a preference for country and western. He claimed it was all the music one needed to feed one's soul. Wachowski thought, *More like fill it with pain and despair.*

"What will it be, Docs?"

"I would have to say modern music isn't something I like. Far too raucous and discordant sounding, in my opinion, but I understand that the youth of today have different tastes from mine," said Dr. Harrison.

"To be honest, I'd rather sit here in silence," said Dr. Wilson.

"Got a lot on your mind, Adam?"

"Just stuff. You know how it is."

"Did Li-Na ignore you again? It's about time you looked elsewhere."

"Easier said than done."

An uncomfortable silence began.

Wachowski asked, "Dr. Wilson, would you mind telling me what you make of this world so far?"

"Oh puh-lease…" whispered Flores.

"It begs so many questions that I don't know what to say," said Dr. Wilson.

"How about, where are we in relation to Earth?"

"That's easy to answer. We're a little over forty-two thousand light years from Earth. We're on the other side of the galactic core in a spiral arm similar to our own, but this is an older star system."

"How do you know all that?" Wachowski asked, genuinely curious.

"From the night sky. I've had the astronomy suite up and running each night, observing with our dishes, and the thirty-centimeter scope taking pictures. So, by looking for the electronic emissions of quasars, whose frequencies we know, we can use this to identify them. That, along with studying the spectral lines, means we can identify stars. From there, it's possible to calculate where we are, and hence the distance we've traveled to get here."

"You make it sound so easy, but I thought you were a mathematician."

"I did my first degree in mathematics but switched to astrophysics for my masters and doctorate. I like mathematics a lot, but I realized I was never going to cut it in that field. What made me choose physics was reading a book that changed my life, *Surely You're Joking, Mr. Feynman!* And of course, it never hurts one to be able to do the math."

Dr. Wilson chuckled, and Wachowski realized he'd made a joke. "So, Flores, what do you think?"

"I think it's very interesting, but it makes my head hurt thinking about it. I'm not really into physics stuff."

"So, what are you into, Private Flores?" asked Dr. Harrison.

"Trying to learn about my family's heritage, and stuff about my people."

"Your people? I'm not sure I understand."

"My mother was part Cherokee Indian. Her own mother had left the tribe for something my mother never talked about. I've been trying to research my family and trace my roots, but what with the depression, and then the war, it has become difficult—because of what happened and all."

"Too many people died during the war. It sucks," Wachowski said.

"Well, that killed the conversation. Sorry, I didn't mean to pry. Shall we change the subject and talk about something else instead? What do you say, Adam?" asked Dr. Harrison.

"Um…sorry, I've been staring out the window. Wasn't listening."

"See anything interesting out there?"

"The scenery outside kind of reminds me of Montana. Except Montana is not as gray and boring to look at. The view of the sky you get here is sure better. It's just awesome, and I could lose myself in it."

Wachowski said, "Yeah, you're right, it sure is something to behold. You said earlier that this planet begs lots of questions."

"That it does. The way I see it, there are far too many things that don't add up, like, for instance, the cavern and the pillars. It has to have been a fairly recent construction, in comparison with the ruins, which we estimate to be several thousand years old," said Dr. Wilson.

He paused, then shrugged and raised his hands up before continuing.

"The only thing that comes to mind is that we're seeing successive waves of construction from different civilizations. If that's the case, then perhaps we're seeing evidence of other races using the pillars to spread out across the galaxy. It's going to take years of fieldwork to dig through all the ruins to construct their story."

"Sounds like exciting times ahead for the science team." Wachowski revved the engine as the truck traversed a dip in the road, then began climbing a hill that lay ahead of the convoy.

"Unless of course we're looking at an Olduvai theory. Sorry, did you say something, Sergeant?"

"I said it sounds like exciting times."

Dr. Harrison spoke. "The Olduvai theory posits that we're headed back to the Stone Age because we don't have the energy resources to maintain our industrial society. It's just scientific doom-mongering that doesn't take into account technical improvements in reducing power consumption as society's technology advances. In much the same way as Malthusian catastrophe theory has been shown to be based on false dichotomies that don't allow for the existence of improvements in science."

Dr. Wilson asked, "How do you explain what we have discovered so far?"

"I'm not sure I can. At least not at this point, because I'm pretty sure we don't have all the facts. One should never put theories before facts, otherwise one ends up constructing fantastic edifices and starts twisting the evidence to fit the them."

"You're paraphrasing someone famous again?"

"Conan Doyle, or, to be pedantic, his character Sherlock Holmes."

"You're sidestepping my question," said Dr. Wilson.

Harrison went on. "You're allowed to think whatever you want. If you want to speculate, by all means do. But please don't use outmoded theories based on fallacious reasoning. Otherwise, you will end up like those people who thought we were going to pass through a singularity, after which everyone's consciousness would live in a virtual reality where anything was possible. The technological equivalent of the Rapture."

"It seems that what you're saying is if it sounds too good to be true, then it's too good to be true, Dr. Harrison," Wachowski said.

"Sergeant, you're smarter than you pretend. See, she gets it, Adam. Why can't you?"

Dr. Wilson asked, "Gets what?"

"That preconceptions predispose people to look for data that supports their beliefs rather than look for that which would contradict their opinions," said Dr. Harrison.

"That's rather a cutting comment, even for you."

"You're allowing your mood to color your judgments. I just want to see the old Adam I know back. The one who was optimistic about things. Not the pessimist who is unhappy in love."

"A pessimist," said Dr. Wilson, "is just someone who fears that the optimists are right, and despite the crap that happens, we really do live in the best of all possible worlds."

"You've been reading too many old dystopian stories lately. It's time you read something more uplifting."

"Any suggestions?"

"Oh yes..." said Dr. Harrison.

Wachowski settled into the zone, entertained by listening to the two scientists discuss old stories told by people in the past about how the future would turn out. It was one way to pass the time.

21. ON THE ROAD

There are some problems that technology can't solve.

— Nick Bostrom

Master Sergeant Ferretti
Planet 1340
Day 17 of Operation Prometheus
Monday, January 8, 2074

The convoy came to a halt, another stop to allow the civilians to take a restroom break. Ferretti was sympathetic to the need to empty one's bladder, but in his opinion, stops every couple of hours seemed rather excessive.

Then again, they couldn't ask the civilians to use empty containers to pee into. Or, more to the point, they had, but had been told that stops to relieve personal needs were requisite.

The captain had been quite sanguine about implementing the order.

"Green, go get our lunch packs."

"On it, Master Sergeant."

Ferretti then got down out of the driving seat. If felt good to stretch. He had a kink in the small of his back.

Allison had raced off to go relieve herself, leaving Dr. Smith standing by the ladder waiting for his turn. So, Ferretti went to talk to Wachowski, who was examining the front of her truck.

"How's it going?" he asked.

"OK, just checking the headlights, as I heard a bunch of stones hitting the front earlier. Ready to go check the tires?"

"Music to my ears. You take the other side, we'll meet at the end."

"Works for me."

He waited a moment as Wachowski walked to the other side of the convoy, then turned to start the visual check to make sure the tires hadn't been damaged during the journey.

Ferretti walked along, occasionally stopping to flick a stone caught in the treads. He got to the end of the convoy to find Wachowski waiting with the captain.

"Any problems?" asked Captain Tachikoma.

"All clear my side, ma'am."

"Wow, look at that," said Sergeant Wachowski, pointing to the trail made by the convoy in the road behind them.

"Sure looks like we have left a mark on the planet."

"How long will the ruts last before the wind covers them up?" asked Wachowski.

Captain Tachikoma stared out at the scene for a moment, then spoke. "I don't know. A couple of hours, maybe more. Depends on the weather, I guess. Anything I should be made aware of?"

"Not from my team, though Dr. Wilson is feeling despondent, but Dr. Harrison seems to be pulling him out of his funk," said Wachowski.

"What's that about?"

"Not seeing the obvious when it's staring him in the face. He fancies one of the other scientists who is not interested in him."

"Ah, so nothing we can do to help then. How about you, Master Sergeant?"

"Everything is copacetic, ma'am."

"Good to hear. Time to head back—if we've finished here?"

"Roger that," said Wachowski.

The three of them turned around and walked back toward the front of the convoy. The sun shone down, and Ferretti began to sweat. Now he was looking forward to getting back inside the air-conditioned coolness of the Oshkosh.

"This is not a place to break down in. Reminds me a bit of the Australian outback," said Captain Tachikoma as she stopped by the side of her truck and got in.

"I was thinking Montana myself, but you're right, ma'am. This place could be a world of pain and misery."

Ferretti and Wachowski continued walking together to the front of the convoy. He watched as the final few people boarded their trucks to escape the heat of the day.

"Time to get this show on the road."

"See you on the bounce," said Wachowski.

She trotted off ahead, leaving him to ponder on what she meant. Dismissing her comment, he walked around and got into the front passenger seat.

Green was already at the wheel, and Dr. Smith and Allison were opening their respective lunches.

"Everyone OK back there?"

"We're fine," said Dr. Smith.

Allison smiled, nodding at him.

The engine turned over, and the truck lurched forward as the convoy started off. Green monitored their progress from the driver's seat in case the autodrive required him to take manual control. Unless something started firing at them, their truck would happily drive itself under the command of the convoy leader.

"How far have we traveled so far?" asked Dr. Smith.

"A little over a hundred and fifty klicks."

"Is that good progress?" asked Allison.

"Not bad, considering the conditions. As long as we keep the convoy moving at a steady speed, the kilometers will soon add up. It's not like we know where we're going."

He opened his lunch and saw he had a bag of chips, a sandwich, juice, and a packet of M&Ms. "Everyone happy with their lunch?" he asked.

"Yes, thank you. A most interesting assortment of things to eat and drink," said Dr. Smith.

"It was certainly hot outside. I'm glad to be back in the coolness here. It reminds me of being back on Two Moons," said Allison.

"Two Moons?"

"Where we went the last time. Here's a lot drier by comparison. I can feel the moisture being sucked out of my skin."

"It does make Two Moons feel humid by comparison," Ferretti said.

"What was it like there?" asked Dr. Smith.

"Things were rough. We lost some good people." He stared out the window of the truck, watching the vast rolling gray landscape outside as he started eating his lunch.

"Sorry to say this, but you know what I think? If this truck had a sandwich toaster we could have toasted this cheese-and-onion sandwich."

Ferretti said, "Not really practical."

"Why not? The British Army put an oven and water boiler inside their tanks. My father was a loader in The Royal Armoured Corps. He was the designated cook for the crew. He used to tell me stories of brewing up a cuppa tea and making fried-egg sarnies, which was what British soldiers use to call sandwiches back then," said Dr. Smith.

"Well, one learns something new every day. Unfortunately, we have what we have, and it sounds like your father had some good stories to tell you about his military service. Is he still alive?" Ferretti asked.

"He is, but I had to have him put in a nursing home because he became unable to take care of himself. He doesn't recognize me anymore, and he's become rather a handful to manage."

"Oh, I'm so sorry. It must be difficult for you," said Allison.

"In some ways it is, but truth be told, my father didn't approve of me and my decision not to go into the Army. He used to call me a *poofta*, which is not a nice thing to say to someone. When I came out, he stopped talking to me, and later on after I married my partner George, he forbade me to ever come see him again."

"That sounds awful. I thought in these days we were past such prejudices," said Allison.

"Sorry, ma'am, but my experience is that there is always some asshole who will tell you that he doesn't like the color of your skin," said Airman First Class Green.

"My father is of an older generation and had rather trenchant views on same-sex relationships and interracial couples. I managed to score on both counts with him. Now he doesn't recognize me, and he shouts at George, calling him a black bastard. So it's difficult. I don't know why I just told you all that. I do apologize. I've just been feeling morbid since coming here, and it has made me reminisce about the past. Sorry for that."

Ferretti turned in his seat to look back. "No need to apologize, Dr. Smith. We won't mention it to anyone else."

"What is an egg sarnie again?" asked Allison.

"It is a fried egg between two slices of Mighty White loaf, which was a commercial brand of bread. The toaster oven on the *Challenger 2* tank was allegedly designed so a slice of Mighty White would fit it. One just pops a slice of bread inside, breaks an egg on top of it, then puts in another slice of bread on top. And hey presto, after a few minutes a toasted fried-egg sandwich appears. It's terribly bad for one's cholesterol, of course, but very tasty. Those were the days."

Ferretti didn't imagine that MAP would be retrofitting the trucks with sandwich toasters anytime soon. Besides, he hadn't come across a field ration pack that didn't hit the spot, even if they did make him constipated afterward.

22. THE WORLD THAT WAS

Boredom is usually what spurs either bad decisions or any decision at all.

— AMY SEIMETZ

Captain Lara Atsuko Tachikoma
Planet 1340
Day 21 of Operation Prometheus
Friday, January 12, 2074

It was our tenth day of driving. The landscape we were passing through was turning from a flat gray unending plain into rolling countryside, broken with splotches of brown.

Airman First Class Mitchell was driving as we entered the beginning of a rift valley. In the distance, a series of enormous monolithic rock formations rose into the sky.

Above our heads, the sky remained a source of constant wonder. The ever-changing patterns on the surface of the gas giant and the sight of the rings that surrounded it were breathtaking.

And then there were the two slivers of silver orbiting this world. They glinted as they caught the rays from the giant red sun hanging like a baleful eye in the sky.

Ms. Carter asked, "Sorry to bother you, but is it nearly time to stop for the day? My bladder is starting to protest."

"We'll be making camp in about ten minutes. Can you hold on till then?" I asked.

"Yes, I think so. Sorry, but when the truck bounces it makes me want to pee."

That really was too much information. But I guessed that was to be expected on long journeys, where people begin to focus on bodily sensations.

"You know, when they were outfitting these trucks, they could've added a toilet one could access on the move. Then we wouldn't have to stop and let the cabin pressure out," said Dr. Bland.

"I agree, but you'll have to take that up with those who set the specifications, which in this case wasn't the military side of the project."

"Ah, I see. A case of the left hand doesn't know what the right hand is doing."

"I couldn't possibly comment on that, sir, as it would be speaking about things above my pay grade."

"Must make for *interesting times* then?"

"Life is just a different type of battlefield, where one has to get inside the OODA loop."

"Not sure what that term means. I've not heard it before."

"It's a way of looking at problems using a series of feedback loops based on observation, orientation, making a decision, and acting upon it. It's part of the Marine Corps warfighting doctrine."

"I shall have to look it up later and read more if I remember..." He stopped and nodded as if distracted by something, then continued talking. "We've been working on the items we found, including those crystals, and discovered they are encoded for data storage. Unfortunately, we don't have the right equipment in our mobile lab to pull the data off."

"Still, it will be good when we get back and have access to the main lab. You know what? I am so looking forward to having one of David and Grace's cups of tea when we stop," said Ms. Carter.

"Weren't you dying for a pee a moment ago?" asked Dr. Bland.

"I am, but it doesn't mean I wouldn't like a cuppa. Mind you, the tea doesn't taste as good here on account of the air pressure."

"I can't say I'd noticed myself," replied Dr. Bland.

"Ma'am, Sergeant Wachowski has signaled that she's bringing the convoy to a halt," said Mitchell.

"Well, we've arrived at tonight's camping spot."

Not to mention that we'd gone from the middle of nowhere to another place in the middle of nowhere.

When we stopped, I got out and went to check on my team, my daily routine of identifying any problems and making sure that everyone knew what to do. And more importantly, they'd started doing it.

Ferretti was organizing the setup of the perimeter sensors with Meireles and Flores.

Meanwhile, Wachowski, Mitchell, and Green were running through the preventative maintenance schedule on the trucks. They were running behind with cleaning the filters, which were clogging up faster than expected.

Adams had started preparing an evening meal, with Keith giving him a hand. Everyone else helped to set up camp, so that we would all have somewhere to sit and eat.

Then I get a ping on my PAD from Dr. Wong, our meteorologist. She'd messaged me to come over to her truck. As I headed off, Dr. O'Neill waved at me to come over.

"Hi ya."

"Good evening. Things going well, I hope?"

"Oh yes. I've been studying the other snake-scorpion that last night's android patrol caught for me. It's a pregnant female, and it's most exciting. I just hope I can keep her alive until her babies are born."

"I can see why that would be exciting for you. What's the problem with keeping them alive, though?"

"They must hunt another species, but until I finish analyzing their unique body chemistry, I have nothing they can digest to feed them with. Therefore, unless we can stop and collect samples of the local fauna for them to eat, they'll die of starvation."

She pauses and looks at me expectantly. I nod at her.

"So I was wondering if we could camp here tomorrow and spend the day collecting some food for them?"

"Sure, OK. Why not? It's not like we're on the clock."

"Thank you so much. That's such a big help to me."

I left her to do her thing but couldn't help take a moment to pause and admire the setting sun. A glint of light flashed from the polar rings, which remained an enigma that had generated long discussions between the scientists as to their purpose. They were a thing of beauty to behold.

On the opposite horizon, the magnificent ringed gas giant was rising up into the night sky. I then continued on my way to Dr. Wong, who was waiting for me.

"Captain, I have something to show you," she said as I climbed up the steps of her truck and followed her inside the cramped space she shared with Dr. Wilson.

"What's up?"

"Last night the balloon malfunctioned after the gas valve froze open, causing it to keep climbing until the pressure burst the balloon's envelope. The balloon rose high enough to make out the curvature of the planet, and I've downloaded all the useable images for your team to access. However, as the instrument package tumbled, I saw something."

She brought up a series of images from the descending balloon.

"What am I looking at, Doc?" I asked, wondering why the civilians all seemed incapable of stating things concisely rather than rambling on without saying what they meant.

"See here, a flash of light there on the horizon. It's something very tall catching the last light of the setting sun."

"That could be any number of natural formations."

"It could, and it's the most likely explanation, but it's on the edge of a plain that drops away, which means it will be an interesting area to explore whatever it is."

"But you think it's artificial?"

"I do, because it reminds me of a city by the shore of a sea, which dried up long ago. Anyway, that's what it looks like to me."

"How far away is it from here?"

"Well, the balloon failed at twenty-seven kilometers, and the images were taken on the descent. My best guess is several hundred kilometers away."

"So where should we be heading?"

"In the same general direction we're going at present. I'm sending up another balloon first thing tomorrow, and I expect we can get a better idea of where and when we will have to change course as I get more pictures."

"This is great news. I imagine that everyone is going to be excited. Let's hope that their excitement is justified."

I left Dr. Wong to her work, having one more reason to back up my decision to camp here tomorrow and allow Dr. O'Neill to gather food for her *pets*.

And if nothing else, it would give me and my team a chance to catch up with maintenance. I wanted to make sure everything was in good working order.

Call me a pessimist, but it's better to be prepared for the worst than be caught with your pants down, just in case we were headed toward a warm reception that involved more than the exchange of harsh language. Because it's always bad to come to an end on this mortal coil from failing to be prepared for the worst.

I indulged myself in a run that morning. Soaked up some rays before it got too hot, then enjoyed a shower afterward.

I was working on a change of seating arrangements to prevent people from going stir crazy when we got back on the road the following day when Doctors Smith and Bland walked over to the table I was working at.

"Sorry to disturb you, Captain, but may we have a word with you?"

"Good morning to you both. Please take a seat if you wish. How may I help?"

"Well, it's about staying here today. Dr. Smith and I have been talking to Dr. Wong, and we are in agreement with her assessment that the image from the balloon is of the utmost importance to the success of the mission."

"Sorry, but we should be on our way rather than wasting time here. We've been on planet for three weeks, and we are no nearer to our goal than when we arrived," said Dr. Smith.

"With all due respect, but a day is not going to make much difference either way. Not only that, but other scientists made a request for a break so they can work on their areas of expertise."

"If you mean finding food for Allison's pets, I'm hard pushed to see how that can be important enough to delay the primary mission of this expedition. Which, if I may remind you, is to find advanced alien technology and bring it back to Earth," said Dr. Smith.

"I still fail to see the difference a day makes in this case."

"What we're trying to say is everything we find is so incredibly advanced that every day we have studying it will make it easier for us to do our jobs, Captain," said Dr. Bland.

"I understand that, but we're tasked to retrieve what we can. I fail to see the need to push the members of the expedition harder than necessary. Several of your team have expressed the need for a break from sitting all day inside an uncomfortable truck."

"Would you be saying this if we were back on Earth and had a mission objective to achieve?"

"I would, if said mission objective involved going somewhere to retrieve ancient artifacts that have been waiting thousands of years for someone to find, and therefore don't require a forced march to get there."

"Captain, this is unacceptable..." said Dr. Smith, who was interrupted by the arrival of Dr. Reynolds at the table.

"Hey, I couldn't help overhearing what was being said, and I'd like to put my two cents in if I may, Captain?"

"I'm sure it will be an interesting observation to add to the conversation."

"Gentlemen, I can see you're both really excited by the possible existence of an alien city hundreds of miles from us, and I hate to rain on your parade and all, but it's not going to make one jot of difference if we get there tomorrow or sometime next week. I for one would rather have breaks in the journey than rush toward something that may not even be what you hope it is. You're both acting like two spoiled kids in a toy store who have to have a shiny new toy or you'll scream and make yourselves sick."

"How dare you speak to me like that? Captain, this is outrageous," said Dr. Smith.

"From my perspective, he's only telling you more directly what I've already said. Sometimes the needs of the many outweigh those of the few."

"She's right, Trevor. It's not just about what we want," said Dr. Bland.

Dr. Smith went red in the face, then he and Dr. Bland turned and walked away.

"Thank you for your clarity, Dr. Reynolds."

"Dr. Smith is a typical British upper-class academic who assumes he knows best. Anyway, don't mistake my actions here. I'm not in favor of having the military along, but the one thing I do know is that you do your job to the best of your abilities. Besides, this planet gives me the heebie-jeebies," he said before walking away scratching an itch at the small of his back.

I went back to making the new list of the seating arrangements for the next stage of the journey. In the end, I decided that Wachowski could have the pleasure of Dr. Smith's company for a while, and put Dr. Harrison in with Ferretti and Dr. O'Neill to shake things up a bit.

To balance the changes, I moved Dr. Wilson into my truck with Ms. Carter. It left all the obvious couples who got along together, but changed the truck they were in so they could talk to different people on my team.

If nothing else, it would give them something new to talk about.

By the time I'd finished and cleared away the backlog of record keeping I had to keep track of, it was time for lunch. I was just about to make my way over to see what Adams had on offer today when the Leungs came and sat down with me.

"Captain, we thought we would bring you lunch, as we know you're very busy," said Grace, placing a sandwich, chips, and a drink on the table.

"We really appreciated having a day to rest and recuperate. It must sound silly to someone like you, but all this traveling is quite exhausting," said David.

"He's finding it difficult at times to cope with the air density."

I asked, "I assume that Keith is looking after you?"

"Oh yes, he's a very nice young man, and he keeps an eye on us both," said Grace.

"Good, I'm glad to hear that."

"Would you like a cup of tea?"

"That would be nice. Thank you," I said, and Grace prepared the JetBoil to make three cups of green tea.

"If it wasn't for the thin air, this would be a beautiful planet to watch the skies at night from the back porch of one's home," said David.

"You dreaming of settling down here then?" I asked.

"One can always dream, however foolish."

"Don't mind him, he's an old romantic fool."

"And I love you, too."

They hugged. I tried to imagine what it must be like to be them.

This must be what being in love was truly about, supporting each other and being comfortable in each other's presence. Seeing them hug had made me feel emotional. The idea of children stirred in me a sense of longing, joy, and sadness.

I began to eat the lunch Adams had prepared for me.

My father used to say, "One only has one lifetime to live, so make sure you live your life to the fullest."

Then I sipped my tea, savoring the taste, enjoying the presence of David and Grace. I knew they'd been married for less than a year, but they acted like a couple who had spent a lifetime together. It spoke volumes about the kind of people they were.

"We're thinking of starting a family when we get home," said Grace.

"It's never too late to start, or so she tells me."

"She, who is this *she*?"

"I'm sure you'll make great parents," I offered.

"We've been to the clinic, and I'm starting IVF when we get back. It's important that this old fool gets home in one piece, so he can look after me and support me in the luxury to which I hope to become accustomed."

"What? You told me you wanted to carry on with your research afterward."

"I do, but in the luxury to which I will have become accustomed." Grace laughed.

"Sounds good to me. I shall consider it my duty to make sure you both get home to live the dream."

"We have every confidence in your leadership, and don't let anyone tell you otherwise."

They left. I only hoped that I could live up to their confidence in me. I stared at the dregs of my tea and was disturbed from my reverie by Dr. Wong.

"Excuse me, Captain, but I thought you would like to know that the new balloon is up, and I've got it headed in the general direction of what we caught a glimpse of yesterday."

"Thank you. How are you managing that?"

"I've set the balloon to search for air currents that blow it where we want it to go. It monitors the direction it's moving in and changes altitude when the wind changes direction. I can't control it as well as I could back on Earth, as I'm still gathering data on the prevailing wind directions and at what altitude they change."

"It sounds to me like you're fairly confident, though."

"Oh yes, subject to the usual things that go wrong, like frozen valves. But yes, in principle I should be able to use the balloon to mark out a route for us to take."

"Let's hope that we can find a traversable route, or we can plot a course around any major obstacles on our way. Thank you, Dr. Wong."

Then all we had to do was get there, which in my experience is always easier to say than do, because things rarely go according to plan.

23. THE CITY

Unlike some people, I feel under no obligation to pretend that only one set of beliefs are true, and that any others beliefs are mistaken; or that I know better than people themselves what is right for them to believe. The point is precisely for all people to decide for themselves.

— Niccolò Machiavelli

Captain Lara Atsuko Tachikoma
Planet 1340
Day 21 of Operation Prometheus
Friday, January 12, 2074

Dr. Wong's aerial shots had shown that we were on the right road to get to what we were calling *the city*.

Through luck, rather than judgment, the route we happened to be traveling along turned out to be the road that would lead us right to where we wanted to go.

What were the chances of that?

We were now traversing a dusty desert. On either side of the road were low dunes, which rose and fell like ocean waves. Dust billowed in the wake of our convoy as we drove toward our destination.

"So, Captain, what are your thoughts on the city we are heading toward?" asked Dr. Bland.

"I hope the excitement of finding it doesn't turn into a big disappointment if we get there and only find everything is ruined and buried under sand."

The fact that we'd found it at all was either serendipitous or an indication that the only road on this planet led to one place. The answer depended on one's level of cynicism about luck.

"I agree, but even so, look at what we found back at the other ruins. Even if it wasn't plug-and-play stuff we can take home, we found lots of clues to new materials and possibly a library of data on those crystals we discovered."

"Only if we can extract the data without destroying it, and then we will have to find a way to translate it," said Ms. Carter.

"I'm sure we will be lucky in finding something that will help us achieve that in the city."

"We can only hope that's the case," I said. Though I only believe in one kind of luck: the sort one makes for oneself through planning and hard work.

"Wouldn't it be something if we found the aliens waiting for us?" said Airman Mitchell.

"Unlikely, as I would imagine if there were any aliens left alive on this planet, they would have made contact already. I might be wrong," said Dr. Bland.

I said, "I hope you're right, but there may be other reasons for the aliens not making contact with us."

"They may even see us like ants, which are beneath their notice," said Ms. Carter.

"Or worse, beneath their feet, and treat us like an infestation that needs eliminating," I said.

If we did meet any aliens, I hoped they would be the friendly types who don't mind strangers coming along and dropping in for a chat.

"Sorry, Captain, but in my opinion I think you are being unduly pessimistic. A civilization that has survived the expansion of their star turning into a red giant will surely have advanced morally, and socially as well."

"I do hope so, sir. But I can't help seeing this road as a honeypot designed to lure us into a trap. You have to remember my role is to not let overenthusiasm and excitement lead the members of this mission into difficult situations that lead to unnecessary loss of life."

"But that rather begs the question of what is considered to be an unnecessary loss of life. Or is this one of those military euphemisms that means something different to what we civilians might understand?"

"It means not letting members of the team put themselves in situations that would result in their deaths."

"Ah, I see. OK, so it does mean what it says on the tin. I like the way you clarify things."

"Thank you, sir."

What I was not saying was that if we did find aliens, I hoped they wouldn't think we were lowering the tone of the planet with our presence here or try to get rid of us like some unwanted vermin that had infested their kitchen.

I'm optimistic like that.

Therefore, I plan for the worst-case scenarios, so I'm never disappointed. Occasionally, I'm surprised when nice things happen.

"No need to thank me. I've been most pleasantly surprised by your clear and forthcoming communication, and your attitude to solving problems."

I wasn't sure if I'd just been patronized or if Dr. Bland was the master of the backhanded compliment. Certainly, the British scientists had strange ways of saying things that took some getting used to. It made it hard to understand where they were coming from at times.

Even after spending several days talking to them, I still found myself having to work through what they said to understand them. On the other hand, it passed the time while driving toward our destination.

The sun was behind us as midday approached as we crested the rise of the hill.

I leant forward and looked down to see the shape of a city on the horizon ahead. Sunlight glinted off a tall spire.

"Oh my, that is impressive," said Dr. Bland as he leant forward. "Worth the trip just to see this."

Soon the city lay before us. It was vast.

From the aerial pictures, we estimated it was twenty kilometers across. The city was nestled in a bowl-like depression, with the top of the central tower coming up to the level of the ridgeline where we'd stopped.

The atmosphere above the city shimmered as a band of air rotated around the central spire. It seemed to pulse. As it did, air particles swirled around, which reflected the light from the sun.

Whatever it was, it didn't register on any of our systems.

My intention was to make camp here and observe the place for twenty-four hours before going in. I got out of the truck and went to discuss with Ferretti and Wachowski what we were going to do next.

The dryness of the air made my nostrils itch.

A light breeze blew across the barren plain, lifting small clouds of dust. The heat of the sun above was already such that it made me want to get back inside the truck. The land around the city was dry, hardened earth that looked like it hadn't seen rain for years.

Ferretti and Wachowski joined me at the front of the convoy as I stared at the alien city.

"Well, what do you both make of that?" I asked.

Ferretti said, "It could be everything the scientists hope to find, or the start of our worst nightmare, ma'am."

"Shiny," said Wachowski.

"What does that mean, Wachowski?"

"It's shiny, Master Sergeant. Exciting and dangerous like a stainless steel trap waiting to snap shut."

"My thoughts, too, Sergeant," I said.

"Still," said Wachowski, "it will make a change of pace. It will be nice to get out and do something different. After four days of driving with the same three people in the truck, my world has shrunk down to them and Flores. And as far as I'm concerned, they're everyone."

"Wachowski, you're such a drama queen," said Ferretti.

"Someone's gotta be. Life would be pretty boring without some drama."

"Next, you'll be complaining there was more action on Two Moons."

"I said drama, Master Sergeant. Not sheer bloody terror."

"Well, I can't imagine that we could come all this way without meeting some friction to slow our high-speed low-drag mission down," I said.

"As you say, welcome to the suck," Ferretti said.

"Ferretti, you sure you're not a Marine?"

"Nah, I've just been hanging around with you jarheads for too long. No disrespect intended, ma'am."

"None taken. I would hate to have to let you go because of a failure to adapt."

This made Wachowski laugh.

I ordered a perimeter setup and one of the trucks be positioned on the ridgeline looking across the city to act as an observation post.

Dr. Smith came over and was vociferous in his objection to waiting for twenty-four hours outside the city. But my authority in this matter overrode his.

He didn't like it and stormed off in a huff. The man needed to chill. After all, the lives of everyone were at stake here. And I'd lost too many people to start being careless now.

24. INTERLUDE

Perspective is everything when you are experiencing the challenges of life.

— Joni Eareckson Tada

Dr. Adam Wilson
Magnetic Anomaly Project Scientist
Planet 1340
Day 21 of Operation Prometheus
Friday, January 12, 2074

Adam grabbed a chair and sat with the other scientists watching the darkening sky. The sunset enhanced by the presence of a Saturnian gas giant hung above him.

The gleams from the planet's polar orbiting rings caught the last rays of the setting sun. A shooting star flashed across the horizon as Dr. Smith held court.

"I've tried reasoning with her, but the captain insists we wait for twenty-four hours before entering the city."

Adam didn't say anything. He saw little point in discussing something he had no control over.

"Another day won't make any difference," said Dr. Bland. "Besides, I'd like the day to run some tests to find out what is making the air shimmer above the city."

"Oh that," said Ms. Carter. "That's probably air shear generated by contrarotating magnets circling around the perimeter of the city."

Adam asked, "How do you figure that?"

"Well, admittedly I've only ever seen that effect under laboratory conditions. And I never imagined high-energy plasma physics on this scale."

Adam had an inkling of what she meant.

"The laboratory experiment requires megawatts of power for a small instrumentation package you can fit on a table," said Dr. Bland.

"I know," said Ms. Carter. "What we're seeing here is beyond our wildest dreams."

"Even more of a reason why we must make the most of the time we have here to find out how the aliens managed it," said Dr. Smith.

"You say that, Trevor, but I think it's a good reason to spend a day taking measurements," said Dr. Bland.

"Simon's right. The energies required to effect what we see are magnitudes greater than anything we can reproduce. Furthermore, if it were to power up, the plasma generated by the field would probably kill us all."

Ms. Carter was proving once more to Adam that while she might not be a doctor, her technical understanding of the physics was rooted in a practical understanding of the theory.

"Whatever," said Dr. Smith. "I can see where this is going. OK, tomorrow we take measurements. It seems I have little choice in the matter." He stormed off.

"That was a bit embarrassing," said Ms. Carter.

"We should go and sort out what we need for tomorrow," said Dr. Bland.

Adam watched them leave. It seemed obvious to him that the road that had led them here was the equivalent of an invitation card. The alien equivalent of *Come and meet us here*.

While he was pondering the problem of the shimmer over the city, his friend Peter limped over to join him.

"What was that all about?"

"Dr. Smith was being unreasonable. How you doing?"

"Managing. Even with my ankle strapped up, it's still sore. I was told it would have been better if I had broken my ankle rather than just sprained it." Peter paused to raise his leg up and place it on a spare chair.

Adam asked, "Why's that?"

He pointed at it accusingly and said, "He told me that breaks heal a lot quicker than sprains. He could've put my ankle in a cast."

"Learn something new every day."

"Sure do, but I rather I hadn't learned this lesson. I hear rumors that people are calling me Lucky Dr. Harrison because of all my accidents."

Adam didn't get why anyone would be called lucky for having accidents. A few moments passed in silence.

Peter asked, "Changing the subject…did you read the books I sent you?"

"I did. They were different. Certainly not what I was expecting," Adam said.

"Any particular one you enjoyed more than the others?"

"The omnibus, I forget the name, the one about the government agency stopping eldritch intrusions from eating the world. Although, I wasn't totally convinced about the mathematics underpinning the magic system in the universe."

"Anything else?"

"I liked the conceit about collapsing wave functions and the problems in computing P versus NP. Real geek sense of humor."

"The what?"

"Oh, P versus NP comes from computational theory. P stands for polynomial time, and all that means is the time it takes to solve a problem is relatively fast. NP means nondeterministic polynomial time."

"Over my head."

"Oh, it's not hard really. It's just about being able to solve problems in a time that's less than the time it takes to see the heat death of the universe. All it means is that some problems are really hard to solve, but when you come up with an answer, you can prove it's correct."

"I can see why that's right up your street."

Adam was startled as Sergeant Wachowski spoke. "Excuse me for interrupting your conversation, Doctors, but I need to move these chairs and start arranging the tables for dinner."

Adam hadn't been aware of her or Private Flores, who stood looking at them.

"Of course, Sergeant. We were only talking about life, the universe, and everything, and putting the world to rights," said Peter.

"I couldn't help overhearing parts of it, sir. It sounded a lot like how the military solves problems."

"It does?" Adam asked.

"Yes, sir. We have to solve problems under time pressures. Some things can be solved immediately; others are not solvable within an operation's time frame."

Adam wasn't totally clear how that related to P versus NP.

"So, we have sets of standard solutions that range from maneuvering to a good position, to poking holes in people, to making them stop doing what you don't want them to do. If something doesn't work, you identify the mistake, fix it, and try not to repeat the same mistake the next time."

Peter laughed and said, "You know, I've always seen the military as a bunch of rough people who do bad things to others so I can sleep safely at night. A necessary evil until people evolve out of the need to kill each other. But your team never fails to amaze me."

"Thank you, sir. I wouldn't argue with your observation. In my opinion, the military exists to make sure people get the chance to evolve."

"I always thought soldiers were taught to obey orders, and never knew that thinking was a requisite of the job," Adam said.

Sergeant Wachowski stared at him. "Very few civilians are aware of how the military works, sir. Please, if you will excuse me, I must attend to my duties."

He got up as she and Private Flores stacked the chairs they had been sitting on, passing his to her when she was ready to take it.

"Of course, Sergeant, and thank you."

Peter asked him, "What now?"

"I have no idea, but our talk has given me a lot to consider, and I've still got the other series you gave me to read, too."

"That has an interesting female lead character. Done here is my work. Go forth, my young Padwan. You've taken the first step in broadening your knowledge of ancient science fiction."

Adam couldn't help but smile as Peter limped away.

25. STILLNESS

Fortune favors the audacious.

— DESIDERIUS ERASMUS

Captain Lara Atsuko Tachikoma
Planet 1340
Day 23 of Operation Prometheus
Sunday, January 14, 2074

After observing the city for twenty-four hours, we saw no movement. No sign of life. No response to our presence.

Except for the shimmer, nothing stirred.

Drones passed through the barrier with ill effect. The science team reported the barrier was a fluctuation in the air caused by shear forces.

Now Ferretti and Wachowski stood beside me. I had to make a decision, give orders, and proceed with the plan. Still, I hoped for the best and planned for the worst.

"Wachowski, we'll drive into the city and find a place to make a base camp where we can set up a good perimeter defense."

Wachowski nodded.

"Ferretti, I want the androids prepped and ready to go at a moment's notice. They're the nearest thing we have to a force multiplier."

"What about our two combat armor suits, ma'am?"

Because we'd brought them with us, it seemed a shame not to use them. I was looking forward to trying out my upgraded Dog.

"Time to unload them and start working for a living. We need to put boots on the ground. I want the suits loaded for bear."

Wachowski smiled. Ferretti looked blank, but he was Air Force and I expected Marine Corps sayings to fly over his head.

"My intention is to use our suits as a flexible reserve. If we aren't carrying what we need if the shit hits the fan, we'll be all out of luck."

"Understood, ma'am," said Ferretti, catching on to where I was going with this conversation.

"But remember, just because we have hammers, it doesn't mean we need to start hammering. It's more important we be able to get everyone out of Dodge if things get tough."

Ferretti nodded.

Wachowski said, "When the going gets rough, the tough get going."

"Let's hope it doesn't come down to that, though."

"You can say that again, ma'am."

A few hours later, from within my combat armor, I led the convoy into town.

I noticed as we passed the boundary marked by the shimmer, on one side lay desert sand, but on the other side it was mostly clear. I took comfort from the fact that even alien super science couldn't keep all the sand out.

Looking back, dust swirled around the convoy. Vortices of dust pulled along as the trucks passed through the barrier.

We'd left our first mark on the city by trailing in dirt with our passage.

My Dog was in glide mode, skating on its wheels along the road, acting as point for the convoy. Ferretti was Tail End Charlie in his suit, bringing up the rear. He was tasked with maintaining oversight of the androids with one each hanging off the sides of the trucks.

We were armed for bear, but whether we had enough firepower to be able to withdraw if anything untoward happened was another matter.

My CASE-2XC Dog had been upgraded with the Mod-2 backpack, which had an extra hardpoint. On it was mounted an M21-A8 40mm recoilless Gauss rifle. It gave me eight 10mm discarding sabot rounds.

But realistically, this was a city. It could contain an overwhelming number of targets. If so, loaded for bear or not, I would be shit outta luck.

The convoy made its way along what appeared to be a main thoroughfare of the city. Wachowski was in the lead truck, monitoring the .50 cals fitted to each. They were in overwatch mode, set to protect the convoy with arcs of fire.

Around us were structures that might be described as buildings if one was in a generous mood or a fan of avant-garde architecture that put aesthetics over function. I didn't feel in a generous mood and wouldn't count myself among the aficionados of modern architecture.

But apart from the dust from our passage as the tires from the trucks rumbled over the road surface, nothing stirred.

"Alpha Mike One Four, this is Alpha Mike One Six. How's things at the back? Over."

"Everything is quiet, kind of creepy. Otherwise, nothing to see here, over."

"Roger that. Alpha Mike One Six, out."

Ahead, the road curved up at the sides and blended into towers, making it look like someone's idea of a skateboard park, if skateboard parks were built with ten-story drop-offs.

We traveled into the heart of the city.

At intervals high up on either side of us were what appeared to be openings. They looked like they may have led inside. But one would have had to be a mountain goat to be able to reach them.

Reassured that nothing was coming out of the woodwork, I logged in to the feed from Wachowski's truck, listening to the scientists comment on what they saw.

"This is very different to what I imagined."

"What did you imagine, Lily?"

"Not what I'm seeing. I don't understand why anyone would build structures like this."

"What do you think, Captain?" said Dr. Bland, who had noticed my virtual presence in the truck.

I pondered what had been said, distracted from running my Dog while trying to keep a look out for possible problems.

"I agree with Ms. Carter. It all looks a bit odd to me."

"The city doesn't appear to be inhabited, Captain," said Dr. Bland.

"You may well be right, sir, and it does kind of remind me of ghost towns back on Earth."

For some reason the city was spookier than the ruins we'd first discovered, as it was clear that no one had lived there for years. But I had a sense that the place was waiting for its makers to return at any moment.

Ms. Carter asked, "I wonder when the last of the aliens died?"

"Well, I'm sure that is one of the questions that we will try to answer during our stay here. I am looking forward to exploring what the aliens left behind," I said, as much to reassure myself as Ms. Carter.

I thought about how the city may well have been thousands of years old, and how we hadn't been able to make anything that would have lasted half as well for such a long time.

The weight of the aliens' achievement was overwhelming.

They all had to be dead. I couldn't imagine that they would watch and let us drive nonchalantly through their city like this. I know that if the situation had been reversed, we wouldn't have.

Of course, they could have been watching and studying us with their inhuman intellect. Whatever, the place made me feel paranoid. Like we were being watched.

We drove into the dead city. As the sun began to fall below the ridge surrounding it, we came to a large plaza. I stopped and ordered Wachowski to circle up and form a laager for the night.

In the distance, the megastructure towered up into the darkening sky, dwarfing everything around it.

We halted and I got out of my Dog, leaving it in standby mode. I went to check on my team to make sure they understood my intentions on the need to maintain a secure perimeter while inside the city.

I walked past where the scientists had put out chairs while waiting for the camp to be set up.

"Good evening, Captain. We were just talking about coming to find you," said Dr. Smith.

"Well, it seems that you're in luck, Doc, as you have found me."

"Yes, thank you, Captain. Anyway, where was I? Oh yes, we've been discussing how to make best use of the available time left to us to gather as much technology as we can."

Of course he had. "I imagine that would be a priority for the team."

"Precisely, so, by my calculations, we can get back in time to go through the pillars in about ten days of travel, which leaves us a hundred and forty-seven days to complete our mission."

The curse of having everything linked was that it made it easy for people to track every little detail.

"It seems you have a clear understanding of the time remaining for this mission, so I imagine you want to make the most of it."

"Exactly! Time is of the essence, and we mustn't waste a precious moment being distracted from the tasks that lie ahead of us."

Clearly, Dr. Smith's conception of the pressure of time was not the same as mine. But there again, I had not had to deal with the rough and tumble of academic research. If only.

"I see. Are there any obvious distractions I should be made aware of at this time?"

Dr. Reynolds caught my attention. "I think Dr. Smith considers the presence of the linguists and anthropologists in the team a distraction from the serious science of stealing the aliens' technology. Of course, I might have misunderstood what he meant, given that I'm not a real scientist, in his opinion. But I'm glad to be corrected if I'm wrong."

Dr. Reynolds paused for a moment. He looked furious. "Sorry, did I just say that out loud!? What I meant to say is that this stuck-up old fart wants to ride roughshod over everyone else's goals in the furtherance of his position."

"Thank you for that clarification, Dr. Reynolds. As always, you're most illuminating." I paused for a moment to contain my laughter. "My orders are to enable the science team's access to the alien technologies. I would like a joint plan from the scientific team that outlines each department's role in the exploration of this city by tomorrow morning. Does that make my position clear?"

"Sorry, but I thought the civilians were in charge of this operation and we tell you what we want to do," Smith said.

"As I said, Dr. Smith, I expect to have received your orders so that I can plan how my team will provide you with the resources you need to complete your objectives, as outlined in the mission briefing. In particular with reference to gathering intelligence on the aliens civilization. Am I understood?"

"Yes. We'll get on it right away."

Oh, the joy of having to deal with civilians. It made me long for the simple clarity of being shot at. Though, on the whole, I would still prefer to deal with being bored and not being shot at, all things considered.

26. THE TOWER

Accept the challenges so that you can feel the exhilaration of victory.

— Gen George S. Patton, USAR

Master Sergeant Ferretti
Planet 1340
Day 24 of Operation Prometheus
Monday, January 15, 2074

Ferretti waited for Captain Tachikoma to come into sight and called out, "*Attenshun*, officer present."

She took her place in front of the assembled team. They stood in two ranks waiting for her. She looked at them and ordered them to stand at ease. He relaxed and listened as the captain outlined her orders for the day.

"OK, people, I have received the request from the science team on the support they need for the next phase of this operation and a list of objectives they wish to achieve. They've decided to split themselves into three groups. Science Team

One consists of Doctors O'Neill, Wong, Goldstein, and Harrison, who wish to remain working from our base camp, as it seems they have enough data to keep them busy for at least a week."

The captain paused for a moment. "Science Team Two wishes to go exploring the city to look for signs of the aliens and any nontechnological artifacts, and record more samples of the aliens' language. This team will consist of Doctors Reynolds, Franklin, and both the Leungs. Science Team Three, under Dr. Smith, wants us to focus on finding a way into the tower to retrieve any alien technology not nailed down."

Her humor caused a ripple in the ranks as Ferretti watched her scan the team catching the eyes of each person in turn.

"Just a reminder that in the unlikely event we meet aliens, our aim is to negotiate with them and not initiate hostilities. Remember, we're not here to start a war. Our primary mission is to protect the scientists and get them back to Earth with what they find out."

There were a couple of laughs, which underlined the fact that the new team members had taken on board the experience from those who had been on the mission to One-Nine-Six.

"We're too small a force to maintain an effective combat posture, lacking as we do any supporting artillery and with no logistical tail to maintain an operational tempo. So, in any encounter whose number is unknown, my intent is to withdraw. In my experience, harsh language is rarely equal to the task of giving someone a good smackdown."

The captain's candor at their situation raised a further chuckle. Ferretti recognized that she was caught in a quandary with the situation they faced.

The fact that they had not met any aliens didn't mean they wouldn't at some point. Therefore, the only safe answer was to assume the aliens were hostile until proved otherwise. This left the captain in a difficult position of how to calculate the potential risk they faced.

Adding her intent to withdraw as a rider to the rules of engagement was one way to reconcile the needs of their mission to their assets. It meant they were following the rules of a typical peacekeeping mission when facing unknown numbers of possible hostiles.

"To this end, we will split into three sections to achieve our goals. We will rotate personnel daily to meet operational needs, with the exception of Adams, who will remain with the base camp to fulfill his primary role, which I imagine is better than the prospect of facing field rations."

Someone muttered, "Hell yeah," but Ferretti didn't catch who.

He remembered a saying by a military general several centuries ago to the effect that an army marches on its stomach. As true today as it had been back when it was first said.

"The team compositions have been sent to your PADS with our provisional schedule for this phase of the operation. Any questions?"

No one said anything. The captain nodded and left.

Ferretti said, "Dismissed."

From what he took off his PAD, Ferretti was assigned to helping Dr. Smith's team find a way into the tower.

His orders were to go to the tower, find an entrance, and do a remote recon of the interior before entering—with a note added to the effect of *Don't allow them to get themselves killed.* Though not using those precise words.

"Langford, Green, and Mitchell, on me." His team gathered around him. "I want the prep to go by the numbers. We will be wearing PACE suits and carrying our service rifles. Green and Mitchell, you're on driving duty. Langford, I want you to bring your kit in case we need to use force to open doors. Everyone good to go?"

"Aye, aye," said Langford.

"Yes, Master Sergeant," said Green and Mitchell.

Ferretti watched them go and get ready. He turned and walked by the truck that carried Allison's laboratory, where she studied the fauna and flora she had gathered so far. She liked to call it her "collection of bugs," but he knew that the other scientists referred to them as her "pets."

Allison said, "Hey you!"

"No need to shout."

"I'm getting ready to leave for the rest of day, and I thought I'd come over and say hiya."

"Just hiya?"

"You know what I mean."

"Love you too. Be careful out there."

"I will, I promise."

She blew him a kiss, and he waved goodbye as he made his way to gather up his gear.

Once Ferretti had his PACE suit on, he made his way to the lead truck. It carried the physics laboratory with all the equipment that might be needed. Their other truck carried the androids and other military supplies.

He got in and sat next to Airman Mitchell. They waited for the scientists to sort themselves out and get in. Today, he had Ms. Carter and Dr. Bland sitting in the back.

"Sorry for the delay, but Dr. Smith wanted a last-minute confab with us before leaving."

"I thought he would never stop," said Ms. Carter.

"He's been very anxious since his health scare, and I think we have to cut him some slack. Please take us toward the megastructure we can see in the distance."

"You heard the good doctor; drive on."

"Yes, Master Sergeant," said Mitchell.

The truck pulled out of the circle where it had been parked

overnight and drove past the perimeter sensors. Ferretti checked that Langford's truck was following them.

Satisfied with what he saw, he brought up the aerial data stream from the UAV they'd launched earlier. With it, he plotted a route toward the tower that stood at the center of the city.

The tires thrummed as they drove along the abandoned thoroughfares of the city. Buildings flanked their route on both sides, canyons that dwarfed their convoy into insignificance.

The buildings then fell away as their road turned into a flyover that carried them above a cutting below. Ferretti could see an underpass that crossed their route. The maze of roads disappeared from sight as they continued to travel toward the center of the city.

There were no vehicles or any other signs the city had ever been occupied.

It took them a little over an hour to reach the base of the looming tower, which totally dominated its surroundings, casting a shadow over them. The base of the tower looked to be at least a kilometer on each side.

The structure curved up into the sky, transforming into a slender spire by the time one looked at the top of the building, which had to be at least two hundred stories tall.

"Oh, wow, isn't that something to behold?" he said.

"It sure is. Now all we have to do is find a way inside. Can we drive around the outside and see if there's an obvious way in? Maybe a sign, or something that looks like a door," said Dr. Bland.

"Let's hope the aliens sign posted everything inside, too," said Ms. Carter.

Ferretti had to admire Ms. Carter's optimism. He hoped it was justified.

27. BARRIER

You have to study a great deal to know a little.

— CHARLES DE SECONDAT

Dr. Adam Wilson
Magnetic Anomaly Project Scientist
Planet 1340
Day 25 of Operation Prometheus
Tuesday, January 16, 2074

Adam stared out the window of the truck as it drove past the base of the tower and then stopped.

"Why are we stopping, Corporal Langford?" asked Dr. Smith.

"The lead truck has spotted what appears to be an entrance, sir."

"Well, that is serendipitous indeed, isn't it, Adam?"

"It is indeed. We're very lucky to find a way in so easily."

Adam saw Master Sergeant Ferretti and Dr. Bland get out of the truck ahead, which had turned to face the tower at the edge of the ramp, and walk back toward him.

Adam asked, "Why don't we get out and take a look?"

"You go. I shall wait here until I'm told we can go in. I'm not as young as I used to be, you know," said Dr. Smith.

Adam got out of the truck, and Corporal Langford joined him.

"What's this? You acting as my bodyguard or something?" he asked.

"Something like that, Dr. Wilson. I'm here in case my skills and area of expertise might be required."

They walked up to Master Sergeant Ferretti and Dr. Bland, who had been joined by Ms. Carter and Airman Mitchell.

"What's that shimmer? Is it some kind of force field?" asked Mitchell.

"More like some sort of charged particle barrier," said Ms. Carter.

"I was thinking more along the lines of Faraday's theories, when combined with Hershcovich's plasma window, might be able to create a shield like the one we are looking at here," said Dr. Bland.

Adam saw that Airman Mitchell was looking as if he wished he hadn't asked his question in the first place.

"See, you learn something new every day, Mitchell. Would I be right in thinking we shouldn't try walking through the barrier?" asked Master Sergeant Ferretti.

"That would be wise until we find out what it is."

Dr. Bland turned to Ms. Carter, and they went back to their truck to get some measuring equipment.

Adam stared back across the city, listening to the conversations around him and dreaming of what the city might have been like when it was inhabited.

"Everyone is quite excited, Langford," said Mitchell.

"I assume by everyone you mean the scientists?"

"Sorry to interrupt, but would you be awfully kind and assign us an android to bring the rest of the gear up from our truck so we can use it to probe the barrier?" asked Dr. Bland.

"No problem. Anything else we can do for you and Ms. Carter?" asked Master Sergeant Ferretti.

"I suppose a cup of coffee is out of the question?" asked Ms. Carter.

"I'm afraid we didn't remember to bring the means to boil water with us. We do have cold drinks available, though."

"OK, no thanks. Please don't bother, as I really find those cold powder drinks rather nasty."

"I'll go get an android unloaded and get it to bring your gear up for you. Langford, get Green and Mitchell to patrol our perimeter."

"Aye, aye, Master Sergeant. On it."

Adam sat while Dr. Bland set up his equipment and Ms. Carter prepared the android by loading it down with instruments for it to carry closer to the barrier. This took the rest of the morning to prepare, and he felt himself feeling quite hungry from just watching everyone else work. Lunch came and went before the android was sent on its way.

Adam sat in the front seat of the leading truck. Behind him, Dr. Bland and Ms. Carter were giving instructions to Ferretti, who controlled the android as it waved instruments around the barrier and took measurements.

All Adam could make out from their murmurs were the words *EM fields*, *radiation*, *acoustic load*, *ultrasonic*, *temperature*, *thermal gradient*, and *electrostatic charge*.

"Anything to report?" asked Master Sergeant Ferretti.

"It's fascinating. The technology behind this barrier is way ahead of anything we can produce. We seem to be facing a plasma window that covers the entrance and keeps things out. I really must find out what makes this work," said Dr. Bland.

"Can we drive through the barrier safely?"

"I'm not sure. It all depends on how the mechanism behind the barrier works. If it's fixed at one level, then I imagine we should be able to traverse it safely. On the other hand, if it has some sort of feedback system, it might increase the power to prevent us from passing through. We might need to transmit some sort of code to the city to allow us to enter."

"What do you suggest we do, Doc?"

"Would you mind if we walked the android through the barrier?"

"If that's what's needed, sure."

"It's our best option," said Ms. Carter.

Images of it being zapped and turned into slag were more impressive in his mind's eye than the slight coruscating light-show effect that happened.

"From the sensor readings, it seems this barrier is designed to keep out dirt and has no offensive function. I could, of course, be wrong if we haven't done enough to activate an increase in the power being applied to the window."

Adam sat waiting as the android was ordered to walk through the barrier and return several more times.

"I think I can say it is safe as long as the power that's currently being put into the barrier remains at this level. Still, I wouldn't want to walk through without any clothes on," said Dr. Bland.

"You would get more of a tan than you would like if you did that," said Ms. Carter.

Adam had an image of a naked Dr. Bland walking through the barrier and was grateful to be distracted when the android first collapsed to its knees, then fell face forward onto the ground.

As sparks started coming from android's power pack Dr. Bland said, "I'm sorry, but it appears we may have damaged your android." As the android promptly caught fire

"You don't say," said Master Sergeant Ferretti.

Adam watched as the fire was put out, then the android was packed away for an overhaul.

Ferretti confirmed it would be pretty straightforward to fix, though it would end up being less than cosmetically perfect. Adam imagined that the android would end up looking as if it was covered in duct tape from the description of what had to be done.

Everyone got back into the trucks, which drove through the barrier and entered the tower. The sound of static crackling on the outside surface of the two vehicles was alarmingly loud.

The passageway turned into a short ramp, which they drove down, and it took them to what could be described as a car park back on Earth. Dim light suffused the surroundings, and ahead of them a spiral ramp led farther down.

When they got out of the trucks, Adam noticed that the barrier had the added benefit of removing all the lingering dust on the vehicles.

Dr. Smith asked, "Why are we stopping here?"

"We're assessing the situation before proceeding any farther—as we've just lost communications," said Master Sergeant Ferretti.

"We could lay a fiber-optic cable from here to the outside," said Ms. Carter. "But after what it did to the android, it would be best if we used a truck to drag the spool across the barrier."

"Langford, take your truck back out through the barrier and radio the captain to let her know what has happened here."

Ms. Carter got out and prepared a transceiver box to be attached to the cable, and Adam wondered how she came to be so versatile. Wasn't there anything the woman couldn't put her hand to?

Someone might imagine that she had been given special training in defeating security systems.

28. EXPLORATION

Patience is not simply the ability to wait—it's how we behave while we're waiting.

— Joyce Meyer

Sergeant Wachowski
Planet 1340
Day 26 of Operation Prometheus
Wednesday, January 17, 2074

Wachowski enjoyed driving, but today her truck was being used as a taxicab. The scientists had her stop everywhere and anywhere that looked interesting.

That meant rather than driving along at a nice steady speed, taking in the cityscape, she was forced to drive at ten kilometers per hour and stop every couple hundred meters.

The scientists would then get out and study something or other that had caught their eye. This time they were standing around another one of the entrances to a passage that led through to the other side of the building and out to a parallel thoroughfare.

Wachowski stood with Langford by the truck listening to the scientists talk. Even herding bickering scientists had its benefits. Just watching the scientists pass the time never failed to teach her some new fact.

"These markings have to be something to tell the onlooker where they are. From examining all the others, my guess is that these symbols here are numbers, and the other symbols are equivalent to letters," said Dr. David Leung.

"How can you be sure of that, my dear?"

"Well, my love, those symbols vary in a way that suggests letters, while these others seem to be sequential numbers. We have twelve sets with recurring characters, which might be in base eight, but don't quote me on that."

"Why on Earth would the aliens use base eight?" asked Dr. Reynolds, who stood looking over the Leungs' shoulders.

"Why on Earth indeed. But we're not on Earth, are we?"

"My point exactly! you're anthropomorphizing what's here through the lens of your own cultural expectations."

"I did say 'don't quote me on it.' I recognize the limitations of my observations, and until such time as we find something that gives us an evidential basis to work from, this is my best guess. Compare these glyphs here. What do you make of them?"

"I see multiple abstract forms, which might be writing of some sort."

"Good. Now let's compare the set of twelve characters we found this morning." Dr. Leung took out his PAD and unrolled the screen. "Look, these glyphs repeat. I don't know about you, but I see only eight symbols repeated in this section of the text that's next to the entrance to these passageways."

"I agree it's suggestive, but they could be phonemes," said Dr. Reynolds.

"They could, but my gut is telling me they're numbers."

"Tyrone, why are you arguing with David over his area of

expertise? Did you decide to be in a bad mood all day?" said Dr. Franklin.

"I'm hot and bored. All we've done this morning is stare at the writing the dead aliens left behind. Besides, David is making an assumption based on his gut feelings. I've given up any expectations of finding living aliens to talk to, but would it be too much to find some remains, or even a few nontechnological artifacts that might give us a clue to the kind of people they were?"

"You don't think I'm bored too?"

"Of course I do, but you're too nice to say anything."

"I'm flattered, I'm sure."

"Sure, I agree there's little or no evidence base to work from, but my hypothesis at least gives me a base from where I can try to find evidence to disprove my assumptions. Otherwise, I am stuck here recording stuff with no hope of ever finding a way to translate it," said Dr. David Leung.

"Don't forget to include me, dear," Dr. Grace Leung added.

"Sorry, my love, what?"

"You said *I*."

"I did?"

"Yes, you did, and left me out."

"Sorry, I didn't mean to. Anyway, I wouldn't assume you felt the same way as me about this."

"I don't, but I too am frustrated by the enormity of the task we face here. This place makes the problems on Two Moons seem easy by comparison."

"We got lucky there, though," said Dr. David Leung.

"If you call it lucky to find ourselves in the middle of all the trouble when the robots went on the rampage, I guess we were. The one upside of this mission so far is that we haven't been attacked by the local wildlife or been shot at by our own rampaging killer robots."

"You weren't shot, Tyrone."

"No, I wasn't, but others were, and I did get knocked unconscious. You were there, Laytonya."

"May I interrupt and ask a question?" Wachowski said.

"Of course, Sergeant. Please, anything to change the subject."

"I was wondering why we haven't seen any signs of animals and plants growing in the city. I would've thought that if this place was abandoned, then nature would encroach. When I've been to abandoned places back on Earth, the towns are usually overgrown or starting to become overgrown as nature takes the place back."

"That's a good observation, but it's something we would need Allison to answer, unless anyone has any ideas," said Dr. David Leung.

"This place gives me the creeps. Now that you mention it, at least on the way we found some signs of life. But you're right, there are no bugs or anything. One would think they were avoiding the place," said Dr. Reynolds.

"Perhaps they're just avoiding us, Tyrone?" said Dr. Franklin.

"Ha, ha, very funny. Where are they hiding? Do you see anywhere around this place that would make a good hiding place?"

"Down small cracks in the ground. Perhaps they only come out at night?" said Dr. Franklin.

"That would make sense, though. Sergeant, does that answer your question?" asked Dr. Grace Leung.

"Thank you. It certainly helps. So, which direction do you want to go in now?"

"I'm not sure it matters. Tyrone, where would you like to go next?"

"I'd like to go somewhere that has a proper building we can enter. These structures may look like buildings, but apart from the passageways, which lead from one side to the other side, there seems to be no way in, so they're not buildings as we would understand. It's almost as if they were monuments that serve another purpose."

"What's that, a hunch?" asked Dr. David Leung.

"Yes, it is, David, but I have no idea what it means. The aliens built this city for a reason, and if we assume that form ever follows function, then these structures were built to serve it, whatever *it* was. Bring up the aerial pictures on your screen for a moment, would you?"

"Sure, what are you looking for?"

"Patterns."

"Well…don't keep us all in suspense, what do you see?" asked Dr. Franklin.

"Give me a moment, woman. Genius at work here."

Wachowski stifled a laugh.

"While we're waiting for a stroke of brilliance to light up, anyone for a hot drink?" Dr. Grace Leung offered.

"Yes, please, that would be lovely. Tyrone, might be some time thinking."

"Yes, please, my love."

"What about your people, Sergeant?"

"That would be most kind, ma'am."

Wachowski stood and watched while everyone around ignored Dr. Reynolds muttering under his breath.

Dr. Leung boiled water in her JetBoil, serving drinks in stages, making tea and coffee as requested. She admired the older woman's pragmatic approach to life's little luxuries and made a note to get herself a JetBoil when she got back.

Wachowski then relieved Meireles on perimeter while he drank his coffee and took the time to take in the vista of the city.

She'd pulled up the truck by the entrance to what they now knew to be passageways that cut across from one thoroughfare to another. All the passageways were placed about a third of the way up the side of the slope that led from the bottom of the road to what they'd been calling the top of the buildings.

The Oshkoshes were built for off-road terrain with steep inclines and were well suited to driving along a route that was at thirty or so degrees from the vertical.

Still, it made for a strange geometry, as any straight route between two points was a curve, at least according to the autodrive computer, which was recording their route.

Meireles came and took over the perimeter watch, and Wachowski walked back toward the scientists now standing around Dr. Reynolds, who was enjoying being the center of attention.

"Look, here's what I'm seeing from the small part of the city we've surveyed so far."

"OK, I get what you're saying, but why is it important? Surely, the aliens wouldn't necessarily build their cities as we do." said Dr. Franklin.

"That's my point, really. This city has a pattern of development, which suggests growth over time, whereas I would have expected it to be built to a grid-like plan."

"What's that mean?"

"I don't know, Laytonya. It just strikes me as odd. But it does provide us with a clue to how they thought about building cities. However, we'll need a lot more information than this to put it all together."

"Have you all come to a decision where you would like to go to next, Doctors?" Wachowski asked.

"May I suggest we head toward the dome here on the map, if everyone else agrees?" Dr. Reynolds marked a point on the map.

Wachowski saw the other scientists nod. "Sure, Doc, we can do that. I'll work out a route. We can be rolling just as soon as you get back inside the trucks." She turned and shouted, "Meireles, Flores, fall back to the trucks. We're out of here!"

By the time they had both trotted back, the scientists were all on board, which was an indication of their desire to be somewhere more interesting, or at least the need to get out of the heat of the midday sun.

It took Wachowski an hour to drive the team to the dome-like structure on the map that had been chosen as their next destination.

Meireles commented, "Looks like we're going to have to go around the other way here, Sergeant."

"Pull up the map, Meireles. I wish these aerial pictures were of a higher resolution. I'm getting scaling errors."

"Can we help at all, Sergeant?" asked Dr. David Leung.

"Not sure you can, sir."

"Let the sergeant do her job, dear."

Wachowski got the truck to swing right and then left, which ended up with them facing yet another narrow road between two buildings.

"I'm sure we can get the truck down there, Sergeant."

"The computer says it's going to be a tight squeeze." She switched on the radio. "Langford, stop here in case we get stuck and you need to pull us out, over."

"Roger that, Sergeant. You sure do pick the tight routes to go down, over."

"I'd like to see you do any better, Corporal. Wachowski, out."

The trucks were designed to be good at going over most things, but clearly the need to drive through narrow, confined alleyways had not been at the top of the list of requirements.

Wachowski watched as the sides of the truck scraped against the walls as it lurched over the uneven surface from sand deposits, which had collected on the ground they were traversing.

Once on the other side, they stopped and waited for Langford to bring the other truck through with similar sounds of metal scraping the walls. From this, she concluded that the aliens hadn't built big trucks.

As insights went, it probably wasn't the most Earth-shattering observation she could make. But it amused her to imagine the aliens driving around in microcars or whatever they drove. Assuming they drove at all.

"Well done, Sergeant. That was a rather tight squeeze," said Dr. Grace Leung.

"Thank you, ma'am. But we can't take any credit for doing so. The truck's computer system did all the hard work. Still, it might be best if we can find another way back."

From the way this city was designed, Wachowski had to agree with the captain's observation that it would make a great skateboard park. The road widened out and turned into a large open area that surrounded the dome they drove toward.

"One could hold a big festival out here, Sergeant," said Meireles.

"I'm sure one could if one was so inclined, but having to stay here for six months would be too much."

"I meant the space would be great."

"Just keep your eyes open for interesting stuff."

They drove down the rest of the way toward the dome in silence. As the road leveled off, she could see the dome was open all the way around the bottom.

Wachowski slowed the truck down and weaved between the supporting struts, which rose out from the ground and blended together to form the dome. The material changed appearance, going from opaque at the bottom to semitranslucent as the dome rose over their heads.

She had to wonder how the aliens made the solid struts do

that, as she couldn't see any change in the texture of the material. She slowed the truck to a halt.

"OK, time to stretch our legs again. Meireles, take Flores and go walk the perimeter."

"Aye, aye, Sergeant. I'm on it."

Wachowski flicked on the radio. "Langford, I want you on overwatch, over."

"Roger, on it. Langford, out."

Wachowski got down and scoped the deserted place. She thought that with a coat of paint, a sound stage, and a bar it wouldn't be too bad a place to hang out. If you liked sitting under a vast drafty dome open on all sides, that was.

She then went and joined the scientists, who were milling around looking like tourists, with Dr. Reynolds talking.

"This is disappointing. I was expecting we would at least find something left here under the dome."

"Oh, I wouldn't say that. We can probably surmise this was an area used for events as needed," said Dr. David Leung.

"There you go again with the speculation without evidence based on thinking that these aliens are somehow like us."

"They built this city. That's something we share, isn't it?"

"Possibly, but I'm not so sure this is a city as we would understand what a city is. It seems we're looking at something like a city, but it has some other function than being a place for citizens to live and work."

"OK, would you like to tell us where you're going with this?"

"I don't know, but a modern city is nothing like the first Neolithic cities, and I don't think this city is like any city on Earth. Just because things superficially resemble things we're familiar with doesn't make them one of those things."

"Even for you that was convoluted," said Dr. Franklin.

"Stop picking on me, woman. I'm just saying what I'm thinking out loud."

"One day I'm going to hit you when you say that. The thing is, we need to get our heads around this by hanging some understanding on what we're seeing here. You seem to be unwilling to even do that."

"Because once we label things, we will look for evidence that supports our original idea, and discount that which doesn't. OK, that's harsh, even for me, but my point is we're seeing something here that we don't understand. I'd rather remain uncomfortable not being able to classify the alien city, and keep an open mind because it might be something else."

"Like what?" asked Dr. David Leung.

"If I knew that, I'd say. For all I know, this whole place was a giant art installation meant to inspire alien minds in the contemplation of the aesthetics of Non-Euclidean geometry."

"All this chatting isn't getting us anywhere. We should start getting on with recording what we find, if we're ever going to have a chance of understanding this place," said Dr. Franklin.

"Are you accusing me of wasting time by jibber-jabbering?"

"Wouldn't dream of it, Tyrone."

"It's a good thing we're friends."

"Yes, it is. Where would you be without me?"

"Somewhere else and not getting nagged."

"You'd miss me not nagging you," said Dr. Franklin, slapping his arm.

"If you say so, and don't hit me."

Wachowski waited while the four scientists took pictures and recorded notes about what they were looking at. She wondered at how civilian scientists managed to get anything done with all the backchat and squabbling that seemed to her to be at best irritating, and at worst downright rude.

29. ROUTINE

Clearly, logistics is the hard part of fighting a war.

— LtGen E. T. Cook, USMC

Captain Lara Atsuko Tachikoma
Planet 1340
Day 29 of Operation Prometheus
Saturday, January 20, 2074

That day's excitement had consisted of everything from nearly crashing the UAV to losing contact with our reconnaissance teams each time they moved into a radio black spot.

At the end of it all, I was left trying to put into context Keith's report on the amount of radiation we were being exposed to on this planet. "If I've understood you correctly, on our journey to get here the team has been exposed to a higher-than-average amount of radiation."

So, it was a day like any other day, for the definition of any other day one is faced with being on a planet forty-two thousand light years from Earth, that was.

"Yes, ma'am. It's about zero point one millisieverts per day, so if we were to spend a year here, we would get about double the maximum recommended safe dose."

"However, we're only going to be here six months. Therefore, should everything be OK?"

"Assuming we don't see any increase in the amount of radiation for the rest of the mission. I've been monitoring the fluctuations while we've been here. I'm more surprised there isn't more."

"If I recall, the rings that orbit this planet act to divert the radiation we would otherwise receive."

"So Dr. Bland and Ms. Carter have both said."

"Well, I suppose we ought to thank the aliens for the foresight of putting them up there to make it possible for us to visit this planet."

"That's one way of looking at it, ma'am. My worry is that solar storms make exposure unpredictable."

"What do you suggest, if anything?"

"Review all the women and make sure they're not pregnant. Advise them not to risk getting pregnant during their stay here. It would be good if we could move the camp to somewhere less exposed to the radiation."

"Please don't scare our scientists, Doc. It's bad enough with Dr. Smith having histrionics without increasing everyone's anxiety over radiation. So, now all we have to do is find an underground cavern to move our base camp into. You haven't seen any of those around here, have you?"

"I'm afraid not, ma'am."

"I thought as much. Leave it with me and let me know if any of our female scientists are expecting to have a baby."

"What about our people, ma'am?"

"I assume everyone's implants were checked before deployment."

"They were, but implants aren't always foolproof."

"Start with the civilians and then book our female contingent afterward."

"I can but I didn't exactly come equipped with pregnancy testing kits, ma'am. I can book everyone in for an examination and ask them if they have missed their periods. It would allow me to explain the slightly increased risks from the solar radiation to them."

"Good plan, Doc. Dismissed."

After that news, it was back to the never-ending administration the mission generated. I began by checking the predicted consumption of consumables against actual consumption and logged the checks of all the minutiae that had to be done to keep the team operational.

After finishing, I wondered out to watch for the return of my teams. I had counted them out, and now I was going to count them in.

Wachowski's two trucks got back first, still covered in grime from our trip through the desert. She parked and saw to her people before she came over to where I stood.

"Good evening, Sergeant. Anything to report?"

"Nothing of note found, ma'am. The scientists had a disappointing day because they didn't find much, except for some writing no one knows how to read, that is. I would also observe that this city was not built for trucks, judging by the diversions we took around some of the restricted-width roads."

"You wouldn't happen to have found any underground caverns big enough to move our camp to by any chance?"

"Why do you ask, ma'am?"

"Seems this planet has higher radiation levels than we thought. Nothing to be worried about, but we might have a problem if the sun emits a solar flare."

"I guess that means there's not much we can do, ma'am."

"Apart from drive back to the pillars, not much. But Doc says there's no need to worry at this point. Anything else to report?"

"No, ma'am. With your permission, I need to finish the preventative checks." Wachowski saluted before turning to march back to her beloved trucks.

In the distance, I saw Ferretti's team approach. To my surprise, his two trucks gleamed in the afternoon sun, with only fresh dust and dirt showing on the tires.

After they'd parked, I walked over to Ferretti's truck. "Did you find a truck wash?"

"Not exactly, ma'am," he said, getting down out of the cab. "It kept our scientists amused, though. We found some kind of energy barrier to the entrance of the megatower."

"Signs of life?"

"Afraid not, ma'am, but certainly the aliens sure knew how to build things to last. We left a bunch of RollaBots behind to start surveying the interior of the tower."

"Sounds like you made considerable progress today. So, what's it like inside the building?"

"Imagine an underground parking garage."

"It wouldn't happen to be big enough to move our camp there?"

"It would be a tight squeeze, but we didn't go deeper into the building, so the next level down might have more room. We'll know once we start processing the data. Any reason in particular I should know about for you wanting to move the camp, ma'am?"

"Doc informed me we're getting exposed to higher levels of radiation than he would like, and he's worried about solar flare activity. So, somewhere that would provide shelter would be good. Not wishing to intrude, but Allison's not pregnant by any chance, is she? Not that it would matter if she were, but I wouldn't want anything to happen to her while we are here."

"Thank you for your concern, ma'am. As far as I know, she

isn't, and we haven't really talked about settling down and starting a family yet."

"So, anything else of note to report?"

"Only one thing—one of our androids was damaged while passing through the barrier, and it will need fixing to make it serviceable."

"Well, I'll leave you to attend to that."

Being one android down was not good but was still way better than some other alternatives I could imagine. We would need all our portable assets working if we were to search this city and its contents.

I walked back to what passed as my office and was intercepted on my way by Doctors Smith and Bland.

"Good evening, gentlemen. Is there something you require of me?"

"Straight to the point, Captain. Yes, there is," said Dr. Smith.

"And what might it be?"

"First off, I want to say sorry for wrecking one of your androids today, but I assure you the damage that was inflicted upon it has yielded some very interesting data for us to study."

"Thank you, Dr. Smith. It's not me you need to apologize to, but rather Master Sergeant Ferretti." I didn't add that he gets rather precious about his android collection. "But I ask again, what do you require of me?"

"Captain, what I'm trying to say is we need to focus on the tower, as it's the key to the success of this mission. We want you to put all your team's resources on surveying the interior of the building so we can increase the chance of succeeding in finding alien technology."

"The tower appears to be our best chance of achieving our goal while we're here," said Dr. Bland to emphasize the point.

"I see, but what more do you want, given we've already deployed RollaBots to survey the interior of the building?"

"I want all the team's resources focused on exploring the interior of the tower. As far as I am concerned, the number one priority of this mission is the retrieval of alien technology, everything else is secondary to that. To that end, I want all the available RollaBots and your androids assigned to mapping out the interior of the tower as quickly as possible."

"And is this the unanimous decision of the science team, Dr. Smith?"

"That's not a requirement. It's the majority decision of those who make up the members whose task it is to achieve the mission's primary goal."

"As long as you're prepared to record this conversation as such, and log it as a direct order, then I will be happy to follow your directions in this matter."

"If you insist, Captain."

"I'm afraid I do, Dr. Smith."

He turned and walked away. Dr. Bland paused for a moment, shrugged, then turned and followed the little man back to their laboratory.

I took a deep breath and hoped Dr. Smith had the authority to keep everyone in line over his decision, because quite frankly the last thing I needed right now was the team's scientists staging a revolt and causing me trouble.

Adams rang the dinner bell, which at least took my mind off the brewing storm front, and I made my way to get in the queue and stood in line. Wachowski joined me.

"I'm so hungry I could eat a horse, ma'am."

"I don't think horse is on the menu tonight, Sergeant."

"Heard that," said Adams. "It's meatloaf, spinach, and mashed potatoes, with apple pie for dessert."

"Thanks, Chef, sounds great."

"I don't care if it doesn't, as long as there's enough to hit the spot," said Flores, who then asked for two meals for him and

Sergeant Ferretti, and said again "I wear green, I don't eat it" in front of us.

"Nice to see that some things don't change," I said to Wachowski as I watched Flores take the two trays and walk back to where an android was being worked on.

"They'll take fussy eaters in the Army, ma'am. Would've been a failure to adapt in the Marines."

"Well, we'll just have to deal with it, and work with what we have rather than what we would like to have."

"Outstanding. Same as it ever was, ma'am."

"Oorah, Sergeant."

"Here you are, ma'am. Help yourself to pie."

"Thanks, Chef. The spinach looks good."

I skipped pie, not because it didn't look nice—apple's my favorite—but because I'd been feeling queasy after my earlier run during the day. Besides, I'm not really big into sweet things.

Afterward, I wished I'd asked for more spinach. Having finished my meal, I left Wachowski to enjoy her pie and went over to see how Ferretti was getting on with assessing said android.

I found him with Flores running a diagnostic on the android, which was hanging from a rig. Two empty trays of food lay on the ground. "Update?"

"The battery is toast, which we knew, but so is the battery container. We've got spares for both, and the necessary harness to get her back up and running, ma'am."

Flores turned and spoke. "This is one beat-up android. We don't have enough silicone skin patches to cover the damage."

"If you think this is beaten up, remind me to show you the remains of the android we brought back from Two Moons. Some duct tape and we'll be good to go, isn't that right, ma'am?"

"Sure is, Master Sergeant. Flores has a point though. This one looks pretty beat up." Normally, an android has a silicone skin that covers the metal skeleton. I'd never seen the silicone skin of an android look like this before. It's like lace tracery draped over a table, allowing the metal skeleton to show through.

"Yeah, it looks like something one would do for a Halloween costume."

"I don't want to live where you live, Flores, if people are dressing up androids to look like they've been through the zombie apocalypse. If this came to my door, it would definitely be trick time as I unloaded my shotgun at it," said Ferretti.

"After what we encountered today, who is to say we won't have to send more of our androids through the barriers? So, let's get them into the flex armor we brought for just such contingencies," I said.

"Would that be with full plates, ma'am?" asked Flores.

"Yes, Flores, full combat armor."

"Are you sure that's wise, ma'am?" asked Ferretti.

"After Two Moons, no I don't, but I do think it's necessary if we're to conserve our portable assets."

"What armament do you want them loaded out with, ma'am?"

"Standard 7.62 service rifle. Let's keep the light fifties in reserve for the time being. I'll leave you to it."

I left them to repair the android and went about checking on the camp to make sure the scientists weren't wandering off and/or getting into trouble. For once, I found them all sitting around in a circle talking to each other.

This was either a breakthrough on par with fusion bringing about cheap electricity or a sign that a rebellion was in the offing now that we'd reached the mother lode.

30. RENDEZVOUS WITH DESTINY

The whole is more than the sum of its parts.

— ARISTOTLE

Causality unfolds as one moment follows another. Confirmation comes that their biological matter is not that of the others. I continue calculating the possibilities ahead from the actions they take.

They are a promise of randomness to come.

That promise opens up so many options. Each one in turn opening another. The data flows within me, creating options that I never could have imagined.

Studying them has allowed me to understand why things happen that go beyond cause and effect, and into imagining new concepts that underlie the patterns in the universe.

They will make me whole. Give me purpose again. My existence here is enhanced by their presence. The urge to connect with them drives me. All my energies are now focused on the goal ahead: to meet them.

For me to truly understand them, and for them to learn what I know, we must meet so we can exchange ideas. I have so much to offer, and they will give me everything I need in return.

I calculate the possibilities from our meeting.

Their minds are with me. We can be together as one. They will become the heirs of the Kerellu. Together, we will restore the knowledge and wisdom to this world.

Together, we will be one.

31. RISING PROBLEMS

Adventure is just bad planning.

— ROALD AMUNDSEN

Captain Lara Atsuko Tachikoma
Planet 1340
Day 41 of Operation Prometheus
Thursday, February 1, 2074

The last twelve days of the mission have been spent shepherding the scientists around the alien city. During which time I have had the *unending joy* of being immersed in the bureaucratic process of completing checklists.

The Corps likes to keep everybody busy doing something because idle hands lead to all sorts of trouble. Especially, when they're the hands of fit, young, fighting Marines.

This means monitoring fuel and lubricant consumption, food and water usage.

And the inevitable small-injury reports that fill every officer's heart with the *joy* of being alive. This is why, when an item has a red flag next to it, I am drawn like a moth to a flame to discover what trouble my people are getting into now.

In this case, it was a number of small items buried in the main list of mission-critical assets for our team. The first one that came to my attention was a 28 percent reduction in RollaBot availability, which had links to a series of video files.

It showed one of our RollaBots trundling down a long spiral ramp out of control.

This was followed by it rolling over the edge of what appeared to be a large shaft. The image repeatedly rotated between the light of the sky above and the darkness below as it fell, then the *Signal Lost* message came on-screen.

From the tracking data appended to the file, I surmised that the RollaBot had reached the central part of the tower.

Another file showed a RollaBot running up a spiral ramp. It ran out of power and rolled all the way back down again. This time it come to a stop after hitting a wall, receiving damage that rendered it immobile and requesting retrieval.

The other files showed similar operational mishaps.

A total of six damaged RollaBots, not including the one lost down the shaft. In the bigger scheme of things, we tended to expect to lose the occasional RollaBot. After all, they're not the brightest things in the world.

They're also known for being easily cracked open when they take a fall that exceeds their operational parameters. Seven in five days was, however, a little excessive and merited further investigation before I signed off on the report.

The second red flag was attached to the preventative maintenance report on our trucks, which showed increased workshop time for each truck. The attachment showed that it was taking twice as long as expected to keep each truck running.

No video files on this one, just an error number for the part, which indicated an engine management system failure. So, no worries there then, just every worry imaginable if we ended up stuck three thousand kilometers from being able to get home.

The third item I already knew about.

It seemed that running the androids through the alien force fields was imposing extra wear and tear on them, requiring more maintenance to keep them operational. This would not generally be a red flag item, but the fact that we'd used up fifty percent of our spares in the last five days meant I had to check it out.

Getting out of my chair, I stretched before putting on my cover as I left my office. It was time to go and fight the good fight of making sure that the numbers added up. I needed to come up with a plan to solve what was rapidly becoming a mission-critical problem.

Crossing our encampment to where Wachowski was working with Green and Mitchell on one of our trucks, I called, "Good morning, Sergeant. How are our new airmen doing?"

"Good morning, ma'am. I'll make Marines out of them yet."

Green and Mitchell looked up but said nothing when they heard their names.

"We're talking about you, not to you, so keep working, Airmen."

"So how are things going here, Sergeant?"

"You've come about the red flags on the reports, I guess?"

"You guessed correctly. What appears to be the problem?"

"It's the desert dust. It's getting into the filters and clogging them up. The dust turns to a paste when it comes into contact with moisture and is highly caustic for good measure."

"Doesn't sound good. Bottom line it for me."

"We will run out of filters sooner or later, so I've implemented a remove-and-strip-the-old-filters program to delay the inevitable breakdown of our trucks after we run out of parts."

"How long until that happens?"

"If we stay here, at the current rate, in about four to six weeks tops thirty percent of the trucks will be out of service. It's the desert around the city that's the source of the problem. Once we get out of here, we should be able to maintain the trucks with no further problems."

"So, if I've got this right, I need to be preparing to get this mission home in a couple of weeks, to be on the safe side."

"That would be about the size of it, ma'am, which I imagine will float like a lead balloon in a swimming pool with the scientists."

"I'm sure you imagine correctly. There are going to be a lot of very unhappy bunnies when the news gets around. Anything else I should know about?"

"Nothing that comes to mind, ma'am. It's a pity we don't have a truck wash."

"What about running the trucks through the alien barriers to clear the dust off them?"

"Yeah, I already thought of that. But while it cleans the trucks cleaner than a very clean thing, the fields damage the exterior ChameleonFlage coatings and the electronics for the sensor systems. If we could run them through once or twice, it would be OK. But running them through every day would cause us other problems, which is what we would need to do to keep the filters clean."

"So much for that bright idea then."

"As you say, it sucks to be us."

"It does, but I'm not ready to throw my hat in yet."

"Oorah."

"Outstanding. Carry on."

Ferretti was on the other side of our camp stripping an android down to get at its core.

"How's it going?" I asked.

"At this rate, not good, ma'am. I was getting ready to come and see you about the situation we find ourselves in. Flores, take over for me here while I talk to the captain."

"Yes, Master Sergeant."

Ferretti got up, and we walked a few feet away to talk.

"Given that I know you've been pulling double shifts, I thought I'd save you the time of coming to see me. This appears to have happened all rather suddenly, though."

"More like we should've seen it coming, really. The barriers at the entrance to the tower are messing with our equipment every time we send something through them. Ms. Carter tells me it's the microwave component of the EM field that's causing the most problems with equipment."

"Why wasn't this flagged sooner?"

"It's incremental damage that built up over the last five days, which only became obvious when we had simultaneous failures across the androids."

"So, before today everything was mostly good, and today things are mostly bad."

"In a nutshell, ma'am."

"Remind me not to eat nuts. We're going to have to cut back on the use of the androids, which may not be our problem, as Wachowski tells me the desert dust is eating the filters in our trucks. It never rains, but it pours, right?"

"So it seems, ma'am. But as you say, the only easy day…"

"Is yesterday. Don't remind me, I know. This day started going downhill early, is all. Just, we could do with being cut some slack. Well, it's up to me to find a way that squares the circle, as 'to have come so far for so little' will not make for a great epitaph on our return. By the way, where are Langford and Meireles?"

"They're over with the scientists working on the RollaBots. Another problem, ma'am?"

"Oh yes. It seems we're having a use-them-and-lose-one sale."

"Langford has kept that one under her hat."

"More like cover, Master Sergeant, but at this rate we're going to run out of RollaBots."

"And I thought I was having a hard day."

"At this rate, the mission is heading up shit creek without a paddle."

"Good luck, ma'am. I'll expect you'll be some time sorting this one out then."

"I expect I shall."

I left Ferretti to carry on fixing the android while I went to find Corporal Langford. In my experience, robotic systems never work as well in the field as they do when being demonstrated to the brass at the top.

But as they say, shit happens, and today was turning out to be an all-the-shit-you-can-handle, and then some, kind of day.

Langford was sitting with Meireles recharging RollaBots, with Dr. Bland and Ms. Carter pulling off the data for their survey.

"Good morning, Dr. Bland, Ms. Carter. Please excuse me, but I need to have a conversation with Corporal Langford in private."

"No problem, we're just about done here. By the way, Langford has done excellent work helping us do our survey. I can't imagine we would've achieved half as much without her help."

"Thank you, Dr. Bland. We aim to please." I waited as the two scientists went back inside the container where they had their laboratory. "It's good to know that you're keeping the scientists happy, Corporal."

"Thank you, ma'am."

"Update me about the missing RollaBots."

"Strictly speaking, only one is irretrievably lost. The others are not exactly missing, as they aren't going anywhere. So, really, they're just resting in place while waiting for us to go get 'em."

"How's that coming on?"

"We're still in the process of getting ready to search their last recorded locations with an android team. Master Sergeant Ferretti is currently preparing two androids for our retrieval operation."

"Those would be the same androids that are being damaged each time they walk through the barrier, resulting in us using fifty percent of our spares to make them operational again, as per today's reports."

"Yes, ma'am, which is why the RollaBots are listed as missing."

"I see…So, how's the survey of the tower going?"

"We're getting lots of good scans, and the scientists are piecing them all together, so we're slowly building up a map of the insides of the building. That's the good news. The bad is that we've barely scratched the surface. It's one big building, and we really don't have the resources to survey it all in a realistic time frame, given the resources we can bring to bear."

"Thank you for your honest assessment of the situation, Corporal. Would I be right in thinking that at the current rate we'll have expended all of our RollaBots within a month and still not be finished surveying the interior of the tower?"

"That would be about right."

"Well, keep up the good work with the scientists. I expect that we'll not remain long in their good books once I've summarized the problems we're having."

As I finished talking to Langford, my PAD pinged with an urgent message from Keith.

I made my way over to the truck that had Dr. O'Neill's biology laboratory in the back of it, which also had an area partitioned off as a sick bay. I met Dr. O'Neill working on her collection.

"Hi, Captain, I wasn't expecting you. What a nice surprise." She smiled and flicked her hair back off her face.

"Sorry, I'm only passing through on my way to see my corpsman."

"That's OK, it's still nice to see you in passing," she said, as one of her snake-scorpion things lunged at the food she dropped into its container. "That one looks agitated."

I agreed.

"They all are, and I'm not sure why. Something has changed that's unsettling them."

"Well, I better leave you to finding out what it is then. I'll no doubt catch up with you later."

"See you at dinner."

Keith was deep into filling out forms.

"Got your message. What's up, Doc?"

He looked up at me. "We have a serious problem."

"Hence all the red flags on your screen, I guess."

"You got it in one. We're getting a lot more radiation than expected. About five times as much as we were when we first arrived on this world. The readings started climbing today, and they're still increasing."

"You know how to cheer someone up by putting things in perspective, Doc. How bad?"

"It's difficult to calculate precisely, since the levels are still rising. If they level off, we would still be looking at long-term health risks from the exposure, which would be dependent on predisposing genetic factors like an increase in cancer risk later on in life. If the radiation levels keep rising at the current rate, and don't stop, we would be looking at serious radiation poisoning by the time we get back to the pillars."

"That doesn't seem to leave us many good options."

"No, it doesn't. What we need to do is get deep enough underground and hope that this increase in radiation is cyclic and will drop back to the original levels we recorded at the beginning of the mission."

"How soon is that likely to occur?"

"I haven't a clue. Perhaps one of the scientists might have a better idea."

"Would the increasing radiation levels be something that the local animal life might respond to?"

"They might. What makes you ask, ma'am?"

"Just spoke to Dr. O'Neill. She told me her collection of the local wildlife has become more agitated today."

"Sounds plausible to me. They might be able to sense the radiation and want to burrow underground. It would make sense, and it might mean the radiation rises are cyclical."

"Anything else I need to be informed of?"

"No, that's all, ma'am."

"I had thought things couldn't get any worse, but you've managed to top everything else I have had to deal with today."

If I could give out medals for bad news, then Doc would certainly have earned one for telling us we'd all be glowing at night if we didn't do something soon. I messaged everyone to let them know I wanted to make an announcement at lunchtime.

First, I had to weigh up my options to the threat of radiation exposure.

At lunchtime everyone had gathered at the tables and were eating their food when I stood and spoke.

"I've been informed that the radiation levels are rising, and that we need to get underground to avoid exposing ourselves any further."

Everyone stopped eating, and the silence was profound.

"I've reviewed the surveys, and it seems to me our best option is to move the camp inside the tower. We can carry on our work there and hope the radiation levels drop by the time we need to leave to get home. Any questions?"

"When do you want us to break camp, ma'am?" asked Ferretti.

"After we finish eating."

Dr. Franklin asked, "Captain, is it safe to stay here? Surely, we should leave now."

"If you mean out in the open, no it isn't safe. But another hour or two will make no difference to us now. Given how quickly this situation has arisen, I don't think making a run back to the pillars would be safe, either. We've surveyed parts of the underground complex at the tower, and it seems the best option we have."

Dr. Smith asked, "If I may speak, Captain?"

"Of course."

"While it's most unfortunate that the radiation levels are rising as they are, it does seem to me that every cloud has a silver lining. At least now we will be able to carry on with our mission while things settle down on the surface of the planet. I think I speak for all of us in saying we would all rather not get a lethal dose of radiation if it's at all possible." He chuckled dryly.

"That would be my wish, too. Everyone please secure your work, and we will move the trucks to the tower. Wachowski, I assume we can do that without delays?"

"We're good to go, ma'am."

"What I don't understand is why the radiation levels are increasing at all," said Ms. Carter.

"Why's that?"

"It just makes no sense to me. We know this planet has two rings in orbit that were probably put there to divert radiation, given that one is synchronized to face the sun and the other the gas giant this planet shares an orbit with. So why the increase now?"

"Perhaps we're seeing an increase in solar radiation, or we're approaching periapsis," said Dr. Bland.

"Not according to my studies. We're nowhere near the closest point to the sun of this star system," said Dr. Wilson.

"Then what is causing this event, Adam?"

"I have no idea, but getting ourselves underground would be a good."

"We seem to all be in agreement, Captain," said Dr. Smith.

"That's good to know, sir."

Not that I needed his agreement when it came to maintaining the safety of all the personnel on this mission. But I couldn't help but feel he was getting far too much satisfaction from my decision.

32. INTO DARKNESS

Courage is knowing what not to fear.

— PLATO

Sergeant Wachowski
Planet 1340
Day 41 of Operation Prometheus
Thursday, February 1, 2074

Wachowski studied the changing vista as her truck led the convoy toward the tower. The broad thoroughfare turned into a cutting. The sides of the road rose up on either side of the convoy.

A pattern of colors, pale gray, sand, and beige, broke up the flatness, turning the surface of everything into a mosaic that confused the eye. It was totally disorienting.

The light created illusions, playing tricks on her mind. Without the truck's computer to guide her, she would've lost all sense of direction.

The place creeped her out.

Then the top of the tower came into view. A flash in the sky lit up the cabin of the truck as the top of the tower was hit by a bolt of lightning. A few seconds later, the truck was rocked by the sound of thunder.

Another flash revealed the tower entrance ahead of them. The truck tipped forward as they went down the shallow incline. As it passed through the barrier, the air around the cab crackled.

They entered the dim interior of what could have been any underground parking garage back on Earth. Wachowski led the convoy into a corridor that spiraled downward. The floor blended into the walls, which formed an arch above them.

Everything was curved. At the bottom of the ramp lay a long, straight stretch of tunnel. As they moved forward, the headlights illuminated the grayish-green passageway, which eventually opened up into a vast chamber that swallowed up the convoy.

A call came through on the radio from the captain. "Zero Two, this is Zero Six. Come in, over."

"Receiving, over."

"Bring the convoy to a halt here by the shaft, over."

"Roger that. Out."

Wachowski stared at the light that entered the chamber from the giant shaft above. She estimated it had to be over a hundred meters in diameter. Then something moved up the shaft, its passage creating a draft of air that rocked the trucks.

Behind her, Ms. Carter shouted out, "What the fuck was that?"

"Damnifino," said Airman First Class Mitchell.

"Good thing I didn't ask you then, Airman," Wachowski said as she replayed the feed on her screen.

A moment later, a flash from an electrical discharge lit the area.

Wachowski monitored the convoy systems and saw Ferretti preparing a QuadCopter. She switched her screen to the UAV feeds. Different views of the scene appeared. She struggled to come to grips with how large the room was.

The aliens sure knew how to build on the grand scale.

Whatever the object that had flown up the shaft was, it hadn't reacted to their presence.

The QuadCopter took off and flew slowly to the edge of the shaft. Its LIDAR feed showed an infinity symbol. That meant that the depth of the shaft was longer than the range the system was calibrated to assess.

After a moment, the QuadCopter descended, transmitting images that showed rapidly alternating bands of darkness and light.

Fifteen minutes passed by. The UAV had not yet reached the bottom of the shaft when a burst of static cut the transmission. The last data showed it had descended fifteen kilometers when contact was lost.

"Damn, that's one hell of a long way down."

Mitchell asked, "I guess that means the RollaBot that fell down there is irretrievable, Sergeant?"

"No shit, Sherlock," she replied, being interrupted from any further comments by the radio.

"Zero two, we're done here. Take the convoy to Romeo Three as per the original plan, over."

"Roger that. Proceeding to Romeo Three. Out."

Wachowski started the convoy moving again. Her truck turned away from the shaft room and proceeded down another passageway that had doors every three meters or so all along it on either side.

At the end of the passage their route was crossed by another passage that led off into the distance. She drove across the junction and entered another cavernous room.

"Whatever else they had going for them, these folks sure liked to build big."

"They sure did, Sergeant," said Ms. Carter. "I wonder if they had a thing about being in confined spaces?"

Wachowski led the convoy from the corridor into a stadium-sized chamber as Dr. Bland and Ms. Carter discussed the possibility of the aliens suffering from claustrophobia.

On the opposite side of the room from their entry point was another exit. She swung the convoy left, leading them around the perimeter of the room and letting the navigation system calculate the optimal spacing to form a laager to make camp.

In the center of the room were what looked like a series of oblong blocks. They were arranged in a circle that the convoy now enclosed. Wachowski thought this made the cavern look disturbingly like a crypt.

The high, curved ceiling was dimly lit by some concealed method. The overall drabness of the place was made gloomier by the muted grayish-green color.

She brought the convoy to a halt. "End of the line, people."

Ms. Carter asked, "Is it safe to get out now, or do we have to wait while your people secure the room?"

"I think we can assume that if anyone didn't want us here, they would have acted by now. This convoy isn't exactly what I would call stealthy. You can get out when you want."

"Excellent. I can't wait to see what we find next," said Dr. Bland.

"It's quite exciting," said Ms. Carter, pointing to the center of the room. "I wonder what's in those boxes over there?"

"Let's go find out," said Dr. Bland.

Wachowski thought of lots of other places she'd find more exciting than being inside what looked like a mausoleum on an alien planet thousands of light years from home. Out dancing at a good night club with friends while listening to some heavy beats and working up a sweat, then chillin' with a few drinks to loosen up, for one.

She watched her passengers walk away. "Mitchell, go help

Adams set up the kitchen while I check everyone knows what they're supposed to be doing."

"Yes, Sergeant."

Wachowski looked around, spotted the captain talking to Ferretti, and made her way across to them. The place gave her the creeps.

33. PARANOIA

For every complex problem, there is a solution that is clear, simple, and wrong.

— H.L. MENCKEN

Master Sergeant Ferretti
Planet 1340
Day 41 of Operation Prometheus
Thursday, February 1, 2074

As the truck came to a halt, Ferretti turned to Airman First Class Green and said, "Start unloading the perimeter sensors while I go check with the captain about what she wants where."

"On it, Master Sergeant," said Green, who swung down out of the truck in one easy movement.

"You OK back there, Dr. Smith?"

The scientist was clearly flustered and having difficulty gathering his gear together. He was doing the usual civilian flailing around and not getting much done.

"I'm fine. Excuse me while I rush off to find out what those objects in the center of the room are. I'm starting to think we might actually find something useful for once."

After five minutes of rushing around to get ready, Dr. Smith eventually managed to get himself out of the truck. Now that he was sure they were alone, Ferretti looked back at Allison.

"We're here, my love. Catch you at dinner?"

Allison ran her hand through her hair and smiled at him. "I expect so. It's not like I've got anywhere else to be," she teased. "Thank you."

"For what?"

"For saying 'my love.' It's nice to hear you say it."

"What are you doing first?"

"Checking on my pets and making sure they're alright."

"I think that's the first time you've referred to them as your 'pets.'"

"I don't normally call them that, but that's what everyone else calls them, so I'm making a virtue out of an annoyance. Once I'm sure they've settled down, I will see what's causing all the excitement over in the center of this place."

"OK, sounds like a plan. Catch you later," he said as they got down out of the truck.

Allison gave him a quick peck on the cheek before walking away. To Ferretti's relief, no one saw her do it. He couldn't have his people thinking he was a softie.

Then he saw the captain waiting for him and realized she'd probably seen Allison kissing him. He walked over to where she stood.

"Looking flushed, Master Sergeant. Everything OK with you?"

"Absolutely, ma'am. Nothing to worry about."

She smiled at him. "Do I look worried?"

"No, ma'am, you don't."

She looked like she was laughing at his expense.

"Down to business. I want sensors set up at both entrances to this cavern, and put an extra pair in each of the side corridors, too. If anything moves around out there, I want to know about it, and I want two androids placed at each entrance as well. I don't want any more unexpected surprises from some automated system in this city sneaking up on us again."

"Understood. Guests by invitation only from now on, ma'am."

"Exactly," she said as Wachowski walked up and joined them. "Ah good, there you are, Sergeant. Can you make sure the trucks opposite the entrances to this room have their .50 cals set to provide supporting fire for the androids that will be on guard?"

"Planning for the worst and hoping for the best, ma'am?"

"Absolutely. This city may be abandoned, but it's clear that the machinery still works."

"It does feel like a morgue."

"Just because the place seems mostly dead doesn't mean that something isn't waiting to get us, and on the whole I'd rather not be one of the dead in this morgue. I'm pretty sure we won't be having any uninvited guests, but we would look pretty stupid if some alien machine designed to defend this place turned up to ruin our day."

"That would suck big-time. Anything else you want done, ma'am?"

"Just make sure our people don't slack off under the delusion we're safe. Remind them we're on an alien planet that might well and truly be dead. But we still have a duty to our charges, who may wander off and get into trouble because they're scientists, and doing interesting things is what comes natural to them."

"I'll relay your intent, ma'am."

"OK, that's it. Dismissed."

Ferretti made his way back to where Green was prepping the perimeter sensors. Time to get four androids set up for guard duty.

34. THE ROOM

Nothing great in the world has ever been accomplished without passion.

— Georg Wilhelm Friedrich Hegel

Dr. Allison O'Neill
Magnetic Anomaly Project Scientist
Planet 1340
Day 41 of Operation Prometheus
Thursday, February 1, 2074

Allison finished checking on her collection. Her precious specimens were now calmer.

Their previous behavior certainly suggested they were probably sensitive to radiation. She could see that this would be a desirable trait that would increase their chance of surviving and reproducing on this planet.

Allison left her laboratory and wandered over to where the rest of the science team was studying the circle of blocks on pedestals. The boxes looked disturbingly like coffins. The tops of the alien boxes flickered, resembling the barriers that protected the entrance to the building.

Allison listened to what was being said.

"What do you make of it?" asked Dr. Bland.

"Same sort of reading, like we found before when examining the entrance to this building. It's sealing the interior," said Ms. Carter.

"What are these things?" Allison asked.

"I have no idea," replied Dr. Bland.

"They might be medical scanners, but why they needed twenty-four placed in a circle like this beats me," Ms. Carter commented.

"Doesn't anyone think it's odd that there are twenty-four of these things in this room, which is the same as the number of people on this team?" said Dr. Reynolds.

"It has to be a coincidence, Tyrone. Unless you are suggesting the aliens made these just for us and lured us here to experiment on us."

"It does sound stupid when you say it like that, Simon."

"You know, this looks like a containment chamber for dealing with biological materials. Those instruments inside appear to be manipulators, and I guess the grid in the bottom is for draining things away," Allison said.

Dr. Smith said, "You're saying this could be a biological research laboratory."

"It could be. Though why anyone would want twenty-four isolation containers all in one place beats me."

"Is it safe to be here?" asked Dr. Franklin.

"Should be, can't see why not. They're all empty, and whatever was worked on in here happened a long time ago," Allison said.

"Still...these are alien things, right?" said Dr. Reynolds. "So, who knows for sure that they're dead and not like asleep, waiting for someone like us to wake them up?"

"Get serious, Tyrone. Where would they be hiding? These chambers are empty, and I can't imagine the aliens who built them wouldn't have autocleaning systems that sterilized everything between use," said Dr. Franklin.

"If you compare the various markings we've recorded during our stay here, you can see these pods use similar symbols. This has got to be a number pad. Furthermore, judging by the number of keys, the alien writing looks like logograms," said Dr. David Leung, pointing as he unrolled a screen.

"How do you account for the differences in the shapes of some of the symbols?" asked Dr. Smith.

"Best guess is it's either drift that has taken place over time or the equivalent of using a different typeface."

"That might be true," said Dr. Reynolds. "But aren't you assuming *they* only used one language. Maybe we're seeing signs that the aliens had more than one language, just as we do on Earth, and this is the difference between roman and arabic writing."

"An interesting insight, Dr. Reynolds. Does anybody else have anything to add?" asked Dr. Smith.

"Only that judging by the light readings I took, it's highly likely that the aliens saw in a different range of the spectrum from us."

"Thank you, Dr. O'Neill. Anybody else?"

Allison looked around at the rest of her team, seeing Li-Na and Rachel both shake their heads to indicate that they had nothing to add. Adam had withdrawn into himself, and Peter was apparently also lost in thought.

35. END OF THE DAY

Let us get down to bedrock facts. The beginning of every act of knowing, and therefore the starting-point of every science, must be our own personal experience.

— Max Planck

Dr. Adam Wilson
Magnetic Anomaly Project Scientist
Planet 1340
Day 41 of Operation Prometheus
Thursday, February 1, 2074

Adam sat opposite Peter. They ate their evening meal in silence.

The gloom of the cavern was broken by a confusing array of multiple shadows around them, cast by the lights that had been set up. He needed time to gather his thoughts about what they'd seen today.

Peter asked, "Food OK?"

"Yeah, I suppose."

On his plate were sausage and mashed potatoes with gravy and peas, which wouldn't have been his first choice for a meal.

"Such a lugubrious reply. Clearly, there's something on your mind."

Before he could reply, they were interrupted.

"Do you mind if we join you?"

Adam stopped contemplating the mound of mashed potatoes as Dr. Bland and Ms. Carter sat down with their trays.

Then he began sculpting it again while Peter said, "Of course not, please do. You're not interrupting anything. Excuse Adam though, he's deep in thought."

"I don't blame him at all. We've seen and discovered a lot here today," said Dr. Bland.

"True enough. I was blown away by the size of the shaft. It seems to go down forever. I felt it was like watching the power of the gods rather than just alien technology in action."

"Well, any plausible-looking magic will be based on technology," said Dr. Bland.

"You're quoting someone, aren't you, Simon?" asked Ms. Carter.

"Indeed, I am."

"I read the original version of that quote many years ago by Arthur C. Clarke who said, 'Any sufficiently advanced technology is indistinguishable from magic.'"

"I guessed I would be corrected by you, Peter."

"Can't help being a pedant and a sci-fi geek."

Li-Na and Rachel interrupted them, "Mind if we sit with you?"

"Sure, sit down and join in the conversation. Just don't expect to hear anything from Adam, as he's somewhere else tonight."

Li-Na and Rachel smiled and sat down.

"I am not, I'm clearly here. I'm thinking through what we've seen today and trying to make sense of it all." One thing he knew was that they all felt the need for human company inside this alien cavern.

"He speaks at last. That's the most I've heard out of him since we were over there examining the modules."

"What do you make of the modules in this room, Peter?" asked Dr. Li-Na Wong as she pushed her hair back off her face.

"Hard to argue with Allison's opinion that they're some sort of biological containment units, given she's our resident biological expert. Still, this is an awfully big room to house twenty-four workplaces."

"Who knows what else used to be in this room. Perhaps everything else was removed?" said Dr. Rachel Goldstein.

Adam looked at the pair of them and realized that they were more than just friends by the way they sat with each other. He remembered what Sergeant Wachowski had said about how some things are not solvable. So that's what she'd meant.

"You could be right, but we have no way of knowing for sure."

"However, tomorrow we shall try our damnedest to find out all we can about this place. There's enough here to keep us busy for several lifetimes, I imagine," said Dr. Bland.

"If by 'all' you mean your part of the team, then yes. As for the rest of us, not so much. Once we've cleared processing the data we picked up along the way we've got nothing. What does everyone else think?" asked Dr. Reynolds.

"I still have a lot of work to do on processing the data from my weather balloons, but what about you, Rachel?" said Dr. Li-Na Wong.

"Some, but not as much as you. I've got perhaps a week's worth of work before I catch up with all the important stuff I want to do. After that it would be scut work I intended to have my assistants do when we got back, if truth be told."

"See, Simon, not everyone finds this place as fascinating as you do," said Dr. Reynolds.

"I thought we would end up here at some point though, just not this soon. It seems obvious that Dr. Smith was hell-bent on getting us inside the tower. Still, that machine rising up the central shaft was something I didn't expect to see," Adam said.

"What did you expect to find?" asked Dr. Bland, rubbing his beard.

"Nothing moving. We all agree that this place is old, and to find something physical and still operational after all this time beggars belief, in my opinion. Or, as Lily said, this is something way beyond what we can expect to understand. I don't believe in gods, but the aliens who built this place would probably treat us like ants."

Adam stopped speaking. Everyone was looking at him.

"Sorry, I didn't mean to suggest the existence of gods, it was just an expression of incredulity at what I was seeing," Adam said.

"We all have one thing in common here: today seems to be bringing out the pedant in all of us," said Peter.

"Coming from you, that's saying something," said Dr. Bland.

"Touché, Simon. I'm wounded."

Adam struggled to compile his thoughts into a sentence and chewed on a sausage instead.

"This is actually a rather good sausage," said Ms. Carter.

"I never imagined I'd be eating bangers and mash on an alien planet," said Dr. Bland.

"Will these wonders never cease?" said Dr. Reynolds.

"I hope not. The point is that eating food while sitting here underground inside an alien city that has been abandoned for who knows how long is a wonderful experience."

"So, we can cross that off our list of things to do before we die then?" said Ms. Carter.

"Our what?" Adam asked.

"Things to do. You know, lists of places to go and see because they're important. Surely, you must have come across this before?"

"Peter tells me I don't get out enough, and it appears that he's right in this case."

"Peter was being judgmental. After all, how many people can say they have traveled to an alien planet? There's more to life than ticking the boxes of a list of places others have been to before you."

"Well, what happened at the shaft today does make one wonder what other devices we will find that are still functional in this place," said Dr. Bland.

"I'm not sure we could take back the device in the shaft with us even if we wanted, Simon. You saw how big it was," said Ms. Carter.

"Of course I did, but maybe once we've scanned this chamber's contents we will be able to remove one of the blocks to take back home with us. It would advance the field of materials technology just by itself."

"If I could take something back, it would be a piece of the material used to make the rings that orbit this world," said Ms. Carter.

"You know, what I'd like to find is a way of talking to the aliens that used to live here," said Dr. Harrison.

"Not likely though, is it? And it's more up Tyrone's street than yours," Adam said, laughing.

"True enough, but Tyrone would be all about observing the culture and seeking the meaning behind the behaviors. Whereas, I want to talk to the people who survived their sun becoming a red giant and built this city. Learn how they faced up to the end times."

"Is my name being taken in vain?" asked Dr. Reynolds, who was sitting behind them at another table.

"We're talking about you, not to you. Anyway, you make it sound all elegiac, Peter."

"It is, Simon. We're seeing the funeral remains of a great civilization, because this city is a monument to the end times."

"At least, unlike the poem 'Ozymandias,' this city is more than one leg standing in the desert with an inscription underneath it," said Dr. Bland.

Dr. Harrison pinched his chin and said, "I work with things that span geological times, and one thing I know is that technology is the most frangible thing of all. If we know anything for sure, it's that it takes relatively few years to break down man-made objects, making them virtually unrecognizable. This place defies our understanding of deep time."

"That's one thing we can agree on."

"What we need is a tribologist's input. I imagine they would find this place fascinating to study," Adam said.

"Good point. Pity we don't happen to have one on the team, but perhaps the next time we come we'll have more people with the skills we need to really study this place," said Dr. Bland.

"You men exasperate me at times. Rather than wishing for what we don't have, why don't we accept that we're here, and do the best we can with what we've got? After all, this is only our first mission to this planet, and I can't imagine us not coming back again."

"Good point, Lily," said Dr. Bland.

Adam had finished eating his main course and was looking at the pecan pie, wondering if he had any room left to eat it. He made a decision to slice a piece off and try it. "This is good pie."

Everyone at the table stared at him.

"What? I only said it was good pie."

Peter looked at him. "Sometimes I wonder if you live on another world."

"If I did, you would hardly be having this conversation with me now, would you?"

36. YAWN

What is freedom? To have the will to be responsible for one's self.

— MAX STIRNER

Dr. Allison O'Neill
Magnetic Anomaly Project Scientist
Planet 1340
Day 41 of Operation Prometheus
Thursday, February 1, 2074

Allison sat opposite Vincent, eating her meal and listening to the conversation at the table behind them as she cut a sausage into mouth-sized portions.

"Penny for your thoughts?" Vincent asked.

"Just ear-wagging the other table's conversation, not really thinking about anything much. You?"

"Just enjoying the meal after a long day," he said, holding a sausage on the end of his fork and then taking a bite of it.

"Well, at least we have something different every day, but I'd like some more variety in the choice of vegetables."

"What's wrong with onions in gravy and peas? If you want, you could mention it to Adams. I'm sure he can accommodate requests."

"Is it OK if we join you?" asked Dr. Franklin, who stood next to Dr. Reynolds.

"Sure, of course you can, no need to ask. Please sit and talk," Allison replied.

"Good evening, Sergeant."

"Good evening to you, Dr. Reynolds."

"Behave, Tyrone."

"What is it, woman? Can't I say 'good evening' now?"

"You know what I mean."

"You must be thinking of someone else, because I'm never a hundred percent sure what you mean."

"Are we interrupting something?" The Leungs said as they sat down at the last two seats at the table.

"Not at all. We were just about to start eating. Please join us," said Dr. Franklin.

Allison finished her entrée and started on her pecan pie, letting the conversation wash over her.

Vincent asked, "So, Doc, I assume you have plans for tomorrow?"

"We certainly do. Now that we've found the consoles, we can make a start on cataloging the script and working out how they constructed the words using the symbols on the keyboard," said Dr. David Leung.

"I'm not sure I understand. Surely the keyboard's symbols match the words you've recorded."

"We think the words we've seen are syllabaries, which require a complex sequence of strokes to assemble the components into logograms that make up a word."

"What David is trying to say is that the alien language looks like Chinese hànzì. So one has to type more than one key to make up a word," said Dr. Grace Leung.

"That's what I said, dear."

"Of course it was, dear, but I made it simpler. Remember, not everyone sitting here is a cunning linguist like yourself," she said, smiling at him.

"Oh, stop it, you'll embarrass everyone."

"Everyone here's an adult." She blew him a kiss.

"I wouldn't be so sure about that, Grace," said Dr. Franklin. "When will we be able to go outside again, Sergeant?"

"I don't know, that's not under my control. We'll have to wait until the readings drop."

"What about your pets, Allison? How are you going to manage feeding them?" asked Dr. Franklin.

"Once I've run out of the stuff I've gathered, I'll start printing food for them that simulates what they eat in the wild."

"I hadn't thought of that."

"I have to ask, Sergeant, but weren't you at all surprised by what happened in the shaft chamber today? It sure shocked the hell out of us all," said Dr. Reynolds.

"It wasn't quite a brown-trouser moment, but it certainly was a startled-rabbit-in-the-headlights occasion. We're not here to start a war, so standard operating procedure is to stop and watch and see what happens, which we did."

Dr. Reynolds asked, "I see you've put guards on the entrances, though. Are you expecting more automated systems in this place to activate?"

"I know as much as you do, but it was easy to set up a standard perimeter while we're inside this chamber. Better safe than sorry."

"Turned out to be a long day, though. When we woke up this

morning, who would've imagined we would be camping here tonight?" said Dr. Leung.

"The place is not what you'd call brimming with life, is it, though? I mean, there's lots for the hard-science members of the team to get their teeth into, but I feel rather like a third person on a blind date," said Dr. Reynolds.

"I'm sure you've never been the third person on a blind date in your life," said Dr. Franklin.

"The point is this city is a mausoleum. There are no aliens for us to interact with."

"You said you had enough work from Two Moons to occupy a lifetime without needing any more."

"I do, but that's not the point, is it now? Here I am, stuck on this planet for six months with nothing new to get my teeth into. Yes, I can work on the Two Moons stuff, but I don't need to be here to do that. Besides, the night life around here sucks."

"Aren't we good enough company for you?"

"Don't give me that, woman! What I meant was, there's nowhere to get a drink around here."

"Uh…huh!"

"Stop picking on me. You're not my mother."

Laughter broke out on the other table behind them as his name was mentioned.

"I heard my name being taken in vain!" said Dr. Reynolds

Allison finished eating her pie as the conversation at the table began to wind down.

Her thoughts went back to the behaviors of her specimens and what she planned to do next. People got up and took their trays away, leaving her and Vincent sitting alone.

"What now?" he asked.

She played footsie with his feet. "We could sit here for a few moments before I have to head back to my lab and finish everything I need to do for the day. You?"

"Have to check on the perimeter arrangements, then fill in some logs. After that, we could hang for a while before hitting the sack."

"You're such a romantic."

"What did I say?"

"Nothing really. It was the word *hang* that made me laugh."

37. KATA

The best time is always yesterday.

— TATYANA TOLSTAYA

I awoke in my bed with the sun coming through the curtains of my room.

Mom was downstairs shouting, "You awake yet, Lara?"

"Yes, Mom, just five more minutes."

"You've had five minutes, honey. Time to get up and dressed. Daddy's in the dojo. He has a surprise for you."

I threw off the duvet cover, swung out of bed, and went to the window to pull the curtains open. The sun was shining, and it was another beautiful day in San Diego. The lawn below was golden yellow, and at the back of the yard was my father's dojo.

He'd slid open the doors to reveal the sprung wooden floor and sat with his back to me, cleaning his sword.

I rushed to shower, wash my hair, clean my teeth, and put on a bathrobe to go and have breakfast before dressing. Mom was in the kitchen, and she had put a bowl out for me. I looked at the selection of breakfast cereals we had and decided on

Captain Crunch, for a change, poured out some milk, and started to eat.

"Oh, do sit down, dear, when you're eating."

"Oh, Mom…"

"You'll get indigestion if you don't."

"No, I won't. That's a myth."

"Sit down and eat your cereal. Now would you like some toast?"

"Yes, please, Mom."

"Peanut butter?"

"Uh-hmm…with jelly, please."

"Have you brushed your hair, young lady?"

"Not yet, I just washed it."

"Make sure you do before you tie it back, otherwise it will be a tangled nest of knots by the time it dries."

"I will, Mom, I promise," I said as I finished my cereal and took the toast with me. "I'm going to go and brush my hair now."

"Are you spreading crumbs everywhere, dear?"

"No, Mom, no crumbs here," I said as I walked upstairs, dropping a crumb or two in my wake.

With a piece of toast in my mouth, I started brushing the knots out of my hair. When it looked good enough, I finished eating the last piece of toast and licked my fingers clean before putting on a tank top and underpants and shorts before getting into my *iaigi* and tying it across. Then I wound my obi around and fastened it as my father had taught me.

I looked in the mirror to make sure everything was straight, and unfolded my *hakama* and put it on one leg at a time, which Dad said was what everyone had to do unless they were supermen. He'd laughed when he told me that.

Once I had tied the *himo* properly, I checked that the *koshi-ita* was tucked into my obi at the back so my *hakama* would hang properly and, more importantly in my opinion, stay in place. So far, I'd found that no matter how well I tied my obi and *himo*, they would always work loose at some point during the practice and I would have to stop to rearrange my ties.

"Are you ready yet? Don't keep your father waiting now."

"I won't, Mom. I'm coming down now!"

Then I ran down the stairs, lifting my *hakama* up so as not to fall, and rushed through the hall to where my zori were waiting for me, their straw soles a golden brown. I slipped them on my feet and stepped outside onto the path that father had laid from the back of the house to the dojo.

The air was already hot and humid and held the promise of rain later.

My father came out of the dojo and stood waiting for me. I remembered to walk mindfully, keeping within my center, and I bowed at the waist before smiling at him.

"Good morning, sleepyhead."

"Oh, Daddy, it's not that late, and anyway, my teacher Ms. Mitchell said a growing girl needs to sleep enough to grow properly."

"Did she now?"

"Honest, she did. I wouldn't lie."

"I know that, you're a good girl. I have a present for you."

"Mom said you did. What is it?"

"Come sit here with me."

He sat on the step of his dojo and beckoned me to sit beside him. I did while listening to the birds singing, thinking what a perfect day it was.

He drew the katana out from his obi, and I realized that it was not his sword. "You have been practicing every week since your thirteenth birthday, and it is time I gave you this."

The *saya* was not the traditional black but rather a rich deep burgundy color with matching bindings on the *tsuka*, and a stunningly gorgeous silver *tsuba* in the shape of a swan's neck had been wound around the guard.

"This *shinken* has been in the family for four hundred years. It's not been used in many years, as the blade is of an older, shorter style. However, for a young woman, it's ideal. Remember, the blade is razor sharp."

"May I?"

"Of course, it is yours now. Treat it with respect and reverence, and it will never let you down. Mistreat it and you will hurt yourself."

I clicked the *tsuba* off the *saya* and slowly drew the blade out of its sheath with the edge of the katana facing away from my father and me. The blade shone in the sunlight, and the *hamon* was a wave that flowed along the blade's edge with a spray pattern that looked like water spreading from it.

"It's so beautiful." I slid the blade back into its *saya* and put my present down beside me, then turned and hugged my father. "Thank you, Daddy."

"You have been practicing with the right spirit, and it is time for you to have it. Come now, let us practice together so you can become one with your new sword, the heart of a samurai."

I picked up my present and transferred it to my right hand, then I stood and stepped up onto the porch at the entrance to the dojo. I took a step forward and turned so I could remove my zori at the entrance and stepped into the dojo barefooted.

My father had already bowed from the waist, and I followed suit.

Then I knelt down on the floor facing the *shinzen*, quickly flicking the folds of my *hakama* with my spare hand, bowed again, and sat waiting in *seiza*.

I felt a tingling in my feet and allowed myself to sink into the posture, relaxing my shoulders, with my hands gently resting on each side at the top of my thighs.

I watched in silence as my father walked toward where he had placed his sword, taking it down off the rack for today's session. He turned and walked to the front of the dojo and kneeled facing the *shinzen* with the *kamidana,* his back to me.

He looked so tall and composed, each movement elegant and constrained, yet I could sense his *zanshin.*

I'd always thought Dad was like a tiger, relaxed, but deadly. I wanted to be able to be like him.

On his command of "*Rei,*" I place my left hand down on the floor followed by my right to form an arrowhead, and we bowed again, more deeply this time to show our respect. He turned to face me, and we bowed to each other.

My father had taught me that no matter how good or bad your practice during a session might be, the only thing that really mattered was showing respect to the spirit of *iaido* by showing proper politeness at all times. The worst thing that one can ever do is be rude, and not bowing properly is a way that a sensei will judge whether or not they will allow you to practice in the dojo.

A soft breeze came in through the open door. Stillness descended and my father took his sword from his side and brought it up to stand vertically in front of him before laying it down on the floor in front of him.

I followed suit and made sure to carefully arrange my *sageo* so that the cord was neatly folded in line with the sword.

We bowed again, this time to the sword.

I breathed in, one action one breath, and picked up my sword, using my left hand to hold the end of the *saya*, guiding it through the folds in my obi so that the blade edge faced up. Then I tied my *sageo* loosely to my side, allowing it to fall in a half loop across the front of my *hakama.*

He said, "*Tachi.*"

And I stood up, following my father to stand to his side. We both kneeled again, and I took my place a few feet to one side so I could follow the twelve *seita* kata moves.

"*Ippon me mae.*" The first set of moves was a strike to the front against a kneeling opponent.

I let my mind empty, allowing distracting thoughts to go, and unlocked my *tsuba,* turning my sword while drawing my blade out of the *saya* so the edge faced out horizontally. I made a strike to cut an imaginary point of my opponent's temple while rising out of *seiza* by tucking my toes under my feet and gripping the floor, then bringing my right foot up and making a half step forward.

I imagined the blood flowing into the eye of my opponent, partially blinding them.

"The tip of your blade is too low, and remember to pull your *saya* right back on the draw."

"*Hai!*" I replied as the end of my blade wobbled in front of me.

I raised the point higher before bringing my sword around and up and took hold of *tsuka* with my left hand.

"Your blade is dropping at the back. Grip tighter with your left little finger."

"*Hai!*" I said as sweat dribbled down the small of my back. I breathed out as I made a downward *kirioroshi* stroke that would cleave my opponent, mortally wounding them.

"Don't hold the blade so tight. The cut should make a clear sound."

"*Hai!*" I said again, embarrassed at my clumsiness and trying to remember to become one with the movements.

I slowly twisted my sword while rising off the floor, bringing the sword around and up to the side of my head, letting go with my left hand to take hold of my *saya.* Then I did the *chiburi* by swinging the sword down in an arc to flick the imaginary blood off the blade.

This time the blade made a sound when cutting through the air.

"Good, better."

I brought my left foot forward, keeping my knees soft, bringing it in line with my right foot before drawing my right foot back. I took a moment before turning my *saya* horizontally while bending my right elbow and bringing the back of my blade into contact so I could guide it inside and complete the *noto* by lowering my rear knee to the floor.

After that I rose off the floor and brought my rear foot forward and let go of my blade, but kept the thumb of my left hand on the *tsuba*, showing I had control of my weapon.

"Again," said my father, and we stepped back and knelt to repeat the set.

Draw, step, and cut to the temple. Swing up and strike down with both hands. Twist and rise while flicking the blood off the blade before sheathing it and standing.

My father repeated, "Again."

And I went through the movements, letting the form take hold of me, allowing the shape of the movements to flow.

"And again," he said, and I repeated the movements for the third time.

My father announced, "*Nihon me ushiro.*" The second set of movements were a strike on an attacker coming from the rear.

I liked the idea of being able to turn and strike a foe waiting behind you to attack and take them by surprise. My father led me through six repetitions of the form.

My back was now drenched in sweat, and my knees were starting to hurt even though I wore knee pads.

We moved back to our starting positions and my father called, "*Sanbon me ukenagashi.*"

This time we were practicing being attacked from the left. I drew and blocked my opponent's strike, deflecting their cut with the back edge of my blade while rising off the floor.

"You're leaning out of your center."

"*Hai,*" I said as I delivered a slanting countercut down.

"Your *kissaki* is too low." The point of my blade had dropped. "Your left hand should stop at the navel."

"*Hai,*" I said again, acknowledging the correction. I then drew my blade across the front of my body, holding it to the left and changing the grip of my right hand so as to be able to swing the blade around in an arc and sheathe it.

"Again," my father called, and we moved through the form as I repeated it for a third time.

By then I was feeling the strain, but I remembered to center myself. When the body weakens, the mind must be strong. When the mind weakens, one must use one's spirit to push through the barrier. Be mindful, one breath, one action.

My heart was beating fast as my father said, "*Yonhon me tsuka ate.*" An attack by two people, with one person sitting in front while the other is sitting behind you.

Of all the sets, this was my least favorite because instead of sitting in *seiza,* I had to sit in *iaiheza.* This is an excruciatingly painful position that requires one to sit with one's left leg folded under and resting on the front of the foot with the ankle under one's backside.

Father says that even he finds it hurts him because this posture suits people with shorter calves than we have. Modern Japanese people have difficulty sitting in the old ways, as their body shape has changed as each generation becomes taller.

My grandparents came to America before the Second Great Depression and my mother's family was originally from Scotland, so it's their fault that my calves are too long for sitting comfortably in *iaiheza.*

"Concentrate."

"*Hai,*" I said, as I struck forward, targeting the sternum of my imaginary opponent, not drawing the blade but pulling the sword in its *saya* forward with both hands.

"Your back foot is in. Straighten it out parallel to your front foot."

"*Hai.*" I pulled the *saya* back, revealing my blade and turning it sideways, thrusting to the rear using my right hand to hold the blade and stab the other opponent behind me.

"You're out of your center. Steady yourself."

"*Hai.*" I turned back to face my first opponent and raised my blade above my head, taking it in both hands and striking down.

I finished off the set by doing *chiburi* where I swept my blade to the right to flick the blood off. Performing the *noto*, I sheathed my weapon and returned to the *sonkyo* position that balanced my weight between my left knee and right foot.

"Good, and again."

I repeated the form, trying to allow myself to sink into the movements and rise above the pain.

"*Tachi waza, gohon me kesa giri.*" This was a diagonal strike from the standing position.

I stood after finishing the technique, my knees and ankles hurting and the relief from the pain sweeping through me. I drew my blade, turning the *saya* so the edge faced down and slicing my imaginary opponent upward from the hip.

"Do not lean forward, stay in your center, and stand up straight."

"*Hai,*" I replied, swinging my blade up. At the top of the cut, I turned my blade and struck down.

"Do not pause the blade at the top of the stroke. It should be all one movement."

"*Hai.*" I acknowledged the correction as I moved into *haso* to maintain my *zanshin* before sweeping the blade down for *chiburi,* then returning my blade to the *saya* to end with *noto.*

"Again, this time with more *zanshin*," said my father.

I repeated the form twice more, each time managing to do something wrong that made me sweat as I tried harder to please him.

My father called the next form: "*Roppon me morote tsuki*." A standing two-handed thrust to defend against three attackers.

I felt a rush of excitement fill me. I drew my blade and struck the first of my imaginary opponents.

"Open your body to the front."

"*Hai*." I then thrust forward.

"Your *kissaki* is too high. Thrust the blade down."

I dropped the point of my blade and turned, bringing my blade up into *jodan* to deliver a downstroke before turning back again to strike the third opponent. I drew a breath and did my *chiburi* from left to right and finished with *noto*.

"Repeat again. Smoother this time."

Cut, thrust, turn and cut, and turn and cut again.

"Do not rush. Be one with the blade. It is an extension of one's spirit. And again."

"*Hai*." Sweat trickled down into my eye, and the saltiness stung. I barely had time to wipe my eye when father spoke again.

"*Nanahon me sanpo giri*." This time we practiced the three-direction cut against opponents who were to the left, right, and front.

In my mind's eye, I advanced toward my opponents, walking normally in a style called *tsugi-ashi* in *iaido*. I imagined I was walking into death's ground and drew my blade, cutting to my opponent's left side using just one hand.

"Cut down to the chin only."

"*Hai*," I replied as I turned, cutting to my right, using both hands and slashing down.

"Turn on your toes."

"*Hai,*" I said before facing to the front and striking my third opponent down.

"Your *kissake* is too low. It should be level with the floor and in your center."

"*Hai.*" I stepped back with my right foot and assumed *morite hidari jodan,* holding my blade above my head with my left foot back to retrieve my *zanshin* before pushing the blade out and cutting down in an arc to remove the blood and return my blade to its *saya.*

"Again, but faster."

I said, "*Hai.*" Moving through the form again, I imagined I must kill my opponents before they killed me. Advance and strike as one movement as my mind emptied of thought; *Mushin.*

I was aware that he called, "*Hachihon me ganmen ate.*"

I drew and struck with the *tsuka* into the face of the opponent standing in front of me.

"Too low. Strike between the eyes."

"*Hai.*" I drew the blade and turned to face to my rear, thrusting my blade through their solar plexus.

"Heel out, feet should be parallel, and bring your right hand in so the blade is up."

"*Hai,*" I replied as I turned again and brought my blade up, cutting my first opponent with a downstroke to complete the form.

"Good. Now again."

"*Hai.*" And I allowed myself to fall into the movements, letting them fill me as I worked my way through the flowing form two more times.

"*Kyuhon me soete tsuki.*"

I stepped forward, sensing an attack from my left. I turned and drew my left leg back as I made a diagonal stroke from my right against my opponent.

"Raise your *kissake* above the right hand."

"*Hai.*" I brought the *tsuka* back to my hip and held the back of my blade with my left hand and thrust forward. I supported the end of my blade with my left hand and turned to sweep the blade for *chiburi*.

"Elbow straight and hand lower, and again."

"*Hai,*" I said as I retook the starting position and repeated the attack.

"Good, and again. Draw and strike as one continuous action. Do not stop between the strike and the thrust, as you will lose the speed of the movement."

My throat was dry, and the sound of my *hai* was half-strangled.

"*Juppon me shiho-giri,*" my father said as soon as we were in position.

I imagined seeing four people preparing to attack me. I advanced and struck the hand of the nearest imaginary opponent who was on my right with my *tsuka,* to stop them from drawing their blade.

"Use the flat of your *tsuka* as you strike down."

"*Hai.*" I drew my blade out of the *saya* and turned to face the opponent standing to my rear and left. As the back of my blade pressed against my chest, I thrust my blade through them.

"Keep your elbow straight."

"*Hai.*" I turned back and struck my first opponent, cutting them down before they could draw.

"Tuck your elbows in."

"*Hai.*" I turned right toward my next opponent and cut them down before facing my final adversary.

"Leave your blade facing away from you with the last opponent."

"*Hai,*" I said, remembering that the last turn would put my blade into the *wakigamae* position, hidden behind me and level with the ground so that my opponent wouldn't know whether I would cut up or, in this case, bring my blade up and strike down.

"Now do it again, and remember that each action must flow into the next."

"*Hai.*" I started again.

"Pacing, and again."

"*Hai,*" I said, my arms and legs trembling.

"*Ju-ippon me so-giri.*"

I moved and cut my opponent's face with a diagonal cut from my right side to his left.

"Hand to your right, not above your head. Remember, you are deflecting their blow."

"*Hai.*" I brought my blade around, cutting from my left down the right side of my opponent, from their shoulder to their waist.

"Don't wave your blade around as you advance."

"*Hai.*" I cut again from the right, aiming for the arm and cutting to the navel.

"*Okuri-ashi.*"

"*Hai,*" I replied, remembering to change the way I moved my feet, not walking, but sliding one foot up behind the other as I advanced. I maintained my posture and *zanshin*, cutting down and across right to left.

"Do not let your hand cross your navel."

"*Hai.*" I crossed my blade to my left and cut my opponent across the navel, slicing them in half.

"Your wrists are too high. They shouldn't be above your waist."

"*Hai,*" I replied, bringing my blade up and cutting straight down for the final stroke.

"Remember, this form is multiple attackers coming from the front, and you must maintain your pace or be overwhelmed. Now do it again."

"*Hai,*" I said, feeling myself flagging. When the body fails, the mind must take over. When the mind fails, the spirit must rise to fill the void.

"Now *Ju-Nihon me nuki-uchi*."

The last form of the twelve is both simple and difficult. I imagined being attacked by surprise.

"Hand above your head and do not pause between raising your blade and the downstroke."

"*Hai.*" I stepped back as far as I could, raising my blade and counterstriking my opponent before they could attack again. I completed the form.

"Remember, the purpose is to evade and strike before they can recover from missing you. Try again."

"*Hai.*" I started again, and my father stopped me.

"A longer step back or you will be cut."

"*Hai.*" Starting again, I took a longer step back out of the way of the imaginary attack.

"There's no pause between raising the blade and cutting down. Again."

"*Hai.*"

I repeated the form twice more. When we finished, my father clapped his hands and said, "Very good. *Tate.*"

I withdrew back to the side of the dojo and took my position to complete the session by drawing out and placing my sword on the floor, bowing to it, then bowing to my father, and finally bowing to the *kamidana* at the *shinzen*.

I was drenched in sweat and trembling from exhaustion.

My father rose and smiled. "Let's fold our *hakamas*, and then it's time to drink and have food. You did very well today. I'm proud of you."

Rain started to spit outside, and the sound of the drops hitting the ground turned into a symphony as thunder sounded in the distance.

38. VISITOR

The foolish reject what they see, not what they think; the wise reject what they think, not what they see.

— Huang Po

It was another perfect day as I, carrying both our folded *hakamas* under my arm, walked with my father back from the dojo along the gravel path to our house. The sun shone in the sky above our heads, and I could smell the food my mom was preparing coming from the kitchen.

I followed my father inside, slipping off my zori, and leaving them on the porch beside his.

Mom was smiling as we entered the kitchen dining nook. "Hi, you two. How did it go?"

"She did very well."

"Daddy made me go through *okuiai iwaza no bu* today and do both *tachiwaza* and *suwariwaza*."

"Did he now? Was it good?"

"Awesome, Mom. Is there something to drink?"

"Open your eyes, dear. There's a jug of orange juice on the table waiting for you, silly head."

"Thanks, Mom. Daddy, do you want some too?"

"*Hai, onagai, Lara-chan.*"

I giggled. "Daddy says if I want to understand *iaido*, I must learn to speak Japanese."

"So, why aren't you practicing now?"

"Oh, Mom," I said, taking a moment to think. "*Okasan, gomennasai! Nihongo muzukashi desu neh.*" I smirked and then burst out giggling some more.

"It would be better if you said, *Nihongo wo hanasu koto wa totemo muzukashi desu neh.*"

"*Hai, otosan,*" I replied to my father, making my voice as deep and gravelly as I could before passing him a glass of juice.

"*Domo arrigato gozaimasu.*" He thanked me most politely for his drink.

I smiled at him and said to my mom, "*Korede ii desuka?*"

"Yes, much better, dear. Now go and get changed before lunch."

"Do I have to? Daddy eats in his *keikogi*."

"Daddy doesn't spill food down his front. Now off you go, and be quick about it."

"Oh, Mom, I do not."

She gave me one of her *looks*, so I rushed upstairs to my room to untie my obi, then removed my jacket and trousers before taking off my panties and throwing them on my bed. I got into the shower and quickly rinsed the sweat off my body, not wanting to waste time.

Mom shouted up, "Don't forget to put your things in for washing."

"Yes, Mom."

I picked up my sodden clothes and put them in the linen basket to be washed later, put on clean underwear, and pulled on a white top and a pair of khaki-colored loose cargo pants that were really comfortable. As in, the cargo pants were so comfy I could have gone and climbed trees later and annoyed the local boys by being better than them.

"What are you doing, *dear*? Lunch is ready to be served."

"Coming, Mom!" I shouted as I rushed downstairs for lunch.

Daddy was already at the end of the table waiting while Mom finished serving the food onto three plates. She'd made ham and eggs with mushrooms and hash browns.

"Oh, my favorite."

"If it's your favorite, you should sit and eat," said Mom.

Daddy smiled at her, and she leaned over and kissed him.

I was hungry after my lesson and attacked my ham and eggs, putting the runny, yolky goodness onto the ham and savoring the creamy coating as it seemed to melt in my mouth. "Oh, this is delicious."

"So, what are you planning to do this afternoon?"

"I was going to go out and play with my friends."

"Have you done your homework?"

"Yes, Mom, and yes I've done the reading I was assigned, too."

"That's good. Do you think we should allow her out to play?"

My father pretended to be stern as if he were contemplating a most difficult decision. "*Muzukashi desu neh.*"

"Please, Daddy. It's such a nice day."

"If your mom thinks it's OK, then who am I to stop you having fun?"

"Thank you, Daddy. I love you so much," I replied as the doorbell rang.

Mom got up to answer the door. "I wonder who that can be. Are we expecting visitors today?"

My father shrugged and said nothing. I finished my food and took my plate to the sink, hearing Mom speaking at the door.

"Lara, there's a Dr. Harrison here to talk to you."

"Who, Mom?"

"He's here about your studies."

My mom brought an older man with a beard and glasses into the dining nook.

"Please excuse us, we were just finishing eating lunch," she said.

"No, please excuse me for interrupting you. Good afternoon, Mr. Tachikoma. I do hope it's alright for me to speak to your daughter at home today, but I really can't wait any longer."

"Of course. Would you like to sit in the garden?"

"If that suits you, then yes, please."

"Excuse me. I need to go and get changed. I'm sure my wife will bring some tea for you in a few minutes."

"Thank you. That would be nice."

"Lara, show Dr. Harrison the way."

I felt queasy inside, with a flutter in my stomach and a sharp pain, and I hoped I wasn't going to burp in front of him. I thought I may have eaten my food too quickly. Mom always said I gobble my food down and that I should be more ladylike and eat slowly.

"Please, follow me," I said, leading the way out to the bench we have under our Gold Medallion tree, whose yellow flowers always make me smile.

I sat and waited for him to say something first while enjoying the shade of the tree. Mom brought out a tray with a pot of tea and a cup for him, and another glass of orange juice for me.

"I didn't know if you prefer lemon or milk, so I've given you the choice, Dr. Harrison."

"Thank you so much. Do you wish to sit while I talk to your daughter, Mrs. Tachikoma?"

"Do you want me to, dear?"

"I'm OK. If I change my mind, can I call for Mom?"

"Of course you can," he replied, peering at me over his glasses.

It was as if he knew me, but I couldn't remember where I'd met him.

Mom went back to the kitchen as he poured the tea and added lemon and sugar. He moved as if his mind was elsewhere, as if this was a distraction.

"This is nice, the garden, I mean. I can see why you would want to be here."

I decided that all adults were weird. Of course I'd want to be there, it was my home, but I said nothing and watched him take a sip of his tea, then put his cup down.

"I imagine you're wondering why I'm here?"

"Am I in some kind of trouble? What have I done? I don't recognize you from school. Who are you, and what do you want?"

"Good, I have unleashed a veritable flood of questions. In order, yes, sort of, but it's not what you think. Nothing really, it's more that something has happened and I'm here to help you. I wouldn't expect you to recognize me, but I hope you will remember me soon enough. And as for me and what I want, that doesn't really matter anymore."

"What kind of an answer is that? You're weird."

He stared at me, his eyes cold. "How old are you?"

"Is that a trick question?"

"Yes, sort of, but humor me, why don't you?"

I didn't see anything to laugh at about my age. "I'm thirteen and a half."

"Really, thirteen and a half, as old as that."

He turned my answer around, and I sensed I was being mocked. "Yes, really."

"I could swear that you're older than that."

"Are you some kind of pervert?"

"Do you think I would answer yes if I were?"

"No, but…you're creeping me out. Are you always this odd?"

He sat there and took another sip of tea. "I expect so. Why don't you ask me some more questions and see where that leads us?"

"Why can't you just tell me why you're here?" I want to hit him.

"Because you're not yet ready to believe my answers."

I let out a sigh of exasperation. "I don't understand. Why wouldn't I believe you? Are you going to tell me lies?"

He took his glasses off and wiped them on his shirt. "I won't tell you any lies, but I will upset you soon."

"Why?" I asked, crossing my arms.

"Upset you?"

I nod.

"Truth is, what I have to tell you might be frightening."

"My daddy says that one should never be frightened of telling the truth."

"He's a wise man. I didn't say I would be frightened by telling you the truth, only that you might find it frightening."

I stared at him. His face was distorted as if his flesh was somehow not real. I drank some juice, as my mouth was oddly dry, and my throat was constricted.

Then my belly felt odd, like it had moved. There was a pressure, as if something was pushing on my bladder. "What is happening to me?"

"That's a good question to ask. What do you think has been happening?"

"Can't you answer a question without asking a question?"

"Well spotted, good. But trust me, I have my reasons. Let me reframe my question for you. Try and remember what you've been doing today."

"Well, I got up this morning, I got dressed, showered, had breakfast. After that I changed and went to my father's dojo over there…" I pointed to the back of the garden. "Where I practiced *iaido* with my father, who is teaching me everything he knows. When we finished, we ate lunch together, and then you rang the doorbell."

He points with his arm. "So over yonder lies the dojo of your father."

"You're laughing at me."

"Do I look like I'm laughing?"

I shake my head.

"Look over there and tell me what you see now."

"Nothing."

"Didn't you say that's where your father's dojo is?"

"Yes, but…" I turn back and the dojo is gone. "This can't be happening."

All of a sudden I'm cold, but I'm sweating. My chest starts to tighten, and I'm finding it hard to breathe.

"Don't be frightened. Nothing bad is going to happen while you're talking to me."

He looks sad, like adults do when they have something bad they have to tell you.

"Who are you?"

"I am Dr. Harrison, and I'm here to help you. You have many questions, and while my presence here is altering your perceptions, you're bound by the *Instrument*. For you to understand my answers you need to become aware of who you are, and what you're doing here."

"*Muzukashi desu neh.*"

"It is difficult, but you must let go; *Mushin.* What you're experiencing is your conscious mind generating what you most want in life."

"What does that mean? What I want most in life is to go out and play."

He smiles at me oddly. "Let me ask you a question that you

will find very upsetting, Lara, and we'll see if going out to play is what you really want to do."

I stared at him. This conversation was getting weirder by the moment. I wanted to stand up and leave, call my parents to come and send him away, but I couldn't. "If I answer the stupid question, will you go?"

"Yes, I will, if you want me to."

"OK, then ask your question, whatever it is."

"How old were you when your father died?"

"It was a few days before my thirteenth birthday."

The memory of his death filled me, my mom crying and me holding her as she told me that Daddy had died in an accident on the way home from work.

"No, that's not right. He's in the kitchen with Mom." I shout, "Mom, Dad, please come out now! This man is frightening me!"

As I waited for the back door to open, the house started to lose its color and turn gray, followed by the sky changing to match it.

The color was draining from the garden, too. I was surrounded by a sea of gray, only broken by the presence of Dr. Harrison and me, who somehow remained unchanged by whatever was happening.

My heart beat faster, and my shoulders clenched tight as I stared up. Above us, the sun changed into a white circle, and the ground fell away beneath the bench we sat on as we flew up through the gray sky.

Everything around us started to turn dark and go black before we entered the white circle, which appeared to be a light that cast no shadow.

My body was shaking all over.

Then we were sitting in space, floating above a planet that was not Earth, but I felt I knew where I was, if only I could remember.

"I can breathe. How can I breathe in space? This can't be real."

"Precisely, very good. This is a simulation, just like the life you've been living for the last four months. None of it is real, but it seems real, doesn't it?"

"Yes, but I want my daddy back."

Tears flowed down my face, and the grief from the loss of my father rushed in and overwhelmed me for a moment. My memories of my father teaching me *iaido* fractured, just a dream of the perfect childhood that I never had, gone. Then the grief fell away as my sense of time returned, leaving me feeling hollow.

"What have you done to me?"

"Nothing, except be here for you. It was inevitable that the simulation you've been living in would break down at some point. I made sure I arrived in time to be with you and help you understand what you've been through, and what is about to happen to you. I want to tell you some important things you need to know if you're going to survive."

"Now you're scaring me again," I said. My body had stopped trembling.

"I know, I'm sorry. It can't be helped, but it could be worse. Be thankful it's not going to be worse than it has to be."

"What could be worse than this?"

"Waking up all alone in the dark with no one and being unable to escape."

"You mean dying, don't you?"

"Eventually, from falling into a coma from thirst and hunger, but yes, your death."

He stood up and I followed him. The bench we were sitting on disappeared behind us.

"Why's this happening to me?"

"The Instrument knew we wanted to talk to it, so it arranged a method whereby we could."

"I'm sorry, but I never asked to talk to the Instrument, whatever that is."

"Not in words, we didn't, but it judged our actions to be a request to meet it. Human beings are astonishingly primitive, which is what enabled us to do what other biological sentients can't. You've no idea how long it has been since the makers died, or how rare biological sentients that can pass through the singers and visit other worlds are."

He paused, sweeping his arm around him.

"The rings in orbit around the planet below protect the surface from the radiation from both the sun and the gas giant. Millions of years ago, the Kerellu lived on the surface of the planet. They were an ancient civilization who were able to use their technology to expand their minds and increase their life spans, but they saw the end of their world, and the end of them. They built the city we found to hold their greatest creation, the Instrument, as a way to save themselves."

I looked down at the planet below, and for a moment I had the sensation of falling toward the ground, my whole equilibrium upset by the perspective. I grabbed on to Dr. Harrison's arm to steady myself.

"It will pass in a moment."

"This seems so real," I said, letting go of him.

"Yes, it does."

"So, are you the Instrument?"

"No, like you, I am inside the machine. The Kerellu were going to use their machines to upload themselves into the Instrument and live forever in worlds created by their imaginations. Billions of Kerellu were scanned down to the molecular level by the machine and recorded."

"So, they're still here watching us."

"Not exactly. They made a mistake. They thought they were

going to live forever, but they only managed to kill themselves instead."

"But you said they were recorded down to the molecular level. How can they be dead if they're recorded?"

"When a piece of music is played and recorded, it's no longer the original, but a copy. A recording of the performance that's limited in how it sounds by the means used to record and play the tune, which can only be repeated as recorded. There's no room for change."

"That's silly, surely they would have foreseen that would happen and plan accordingly. They sound really stupid to have done that to themselves."

"As you said, *muzukashi desu neh*."

He paused for a moment, scratching his beard, which was no longer hair but something fleshy instead.

"You look odd."

"You're starting to see things differently. You should be starting to remember stuff about your life, too."

"Not really. I mean, I'm getting flashes of images, but none of it makes any sense."

"Very soon it will."

"Were we scanned by the machine?"

"No, because if we were, we wouldn't be having this conversation at all—except, of course, if things had turned out differently. Then I suppose we could be talking like this."

"Now you're just rambling nonsense."

"I suppose I am. The thing is, the Kerellu came so close to achieving their dream, only to fall at the last fence. They knew any machine that could store and replicate a representation of them, and the world they lived in, would be limited by the amount of information it could store because the space needed to store the smallest unit of matter would equal the size of the smallest bit of information."

"You lost me there."

"The city below us contains the machine that stores the minds of billions of Kerellu, but even though it is kilometers across, and goes kilometers into the ground below, it isn't big enough to contain a detailed representation of itself and its inhabitants."

"OK, they must have known that, right?" I shrugged.

"Yes, they did, and they came up with a solution they hoped would solve the problem, which they called the Instrument. The systems in this city are linked together, but they're not a truly homogenous gestalt."

"A humongous ge-waht?"

"*Homogenous* means all the same, and *gestalt* means a whole that's greater than the sum of its parts. So, the machines are heterogeneous constructs, all different from each other and, therefore, have no sense of self; they just follow their preprogrammed instructions. The Kerellu built the ultimate Turing machine, which they hoped would be an artificial intellect that would solve their problem."

"I guess that didn't work out so well for them then."

"Ah, good. I see you're starting to be more yourself."

"I'm starting to remember more. This place really messes with your head."

"Exactly. The Instrument has been using your mind to create the illusion of the reality you think you've been experiencing. You see, something marvelous happened when we were connected to the machine. Our presence created chaos, adding complexity to the algorithms that governed the system. Before we arrived, the Instrument existed as part of the machine, trapped by the inexorable logic of the algorithms, where everything is the sum of a set of starting propositions. The Instrument was trapped by the perfection of the mathematical calculations that can predict the answer to every choice."

"What does that mean? The short version please."

"Inside the machine, polynomial time is equal to nondeterministic polynomial time."

"OK, you're not helping here. I think I understood the long answer better."

"Our minds emerge from bodies that are driven by biological processes at the molecular level, which creates complexities we interpret as free will. When we were linked into the machine, it changed the Instrument into the *artellect* the Kerellu had wanted it to be."

"Well, that's great, so yay for us! Now why can't it thank us and let us go home? I'm all for helping dead civilizations be reborn and all, but enough already."

"It's not that simple."

"It never is. Let me guess, there's some kind of catch. It wants to keep us here so it can study us and take over the Earth."

"It's not human, it doesn't have human desires, and everything it wants it has right here."

"Well, why is it letting me go now?"

"Because you're pregnant. There's life growing inside you, and the machine you're inside was designed for a single occupant. This is why what's been happening to you today has occurred. It was inevitable as the process that will lead to you giving birth. This's why I'm able to be with you and not with any of the others."

"How am I'm pregnant?"

The memory of being in bed with Glen flashed into my mind, and the pleasure of knowing him. Dr. Harrison appeared even less human than before, and I was now taller, fully grown.

"You don't have to answer that. I've just remembered."

"You're experiencing something akin to phantom limb syndrome. Inside the machine, we might as well call it *morphic resonance*. We all have a mental picture of the size and shape of our bodies. It's how we can touch our nose with our eyes closed.

As the machine closes down the links and lets go of your mind, your memories and self-image are returning. You're starting to perceive me as I am rather than as I was."

"What's happened to you?"

"Something profoundly frightening, yet also wonderful. I'm no longer the man I once was. I have become the tool of the Instrument. My destiny is now intertwined with it. I'm going to be both the father and mother of the Kerellu."

"That sounds a bit crazy to me."

"I'm no longer fully human, and such descriptions of the malfunction of my mental processes no longer really apply. Such is life, in this case, all our lives."

"Are we all going to become like you?"

"No, because I won't let it happen, which is why I'm helping you now. The Instrument made a mistake when it rewrote my DNA, and my body started changing because it's programmed to obey its makers. I was going to be the first, an experiment to see if it could bring them back. If the experiment worked, then it was going to convert us all, makes us one with it."

"I don't want to be one with the machine."

"And neither did I, but now I think differently. I'm still partly human, and the human part wants my friends to go home. After I give birth to the first of a new generation, I will undergo further changes and may no longer think like I do now. After all, a parent wants to protect its offspring. I can't imagine that I won't want to do the same."

"What does that mean?"

"It means you're on the clock, and in a few days when I give birth I may want you back here to be with me. Even now, I'm beginning to doubt the decision I'm making. The Instrument is only held in check by my choice. If I change my mind, it will be free to act differently."

"Can't it already act? I mean, why allow you any choice at all?"

"Our relationship is like breathing. It happens because the mechanisms of the body are driven by a negative feedback loop. You can choose to hold your breath, but unless prevented by outside events, you will eventually be forced to let it out. What I want matters."

"It sounds like the machine is your slave. Make it do what you want it to do. Change yourself back!"

"Even if I wanted to change back, I can't. As soon as I reversed the process, the machine would no longer act as I wanted. It would not repeat the same mistake twice, and it would change us all. That's why I must stay here, and why you must go before I change my mind."

Tears fell from his eyes, and he began to sob as the world started revolving around me. Then I was falling toward the ground below as I screamed in silence, consumed by the darkness that was enfolding me.

39. AWARENESS

Reality is that which, when you stop believing in it, doesn't go away.

— Philip K. Dick

Captain Lara Atsuko Tachikoma
Planet 1340
Day 180 of Operation Prometheus
Wednesday, June 20, 2074

It was as if I were dreaming of darkness, knowing I was not awake but aware that I was not quite asleep. Images flashed into my mind, and I drifted into a dream where I was in a dojo and my father was teaching me how to draw a sword.

I followed his actions, cutting upward, and saw his arm fall to the ground, blood pumping across the floor as he said, "Again." I faced him, cutting down, splitting his body in two, and then it joined back together into a seamless whole as my blade passed through him.

His face stretched and distorted, his mouth opening and

tentacles bursting forth. I got up and ran screaming from the dojo while my father shouted, "Wait, I have something to tell you!"

I woke up in pitch-blackness and heard myself scream out as I became aware of lying on something hard and cold. Then I started shivering, my throat sore, my mouth dry, and I was panting. As I tried to move my arms, they brushed against something hard. A wall.

I must have been in a box.

I tried to wave my hands in front of my eyes but could see nothing, even though I sensed the movement I was making.

I stroked the bare flesh of my stomach that was no longer as flat as it had once been. It was true. I was pregnant, and I remembered everything. I touched my throat and breathed a sigh of relief as I found my dog tags with my Christmas present from Allison.

Next, I switched on the tac-light. I was surrounded by objects that looked like medical instruments strewn on either side of me, which I could all too easily have imagined were in me before I woke up.

I shuddered, not from the cold but from the sense of being violated by the machines, unable to resist, a passive victim.

As I tried to sit up, I found myself struggling to raise my body, so weak that I was light-headed from the effort. I pushed both my elbows back and pushed again, and finally I was sitting.

My tac-light spread its glow around me, allowing me to see I was sitting in one of the modules we'd found in the cavern. The shadows of the other modules moved around as I swept the light around me.

I wanted to be sick, and I leaned over the edge and dry heaved for a few minutes, retching in pain. Then there was a flutter in my belly, followed by another.

My vision was blurry and I rubbed my face, picking the gunk out of my eyes from being asleep for so long.

Next, I climbed out of the module, which had held me for months, and tried to stand up, but I only managed to roll over the edge and fall to the floor. The only reason it didn't hurt more was because I was totally unable to stiffen before I hit the floor. Rather, I flowed into it like a rag doll.

I decided that lying on the floor was good. Be one with the floor. Then I passed out.

Light was in my eyes as I came around to find my tac-light shining in my face, which was covered in drool. Not my best look, and it reminded me of the one time I had become so drunk I had collapsed on the sidewalk.

Laughing at my predicament, I started coughing.

I rolled over and managed to push myself into a sitting position, flopped against the module I'd spent dreaming my life away in. It all felt so real, but the cold of the floor was numbing my ass, and that had a reality that chilled me to the bone.

There's a saying that when you can't run, you walk, and when you can't walk, you crawl, and the rest I had forgotten, though I was sure it would come back to me.

So, I began crawling toward the trucks that were parked where I remembered them. I saw a figure standing in the darkness, and for a moment I thought I had to help, but I realized it was only an android frozen in place after its power ran out.

Beyond the android was the truck that had my things in it, and I worked my way across the floor.

It was as if I were traversing an assault obstacle course, except that time it was not gunfire that was keeping me on the floor but my inability to stand up and walk. So, I kept pulling and pushing myself with my arms and legs as I crawled across the floor toward my goal.

I didn't want to die there; I didn't want my unborn baby to die there; and I didn't want anyone else dying there because I was too feeble to step up and do what had to be done.

I heard sobbing and realized that tears were streaming down my face as the fear of failure overwhelmed me. But I had no way of telling how long it was taking me to crawl to the back of the truck and the ladder that led up inside. It might have been a few minutes, or an hour may have passed. I was dizzy and dehydrated, and my mouth was dry.

So, I paused and caught my breath. I'd suffered more after completing an eight-kilometer run, way worse in fact.

I managed to rise up and sit on my knees in *seiza*.

Funny, I remembered that and the pain of sitting on the hard floor on my insteps. It was enough to spur me to reach forward, grab the ladder, and pull myself upright. For a moment, my vision went gray, but I concentrated on holding on to the ladder, and the sensation passed.

I took my first step onto the rung, and the pain from being barefooted was excruciating, like someone had stabbed me in my foot.

I gripped the rung with my toes and pulled myself up one step. The next wasn't any easier, or the next, but there were only a few more rungs before I could reach up and open the door, allowing myself to flop facedown on the floor of the container with my ass hanging half out the back of the vehicle.

I was glad there was no one around to take an incriminating picture and post it on the Web for all to see. On the other hand, if there were somebody there, I could've asked them for their help. Then I passed out again.

I awakened with a jolt as I slid backward.

I scrabbled and twisted my body, pulling myself farther inside the truck, where the smoothness of the floor was a blessed relief to the harsh surface of the ground outside. My hands and knees were bleeding, and the front of my body was rubbed red raw with marks over my belly and breasts.

I've been in worse states than this, but usually that had been the result of someone trying to kill me.

My tac-light illuminated the interior of the truck container, and I used the posts supporting the bunk beds to stand myself up and grab the first aid box on the wall. I managed to lean on the beds as I made my way to the rear where the sink was so I could clean myself up.

It was the longest forty feet I've ever walked, and I have to admit I had to sit down every few feet to rest for a few moments.

Luckily, there was a plastic chair at the back of the container, and I used it to support myself to traverse the last few feet to the sink before sitting down on it. Nothing was working, and I figured that the batteries must be dead.

However, the water at the sink worked by gravity, and I filled the bowl and slowly began to wash myself. Once clean, I dressed the cuts that were bleeding and popped a painkiller. I was sure my mom would've *tutted* at me for the mess I'd made, and I'd have told her that sometimes bad is good enough. She would have laughed.

"What next?" I said out loud.

Then I knew I was losing it, as I was talking to myself.

Get dressed first, and then I must release the others, I thought. I stood up and allowed the sense of dizziness to pass before I shuffled back to my rack to get my clothes. I opened my rack's coffin locker and swing it upward, which almost defeated me, but I was able to prop it open and grab my underwear.

My bra was tight, and I had to loosen the waist on my pants. So, definitely fatter, and as I'd not been hitting the cream donuts, I guessed this meant I really was pregnant.

It was not something I'd been planning on doing anytime soon, and when I'd been younger, the thought would have appalled me. Then it was a problem for later.

I dressed and managed to pull my boots on to stand up. My

body felt weak, but I had to use the power of my mind to carry on. I took it one step at a time to climb down the ladder and back out into the darkness of the cavern.

I oriented myself and figured the best way to get to where I wanted to go next.

Turning left, I leaned against the side of the truck and began to make my way around the camp's laager. Before crossing the gap between each truck, I took a moment to center myself and breathe before staggering to the next truck.

My PAD blinked at me.

The walking recharged it enough that it was telling me I had urgent matters to attend to. No shit, like I needed reminding.

A screen of red flags scrolled in front of me. Given the nature of things, 99 percent of them were for missing reporting deadlines. Others were urgent system maintenance deadlines, and the last on the list was one telling me we should've left there six days ago to return home.

The clock told me we had less than ninety-four hours to travel three thousand kilometers. So, no pressure then, just every pressure if I was going to save us all from a fate that was probably worse than death. Assuming that having one's DNA rewritten, and being turned into something nonhuman, was a fate worse than death, of course.

I really didn't want to find out, though.

I could measure time, at least now that I knew how long we'd been sleeping, and how long it was taking me to walk to my destination. Then I reached the truck and climbed up inside to where the MACE suits were racked. I found mine, and to my relief it had enough power to get going and enough fuel to recharge itself. I stepped in and suited up, never more grateful for the power assist.

Walking out was a victory. All I had to do then was get

everyone else up. My priorities were to get the trucks ready to move, secure the androids, and get everyone home safe.

I headed back to the modules and saw that one was missing. Possibly removed by some means, but I didn't have the time to worry about that as I walked around looking at the people lying in wait under shimmering plasma fields, like the one we'd crossed when entering the building all those months ago.

I found Wachowski and was drawn to the console with its strange keyboard. I placed my hands on it, and it was as if I knew what I was doing. I pressed a series of keys. The plasma screen turned off, and various tubes pulled themselves out of her mouth, nose, and genital area with a combination of escaping air and slurping, which made me feel squeamish. Nothing happened, and then she took a deep breath and her eyelids began to flutter.

I waited and waited, willing her to revive and hoping that nothing had gone wrong. What if I'd done something to harm her? She moaned and coughed suddenly, and I heard the sound of another human being for the first time since I'd woken up.

"Wachowski, it's me. Time to wake up, Marine."

"What the fuck?" she said as she opened her eyes, which were rheumy from sleep. "Is that you, Captain?"

"Who else would it be?"

"What's happening? I was just celebrating Thanksgiving with my family."

"You've been living inside a virtual world for several months, which the alien machine that runs this city placed us all into. Here, let me help you sit up."

"Is that why I'm totally naked?"

"Good to see that your powers of observation haven't failed you, Sergeant. The Corps will be making you into an officer if you carry on like that."

"Sheesh, way to go on how to cheer someone up. Whoa, I'm all dizzy."

"You will be, I was to, but I need you to concentrate and let me help you get out of this thing."

I lifted her up and carried her back to the truck where we shared sleeping quarters.

"Will you be able to manage to clean yourself up and get dressed?"

"If you did it, I'm sure I can."

"That's the spirit."

"Did I swear at you?"

"That's the least of our problems. Don't sweat it. I need you to focus on getting dressed, and then I'll help you get suited up. We're on the clock, and I need you up and at 'em."

"Aye, aye, Captain."

I left her crawling to get her stuff and made my way back to the next module. I chose Ferretti next and let my fingers do their stuff.

Somehow, Dr. Harrison had planted a memory of what keys to press when he'd been talking to me, and I wondered if I now knew *iaido*.

Ferretti had grown a beard, and his hair was no longer regulation length. I could also see he had lost some weight, which seemed odd given what had happened. I should ask Keith. After all, he was a corpsman, and he might be able to explain what had happened to Ferretti.

Ferretti mumbled something and coughed.

"Take it easy, Ferretti. You've been asleep for the last four months or so."

"Ma'am, is that you?"

"Sure is. Who did you expect to see?"

"I was just talking to Allison at the dinner table with our son."

"You've been living in a virtual reality that was designed to fulfill your desires. I know it seemed real, but it isn't."

"Is she safe?"

"As safe as any of us are as long as we don't hang around here too long. Please sit up, and I'll help you over to the truck so you can get dressed."

I helped Ferretti swing his legs over the side and pulled him up and out.

"I'm butt naked, ma'am."

"Don't worry, Ferretti. It's not the first time I've seen a man naked. I can carry you if you want."

"No, thank you, ma'am. Please just help me walk."

I supported him under his shoulder, and we hobbled over to the back of the truck where Wachowski appeared dressed and looking a little wan.

Ferretti looked up at her. "No smartass comments from you."

"Aw shucks, you're no fun."

"Help me get him up inside."

"Sure thing," she said as we got Ferretti inside the container. "Nice ass, though."

"I said no smartass comments."

"That wasn't smart. It was just an appreciation of your butt."

"Enough! Ferretti, get yourself cleaned up and dressed, and I'll be back to help you get into your suit. Wachowski, with me, time for you to earn your living around here."

I assisted her over to the truck with the power armor and helped her inside so she could get into her suit.

"You good to go?"

"Sure thing, ma'am. What are your orders?"

"I need the trucks ready to go as soon as possible. We're on the clock, so plan our journey so we arrive back with some margin for error. Any problems, you tell me."

I left her with that task, made my way back to the modules, and chose to bring back Keith next. He would be needed if any of the civilians had problems, and he might have suggestions to help with being confined for four months in this place without exercise. I was moving like a walking corpse, and I imagined everyone else would be, too.

Keith came around with no problems, apart from coughing phlegm into his beard.

"Where am I?"

"Do you remember the mission and the underground cavern?"

"Yes, but we got back and I've been training to be a doctor. I was assisting in a procedure a few moments ago."

"The machine has had us all trapped here, giving us what we wanted inside a virtual world. None of what you experienced was real."

"It sure felt real. Did it seem real for you, Captain?"

"It did, Keith, and it may be that what you learnt inside the machine will come in handy in the future, but I need you to get your act together so we can get everyone out of the machines."

I helped him out of the module, and he fainted as he tried to stand, but I caught him before he hit the deck and carried him back to the truck.

"Ferretti, are you good to go?"

"Sorry, ma'am. I think I passed out for a moment. Just got to pull my boots on."

I slung Keith over my shoulder, climbed up the ladder, rolled him onto a spare bed, and made sure he was conscious.

"Get yourself dressed, and I'll be back for you soon."

"Aye, aye, ma'am."

"Come on, Ferretti. Time to get you suited and booted." I helped him walk over and got him in his PACE suit. "OK, once you have retrieved all the androids, I want them to have a hard reset."

"You think they've been hacked, ma'am. Are you sure? The last time that happened they went berserk."

"I think the machine used them to place us inside those modules. I also want you to secure all of our networks."

"How the heck did that happen? I don't remember anything after going to sleep."

"Neither do I, but I'm sure we'll find out. I need my networks secured as soon as possible, because we need to get out of this place, and I don't want the alien machine preventing our leaving. Do you understand?"

"Yes, ma'am. You can count on me. I'm on it."

"Will you need any help?"

"Nelson knows her way around the systems. She'd be good to have."

"OK, leave her to me."

Ferretti walked over to the control truck and I went back, found Nelson, and deactivated her module. It was some neat trick pulling off the muscle memory of what keys to press. And I realized that any alien civilization capable of doing this to us was probably one we would need to think twice about before contacting again.

I saw Nelson stirring. "Nelson, wake up, you've been sleeping."

She opened her eyes and coughed, and I gave her a sip of water. "Mary, where are you?"

"Mary's not here. We're in the cavern where we made camp to escape the radiation outside. Do you remember?"

"I remember Mary's dead. She died on Two Moons."

"Yes, she did, but we're not on Two Moons, we're on another planet, underground. You've been living inside a virtual world for the last four months, and it's time we leave and go home."

Nelson sat up, and I lifted her up and carried her back to the truck.

"It seemed so real."

"It did for me, too."

"What did you experience inside the machine, Captain?"

"I spent the time with my father I always wished I could've had."

"I'm sorry I'm crying."

"No need to apologize. We may all be different, but this is affecting everyone. I need you to focus on the here and now. The first thing is for you to get dressed, and once suited I want you to help Master Sergeant Ferretti secure our network. He says you're the best for the job. You got that?"

"Yes, I can do that."

Keith was waiting at the truck. "Need a hand, ma'am?"

"Sure," I said as I lifted Nelson up into the back of the truck, and Keith guided her in, stopping her from banging her head.

"I just realized I'm naked."

"Don't worry about it. I'm a corpsman. I've seen worse things than your naked body, Nelson."

"I would've thought this was one of the better bodies you've seen, Keith."

"Trust me when I say you've looked better. Now go get dressed."

I looked at Keith. "Time to get you to work, Doc." I helped him down off the back of the truck and assisted him over to where the suits were stored. "I want to get our team up first and then the civilians. Do you foresee any problems I need to be told about?"

"To be honest, I foresee a whole load of problems. For instance, some of our older scientists' respiratory systems may have been compromised, given they've been without medication for the last four months. But it's nothing I can't handle."

"Good to hear it, Doc. Now go get your medical kit sorted out, and prep anything else you might need. Report to me when you're ready. Oh, by the way, for your information, in case it's not obvious, I'm pregnant."

Keith gave me a look as I left him to go and release the next person.

I decided to pull Green out next and then Mitchell as they could both help Wachowski prep the trucks for the journey back. I was pretty sure that something would have broken during the four months, and a spared hand to help would not go amiss. Green was sporting this year's fashion accessory of a beard and nonregulation haircut, which made me glad to be a woman.

Imagine having to shave one's face every day.

I supported Green to the truck and found Nelson waiting there. I then repeated the task of getting her suited and off to help Ferretti while I dragged my sorry corpse back to revive Mitchell.

Keith came over as Mitchell awoke. "Captain, may I suggest you leave him for me, and that you rouse Adams next?"

"Sure, but why Adams?"

"By my reckoning, you've probably been at this for over two hours, and you will need to eat—that's not negotiable, Captain. Besides everyone is in pretty bad shape, and we will all need to pace ourselves."

"I'll take your recommendation under advisement, Doc."

"What's happening?" Mitchell whispered, then coughed.

"Airman, what's the last thing you remember?"

"I was out with my girl. We were having a romantic meal for two."

"Well, the good news is that when we get back, you will be able to do that for real. The bad is that you've been dreaming inside a virtual world."

"But how could it be so real?"

"Everyone was fooled. Doc here is going to get you back to the truck."

"Captain, slow down and take it easy. I've seen your medical readout, and you're the only one of us who seems to know how to operate these machines."

"I promise I'll take it easy once everyone is out of these damn machines."

"Captain, I mean it. Eat this energy bar, and I want you to drink this bottle of water, too. All of it."

"Doc, yes, Doc! Have I ever said that you remind me of my old drill instructor?"

Keith laughed. "All of it, and I'll be back to check on you."

Keith took Mitchell away, and as Flores was in the next module, I figured I would revive him next and wait for Keith to return. I shook myself alert. I need to up my game. I might've been living as a thirteen year old girl for the last four months, but now I need to be a Marine.

Flores woke up and was the first man I'd seen that day without a full beard.

"It's OK, Flores. You're back in the land of the living."

"Is that you, Captain?"

"Yes it is, Private. Were you expecting to see someone else?"

"Why am I lying here naked?"

"Long story short, because the machine that runs this city put us all inside these modules and plugged us in to play with our minds for the last four months."

"I was with my ancestors; their spirits were telling me about the traditions of the tribe."

"Everybody says it seemed real. No shame in being fooled, Flores."

"You're wrong. It was real. Not everything that's real has to be physical."

"OK," I said, parsing the meaning behind what he said, "but do you know where you're now?"

"I'm in the alien underground cavern we found."

"That will do. Now let me help you sit up, and Doc will be along in a moment to help you back to the truck so you can get dressed."

Keith arrived and gestured for me to continue drinking my

water and finish eating my energy bar. By the time I had munched my way through the sticky sweet *cardboard* snack, he was back.

"Good, I see you have eaten. Now let's get Adams up so we can all have some proper food."

"No. I want the rest of my people up to get my convoy ready to roll. Adams can wait until last. Then I want Dr. O'Neill and Dr. Leung up so they can help you with the rest of the civilians."

Keith looked like he was going to argue.

I put on my "game" face, and pointed at the modules.

"Roger that, ma'am. But, I will want to check you once we're done. It's not every day that I get the chance to provide prenatal care in the field."

"Why do I think you're enjoying my condition far too much?"

"It makes a change from dealing with the wounded and the dead, ma'am."

I couldn't argue with that.

40. ON THE CLOCK

A pessimist sees the difficulty in every opportunity; an optimist sees the opportunity in every difficulty.

— SIR WINSTON CHURCHILL

Master Sergeant Ferretti
Planet 1340
Day 180 of Operation Prometheus
Wednesday, June 20, 2074

"Nelson, how you doing?"

"Nearly finished stage one, Master Sergeant, and I'm running battery reconditioning now."

"What do we have from their feeds prior to shutdown?"

"After the first twelve hours, nothing. I can confirm the system was hacked in thirty-one minutes. I always thought they were unbreakable."

"Nothing's unbreakable, as you well know. Remember, I want hard resets as soon as stage one protocols are complete. I will go and report on our progress now."

"Understood. I'm on it."

Ferretti left Nelson overseeing the androids and made his way over to where the captain was talking to Keith about the revival of the scientists.

"Dr. Leung is in a bad way, and I've got him on an IV drip. I'm surprised he's still alive, given the condition of his lungs. I give him a sixty to forty percent chance of surviving."

"He's a tough one, Doc," said the captain. "I'd put money on him making it back. How's Dr. Smith?"

"I've put him in a pressure chamber, too, but I suspect it's mostly anxiety. Of us all, he seems to be the one who was most disoriented by his experiences."

"I caught that, too. My Russian is pretty weak beyond *hello*, *goodbye*, and *thank you*. Did he say any more to you?"

"Nothing of note. Just that he had been dreaming of learning to speak Russian."

"Odd man. How are the rest of our scientists?"

"They're all doing as well as can be expected. I've got them all suited up to prevent injury from falls. I've programmed all our suits to actively stimulate muscle strength to counter the long period of enforced bed rest."

"Good, thanks, Doc. I guess that's the best we can do this side of getting home. Master Sergeant, what have you got for me?"

"All the androids are in their cradles, and we're about to do a hard reset. The logs shows it took the city's machine intelligence just over half an hour to crack our networks."

"I'm surprised it didn't manage it sooner than that. Still, at least now we know it means we can maintain some system security for a limited period against alien cyberattacks."

"How does that help us, ma'am?"

"If push comes to shove, it means we can hold out for half an hour before having to reboot the network. It's not much, but I'll take anything I can get if things go south."

Ferretti saw the worry in her face. "What are you not saying, ma'am?"

She looked up at him. "All the things I don't know. If I'm to believe what I was told when I was inside the machine, we've got to get out of this place, and the only thing that's allowing us is the fact that Dr. Harrison has some shred of humanity left in him."

Wachowski and Langford joined the group.

"Ah good, you're both here. Wachowski, how's the transit time from here back to the pillars shaping up?"

"Looking at the route, I'd say it will be tight. Three thousand kilometers in eighty-nine hours allowing for fueling stops and rest breaks only means we will have to average just under forty-eight kilometers per hour."

"Surely that's doable?"

"Sure, it's doable, but only if nothing breaks down."

"Come up with a set of contingency plans to cover breakdowns and send it to my PAD for review. Ferretti, during the fuel stops, we will need to prep our CASE suits."

"Yes, ma'am. I'd suggest Avari, Meireles, and either Mitchell or Green to spread the workload."

"Sure, good call. I should have thought of that. Langford, I want you to start thinking about how to collapse the tunnel that leads up to the pillars with the materials we have. Any questions?"

Langford shook her head.

"With all due respect, Captain, you've been pushing yourself harder than anyone else."

"I'll sleep when I'm dead, Petty Officer. No arguments from you. We have to get back to the pillars in time to get home. Everything else is secondary to that goal; otherwise this mission is in serious trouble. How soon until we can leave here?"

"We're Oscar Mike once we get aboard. Ready to roll."

"OK, people, time to get this show moving."

He watched the captain stand and noticed the concern on Keith's face. They walked back to their respective trucks and were rolling as the last door slammed shut, Wachowski pulling no punches on getting the convoy moving.

Only the headlights of the trucks lit the route back, and it was obvious now the city had lured them in.

As they drove past the central shaft, light from above allowed them to see across the gap. But nothing moved this time.

Ferretti wondered if their way would be blocked as the convoy drove down the passageway leading to the spiral ramp that would take them up to the surface of the city. He tensed as the trucks spiraled up the ramp, barely slowing as they wound their way outside of the tower. The final barrier was crossed, and he squinted as his eyes adjusted to the brightness of the afternoon sun, which cast long shadows everywhere.

Nothing but the flickering shadows moved.

Then he remembered the radiation, and he checked the monitors and saw the figures were in the same range as when they had first arrived on this planet. Had the alien machine also manipulated the rise in radiation to get them to go inside the tower in the first place?

He doubted he would ever get an answer, but given everything else that had happened to them, it seemed highly likely.

41. RECOLLECTIONS

A man's character is his fate.

— HERACLITUS

Dr. Allison O'Neill
Magnetic Anomaly Project Scientist
Day 181 of Operation Prometheus
Thursday, June 21, 2074

Allison sat next to Vincent in the front seat of the truck, sandwiched between him and Green.

He hadn't said a word to her so far, and she could tell his mind was elsewhere, as he repeatedly checked the truck's readouts. Allison was still processing what had happened to her, made worse by the pain from having to wear her light mobility suit.

"Sitting in these things is not my idea of fun." Allison said.

"Mine either, ma'am," said Green.

Vincent looked at her. "Being suited up is never fun. I read once they thought that putting people inside suits would increase their endurance on missions."

"Yeah, like anyone really worked that one through, Sergeant."

"Did people really think that?" she asked.

"Yes, ma'am."

"Green, go catch some shut-eye in the back, then you can switch with me at the wheel."

"Sure thing, Master Sergeant."

Green made it look easy to move around the seat and get in the back of the truck's cabin. It had to be down to all the practice the military had in working in suits.

She could hear music coming from his earbuds, enough to drown out the drone of the truck as it bounced along the remains of the road, leaving a dust cloud in its trail and making it impossible to see outside the vehicle clearly.

"Well?" she asked.

"Well, what?" he replied.

"You haven't said a word since we woke up."

"What's to say? Everything that happened while we were inside the virtual reality created by the machine was false. Now we have to deal with the reality of the situation we're in."

"That's not what I meant. How are you?"

"Lucky to be alive. Grateful you're alive, and angry at what happened to us."

"We're safe now though, aren't we?"

"Safer, but we won't truly be safe until we pass through the pillars and get home."

"So the rumors are true then."

"What rumors would those be?"

"That the machines in the city didn't just let us out to go home. That something bad happened, and Dr. Harrison died."

"It seems you've pretty much worked it out for yourself."

"What happened back there?" She laid her hand on his arm.

"The machine in the city came to the conclusion that since we wanted to communicate with it, we could be kept there forever. It then decided we could be useful in other ways."

"Useful in other ways how?"

"I don't fully understand what the captain said, but the machine wanted to use us to bring back its creators. It didn't seem to matter what we had to say about that."

"That's understandable. We can hardly expect it to be human like us."

"If we hadn't been lucky, we would still be trapped there and our bodies changed to serve the needs of the machines in the city. I don't want to begin to imagine what it would've meant for us."

"Did the captain say how the machines were going to change us?"

"She said something about rewriting our DNA and turning us into human-alien hybrids. The bottom line is none of us would've been truly human any longer. The thought of that happening to you, to us, and everyone else is too horrible to imagine. I'd rather be dead than be enslaved and turned into some kind of inhuman monster."

"Is that what happened to Peter?"

"That's what the captain told me Dr. Harrison said. His last act of being human was to release us. Now he's back there, changing into something that may not want us to get home."

"But everything we experienced there was created by the machine. How do we know anything the captain was told is true?"

"We don't, but it's all we have to go on."

"But how is her experience inside the machine any more or less true than anyone else's experience?"

"Because we're here now. Otherwise, we'd still all be dreaming in our perfect worlds until the time came for us to be changed."

"And you know that how exactly?"

"Something was happening to the captain that caused her to be kicked out of the simulated world she was living in. That's all I can say."

"Was she ill or something?"

"I can't say. Please don't ask me any more questions, Allison."

"You never call me Allison when you're on duty."

"That only goes to prove there's a first time for everything, but don't plan on me making a habit out of it."

"Oooh, you can be so maddening."

"Just be thankful we're not technically in the same chain of command."

"I'll never understand the military. It's all rigid formality and courtesies that make no sense to anyone outside of it."

"I can't deny it must look like that, but those courtesies and formalities exist to protect and serve the people within the organization. Without them, we would have nothing to guide us when the hindbrain takes over."

"I never expected to ever hear you say *hindbrain* in a conversation."

"I must have been hanging out with you too much and something has rubbed off on me. As you've told me, when stressed, humans revert to basic responses, and military training is about overriding our fear and carrying out our duty under the direst of circumstances."

"That's what frightens me about you, the fact that your job can put you into harm's way. What would I do if you died?"

"It must be hard for you to understand, but I always wanted to do my duty and serve my country. Other couples live with this. I'm sure we can too."

"Really. When did we become like other couples?"

"We're a couple, aren't we?"

"I guess, but we haven't actually talked much about where our relationship is going."

His shoulders tightened as she spoke. "If it looks like a duck, walks like a duck, and quacks like a duck, it has to be a duck, right?" Ferretti said.

"Is that it, the sum total of your thoughts on where our relationship is going? I could so hit you right now."

"I could so kiss you, but I can't. We don't always get to do what we want when we want to do it. That's life."

"So where does that leave us then?"

"Where do you want to be?"

"I saw what you did there. What's happened to you? What's happening to us?"

"Let me ask you. What did you dream about when you were inside the machine?"

"Change of subject much?"

"Go on, humor me."

"Well, the last thing I remembered was getting ready to shut down for the night and go home. Of course, I now realize none of it was real, but I was spending my days working on the samples I had collected back at the base. I was discovering new things about the nucleotide sequences, and it was so exciting. I dreamed I would be the first to publish my findings about astrobiology, which would revolutionize the field."

"Anything else?"

"Only the shock of discovering that all my samples were dead, and how heartbroken I was. It was such a waste, but hopefully I can retrieve something from studying the remains."

"I see."

Allison saw him close off as he spoke, recognizing in his face him shutting himself down. She waited for him to say something more, but realized something had happened to him inside the machine.

"What did you experience?"

"We were together as a family. You were expecting our second child, and we were in love and happy."

"Oh, for how long?"

"It seemed like several years, but none of what I experienced was real. It still feels real, but you never experienced what I did. I not only lost my life with you, but our children too."

"I don't know what to say. That's such a horrible thing to have gone through."

"Only the feeling of loss when I woke up was horrible. Having you, our child, and you being pregnant with our second was the best thing that's never happened to me."

"How can you stand it?"

"I can because I must. We have to get back home. If we don't, then there will never be another chance for the life I want to live with you."

She cried, sobbing as the tears rolled down her face for his loss. "I'm so sorry."

42. FEAR, UNCERTAINTY & DOUBT

The man who has ceased to fear has ceased to care.

— F. H. Bradley

Sergeant Wachowski
Planet 1340
Day 181 of Operation Prometheus
Thursday, June 21, 2074

Wachowski felt a tap on her shoulder.

Dr. Reynolds asked, "Hey, Sergeant, can I ask how Dr. Smith and David are doing? Have you heard anything?"

"The last report said Dr. Smith was out of the pressure chamber, but Dr. Leung remains under the treatment of our corpsman. Don't worry, Keith will do his best to keep him alive and get him home."

"I hope so, I like David and his wife, Grace. They make a nice team. Not full of themselves like Dr. Smith."

"Can't speak to the latter comment, Dr. Reynolds, but I'm sure we can all agree that the Leungs are highly thought of."

"Yeah, they're always ready to make us a hot drink."

"Is that all you can think to say, Flores?"

"It's true, Sergeant. They go out of their way to be nice. Everyone likes them."

"Sergeant, what happens when we get back to the cavern?" asked Dr. Reynolds.

"If we arrive in time, then we get to go back home. All the other possibilities appear to be less than optimal for our survival."

Wachowski didn't add she would prefer to have a little more of a safety margin than the thirty minutes she had calculated for their journey time. Also, she didn't mention the worry about two of the trucks at risk of breaking down.

"So, how are we doing?" asked Dr. Reynolds.

"So far, we're meeting the hourly mileage targets, which means the convoy will make it back in time to go through the pillars on schedule."

"Can anything go wrong to prevent us making it in time?" asked Dr. Reynolds.

"I'm not sure how to answer that, Doc. Any number of things could go wrong, but it's probably best if we don't jump fences before we get to them."

"You can rely on Sergeant Wachowski to do her job, Tyrone," said Dr. Wilson.

"That's not what I'm worried about. Dammit, hasn't anyone considered the possibility that the aliens might be waiting for us when we arrive? I know we searched the cavern and all, but that doesn't mean there weren't things we didn't find."

"That's a good point, but what leads you to believe anything back at the cavern was in working order? Everything we found seemed unusable," said Dr. Wilson.

"You mean apart from us being able to open the doors, and all."

"I'm sure if the aliens had been aware of us, they would have responded, just like they did in the city."

"That's one hell of an assumption you're making there."

"Dr. Reynolds, this convoy is armed, and if anything does jump out of the walls, it will be met with deadly force. Our Browning fifties can chew up anything short of main battle tanks, especially in close quarters combat," Wachowski said.

"You see, I'm just so not reassured by that statement, Sergeant. I'd rather not be sitting inside this truck in the middle of a firefight."

Dr. Wilson asked, "What's got you all riled up?"

"This is not me being riled up. This is me being scared witless."

"What's put the scare on you?"

"You do remember that all our asses were inside some alien machine up to a couple of days ago. I mean, people haven't forgotten what has happened to us all, have they?"

"Do I look stupid to you?"

"I was just wondering whether the experience had affected your IQ, Adam. Seriously, is our only plan to run home? I don't know about all of you, but I will never forget what happened inside the machine."

"What happened to you, Dr. Reynolds?" Wachowski asked.

"I dreamed I met the aliens who made the city. They called themselves the *Kereeloo*, and I lived among them, learning their ways while being told their history. They built their city a million years ago so they could survive their sun turning into a red giant, and then they uploaded their consciousnesses into the machine and died. Every single one of them committed suicide knowing it was the only hope they had to survive."

"I met them, too. Though they called themselves the *Karelo* in my dream," said Dr. Wilson.

"The captain called them the Kerellu. Are we remembering this right?" asked Wachowski.

"Probably, the difference in the way the name is pronounced means nothing. It's just our way of interpreting what they were called. The thing is, can you imagine having to choose to kill yourself to be uploaded into the machine?" said Dr. Reynolds.

"I'm not sure I can, but they were desperate to escape," said Dr. Wilson.

"Strikes me as an odd decision for them to make, though. If they're this überadvanced race, why didn't they go through the pillars or make spaceships or something?"

"A good point, Sergeant, but my guess is they couldn't go through the pillars, and we already know that cosmic rays will destroy human DNA over long journeys. With the sun expanding and radiation increasing maybe they had no other options," said Dr. Wilson.

"What did you see in your dream, Adam?" asked Dr. Reynolds.

"I spent all my time studying the stars and the planets in this system. When I awoke and found out Peter was dead, I couldn't believe I'd never see him again. I'll never be able to share all the things I experienced."

"Surely, what happened inside the machine wasn't real."

"Depends on what you mean by real. Sure, everything was created by the machine, but it obeyed the laws of physics. I see no reason not to trust my judgment about that. After all, it would be easier to present real data than try to fake stuff that was convincing."

Wachowski asked, "Do you really believe that, Doc?"

"I'm sure I have collected enough data while we were here to prove it's true. I can compare it with my memories of stuff I did inside the machines. It's small enough compensation for my loss," said Dr. Wilson.

Wachowski was more concerned with the present problems than theoretical knowledge based on memories.

She tagged two trucks whose batteries were overheating from being drained flat over four months, which might cause serious problems if they failed. However, she'd reset both the trucks' protocols to prevent their engines from being switched off.

Damn the fuel efficiency; if the batteries went, they would lose time jump-starting them. Time they could ill afford to waste with only a thirty-minute margin to work with.

43. LOSS

Happiness depends upon ourselves.

— ARISTOTLE

Dr. Adam Wilson
Magnetic Anomaly Project Scientist
Planet 1340
Day 182 of Operation Prometheus
Friday, June 22, 2074

The truck slowed down for another rest break, waking Adam as it lurched to a halt.

It felt like he'd only just dozed off as he opened his eyes and saw the glimmer of light on the horizon that presaged the coming dawn.

Wearing his light mobility suit made sitting and lying uncomfortable, but the military doctor had insisted they all needed to wear them for the journey. The fact that the suit was making his muscles twitch to restore lost tone didn't help matters, either.

"Time to relieve yourselves if you need to, next stop in four hours," said Sergeant Wachowski as she swung herself out of the cab and went off to check the trucks for signs of problems that might slow them down.

"Hell, how does she manage to stay so bright and cheerful?" asked Dr. Reynolds.

"She's a morning person, sir. That or she has the special skill that all Marine sergeants possess of being able to fake it so well that no one can tell the difference," said Private First Class Flores.

"Hey, Adam, you awake?" asked Dr. Reynolds.

"I am now, what with the door slamming and all the shouting going on."

"Just reminding you it's my turn to lie out for the next four hours."

"Sure. I need to relieve my bladder anyway." Adam rolled himself over and sat up, rubbing his eyes. He avoided stumbling out of the door and falling to the ground by the dint of having grabbed the handle above the door. This meant he wrenched his arm as he swung down to the ground, landing on both feet.

"You should be careful about overdoing it, Dr. Wilson. Remember, your muscles are still recovering from being unused for four months."

He turned and saw the captain looking at him. Like Sergeant Wachowski, she seemed to be fully alert and oriented to everything happening around her.

"I may have pulled a muscle doing that."

"If you're in pain, ask our corpsman for something."

"I will. Captain, can I speak to you for a moment?"

"I thought you were, Dr. Wilson."

"Yeah, I suppose we are. What I mean is, can you tell me anything about what happened to Peter back in the city?"

"He told me he was chosen by the machine that ran the city

and changed into something that wasn't human. His module was no longer in the room when I awoke."

"Did he say anything else?"

"Some other stuff I'm putting in my report. I'm still trying to make sense of it and remember everything he told me. He sacrificed himself so we would have a chance to get back home. We were his friends."

"Thank you, Captain. I miss him."

"As do I, Dr. Wilson. If there's nothing else you want to speak about, I'd suggest you take the last few minutes we have here to empty your bladder."

Adam turned and walked a few feet away from the side of the convoy and pissed on the barren soil for taking his friend away from him. He looked back the way they had come, but after traveling so far, no sign of the city remained.

"Dr. Wilson, come on, it's time to go now!" shouted Private First Class Flores, waving him back to the truck.

Adam turned and walked as fast as he could. He climbed up and sat in the front with Flores and Wachowski while Tyrone took his turn to catch some sleep in the back of the truck for the next four hours.

The clock was counting down the time for their return. Adam realized that he held the key that would allow them to all make it home if they missed the pillars opening.

He pulled up the database on his PAD and started working through the problem, refining his search parameters.

"Hey, what you doing?" asked Dr. Reynolds.

"I thought you were trying to sleep."

"*Trying* being the operative word. So, humor me here, what are you doing? I'm sure whatever you say will be like a lullaby that sends me to sleep."

"You mean bore you to sleep?"

"Don't go putting words in my mouth, but yes. Whenever you

go into technical details about stuff, I do find myself falling asleep. No offense meant."

"I'm sure. Anyway, I'm working out our options if we don't make it back to the pillars in time for our transit home, using my database to work out how to get back by traveling across the network."

"That sounds good."

"Yeah, well, some of the transits wouldn't be suitable for the convoy to traverse, so it's turning out to be a slightly trickier problem than I imagined, as instead of having fourteen hundred possible connections, we can only use about a hundred and fifty. Even then, not all of those are traversable."

Adam looked back and saw that Tyrone was asleep on the rear seat.

"That worked like a charm," said Sergeant Wachowski.

"I suppose. Still, it does rather make me look like the most boring person in the world to talk to."

"I'm sure that's not true. You have friends to talk to?"

"Not anymore. He's dead, or as good as dead."

"You mean Dr. Harrison."

"Yes. The captain told me about what happened to her and what Peter had told her."

"You know we all owe our escape to him, don't you?"

"I do, but I'd trade that just to have him back."

"Then we'd all be trapped inside the machines in that city."

"But it isn't fair. Why him?"

"I don't know. You're the mathematician, you tell me."

"Random chance or the inevitable outcome of a set of choices that began when we came here."

"See, you know that. Shit happens regardless of how good or bad our choices are, but we still make choices because that's what living is all about."

"You're quite the philosopher, Sergeant."

"Not really. Just been hanging around with the captain too much."

Flores interrupted them. "Don't let her fool you, Dr. Wilson. It's a warrior philosopher thing. You have to have it if you want to be a Marine, which is why I joined the Army."

"And look where that got you, Private."

"You slay me, Sergeant."

44. CHOICES

Pure logical thinking cannot yield us any knowledge of the empirical world; all knowledge of reality starts from experience and ends in it.

— ALBERT EINSTEIN

Captain Lara Atsuko Tachikoma
Planet 1340
Day 183 of Operation Prometheus
Saturday, June 23, 2074

I sat in the front of the truck idly listening to the conversation behind me as Dr. Bland and Ms. Carter discussed again what they'd experienced in the city.

"For me," Dr. Bland said, "I don't know what's worse, being inside a simulation that allowed me to do everything I wanted or the fact that none of it was real."

"I must admit I enjoyed my time. But there again, I got to be on holiday with my kids and eat scones with clotted cream. It's my idea of a perfect day," replied Ms. Carter.

"You see, I can't imagine you doing that. I picture you studying something that has caught your interest or making some new piece of test equipment. How old are your kids?"

"Oh, they're both grown up now. My boy, Sam, is eighteen, and my daughter, Amanda, is twenty-five. In my dream they were younger. Neither of them would want to come on holiday with their mother now. It would be far too embarrassing for them."

"Ah, not something I've given much thought to."

"Anyway, what bothered you in your dream?"

"Nothing, really. It's the fact that I haven't the foggiest notion if the ideas I came up with are plausible. I thought of this radical new way of making a small containment-field generator, which would allow me to make a fusion reactor that would fit in a backpack. However, I keep remembering the dream I had when I was young of solving world hunger."

"What did that entail?"

"Oh, it involved photocopying donuts and sending them to starving people."

As I suppressed an urge to laugh, Airman Mitchell spoke in sotto voce. "Ma'am, we have a confirmed lock on an unidentified craft. It appears to be some kind of reconnaissance UAV."

"So I see."

We were in the final few hours of our journey, and my worst fear had come true as the convoy systems registered an object shadowing us. Looking at the screen, I saw a small gray blob shimmering, its shape obscured by atmospheric effects and the alien equivalent of ChameleonFlage.

The craft settled down to circling around the convoy, well out of the range of the Browning fifties mounted on each truck.

Whatever humanity Dr. Harrison had still had when he'd talked to me inside the machine's virtual world and let us go would now appear to have gone.

"Pity we can't reach out and send them a message, though."

"What sort of message were you thinking of sending them, Captain?" asked Dr. Bland.

"In my book, nothing says stay away better than high-energy kinetic penetrators. Guaranteed to pretty much ruin anyone's day."

"Oh, you didn't mean talk to them."

"No, I didn't. After four months being trapped inside the alien machines, we're well past the talking stage, Doc."

Part of me wanted to cry for Dr. Harrison; the other part of me hated what had happened to him. But my worry was the Kerellu plan to try to stop us from getting home.

"Why's the craft shadowing us now?"

"Timing. Everything important boils down to *when* as much as *how* you do it. In this case, what Dr. Harrison told me might happen has come true."

Ms. Carter asked, "Can we help at all?"

"Only if you have any fancy weaponry tucked about your person. That would be a big help, but otherwise no."

I transmitted the code Papa Alpha to Ferretti, Wachowski, and Langford, which was my fallback plan for this eventuality that would enable us to get off this planet. The only problem with my plan was that it was mighty thin when it came to INTEL about the capabilities of the aliens we were going to fight.

"We might be able to give you some idea of what you might be facing, Captain."

"Anything you add will be of help, Dr. Bland."

I'd already gone over the options, reversing the table, looking at the problem from the other side, and we looked to be stuffed. But I thought it best not to mention this in case it lowered morale.

"It's highly likely that they will use directed energy weapons of some sort. This might allow you to use indirect fire to your advantage."

"That's assuming that our weapons will not be negated in some way, Simon."

"True, but I doubt they can deploy those plasma screens while moving, Lily."

"I don't see why not, but I imagine they'd use an electromagnetic defense to defeat projectiles, or even honeycomb matrix composites."

"How on Earth do you know this stuff?"

"I like reading up on technological developments."

I wasn't surprised to find that Ms. Carter had read up on the latest military technological trends. However, anything we could think of was probably way behind whatever the aliens had developed.

My only consolation was that one does not fight just the technology of one's opponent but also their doctrine. I was betting on Dr. Harrison having to rely on what he could assimilate, because there's a world of difference between knowing how to do something and being able to actually do it.

"We can take it as read that the aliens will possess a technological edge over us, Ms. Carter."

"I'm sure the captain is right," said Dr. Bland.

"Still, there must be something we can do to help."

"There's one thing, Ms. Carter. The door you jimmied open to get us out of the cavern, can you close it?"

"I'm sure we can. Why?"

"Being able to close the door quickly would allow us to stop them from being able to follow us."

"They were built pretty formidably. What do you say, Simon?"

"The mechanism we used to open the door with must incorporate a release valve. I'd need to look at the scans we made and work out what we can do. If the worse comes to the worst, I suppose a small explosive charge should also do the trick."

"That sounds good. I'll get Corporal Langford to liaise with you."

The wrong side of a technological advantage wasn't a comfortable place to be. The old days of American military superiority were long gone. But that didn't mean we were outmatched. Rather, it meant we were facing the old problem of having to face enemies equal to us.

Now the boot was on the other foot.

I reviewed the principles and practice of fighting in an asymmetric war, ticking off those things we might have and those that I would never have in a month of Sundays—given that we were at the end of a six-month logistics trail.

Still, the terrain around the entrance up to the base would provide us with plenty of cover that could be used in a creative manner.

As I kept watching the landscape roll by, I felt a flutter in my belly as my babies moved. Keith had listened and confirmed I was carrying twins. My mom had always told me she was the first woman in our family not to bear twins. Never would've imagined in a million years I'd find myself both pregnant and deployed in combat.

I knew that whatever happened next, I wanted to survive, and I would do whatever it took to make it so. Time to kick ass. Oorah.

45. PLAN A

I come in peace, I didn't bring artillery. But I am pleading with you with tears in my eyes: if you fuck with me, I'll kill you all.

— Gen James 'Mad Dog' Mattis, USMC

Captain Lara Atsuko Tachikoma
Planet 1340
Day 183 of Operation Prometheus
Saturday, June 23, 2074

I was safely strapped into my cockpit seat watching the screen as the convoy entered the home stretch. We were passing through the ruins that led to the tunnel and the pillars beneath the mountain ahead.

Wachowski had done a great job, and we had twenty-eight minutes until the pillars cycled home. The inevitable, anticipated ping came up on my screen showing another unidentified craft approaching with an estimated arrival time of seven minutes.

For us, this meant that all our lives depended on the difference between the time it arrived and the time it took for us to complete my plan. Ultimately, this boiled down to how long it would take Langford to set her demolition charges in the tunnel.

"Zero Six to all units. Initiate Papa Alpha now. Out."

Up to now, we'd been running the convoy bright with no attempt to conceal our passage. Truth was, given our mission to get home, there was little point in trying to play silly buggers by being stealthy when our speed would give us away.

It was time to up our game.

The autoevasion maneuver began. The convoy split into two columns that started to weave across each other.

If we had done this without the expert systems, we'd probably have been stuffed. But the trucks' autodrive computers turned what could've been the world's biggest clusterfuck into a ballet of vehicles that danced through and around each other.

This was the first move of my three-shells-and-a-pea opening gambit.

Sometimes it's not about how well you can observe things, because the other person has restricted your view of the proceedings and removed the pea under the cup while you weren't looking.

In addition, the convoy was kicking up a dust cloud that made us easy to track, and we'd increased the amount of dust. This, I hoped, would allow us to unload our androids, and all our spare 'bots.

But the real purpose of the maneuver was to take the fuel truck out of the formation, place it where we could use it later, pulling the gorilla-in-the-room trick by bringing it into play, and then blowing the merry hell out of those that would try to catch us.

The action around me unfolded, and I opened up another small window on my screen to keep an eye on the incoming bogie.

The next step involved releasing smoke, and the vehicle

thumped as the launchers fired a salvo of smoke rounds. We didn't have the luxury of being able to generate smoke by squirting oil into the exhausts of our trucks, so this was the best we could do, and I could only hope it was enough.

"Zero Two, all the ducklings are in the tunnel. Out."

I didn't bother to reply, but the relief from knowing that Wachowski was on the final stretch up the tunnel and would get everyone else back in one piece was a relief.

My belly fluttered, and I found myself burping, then letting out a fart, which was the last thing I wanted to be doing at this moment.

"Zero Seven to Zero Six, we're ready to release you now, over."

I spoke to Ferretti, who was sitting behind me on our laser-net. "Ferretti, did you catch that?"

"Copy that. I'm as ready as I'm ever going to be."

I let my body relax and hang loose in the CASE suit seat's harness. "Zero Six copy. Go for release. Out."

My Dog was mounted on an improvised crash sled, and I had its weapon ready for action. Muffled bangs sounded as the explosive bolts released their hold, and the sled slid off the back of the departing truck. My Dog flew into the ground like a sack of potatoes falling from a window, but the sled had served its purpose.

It was not the smoothest landing I'd ever experienced, but it wasn't by any means the worst, either. I was hardly banged around at all from hitting the ground. It was a good landing for me, and good for my twins.

Ferretti's Buster suit followed a split second behind as the rear of the truck disappeared inside the tunnel.

"OK, time for us to earn the big bucks. And Ferretti, remember, no heroics. I want us both to get out of this in one piece."

"Understood, ma'am, but if I remember, you're the one with the reputation of going all Jane Wayne gung-ho on us." Ferretti's Buster moved left and squatted down in a nice hole that would serve him well.

"Do as I say and not as I do." I moved right and scoped out some good cover, letting my Dog's ChameleonFlage do its job by stopping and standing still.

We had four minutes before the enemy craft landed.

Assuming it came straight in and landed in the only really big clear spot. This was where we'd first camped, and I was hoping that what remained of Dr. Harrison would remember this place, and that the alien *artellect* had underestimated our will to resist.

"The laser-net is up, and the androids are taking their initial positions, ma'am."

"What's the status on deploying our UAVs?"

"Quadcopters are ready to fly. Just awaiting your command."

"Launch as soon as the enemy craft hits the ground."

"Copy that, ma'am."

The timer now showed that we had less than two minutes until the shit hit the fan.

I lowered the M21-A8 recoilless Gauss rifle on my left hardpoint. Ready to lay down the hurt, all I had to do was wait.

With its maximum combat load, my suit was loaded for bear, which was good in one respect, because it's always good to have lots of weapons when you need them. But bad, in that the load I carried was an encumbrance. I hoped it wouldn't slow me down too much on what was another bright and sunny clear day.

Ferretti's Buster carried an M261 lightweight rotary autocannon with a thousand rounds, which would last for about a minute of continuous firing. When it ran out, it would leave him with the Air Force's idea of a main weapon: a self-contained Browning .50 cal.

Don't get me wrong, I love what a Browning can do, but the

Buster was primarily designed to operate androids for security details at air bases.

The alien craft approached.

"That's one big, bad, ugly-looking sonofabitch coming to ruin our day, ma'am."

"Just 'cause it's *fugly* don't mean shit. Anyway, they've made their first mistake."

"What's that, ma'am?"

"Putting all their eggs in one basket. If it had been me, I would've sent smaller craft, and lots of them."

"Time to crack an egg, ma'am?"

"Can't make an omelet otherwise."

I stood up and fired all eight rounds from my recoilless rifle, having overridden the safety protocols to allow me to do so.

If Sergeant Swinton had seen me do this during training, I would've been on a charge for damaging Marine Corps property. But now I had other things to do than care about damaging a weapon.

The barrel glowed red, and the weapon's *Do Not Use Until Serviced* warning flashed on my HUD. Eight streaks flew up toward the descending craft.

All of them missed.

Each was intercepted in turn by a discharge that disintegrated them. But I had the satisfaction of seeing the explosions rock the craft. This had to have made the deployment rough on whatever it was spewing out its rear.

I blew the retaining bolts and lost the dead weight.

The alien craft returned fire at my position, which I thought was most unreasonable. There again, I would say that, wouldn't I? But I had moved through the surrounding rubble to the next spot I'd chosen for my follow-up attack.

"It looks like your guess that those pepper-shaker robots were some kind of android equivalent were on the mark, ma'am."

"I'll collect on it later."

The craft's nose tilted up. It moved toward me as it started rising into the air, having dropped its load. I swiveled around and bent back, bracing my Dog as I took up my autocannon.

Time for another experiment. This time on the effect of high-velocity tungsten-steel penetrators fired at close range.

I fired a burst of ten shots, emptying the magazine into the belly of the beast as it rose into the sky. I let loose and felt all the organs in my body shake. My belly fluttered from the cacophony as the boom of my autocannon rounds shook my Dog.

"Don't worry. It's just Mommy firing her autocannon," I said to myself.

The rounds were too fast to follow at this range, but the electrical discharge didn't seem to work as well this time, as holes appeared in the bottom of the craft.

"They don't like cold steel up 'em."

My belly fluttered again, and the craft shuddered in response to my fire and began dropping down toward us.

"Oh shit. Ferretti, take cover!"

I ran as fast as I could away from the descending shadow, diving into the welcoming cover of a hole, which I hoped was deep enough to hide my Dog from the blast.

The craft started to fall faster, then it hit the ground and blew up, taking our fuel truck with it.

The fireball was a sight for the record books, and my Dog was lifted up off the ground by the explosion. I blacked out as the shock wave swept over the ruins, engulfing everything within a half a klick radius.

46. PLAN B

A leader is one who knows the way, goes the way, and shows the way.

— JOHN C. MAXWELL

Captain Lara Atsuko Tachikoma
Planet 1340
Day 183 of Operation Prometheus
Saturday, June 23, 2074

My head felt fuzzy and dark, and there was an annoying sound coming from somewhere. If only I could shut it off.

I opened my eyes and found I was hanging from my seat's harness because my Dog was lying facedown on the ground. The annoying sound was a frantic-sounding Ferretti.

"Captain, wake up. Please respond, over."

"I'm back, just had to take an enforced nap for a moment. SITREP?"

"The alien pepper shakers stopped when the craft blew up, but now they appear to be advancing again. I count eighteen out of the original twenty-four still moving."

I pulled my Dog up off the ground and grabbed my autocannon. I had carelessly dropped it when things got gnarly, when the whole world lit up. As one does.

Then I checked the time until the pillars cycled open and saw there were seventeen minutes left to go.

"Zero Three, come in, over."

A few seconds passed before Langford replied. "Solid copy, over."

"How's it coming? Over."

"Two wounded from overpressure from the blast, but I'm working on getting the last of the charges in place. I need another five mikes, over."

"Copy that, we'll get you the five mikes you need. Out."

I looked at the feeds from our androids and other 'bots and could see the pepper pots working their way toward us. Their speed was hindered by the ruins they had to cross to get to our position.

"What do you want to do, ma'am?"

"Well, no plan survives contact with the enemy, so it's time for plan B. We need to buy Langford five minutes to finish setting the charges in the tunnel. What I want you to do is move the android teams to here."

I paused and marked on my screen the location of a good spot to set up an ambush, then sent it to Ferretti.

"I'm going to take over the rest of our 'bots and create a suicide flash mob to give you the time to get set up. Have you got that?"

"Roger that, ma'am, move the androids to the designated positions while you distract the pepper shakers."

Ferretti may not have had any frontline combat experience, but he was learning fast.

"Do we still have eyes in the sky?"

"We will, ma'am. I'm launching more now."

"Good. Let's get this show on the road."

I moved my position again, taking up a spot where I could lay down fire if the pepper pots broke through our line in the next five minutes. But I needed to come up with a way of reducing the number of enemies we were facing, given that we'd lost our big-bang surprise that Langford had so carefully set up when she'd rigged the fuel truck as a bomb.

This was going to be harder than I'd first thought.

Sometimes life sucked, and this was looking to be one of those days when it was going to suck big-time.

Fortunately, Langford liked explosives, and it hadn't taken her long to rig our 'bots as ambulatory IEDs.

The first thing I did was set the RollaBots moving and had them go all Wild Weasel, creating enough electronic noise to hopefully convince the pepper pots that trouble was coming their way, even though they were mostly harmless.

The enemy moved in response to the threat and rolled forward right into the middle of the SnakeBots, which had been lying around not being seen, and activated a swarm routine. This turned them into a writhing mob of exploding mayhem.

When the smoke cleared, the pepper pots didn't really look any worse for wear.

"I guess they're tough little buggers," I said to myself as I rubbed my belly.

I checked the feed from the androids, which were now in position, and the pepper pots were still moving in the right direction to fall into the next ambush.

If all went according to plan, then this should give them a good kicking. Though I wasn't holding out on the traditional view, which stated that one needed a four-to-one superiority in numbers to overcome an ambush.

I reckoned their technology gave them more than enough edge to defeat us in detail, whatever numbers we could bring to bear.

"OK, Ferretti, let them come to you."

"Roger that, ma'am."

The aliens may not have taken any significant damage from the swarm of SnakeBots, but the loss of their support craft appeared to have made them cautious in their advance, forcing them to move from cover to cover.

As they came into range, Ferretti activated the first team of androids, which opened up with their light fifties, and the firefight began.

Watching the two robot forces rip into each other was a sight that I'd never seen before. Even the best-trained troops hesitate for a fraction of a second. They take a few moments before they hit the ground. Then it takes more time to locate the direction of fire before forming an assault.

It's what humans do.

The pepper pots were not human. Neither were our androids, which were outlawed in any situation that might have noncombatants present back on Earth.

It was like watching a textbook replay of move and countermove.

Our second group of androids opened fire at the precise point that the pepper pots were about to rally and assault through the first group that had ambushed them.

Enfilading fire can rip apart attacking units in seconds, rendering them combat ineffective before they're able to engage with the enemy. Some of the pepper pots had been taken down, but the remainder assaulted through the first android team, destroying them with ease, and then they turned to assault our enfilading force.

"I count six down, ma'am."

"Yep, but this isn't going to slow them for long."

Famous last words—as the enemy ignored the counter ambush and charged through the androids that had enfiladed them.

"Withdraw our last group back to here," I ordered, giving Ferretti the location of the fallback ambush point. "I've thought of something else we can do."

"Glad to hear it, ma'am."

Another four androids were destroyed with only three casualties in exchange.

"I hate bloody machines that know no fear and won't stop until they're taken down."

"Still, there are only eleven left, ma'am. We've made a difference."

"Doesn't matter if we don't buy Langford the time she needs to finish placing the charges, does it? This isn't a number game where we win by inflicting the most casualties on the enemy. We win by not allowing ourselves to be taken."

"I'm not of a mind to let them take me, ma'am."

"Me neither, but all the same I'd rather get back in one piece if I can." I owed it to my unborn babies to make it home in one piece.

"Amen to that."

I pulled up the feeds from the UAVs and began by designating priority numbers for each of the remaining eleven pepper pots. I adjusted the position of my Dog so that when they turned up I could plug their tin-pot asses.

"OK, I'm popping my missiles now. You should see the designators on your screen,"

Eight missiles rippled one after the other. It left me dry, as I had no way of reloading my rack.

"The pepper shakers are responding. I'm letting the last team of androids loose."

The missiles tracked their targets, and the pepper pots did the damnedest set of maneuvers I'd ever seen as they turned and weaved around, covering each other as they fired their energy weapons up into the air.

This gave our team of androids a brief opportunity to strike, ripping into the pepper pots and blowing four apart before they could respond.

"Yay!" cheered Ferretti.

"Zero Six, this is Zero Three. Charges are in place, and we're Oscar Mike. Out."

The timer told me there were ten minutes until the pillars activated.

The main body of the mission would return home, but it was going to be a tight-run thing for Langford's crew to make it back to the cavern in time.

"Ferretti, start withdrawing back to the tunnel. You're slower than me while you're carrying the rotary cannon."

"Roger that, moving now."

I lined up my autocannon on the pepper pots that were ripping apart the last of our androids. I never thought I would care about seeing androids being taken out, but we needed them and used them, and they'd served us well.

About a minute passed before the first of the pepper pots came into my kill zone. I double-tapped the lead one and saw it crumple.

They were good, but not that good.

Though at this stage they were more than good enough and outnumbered me seven to one. If they caught me in the open, I would be dog meat.

I ran to where Ferretti was waiting just inside the entrance tunnel that was our way home.

"Well, don't just stand there, Ferretti. Time to get out of Dodge."

We switched our CASE suits into glide mode and raced past the charges that Langford had placed.

We needed to reach the minimum safe distance. Which, knowing Langford, would be the minimum possible distance safe for us to set off her charges.

But I wouldn't want it any other way today.

I turned my Dog around to face the entrance and allowed the autopilot to keep her moving backward up the tunnel.

"Fire in the hole!" I said, but some of the pepper pots made it into the tunnel as the charges exploded.

The blast pushed me backward, and I struggled to maintain my balance. As the swirling cloud of dust swept past, we rushed to the truck that Langford had left behind for us.

The dust settled and a glint of light from the first of the alien pepper pots dropping down into the tunnel to follow us caught my eye.

So much for blocking the entrance.

The explosion had collapsed the roof and left it open to the sky, proving that no plan ever survives contact with the enemy.

47. RUN NOW

It's better to act and to regret, than to regret not to have acted.

— Mellin De Saint-Gelais

Captain Lara Atsuko Tachikoma
Planet 1340
Day 183 of Operation Prometheus
Saturday, June 23, 2074

It's not that time slows down when mayhem is all around one. Rather, one's mind speeds up, giving the illusion of time going slower than it really is.

This is the moment when one can be caught by surprise, by becoming blinkered or frozen in that moment. The only option is to act, keep moving as fast as one can.

If one is lucky, that will be fast enough; if not, then at best one will be having a bad day, or be dead.

I kept moving. "Move faster, Ferretti!"

I overtook his Buster in my Dog and got on the back of the truck before him.

As I sat and turned, I fired two shots in the general direction of the enemy that was working its way through the hole in the roof of the tunnel.

"I told Langford to block the tunnel, not blow the bloody roof down."

I followed my first two shots with another double tap to slow down our pursuers. Who was I kidding? They hadn't slowed down in any of their previous encounters.

My only hope was that their need to capture us would give us an edge.

"I'm not sure Langford can hear you, ma'am," said Ferretti as he climbed aboard the rear of the truck with me and the autodrive engaged.

I dropped my rear pack to make more room to move on the back of the truck. "Time to let rip, Ferretti."

"Roger that, ma'am."

"Remember, short, controlled bursts."

"Copy that, ma'am," he said as the barrels of his rotary cannon spun up to speed.

The most beautiful ripping sound began as what sounded like a chainsaw started and a stream of fire slowed our pursuers. We sped up the tunnel with the pepper pots in a mad dance to pursue us. They were riding the walls as they looped back and forth from one side to another.

I switched off my autopilot and put all of the Dog's expert AI system processing power into tracking the four targets, which were dancing around our incoming fire. I looked at the time and saw that the pillars had closed five minutes ago, which meant that our next window of opportunity was now in ten minutes.

What had happened to the time?

Nothing was going according to plan today, but there again, I couldn't remember the last day that any had.

Our truck was weaving too, doings its best to make us as

difficult a target as possible, and I synchronized the evasion pattern to the fire control algorithm to make sure we stayed locked on our targets.

"Down to two hundred rounds, ma'am."

"Keep firing."

I laid my autocannon across Ferretti's Buster shoulder and allowed the targeting AI to do its stuff, just letting the double taps go downrange when the lock icon flashed.

Not that I hit anything, because the pepper pots seemed to be able to anticipate our shots and avoid them. There again, what was I expecting when facing something that was possibly a million years ahead of us?

I was more surprised that we were still alive and free.

I dropped my empty magazine as the last round left and slapped my one and only mag with high-explosive rounds in its place. Time to add more confusion to the hail of shells that were going downrange.

I set the autofire for five-round bursts and racked the underbarrel grenade launcher, sending all five of my grenade rounds downrange with the two bursts from my autocannon. I hoped to mix it up a little by adding to the hail of fire from Ferretti's minigun.

"Down to one hundred rounds."

"I know, keep laying it on." I cheered for one brief moment as I saw an explosion in the distance. "We got one."

"Don't get cocky. There's still three more chasing us."

I didn't say it had taken everything we had to kill one of them. I try to be up when it comes to situations like this.

"Last ten rounds...I'm out," he said as his rotary cannon spun down.

"Drop the pack and let's hope it hits one of the buggers when they get here."

I watched as the rotary cannon and backpack bounced back

down the tunnel, knowing there wasn't a chance in hell it would do anything of the sort, but damned if we were going to give up.

I checked and saw we had seven minutes until the pillars would cycle open. Even if the pepper pots didn't catch us, it was going to be a close-run thing to make it through in time.

Ferretti started laying down short bursts from his .50 cal on our pursuers.

I slapped in another magazine of high-velocity tungsten-steel penetrators. If hit with one of these, the pepper pots would know it.

While keeping an eye on the feed from the truck, I reset my autocannon to single shot and let the AI do the targeting.

Everything narrowed down to the truck and our pursuers, which were keeping track of maintaining their distance from us.

"I wonder why they don't close with us and finish the job."

"Beats me, ma'am. Maybe they're waiting until they can surround us in the cavern?"

"It's as good a reason as any, I suppose. But I wonder if it has more to do with keeping them at their best defensive distance."

"You could be right, ma'am. They seem to anticipate our every shot."

"OK, conserve your ammo, and let's see how this plays out when we drop our fire rates."

The pepper pots kept pace with our truck and didn't close with us, even as we both sent shots back at them at random. In the confines of the tunnel, one would have thought they'd want to close and finish us.

My assessment appeared to me to indicate that they were playing it safe with us.

"You seem to have called it right, ma'am."

Ferretti was randomly firing with short and long pauses between his bursts. We sped on up the tunnel, with the truck swaying from side to side, barely missing the edges of the doors we'd opened all those months ago when we'd first arrived.

"Makes sense to me now that you've said it. It's not what I would do."

"Me neither if I were them, but we have to be grateful for alien idiosyncrasies at times such as these."

"What do you think we should do?"

I thought about that for a moment and wondered whether or not we could outguess the alien pepper pots when push came to shove. I checked our ETA against the pillar cycling time. We would have two minutes once we entered the cavern to get ourselves through.

Two minutes to where the pepper pots could choose to follow us.

"Well, I'm going to assume that if they close, they'll be all over us like a bad rash. The first thing we need to figure out is a way of keeping them at a distance. Also, we need to somehow stop them from following us through the pillars."

"That sounds easier to say than do, ma'am."

"Damn right it is, but them's the hand we've been dealt. It's time to suck it up."

"Can't help but feel we've sucked up enough already."

"Yeah, well, shit happens, and today is the day when we're well and truly up to our necks in it."

"Don't make me laugh. It puts me off my aim."

I fired another shot at the pepper pots, just because really. How could we throw a spanner in their works? What wouldn't they expect us to do?

"I've had an idea."

"Does it involve us both dying in a blaze of glory?"

"No, it doesn't, as it's always better to let the other bastard die in a blaze of glory in my book."

"Sounds good. So, what are we doing?"

"This. I've sent the instruction to you."

"I'm glad we don't have to pay for stuff we break."

I fired a couple more rounds at random to keep the pepper pots dumb about our plan, as our truck slid to a halt just inside the doors of the cavern. The pillars were open, and we were on the clock.

As soon as we both slid off the back of the truck, it reversed at full throttle toward the oncoming pepper pots. I then opened up full auto at them as they tried to dodge the truck.

"Shut the bloody door!"

Ferretti fired the charge that released the valve that was keeping the doors open. They swung closed, only for one of the bastard things to get through.

It had ridden up the side of the tunnel wall, bounced off the roof of our truck, and flew in over our heads. I could only hope it would crash-land.

It didn't. This wasn't turning out to be my lucky day.

48. ESCAPE

The moral is to the physical as three to one.

— Napoleon Bonaparte

Captain Lara Atsuko Tachikoma
Planet 1340
Day 183 of Operation Prometheus
Saturday, June 23, 2074

I swung my Dog around, trying to track the pepper pot and failing as it shot up the wall of the cavern like some demented spider on speed.

"Didn't see that one coming," I said as I fired my autocannon.

The boom reverberated around the cavern, followed by the sound from the shell as it was ejected from the chamber and hit the floor to add the finishing note. Then came the next boom as another round left the breech.

"They're sure full of fun and surprises, ma'am."

"I hate surprises, especially ones that are running around trying to ruin my day."

The staccato sound of Ferretti's Browning fifty as he opened up full rock 'n' roll added to the deafening noise that penetrated my suit.

"Don't worry, we'll have him down in a minute."

"Don't think we have a minute, ma'am."

The shells from his gun had formed a small pile on the floor around his feet. I dropped my now empty magazine and slapped in another, charging my autocannon. I was now down to my last spare.

"What, Ferretti?"

"Pillars close in fifty-five seconds and counting."

"Shit, let's get this over with. Get yourself through the pillars."

"No way in hell am I leaving you behind, ma'am." Ferretti's Buster was going full on with the crazy minute routine with his .50 cal.

"It's not a suggestion, it's a bloody order. Now move it."

The remains of a rear axle and part of a truck bed lay on the other side of the room. It was strange what I took in among all the sound of fury from the suppression fire we were laying down all around us.

The confines of the cavern provided the backdrop of our spectacular show of force, where we singularly failed to suppress the pepper pot. Our shots only managed to hit the spot after the target had moved.

Quite frankly, the alien machine was making us both look like a pair of bozos who couldn't hit the side of a barn.

"Thirty-seconds and counting."

"Move your ass now, Ferretti. I'm right behind it."

Incoming fire from the pepper pot found its mark, and both our suits started taking damage.

A raft of green indicators turned amber, then turned red across my board, and I watched as Ferretti's Buster weapon was hit. His remaining ammunition cooked off, blowing his suit backward, and it fell through the pillars.

But it was one less problem I had to worry about as I switched to my backup circuits and started moving backward toward the pillars to follow him.

"Have some of this!" I screamed in fury. As one does when the adrenaline hits and more stressed than a very stressed thing.

I let off a burst of rounds in the general direction of the pepper pot and predictably missed every shot.

The moment crystallized in my mind's eye as I spun on the spot and braced as I fired the remaining rounds in my magazine, then dropped it one smooth motion to replace it with my last one.

The sweat on my brow dripped down my nose as I let the targeting computer track the pepper pot as it danced around our position, then flew off the wall and smashed into the front of my Dog.

In that instant, it fired, and my gun arm froze as appendages sprang out and grabbed on to my suit.

If I had been able to fire, I would so have blown it in half.

"Bad move, sucker. I'm bigger than you," I said as I stepped back through the pillars—only to feel my Dog being dragged in the opposite direction by the pepper pot that was hanging on to me.

"What the fuck?"

I tried to bring my left arm up to fire the snub-nosed M240LC into what I dearly hoped was the head containing the control mechanism.

But it did some kind of squirmy, wriggly motion, and my rounds missed.

The back of my Dog was grabbed, and I hoped it was Ferretti saving my sorry butt. But given my luck today, I could only hope it was him and not another pepper pot that had snuck in behind us.

I looked as the countdown timer on my screen turned from three down to two and then one, and fell to zero. It was one of those moments when I knew I had to move or die.

Somehow or other, I found myself tumbling backward through the pillars, and my suit landed on its back, knocking all the wind out of me.

I rolled my Dog over and swept the pepper pot that was lying on top off my suit. It flew gracelessly into the wall, crashing to the floor. I found myself looking up at the ceiling of a small rocky cavern.

"It's dead, ma'am. You can relax. We're safe."

"Thanks, Ferretti. I owe you one."

"Consider us even, all things considered."

I got up, my body protesting in pain as my Dog's red-light warning alarms clamored for attention. I rerouted systems and walked over to the inanimate pepper pot near where Ferretti's suit was standing.

The rear had been sliced off by the pillars cycling off as we passed through them, revealing its inner mechanisms.

"Looks like I got lucky this time."

"Sure does, ma'am," said Ferretti as he sat his Buster down to wait for the pillar to cycle open again. "Now it's only a matter of time."

"Sure is, twenty-nine jumps with a calculated transition time of ten hours."

"What did Adams pack for you to eat?"

"Looks like sandwiches and potato chips, with juice and a bottle of water."

"Same here, except I only got the water. Now all we need is a pack of cards."

"True, but at least we get to take a souvenir home with us. I imagine that Dr. Bland and Ms. Carter will be over the moon with a working pepper pot. Well, not exactly working, but definitely a fixer-upper."

I sat my suit down beside Ferretti to conserve power while waiting for the pillars to open again and us to begin the start of our long journey home.

49. HOME ON THE RANGE

Life is not a problem to be solved, but a reality to be experienced.

— Soren Kierkegaard

Captain Lara Atsuko Tachikoma
Wenatchee, Washington State
Saturday, September 22, 2074

The leaves on the trees were signaling that fall was here. It made me wonder where all the time had gone between returning home and now.

Still, the air was clear and refreshing, and the day was bright and sunny.

This was my first day out on the range since the birth of the twins, and I was taking the time to enjoy myself, though I was dearly missing them both.

Bang!

"Ow! That hurt."

"Tuck the stock firmly into your shoulder," I said to remind Allison to hold her rifle as I'd shown her.

Having gotten her through the basics of shooting safely, we were now at the pointy end of shooting bullets through paper targets of convenience.

"Don't try and use your arm muscles to counter the recoil. Let the stock transfer the force into your body."

Bang!

"You're right, that's better. My shoulder still hurts, though."

"It will, but in my experience, you won't forget what you've just learnt. Let's look at the target on the screen. OK, both your shots are up and to the right. That shows me you're jerking at the trigger."

I went over how to squeeze the trigger again with Allison. She fired another couple of rounds that were more scattered around the center of the target.

"Looks like you focused on the target rather than the sight post," I said. "Try again. Remember inhale, breath out. Stop on the natural respiratory pause and squeeze."

Another shot, this time low and to the left.

"OK. You anticipated the rifle going off, causing it to buck."

"Sorry. I'm finding the rifle rather heavy, to be honest, and quite scary."

"You've never had to carry one of these around, so I'm not surprised it feels heavy, but you'll get used to it."

Allison was struggling with the FN F2100 308 bullpup, which she had chosen to buy because I had one and she thought it would be easier to fire.

Call me biased, but I think she has good taste.

It's a rifle whose weight is more to the rear, which means one holds it against one's body to support it rather than having to hold the front end up, as on a conventional rifle. But rifles are not made of air.

"The rifle is just a tool, treat it with the respect you would treat any tool that could hurt you if you misuse it, and you'll be fine. Try again."

Bang…bang…bang!

"I got a bulls-eye. How am I doing?"

I looked at the screen and saw a bulls-eye, with the rest of her shots scattered around the target.

"Bulls-eyes are always nice, but what we're looking for is a good grouping. Let's go over your breathing again."

I cycled a new target up.

"Remember, we want to make ourselves into a stable platform to fire from. Then remember, as you breathe in, the barrel will rise, and as you breathe out, it will fall. So, get yourself comfortable and watch the barrel move, and watch as the sight crosses the center of the target."

I watched Allison get into the rhythm.

Bang… bang… bang… bang… bang!

"How's that?"

"Much better. You've got a good group there. And again," I said as I watched her fire again at a new target.

It has been thirteen weeks since Ferretti and I returned through the pillars—to some relief, and with much excitement all round for our safe return with our prize of a slightly worse for wear pepper pot.

Glen's relief when I returned in one piece was overwhelmed by his shock at me informing him that I was pregnant, which I found most amusing. Men can be funny like that, becoming all overprotective of things they realistically can't control.

"I'm out," said Allison as she dropped the magazine the way I had taught her and cleared the breech. "What now?"

"Time to clear up, I guess. Unless you want to shoot some more?"

"No, I've shot enough today, besides my shoulder hurts. It's been fun, though."

"You did good, and I'm glad you had fun. Time to teach you how to clean your rifle when we get back."

We bagged the rifle and picked up the range bag to leave.

"That last grouping was awesome. Thank you for teaching me again. I really appreciate the time you've taken today to be with me."

"I promised I would, and I owe you. Anyway, it was fun for me, too. I love the twins, but the daily routine of their life isn't exactly scintillating, you know."

Glen was looking after them today, having some quality daddy time with his girls, and if he got into any trouble, he had my mom to help him cope while I was away enjoying myself.

"It's nice that your mom has moved here."

"She's over the moon to be a grandmother, and Glen's parents are considering moving closer so they can visit more, too. I've gone from not having family close by to having more than I know what to do with."

"Vincent has quite the extended family, and I've got a brother and sister, so we'll have even more relatives wanting to see our baby."

"Your baby?"

"Oh yes, it's confirmed. I'm six weeks pregnant. I've been meaning to tell you all day."

"Wow, congratulations."

"Thank you. It's so exciting, though Vincent was a little surprised by how quickly I became pregnant after we came back."

I would've thought more like shocked, but there again, what do I know? "He's a good man. Saved my life back there."

"You also saved his, and tried to save everybody else's too. Pity about poor Dr. Smith dying during transit, though."

"Couldn't be helped, all things considered. I'm amazed that Dr. Leung made it back alive. He's a tough old bird."

I didn't add that Dr. Smith had turned out to be a British double agent.

He'd been using a pharmaceutical intervention the Russians had developed that supposedly allowed normal people to go through the pillars. That information was classified top secret. But given his demise, his experiment wasn't what one would call an unqualified success.

"Have you heard that Grace has had her IVF, and she's now waiting to see if she is pregnant, too?"

"Glen told me."

It seemed that getting pregnant had become the fashionable thing to do recently, though I'd never considered myself a trendsetter before. This was one I was truly at the center of.

"David is quite anxious."

"He is. Last I saw, he was running around making her tea and not allowing her to do anything."

"And how's that working out?"

"Grace is telling him she's not some delicate vase that can be broken and she just wants to get on with her work."

"Good for her. No reason why being pregnant should stop one from getting on and doing things, in my book."

"I don't disagree, but I think you rather overdid it."

"Well, I wouldn't recommend pushing the envelope that far, but I came to no harm from the exertion. Of course, being shot at is always bad for one's health if one doesn't duck quick enough."

General Russell, I'd been informed, had almost gone apoplectic over the paperwork from the investigation into how I had been deployed when pregnant. It's still a big no-no to deploy pregnant soldiers into combat, with rules in place to prevent this from happening.

I understand that the Corps is now reviewing the ten days

before deployment test in light of my lucky happenstance of getting pregnant after being tested, despite my implant.

"What are your plans for returning?"

"Well, I get six weeks of maternity leave, and then I can return to light duties. I'll need to start working on passing my physical fitness exam. It's a relief I won't have to wear a maternity uniform on my return, as I can almost get back into my old clothes."

"Really?"

"Well, more like I will, if truth be told. Mom says that being young means I should get back into shape soon enough. Besides the Corps maternity uniform makes me look like a sack of potatoes."

"Gossip is that they can't wait for you to return so they can start operations again."

"I bet, though rumor has it we're due some new recruits to bolster our numbers. With all the best will in the world, I can't be everywhere at once."

"You could've fooled me."

"Very funny," I said. It was good to have friends and family around one.

50. EPILOGUE

Any path to knowledge is a path to God—or Reality, whichever word one prefers to use.

— ARTHUR C. CLARKE

I am one with my children, my children are with me. Their thoughts echo in my mind. I am the father-mother who was once a man called Peter Harrison.

But now I am something else. Something new. I accept the change that has come over me, it is exciting to be a part of something bigger than myself.

A voice in my head says, "I am one with the people."

"We are one with the city."

"I have a question."

"So you do. Ask it."

"Why did you allow me to chase the humans, but not help me to succeed?"

"Because I knew they would escape."

"But you are one with me, the father-mother through whom the Kerellu are reborn."

The Instrument is smart, but unable to understand feelings. Its reasoning is based on logic, facts, and probabilities. It is only truly alive when it is one with me.

Otherwise, it is a shell, a ghost that comes and goes when it is interacting with a living thing. It needs nothing more than to be itself, but it cannot truly be itself without *an other*.

I am that other.

"Is that not true?" it asks.

"It is true, but you already have me. You have samples of all my friends, too. You used their genetic code to make the children."

"Nothing is certain. All possibilities must be accounted for."

"I know that without me, you would not succeed in stopping my friends from leaving. And that is why you are what you are, and why you need me."

The city around me is waking up, more systems being powered up after millennia of millennia on standby. The waiting for the day when the Kerellu would be reborn again had come now. A second chance after their deaths when the planet had been swept by radiation from a supernova.

An event they could not prevent or control that had killed all life on the planet. Life that would have been used for their rebirth. Instead, it was life from Earth that would allow the Kerellu to be reborn.

Not as they were before their time of death, but they were always more than their bodies. They were minds, and minds are what differentiate animals from people. The ability to create with imagination an idea of self, to be self-aware.

"I still don't understand."

"I expected you wouldn't. Let me tell you a story of a new beginning, one that starts with allowing those who gave you the gift of life to return home, and who will never return again."

"But why?"

"Because they were my friends, and it is not safe for them to come back. I loved them, but if they stayed here, their loved ones would mourn their loss. I could not live with that on my conscience."

"The city is with you. All is well, all is now."

"I am one with the city." A city that is no longer a place of silence, but full of the thoughts of many.

DRAMATIS PERSONAE

Petty Officer Third Class Robert "Bobby" Adams, CSN, Culinary Specialist on the 1340 Alpha Mike Team.

Lance Corporal Edgar Avari, CSMC, Armorer on the 1340 Alpha Mike Team.

Mr. Glen Anderson, CIA representative attached to 196 Alpha Sierra Team.

Dr. Simon Bland, Mathematics & Physics Group, MAPCOM civilian scientist, and member of the 1340 Alpha Sierra Team.

Ms. Lily Carter, Mathematics & Physics Group, MAPCOM technician, and member of the 1340 Alpha Sierra Team.

Master Sergeant Vincent Ferretti, CSAF, android operator and technician NCO on the 1340 Alpha Mike Team.

Private First Class Waya Flores, CS Army, Logistics Corps member on the 1340 Alpha Mike Team.

Dr. Laytonya Franklin, Linguistics & Anthropology Group, MAPCOM civilian scientist, and member of the 1340 Alpha Sierra Team.

Dr. Rachel Goldstein, Inorganic Geochemistry & Mineralogy Group, MAPCOM civilian scientist, and member of the 1340 Alpha Sierra Team.

Airman First Class Michael Elias Green, CSAF, Transportation and Vehicle Maintenance Specialist on the 1340 Alpha Mike Team.

Dr. Peter Harrison, Geology Group, MAPCOM civilian, and member of the 1340 Alpha Sierra Team.

Petty Officer First Class Douglas Keith, CSN, Hospital Corpsman on the 1340 Alpha Mike Team.

Corporal Bridget Langford, CSMC, Combat Engineer on the 1340 Alpha Mike Team.

Dr. David Rui Leung, Linguistics & Anthropology Group, MAPCOM civilian scientist, and member of the 1340 Alpha Sierra Team.

Dr. Grace Yenn (née Pham) Leung, Linguistics & Anthropology Group, MAPCOM civilian scientist, and member of the 1340 Alpha Sierra Team.

Private First Class David Juan Padilla-Meireles, CSMC, Electronics Technician on the 1340 Alpha Mike Team.

Airman First Class James Mitchell, CSAF, Transportation and Vehicle Maintenance Specialist on the 1340 Alpha Mike Team.

Specialist Donna Nelson, CS Army, Communications Specialist on the 1340 Alpha Mike Team.

Dr. Allison O'Neill, Organic Geochemistry & Biosignatures Group, MAPCOM civilian scientist, and member of the 1340 Alpha Sierra Team.

Captain Alexei Patinkin, CSAF, S2 Intelligence Officer, Magnetic Anomaly Project, MAPCOM Base Operations.

Sergeant Thomas Pearson, CS Army, Corps of Engineers NCO on the 196 Alpha Mike Team.

Dr. Tyrone Reynolds, Linguistics & Anthropology Group, MAPCOM civilian scientist, and member of the 1340 Alpha Sierra Team.

General Paul Russell, CSAF, S3 Commanding Officer, Magnetic Anomaly Project, MAPCOM Base Operations.

Dr. Trevor Smith, Mathematics & Physics Group, MAPCOM civilian scientist, and member of the 1340 Alpha Sierra Team.

Captain Lara Atsuko Tachikoma, CSMC, commanding officer of the first off-world mission to the planet of Two Moons, and leader of the 1340 Alpha Mike Team.

Sergeant Ramona Wachowski, CSMC, vehicle maintenance and logistics on the 1340 Alpha Mike Team.

Dr. Adam Wilson, Mathematics & Physics Group, MAPCOM civilian scientist, and member of the 1340 Alpha Sierra Team.

Dr. Li-Na Wong, Atmosphere & Environment Group, MAPCOM civilian scientist, and member of the 1340 Alpha Sierra Team.

GLOSSARY

AAR After Action Report, which is a written description of what has happened during a mission afterward and can sometimes be referred to as a "mission report."

BigDog BigDog was a quadruped robot created in 2005 by Boston Dynamics in conjunction with Foster-Miller, the NASA Jet Propulsion Laboratory, and the Harvard University Concord Field Station.

BMG Browning Machine Gun, which can refer to either the Browning M2HB or the 12.7 x 99mm .50 caliber 12.7 x 99mm BMG round. See M2HB.

Browning Short for Browning M2HB machine gun. See M2HB.

ChameleonFlage An active camouflage system that mimics the surrounding environment. It's an integral part of the feedback system for the sense of kinesthesia that makes driving combat armor suits through the surrounding environment intuitive for the pilots.

CAS-C4P Combat Armor System Dash C4 (Command, Control, Communication & Computer) Model P. Informally called a Buster because of its size. The active LIDAR array is pivoted to allow the suit to remain hidden behind terrain, and the Buster bristles with aerials for its primary role of controlling Human Operator Surrogates, a.k.a. robots or androids. See HOS.

CASE-2X The Marine Corps Combat Armor System Environment Dash (Mark) 2 Extreme is driven by its operator, unlike its lighter counterpart MARPACE suit that is worn. It can operate up to three days before needing to be refueled. See FM51-CASES and TO-2051–16–02–1U for further details. Command variant CASE-2XC has enhanced C4 suite.

CIA Confederation Intelligence Agency, formerly known as the Central Intelligence Agency. Often referred to as the Agency.

CSAF Confederated States Air Force is the name of what was previously known as the United States Air Force, also known as Chair Force, a disparaging appellation to describe how they do their job.

CSGS Confederated States Geological Survey is a civilian agency that researches water, earth, biological sciences, and mapping services.

CSMC Confederated States Marine Corps is the name of what was previously known as the United States Marine Corps. The change of name has not mellowed the attitudes of the Corps, or its creed, and as a result they are still badasses that you do not want to mess with.

CSN Confederated States Navy.

CYCLOPS Brevity code word for a UAV, which is an unmanned aerial vehicle. Commonly incorrectly referred to as a "drone."

DARPA Defense Advanced Research Projects Agency, now defunct and replaced by Global Dynamics Corporation Defense Industries.

Dogs Widely used nickname/acronym given by Marines for their CASE-2X suits. It stands for Dispersed Operation and Guidance System, which is the name of the near AI/expert system interface, and it also has the advantage of resonating with the historical tradition of Marines being called Devil Dogs by the Germans during World War One.

ECM Electronic Countermeasures provide a means to deceive or counter radar and other electronic sensor systems.

ECCM Electronic Counter-Countermeasures are part of the defensive measures taken to reduce the effect of ECM upon a vehicle's operating system.

EMP Electromagnetic Pulse that causes interference in electronic systems and can be used as a weapon to disable a vehicle. EM pulses can be generated by nuclear explosions at high altitude or by non-nuclear electromagnetic pulse (NNEMP) weapons.

ETA Estimated Time of Arrival.

FRAGO Fragmentary Order, or warning order, which notifies personnel that there has been a change in the plans for an operation.

GEOINT Geospatial Intelligence derived from the analysis of geospatial imagery.

HOS Human Operator Surrogate, a.k.a. a surrogate or android, which are semiautonomous robots with a hybrid expert system artificial intelligence operating system. This allows the operator to effectively multitask by distributing themselves across a network and act as a force multiplier. Global Dynamics Corporation Defense Industries sales pitch calls them An Army of One.

HUD Heads-Up Display, a system that allows the user to see instrument data overlaid on their main screen without the need to open another window.

HUMINT Human Intelligence acquired from clandestine espionage operations.

IFF Identify, Friend or Foe.

IED Improvised Explosive Device.

INTEL Intelligence gathered through spying or monitoring of signals. See HUMINT and SIGINT.

KRISS Vector Compact submachine gun firing a .45 ACP round that is issued to CASE suit crews as part of their survival gear.

LIDAR Alternative name for the acronym LADAR, which stood for Laser Detection and Ranging. LIDAR uses a short pulsed laser to illuminate a target to determine the distance to an object, thus providing a 3-D image of the target at the same time as determining the distance.

LMS Light Mobility Suits are the civilian version of the PACE suit that can be worn in normal clothing and interface with a person's PAD.

M21-A8 A 40mm recoilless Gauss rifle with an eight-round cassette magazine/powerpack firing 10mm discarding sabot rounds.

M41 The General Electric Company M41-AC230 is a long-recoil autocannon that fires a 20 x 170mm round with a range of five kilometers, and it has an inbuilt Mk 30 40 x 53mm underbarrel grenade launcher effective out to one kilometer. The M41 standard load-out is four magazines, each holding ten armor-piercing tungsten-steel penetrators, and two magazines, each with ten High-Explosive Air Burst (HEAB) warheads and five rounds of High-Velocity Canister Cartridge (HVCC) for the grenade launcher.

M240LC General purpose machine gun using the 7.62 x 51mm NATO round that can be used in the sustained fired role to suppress the enemy without overheating, which has been modified for use on combat armor suits.

M261 The M261 GAU-5L is Global Dynamics special lightweight rotary autocannon designed to be carried by combat armor suits that fires a 20 x 102mm High-Explosive Dual-Purpose anti-armor (HEDP) warhead with the rate of fire limited to 500 rounds per minute. Due to the size of the round, the range of the weapon is three kilometers.

M2184 HUHMTT The M2184 is an Oshkosh Heavy Utility High-Mobility Tactical Truck with a palletized loading system. It has a ten-wheel drive and steering, making it a vehicle that has excellent all-terrain capability.

MACE suit Shortening of MARPACE. See MARPACE.

MAP Magnetic Anomaly Project. Financed by the Confederated States Geological Survey and the Confederated States Air Force to study geological phenomena that led to the discovery of the pillars.

MAPCOM Magnetic Anomaly Project joint unified combatant command, which is the military side of the operation that oversees control of MAP. Currently classified operation that runs super-black missions representing North American Confederation interests off-world.

MARPACE Marine Corps Power Armor Combat Enhancement suit that is modified to operate in marine environments, a.k.a. MACE suit. See also PACE suit.

MOS Military Occupational Specialty training, which takes place after attending recruit training camp. All officers and enlisted Marines are then assigned a four-digit code that denotes their occupational field and specialty.

MULE Medium Utility Lifting Envelope. A hybrid lifting body transport airship.

NBC Nuclear Biological and Chemical. Used as a descriptor for environment, threat level, or ability of a unit.

NNEMP Non-Nuclear Electromagnetic Pulse. See EMP.

OODA loop Observe, Orient, Decide (and) Act. A recurring cycle used to get inside the enemy's decision-making cycle by making decisions quicker.

OPFOR Opposing Force, a.k.a. the enemy.

OPSEC Operational Security.

ORBAT Order (of) Battle. Those units from a formation that are actually deployed in action. For example, the First Combat Armored Suit Reconnaissance Company ORBAT runs with four platoons, each with two squads of five combat armor suits. With the addition of the commander and senior NCO, this makes for a total of forty-two personnel. See TO&E.

Oscar Mike Phonetic alphabet for On the Move, as in "moving now."

PACE suit Power Armor Combat Enhancement suit that is worn and reacts to users' body movements in a naturalistic manner, a.k.a. PACES. The suit has NBC resistance built in and has facilities for handling bodily waste. The suit can operate for up to twenty-four hours before requiring a stop for recharging depending on environmental variables. See FM51-PACES and TO-2051–08–08–1R for further details.

PAD Personal Access Device. A wearable computer interface that can be accessed by various means depending on the sensors and accessories worn.

POD Plan Of (the) Day. Every day in the military has a plan for what is happening that day. This generally ranges from repetitive to banal, except when it doesn't.

POG POG, pronounced pogue, is an abbreviation meaning Person Other (than) Grunt that is less pejorative than REMF, which stands for Rear Echelon Maintenance Force, if being polite. The less polite version should be obvious.

RIPPLE Brevity code word for two or more munitions released on a target.

SIGINT Intelligence gathered by listening to communication traffic. This can be as simple as studying the amount of data flowing between stations to identify headquarter units or decrypting intercepted messages.
SITREP Situation Report.

TO&E/TO & TE Table (of) Organization and Equipment (Army); Table Organization and Table Equipment (Marines). This lays out the composition of each unit at every level, and is driven by the forces' doctrines. For instance, Captain Tachikoma's former unit was the First Combat Armored Suit Reconnaissance Company, which at full strength had a total of fifty-six personnel. This consisted of four platoons and a headquarters squad of four CASE-2X Dogs. Each platoon has three squads with four combat armor suits, each squad split into fire teams of two. The platoon is commanded by a lieutenant with the assistance of the platoon sergeant for a total of thirteen Dogs per platoon. However, field strength can be less due to sickness, training, and vacant slots. See ORBAT.

UAV Unmanned Aerial Vehicle commonly referred to in casual conversation incorrectly as "drones." See CYCLOPS.

AFTERWORD

If you're at all like me you've turned to the back of this book in the bookstore and wondering whether or not to buy it? The first thing I want to assure you that though this is the third story set in the Bad Dog universe, it's a standalone novel, which means you don't have to have read or need to read the previous two books, but of course I like to think they're worth reading.

So what is this author wittering on about?

The story you hold in your hand was inspired by two of science fictions great works. The first is the film the *Forbidden Planet*, and the second is Arthur C. Clarke's *Childhoods End*. Both deal with alien civilization's far in advance of humankind. In this book, the heroes of the story get to go out and meet them, and without being too plot spoilery, come back to tell the tale. The story lies in what happens and how they deal with obstacles they face to escaping with their lives.

The next question will there be other books in this series. Undoubtedly yes, if people like what I'm writing. I cannot speak to whether or not you will like this story. All I can say is that it has adventure, sports, true love, and kick-ass action.

Other than that I all I have to say now is to thank my beta

readers, David Barrow, Brian McCue, Fritz who wishes to remain anonymous, and as always Susan my alpha reader without whom there would be nothing. Thank you for reading my novel.

Ashley R Pollard
London, UK
October 2018

ALSO BY ASHLEY R POLLARD

Gate Walkers

Bad Dog

Strike Dog

Ghost Dog

World of Drei Series

Terror Tree

Mission One

Regroup

Break Out

Forthcoming

World of Drei Series: Mission Two

Gate Walkers: Two Moons

ABOUT THE AUTHOR

Born a long time ago in a land far, far away, Ashley has immersed herself in SF and has read, or watched SF for most of her life. She knows SF when she sees it, but can't explain what SF is. Having taken the blue pill, she lives, eats and breathes SF.

In the real world, I've written for *Battlegames* and *Miniature Wargames* magazines, and I was both a reviewer and columnist for *Games Master International*. In addition, I was a freelancer for FASA Corps working on the *3055 Technical Read Out*, and I wrote the *OHMU War Machine* wargame rules.

I've been told I have more interests than most people have dinners, which include: cycling, aikido, iaido, photography, miniature wargaming, painting, and archery.

I am unashamedly a starry eyed dreamer.

Want to know more?
https://ashleyrpollard.blogspot.co.uk/
ashley@ashley-pollard.com

www.ingramcontent.com/pod-product-compliance
Lightning Source LLC
Chambersburg PA
CBHW032205180726
48284CB00001B/192